"BROTHERHOOD OF WAR is a cracking good story. It gets into the hearts and the minds of those who by choice or circumstance are called upon to fight our nation's wars."
—William R. Corson, Lt. Col. (Ret.) U.S.M.C., author of *The Betrayal* and *The Armies of Ignorance*

"A large, exciting, fast-moving novel."
—Shirley Ann Grau, author of *The Keepers of the House*

"Griffin has captured the rhythms of army life and speech, its rewards and deprivations...a well-written, absorbing account of military life."
—*Publishers Weekly*

"A good, solid read about military life. THE BERETS reflects the flavor of what it's like to be a professional soldier."
—Frederick Downs, author of *The Killing Zone*

By W. E. B. Griffin
from Jove

BROTHERHOOD OF WAR

THE BERETS
BROTHERHOOD
OF
WAR
BOOK
V

BY W.E.B.GRIFFIN

A JOVE BOOK

The Berets was written on a Lanier "Super No Problem"
word processor maintained by Gene Vajgert.

THE BERETS

A Jove Book/published by arrangement with
the author

PRINTING HISTORY
Jove edition/February 1985

ISBN: 0-515-07909-X

Jove books are published by The Berkley Publishing Group,
200 Madison Avenue, New York, N.Y. 10016. The words
"A JOVE BOOK" and the "J" with sunburst are trademarks
belonging to Jove Publications, Inc.

PRINTED IN THE UNITED STATES OF AMERICA

AP WASHINGTON
FOR NATIONAL WIRE 825PM JULY 19 1961 APW 31/233
SLUG: SALINGER: "NO COMMENT" RE AMERICANS CAPTURED AT
BAY OF PIGS

WASH DC—July 19: Presidential Press Secretary Pierre Salinger
refused comment tonight on the question of American military personnel captured in Cuba during the failed Bay of Pigs invasion of
Cuba, and was either unable or unwilling to identify with whom
President Kennedy has agreed not to publicly discuss the issue.

Salinger was questioned by the Associated Press at 8:05 P.M.
following tonight's nationally televised Presidential Press Conference, seeking clarification of the following exchange:

Meg Green *(Chicago Sun-Times)*: "Mr. President, there have been
recurring rumors of American soldiers captured when the Bay of
Pigs operation failed, and rumors that at least two such prisoners
have been executed. What can you tell us about this?"

President Kennedy: "I'm sorry, Meg, I've agreed not to get into
that in public."

Meg Green: "Agreed with whom, Mr. President?"

President Kennedy: "Charley Whaley, I think you were next."

Charles Whaley *(Conservative Digest)*: "Mr. President, were any
American military personnel taken prisoner during the Bay of Pigs
invasion?"

President Kennedy: "I just answered that."

When pressed for clarification, Presidential Press Secretary Salinger said, "Obviously, I have no comment on that." END NOTHING
FOLLOWS.

I

(One)
Key West, Florida
1430 Hours, 28 November 1961

Tom Ellis had never been on a yacht before, nor had he ever been farther at sea than up to his waist in the waters lapping a Cuban beach. He was a fair-skinned young man, slightly built with light brown hair, who looked to be about seventeen. He was in fact twenty. He was the sort of pleasant-faced young man whom older people were prone to call "son." They seldom did so twice. Tom Ellis did not like to be called "son," nor to be thought of as a pleasant young boy, and when that happened, ice came into his eyes, enough to chill whomever he was looking at.

He wasn't sure that *Over Draught II* was technically a yacht. That word called to his mind the President and Jackie on his sailboat, or that rich Greek and his opera singer on his private ocean liner. Maybe there was a word that he didn't know that properly described a boat like this one. He didn't think it was *motorboat*. In the end he decided that *Over Draught II* was indeed a yacht. Yachts were luxurious boats designed for plea-

3

sure, not work, and the interior of *Over Draught II* was as luxurious as anything he had ever seen outside of the movies. The floors were carpeted, and there was a king-size double bed in the teak-paneled master stateroom. To his eyes the main cabin seemed a floating version of a penthouse living room. Set discreetly in a corner was a bar with its own little sink and refrigerator. There were softly upholstered chairs, nice paintings, a twenty-four-inch television, and a stereo.

On the back of the boat, chromo-plated lettering, like the *Plymouth* FURY or CADILLAC *Sedan De Ville* things you saw on cars, identified the boat as first a Bertram and then as Sport Fisherman 42, which he decided made reference to the length of the boat.

The owner was aboard, a middle-aged, silver-haired man in expensive clothing who looked the sort of guy who would own something like this. The captain had a friend with him who was also middle-aged and tanned. The captain, a good-looking guy of about thirty with blond hair, dressed very casually in washed soft khaki pants and a polo shirt, had introduced him to the owner and to the other member of the crew, who looked like a younger version of the captain. They could have been brothers, Ellis decided. The young blond guy was the mate and Tom Ellis was sailing aboard *Over Draught II* as the deckhand.

"I hope you know how little I know about boats," Ellis told the mate when he was showing Ellis where to put his stuff in the little cabin up front.

"No big deal," the mate told him. "We're fueled and stocked, and all we have to do is untie her and take her out."

"What if I get seasick?"

He was embarrassed to ask the question, but he had long ago learned that it was less embarrassing in the long run to ask embarrassing questions up front than it was to make an ass of yourself later.

"It's like a mirror out there today," the mate said. "I wouldn't worry about that. But just to be sure, if you start feeling funny, take a couple of these."

He handed Ellis a small plastic vial. The label said it was Dramamine.

"This stuff work?"

"Ninety percent of the time," the mate said. "There are some people who seen determined to get sea sick. It doesn't work on them."

The boat shuddered as the engines were started, one at a time. Ellis looked at the mate with a question in his eyes.

"Now we'll untie her," the mate said with a smile, and motioned Ellis ahead of him out of the little cabin.

When they were on the back of the boat, on what Ellis—for lack of a better word—thought of as the "veranda," the mate pointed to the half-inch woven nylon rope tying the boat to the pier.

"You handle that," he said. "I'll go forward. When Captain Bligh gives the order, you just untie it, bring it aboard, and stow it in the locker."

He pointed to a compartment built in the low wall that surrounded the veranda.

"Got it," Ellis said.

If they had told him about this job earlier than they had, Ellis thought, he would have found out something about boats, learned the right words. There were certainly books that he could have looked up in the library. He watched as the mate made his way to the front, nimbly half running along a narrow walkway.

"Let loose the lines, fore and aft," the captain called down from the roof of the cabin. Ellis had noticed that the boat had two sets of controls, one up on top and one in the cabin. For when it rained, he thought. Or for when there was a storm.

With his luck in this sort of thing, half a mile out in the ocean there would be a hurricane.

The mate signaled to him to untie the ropes. He had to jump up on the wharf to do it. When he was done he quickly jumped back onto the veranda.

The sound of the diesel engines changed, and the nose of the boat moved away from the wharf.

An ounce of prevention is worth a pound of cure, Ellis told himself. He took the vial of Dramamine pills from his pocket and popped two of them in his mouth.

Over Draught II moved into the wide part of the harbor, then started out of it, moving between two lines of things bobbing around in the water.

"Buoys," Ellis said aloud, pleased that he knew what they were. Like the soap, which should really be pronounced "Life *boo*-wee" rather than "Life Boy."

When they hit the first swell of the deep water and the whole damned boat went up and down, Tom Ellis was glad that he'd taken the Dramamine. Soon the dull murmur of the diesels changed to a dull roar, and the boat began to pick up speed through the water.

Thirty minutes later he was reasonably sure that he was not going to get seasick and make an ass of himself. It was actually pretty nice in the back of the boat, sitting in one of the cushioned chairs bolted to the floor and watching the water boil up alongside the boat and fan out in back.

The mate came back and smiled at him.

"You doing all right?" he asked.

"Fine," Ellis said. "How fast are we going?"

"Oh," the mate said, and looked over the side, "I guess eighteen, twenty knots."

Ellis did the arithmetic.

"About three hours?"

"About that," the mate said. "There's chow if you're hungry."

"Food?" Ellis said incredulously. "Thank you, no."

"You'll change your mind," the mate said. "You work up an appetite on a small boat."

Ellis doubted that but said nothing.

"There's a couple of six-packs too," the mate said.

"Maybe later," Ellis said.

Two hours later Ellis made himself a ham-on-rye sandwich and washed it down with a Seven-Up. It wasn't as bad as he thought it would be. He reminded himself of the philosophical wisdom that things were seldom as bad as you thought they were going to be.

When he finished his sandwich, he climbed the ladder up to where the captain was driving the boat.

"Is it all right if I come up here?" he asked.

"Sure," the captain said. "Glad to have the company."

"How much farther?"

"Thirty minutes, maybe forty-five," the captain said. "I suppose you're all set."

"Yes, sir," Ellis said.

Thirty minutes later there was a blip on the radar screen. The captain pointed it out to Ellis.

"That's probably them," he said.

"How can you tell?"

"You ever read a dirty book called *Tropic of Cancer* by Henry Miller?"

"Yeah, when I was in high school."

"We're within a few seconds of the Tropic of Cancer," the captain said. "And that's where we're supposed to meet them."

Two minutes later Ellis began to make out the faint outline of a boat on the horizon and just a little left of straight ahead.

"That's probably them," the captain said. "She's not moving."

As they approached the other boat Ellis could see it more clearly. It was about as big as *Over Draught II* but narrower and rode lower in the water. The hull was gray and the superstructure a garish blue.

The captain slowed the *Over Draught II* as they approached, and then slowed it further when they were closer. When they were fifty yards away from the gray and blue boat, he threw the *Over Draught II* into reverse momentarily. They stopped dead in the water, and the boat began to roll slightly with the swells. Ellis felt a pressure in his temples. He was also a little dizzy and felt a clammy sweat.

"Jesus Christ, God!" he prayed silently. "Not now, please!"

There was a small boat tied to the back of the other boat. Three men in khakis—Cubans—climbed off the gray boat and into the smaller one, and there was the sound of an outboard motor starting.

Ellis went inside the *Over Draught II* and returned with a plastic attaché case. He handed it to the mate.

"It's not locked," he said.

The mate nodded.

When the small boat came to the rear of the *Over Draught II*, one of the men in it threw a line to the mate. He caught it and tied it to a brass stanchion. Ellis looked down into the boat. There was a black-plastic–wrapped object in the boat, around which rope had been wound and formed into a sling. When one of the Cubans in the boat saw Ellis, he tossed the loose end of the rope to Ellis, who failed to catch it. He caught it on the second try.

The Cuban in the boat stepped from it to the teak dive platform on the back of the *Over Draught II*, then climbed up a built-in ladder.

The mate and Ellis pulled the black-plastic–wrapped package onto the *Over Draught II*.

The captain handed the briefcase to the man who had come aboard. He put it on the wet-bait well and opened it. It contained currency, twenty-dollar bills in packets of fifty bills each. These were bound with a paper strip reading *$1000 in $20*. There were fifty packets.

As if he were dealing with people who were beneath him and were likely to try to cheat him, the Cuban arrogantly selected a packet of twenty-dollar bills, ripped them free of the paper strip, and counted them.

"It's all there," the captain said, annoyance in his voice.

"We will see," the Cuban said, tossing the loose bills on top of the others and selecting another packet.

By then the mate and Ellis had laid the long black-plastic–wrapped package on the deck.

Ellis dropped to his knees beside it and with a quick gesture pulled up his left trouser leg and came out with a knife. He inhaled audibly and plunged the knife tip into the plastic. It was tough and it took him a little while to saw through enough of the plastic to make a flap. He pulled the flap aside. There was a face, eyes and mouth open. The peculiar odor of decaying flesh seemed to erupt from the plastic. Ellis's face turned white, and he jumped to his feet, turned to the Cuban—(who was still counting money)—spun him around, and then put the tip of the knife against his carotid artery, where the jaw meets the neck. A torrent of gutter Spanish erupted from Ellis.

"Ellis!" the captain said in alarm.

"That's not Commander Eaglebury," Ellis said in English. Another torrent of angry Spanish erupted, and the Cuban yelped as Ellis nicked him with the point of his knife.

There was the sound of actions being worked. The "owner" and his "friend" stepped to the door of the main cabin. Each held an Armalite AR-15 .223 Remington automatic rifle in his hands.

"Are you sure, Ellis?" the "owner's friend" said.

Ellis didn't reply.

There was a yelp of pain and terror from the Cuban as Ellis nicked him with the knife, and the Cuban said something very quickly to him.

"The lying sonofabitch says he must have made a mistake," Ellis said. "He says that he just happens to have another body, which must be the one we're after."

He moved the Cuban to one of the fighting chairs and forced him into it with the knife point, nicking him again. Blood was running down the man's neck and onto his khaki shirt. He was wide-eyed with terror and moaning a prayer to the Blessed Virgin Mary.

Ellis leaned over the rail and spoke to the Cubans still in the boat. "Untie it," he said in English to the mate. "I'm sending them back for the right body."

"And if they just take off?"

"Then I'll slit this sonofabitch's throat and feed him to the fish," Ellis said.

"Take it easy, Ellis," the captain said.

"Jesus *Christ*!" Ellis said in moral indignation. "What a rotten fucking thing to try to do!"

And then he thought of something.

"Hold it! Take this one with you," he said, and then repeated that in Spanish. He turned to the mate. "Help me get this over the edge," he said.

The body was lowered into the boat. The smell of decaying flesh turned Ellis's face white again.

Halfway back to the gray and blue boat, the Cubans in the small boat heaved the black-plastic–wrapped body over the side. It disappeared from sight for a moment and then bobbed to the surface.

Five minutes later a second body was hauled onto the *Over Draught II*. Ellis took his knife again and slit the wrapping. He looked at the captain and nodded his head. The captain saw there were tears in his eyes.

"Give this . . . person . . . the briefcase," the captain ordered icily. "And allow him to get into the boat. But don't turn it loose. We'll take them with us for a thousand yards or so."

"I'd like to slit his fucking throat," Ellis said.

"No, you can't do that, Ellis," the captain said evenly, then ran quickly up the ladder to the flying bridge.

"Is there some tape or something," Ellis asked, "to seal the body bag again?"

"I'll get some," the mate said.

Ellis dropped to his knees and waited for the tape, holding his nostrils closed against the smell of the putrefying flesh.

The *Over Draught II* moved slowly through the water for a thousand yards and then cut the small boat free. The moment it was free, the captain opened his throttles.

The gray and blue boat made no move to pursue them, and when it was clear that they were not going to fire on the *Over Draught II*, the "owner" and his "friend" put their Armalite AR-15s down. The owner went into the cabin and returned with a blanket, which he laid over the black-plastic–wrapped body.

"I think we'd best leave him there," he said gently to Ellis.

Ellis nodded, sat down in a fighting chair, and stared out over the stern, carefully not looking at the blanket and what it concealed.

Fifteen minutes later he got up and walked into the cabin. He went to the refrigerator and took out a can of Schlitz.

"Jesus!" the "owner's friend" said in awe. Ellis looked at him and then out the window, where the other man was pointing.

A hundred yards to their right the water was turbulent, and a large gray-black submarine sail rose from it. Before the hull was visible, figures could be seen on the top of the sail, and an American flag appeared, flapping in the breeze.

The captain slowed the boat and maneuvered closer to the submarine until, at about the moment the submarine stopped dead in the water, he was ten yards away from her.

An officer with an electronic megaphone appeared on the sail. "Captain's compliments, Captain," he said. "Will you come aboard, please?" his amplified voice boomed.

A moment later the captain appeared at the cabin door.

"They want you, too, Lieutenant," he said.

Ellis, beer can in hand, followed him.

Sailors on the submarine threw mats of woven rope down from the deck to form a cushion between the submarine and the *Over Draught II*. After that, two sailors jumped onto the boat and pulled her alongside with boat hooks.

The captain grabbed hold of a ladder on the submarine's side and began climbing. Ellis took a final swallow of his beer, threw the can into the sea, and followed him.

The captain got onto the deck. He saluted the officer standing there and then the national colors.

"Permission to come aboard, sir."

"Permission granted," the navy officer said, returning the salute.

When Ellis climbed up, the navy officer smiled at him.

"Welcome aboard, sir," he said.

Ellis saluted him crisply and then the colors, as the captain had done.

"Permission to come aboard, sir?" he said.

"Permission granted," the navy officer said.

"Will you come with me, gentlemen?" another navy officer in stiffly starched khakis said, and led them to an opening in the sail. They climbed an interior ladder and found themselves on the top of the sail.

An officer wearing the silver eagle of a navy captain on his collar smiled and offered his hand.

"Lieutenant Davis?" he asked.

"Yes, sir."

"And you're Lieutenant Ellis?"

"Yes, sir."

The captain handed Ellis a cryptographic machine printout.

OPERATIONAL IMMEDIATE
NO. 11-103 2305 ZULU 28NOV61

SECRET

FROM COMSUBFORATL
COMMANDER USS GATO

DP. IMMEDIATELY RELIEVE COMMANDER NAVAL AUXILIARY VESSEL OVER DRAUGHT II REMAINS LT COMMANDER EDWARD B. EAGLEBURY USN. TRANSPORT USN YARD PHILADLEPHIA. LIEUTENANT THOMAS J. ELLIS, USA, TO ACCOMPANY.

CZERNIK REARADM USN.

Ellis handed it back to the captain, who handed it to Lieutenant Davis.

"You have luggage aboard that boat, Lieutenant?" the captain asked.

"No, sir," Ellis said.

"We can probably fix you up aboard," the captain said.

Ellis was surprised first to hear a strange whistle and then to see the captain come to a salute. He looked where the captain looked.

A steel stretcher—Ellis knew the correct nomenclature but couldn't think of it—had been lowered onto the *Over Draught II*. The plastic-wrapped body had then been strapped into it and was now being hauled back aboard. Half a dozen officers and ten sailors were standing at attention, saluting, as a sailor blew on a funny-looking whistle.

After he had been captured, interrogated, and executed as a spy by security forces of the People's Democratic Republic of Cuba, the remains of Lieutenant Commander Edward Eaglebury, U.S.N., were being paid the appropriate naval honors as they came aboard a United States ship of war. When they had the black-plastic–wrapped bundle on the deck, it was hurriedly taken into the sail.

"Permission to leave the bridge, sir, and the ship?" Lieutenant Davis asked when the whistling stopped.

"Granted," the captain said. "Well done, Lieutenant."

"Ellis is the one who did things well, sir," Davis said. He offered his hand to Ellis. "See you around sometime, I hope, Lieutenant," he said.

"Thank you for everything," Ellis said.

Ellis watched as Davis emerged from the sail and nimbly made his way back onto the Bertram yacht. As soon as he was aboard, the mate, who was at the controls, pulled the boat sharply away from the submarine.

"Make turns for fifteen knots," the submarine commander said softly, and an enlisted man standing behind him repeated the order into a microphone. Water churned at the rear of the submarine and she began to move. Ellis looked forward and saw the last of the sailors scurry into a round opening in the deck.

"You have the conn, sir," the captain said to an officer

beside him. "When you are ready, take her down. Lieutenant Ellis and I are going below."

"Aye, aye, sir," the officer said, and then called over his shoulder: "Captain leaving the bridge."

"Captain leaving the bridge," the sailor parroted.

"Right this way, Lieutenant," the captain said, gesturing for Ellis to climb back down the ladder.

They climbed down what seemed to Ellis like three or four floors, into a room jammed full of officers and sailors and an awesome display of gauges and controls.

"I don't quite understand your role in this, Lieutenant," the captain said. "Is that a question I'm permitted to ask?"

"I was with Commander Eaglebury in Cuba," Ellis said. "He jumped in with my 'A' Team a couple of days before the Bay of Pigs."

The captain's eyebrows raised in surprise.

"Your 'A' Team? Eaglebury went in as a Green Beret?"

"Yes, sir."

"I see," the captain said. "This your first time on a submarine?"

"Yes, sir."

"Well, we'll try to make you comfortable," the captain said. A Klaxon horn sounded.

"Dive, dive, dive," a voice said over the loudspeaker.

Ellis had no idea what was going on, but he was impressed with a feeling that everyone seemed to know what he was doing and was doing it without orders. After a minute or so the activity seemed less frenzied.

"And now we dive?" he asked as he felt the deck tilt slightly forward.

The captain pointed to a gauge. It read DEPTH IN METERS, and the indicator was inching past fifty.

The officer who had been left on the sail came up to where the captain stood.

"Take her to two hundred and fifty, Paul," the captain said, "and make turns for forty knots."

"Aye, aye, sir."

"Sparks?" the captain said, and a sailor stepped up to him. "Yes, sir?"

"Message COMSUBFORATL," the captain said. "Reference your operational immediate whatever-the-number-was, in compliance."

"Aye, aye, sir," the radioman said.

"You can send messages from down here?" Ellis asked, surprised.

The captain smiled at him. "No, and we can't make forty knots, either," he said.

The officer who was running the ship chuckled.

"I'll be in the wardroom," the captain said. "I need a cup of coffee, and I wouldn't be surprised if Lieutenant Ellis could be talked into having one."

(Two)
The Situation Room
The White House
Washington, D.C.
2105 Hours, 28 November 1961

An army warrant officer ran the tape from COMSUBFOR-ATL through the cryptographic machine. Soon a printout appeared, which he then carried to a vice-admiral standing with his hands on the hips, watching the ship location chart on the wall. He waited until the admiral finally noticed him and handed the printout to him wordlessly.

"Thank you," the admiral said absently, and read it.

OPERATIONAL IMMEDIATE
NO. 10-105 0105 ZULU 29NOV61

SECRET

FROM COMSUBFORATL
CNO ATTEN: THE PRESIDENT

MESSAGE FROM USS GATO RECEIVED 0047 ZULU 28NOV61 INDI-
CATES REMAINS LT COMMANDER EAGLEBURY RECOVERED. GATO
PROCEEDING USN YARD PHILADELPHIA. ETA 1230 ZULU 29NOV61.
                              BERRY REARADM FOR COMSUBFORATL

The admiral looked around the room and then walked across it toward a slight and balding man in a mussed gray suit, sitting at a small stenographer's bench—not unlike a school desk—and bent over a sheath of yellow teletype paper. The man showed no sign that he was aware that the admiral was standing over him.

"Got a minute to spare, Felter?" the admiral asked dryly.

The small man closed the sheath of Teletype messages and stood up.

"Sorry," he said. "I was . . . what do I say? . . . 'concentrating.'"

"We've heard from COMSUBFORATL," the admiral said, and handed him the message. After he had read it, the admiral continued: "You're going to see the President?"

"Just as soon as I finish the summary," Felter said.

"Then you can give him this," the admiral said.

"Yes, sir," Felter said.

The admiral walked away. Felter sat back down and resumed reading the sheath of Teletype messages in front of him. When he finished he got up from his stenographer's bench and went to a desk occupied by a navy chief officer. He smiled at him and made a gesture with his hand, asking for the chief's chair.

He sat down, pulled open a desk drawer and took from it a sheet of paper. The paper had three lines of type printed at the top.

TOP SECRET (*Presidential*)

Eyes of the President Only

Duplication Expressly Forbidden

TOP SECRET (*Presidential*) was repeated at the bottom of the sheet.

Felter rolled the sheet of paper in the IBM electric typewriter and began to type very rapidly. At the top he wrote in the date and the hour and ONE PAGE ONLY. Then beneath that, in short paragraphs, he summarized the intelligence information that had come into the situation room since the last summary at noon. He stopped toward the end of the page in order to decide between an assassination of a Turkish lieutenant general and the recovery of the remains of Lieutenant Command Edward B. Eaglebury.

The assassination went in. It was the more important of the two items. Then he ripped the sheet of paper from the typewriter and stood up.

"If there's no call for these by 0800, Chief," he said to the chief petty officer, handing him the sheath of Teletype messages, "will you have them shredded, please?"

"Yes, sir," the chief said.

Felter folded the summary in thirds, put it in an envelope, and walked out of the Situation Room. There was a marine guard at a small desk by the elevator. When he saw Felter he opened a drawer, took a Colt .45 pistol from it, and laid it on the desk.

"I'll have to come back for it," Felter said. "I'm going upstairs, not out."

"Yes, sir," the marine guard said, and put the pistol back in the drawer.

Felter got in the elevator and rode it to the Presidential Apartments.

"Are you expected, sir?" the Secret Service man in the foyer asked when he stepped off the elevator.

Felter shook his head no.

"Just a moment, sir," the Secret Service man said, and went to the double door at the end of the corridor. He knocked and then opened the door immediately.

"Mr. Felter is here, Mr. President," he said.

Then he turned to Felter and nodded his head to him.

"The President will see you, Mr. Felter."

Felter pushed the door open and went inside. The President was in his rocking chair with a glass of whiskey in his hand. The Attorney General was sitting in an upholstered chair, also with a drink in his hand. There were two nice-looking women sitting in other chairs, each with a drink.

"I hope this is a social call, Sandy," the President said.

"I have the summary, Mr. President," Felter said. "And this."

He handed the President the envelope with the summary. The President took it, read it, and handed it to his brother. Then he took the message from COMSUBFORATL and read that.

The Attorney General laid the summary faceup on a table.

"Are you finished with that, Mr. Kennedy?" Felter asked, walking to the table with the evident purpose of reclaiming the summary.

"I will be, Colonel," the Attorney General snapped, "just as soon as I Xerox a copy for the Kremlin." Bobby did not like Colonel Felter—probably, the President thought, because they were so much alike.

"Easy, Bobby," the President said almost sharply. He walked to the table and picked up the summary and held it out to Felter.

"Would you like to inform the Eagleburys, Sandy?" the President asked.

"No, sir."

"All right," the President said, noting that the pout had returned to his brother's face. He thought he had asked a simple question and gotten an immediate, direct answer. He understood Felter's directness and his brevity. Bobby thought Felter's brevity was insolent.

"Would you like to represent me at the funeral?" the President asked.

"If I can be spared here, I would be honored, sir."

"Well, you plan on it," the President said. "We'll see how things are going. I imagine Colonel Hanrahan and his people would like to participate."

"Yes, sir," Felter said.

"I'd like to go myself," the President said.

"Jack, you're not going to have the time," the Attorney General said.

"I probably won't," the President agreed. "But set it up anyway, would you, Felter? Very quietly. If I can find the time, I'll go."

"Yes, sir," Felter said.

"And check to see that the navy yard in Philadelphia knows what's going on. I'm sure they'll want to do things right."

"Yes, sir," Felter said.

"Tomorrow will be time enough," the President said. "First thing in the morning. Go home now, Sandy. You've been here all day."

"Yes, sir," Felter said.

"That is not a suggestion, Felter," the President said.

"Yes, sir."

"Good night, Colonel Felter," the President said. "I really don't want to hear myself saying that again."

Felter nodded at the President, turned around, and walked out of the room.

When the door had closed after him, the Attorney General said, "I don't know what you see in that creep, why you put up with him."

"He's bright—brighter than you, Bobby." The President chuckled. "You never like people who are brighter than you and who let you know it."

(Three)
Headquarters
The U.S. Army Special Warfare School
Fort Bragg, North Carolina
1000 Hours, 29 November 1961

The sergeant major of the Special Warfare School was a tall, crew-cutted, muscular master sergeant named E. B. Taylor. The office phone was ringing.

His chief clerk, a younger version of Taylor, a staff sergeant, took the call, then rapped his desk with his knuckles twice, the signal the call was for the sergeant major.

"Sergeant Major," Taylor said.

"I have a collect call for anyone from Lieutenant Thomas Ellis," the operator said. "Will you accept the charges?"

"Put him through, Operator," Taylor said with a smile and a gesture that the clerk should listen in. When Ellis came on the line, Taylor's voice became oily with mock humility: "Yes, sir, Lieutenant Ellis, sir. How may I be of service to the lieutenant this morning, sir?"

"I'm in Philadelphia," Ellis said.

"Good for you, sir!" Taylor said. "I'm sure the colonel will be thrilled to hear that, sir! How nice of you to call and tell us, sir!"

"You better ask the colonel if he'll talk to me," Ellis said.

"Oh, I'm sure the colonel will be delighted to talk to you, Lieutenant, sir," Taylor said. "Just one moment, please, sir."

He took the telephone from his ear with his right hand, covering the mouthpiece as he did so. He pushed the intercom switch with his left.

"Colonel, Ellis is on the horn, collect. He sounds like a lost soul."

"From Philadelphia?"

"Yes, sir."

"Ellis," Colonel Paul T. Hanrahan demanded, falling easily into Taylor's game, "who told you you could go to Philadelphia?"

There was no reply, and disappointing Sergeant Major Taylor, Colonel Hanrahan took pity on his young lieutenant. "It's okay, Ellis," Hanrahan said, changing his tone. "Colonel Felter called last night and explained the situation. Everything going all right so far?"

"The navy's taken over," Ellis said. "They put him in a casket on the sub, and then they had a little ceremony when they took him off. His father and his sister were on the dock. That was a little rough. Anyway, they're going to bury him tomorrow. I'd really like to stick around for that, and the sister asked me if I could, but I don't have any clothes or uniforms, and—"

"If someone—Sergeant Major Taylor, for example—were to go to your room in the BOQ, do you think he could find enough clothes for you to wear? Or is it the garbage dump rumor has it?"

"Yes, sir," Ellis said. "There's greens and blues in the closet. But how would you get it here, sir?"

"We're coming up there this afternoon. Colonel MacMillan, Major MacMillan, Major Parker, Mr. Wojinski, and me. We'll bring it with us. You go get us hotel rooms."

"What hotel, sir?" Ellis asked.

Good question, Colonel Hanrahan thought. One he hadn't thought of. He needed an answer right now too.

"The Bellevue Stratford," he said. It was the only Philadelphia hotel whose name he could call to mind. It was famous and therefore probably expensive as hell, but it was an answer. "If you can't get us put up there, leave word there where you are. Got it?"

"Yes, sir," Ellis said. "The Bellevue Stratford."

"We'll see you later today," Hanrahan said. "Try to stay out of poker games." He hung up and pursed his mouth as if to whistle. He didn't have to. Sergeant Major Taylor was standing in the office door.

"You were on the horn?" Hanrahan asked.

"The lieutenant's luggage, containing a green uniform and a dress blue uniform, complete to his medal, the Good Conduct Medal, is in my office, Colonel."

(Four)
Skeet and Trap Range
Fort Rucker, Alabama
1130 Hours, 29 November 1961

Colonel Jack Martinelli was a good shot, and he took his skeet shooting seriously. He had a matched set of Diana Grade Browning over-and-under shotguns, the stocks of which had been fitted for him at the Fabrique Nationale des Armes de la Guerre at Liege, Belgium. The set consisted of two actions and stocks, and four barrels and forearms. The 12- and 20-bores fitted one action and stock, and the 28-bore and .410 gauge the second.

Today, Colonel Martinelli was shooting the 28-bore against an opponent worthy of the effort. He would have preferred to be shooting the .410 gauge, the expert's weapon, but his opponent, Lieutenant Colonel Craig W. Lowell, did not own a .410. Lowell was firing a side-by-side 28-bore Hans Schroeder shotgun, which had been made for him in the small Austrian village of Ferlach.

Colonel Martinelli, who knew about guns, was aware that the Schroeder was worth more than his entire matched set of Diana Grade Brownings. He was also aware that it was not really a skeet gun. In his skilled judgment, not only were side-by-sides less suitable for skeet shooting than over-and-unders, but Lowell had had the gun bored modified and improved modified, because it was a hunting gun. A skeet gun is supposed to be bored skeet and skeet.

Lieutenant Colonel Lowell was thus firing the wrong type of shotgun with inappropriate tubes, a double handicap. Despite that, he was beating Colonel Martinelli, and rather badly. Colonel Martinelli was a large, stocky man with dark hair and a somewhat swarthy complexion, which darkened even more every time he missed. Lieutenant Colonel Lowell was a large man, lithe, blond, and mustachioed. His friends called him the Duke.

Over their civilian clothing, brightly colored slacks and knit sports shirts (the sort of clothing normally worn on golf courses), both officers wore sleeveless skeet vests. Colonel Martinelli's was festooned with insignia testifying to his membership in the National Skeet Shooting Association, his life membership in the National Rifle Association, his certification as a shotgun instructor, as a Distinguished Shotgun Marksman, and as someone who had broken without a miss 25, 50, 75, 100, 150, and 200 clay targets in a row.

Lowell's vest bore only his NRA Life Member Patch and a small embroidered Combat Infantry Badge.

It was technically against regulations to wear an issue qualification badge like that, and as he stepped to Station 1, beneath the High House, Colonel Martinelli remembered with some annoyance that Lowell had once said that the Combat Infantry Badge was the only marksmanship badge that meant anything, marksmanship against targets that were shooting back being inarguably more difficult than shooting at defenseless clay pigeons.

Colonel Martinelli was Artillery, and he had heard more than his fair share of rounds fired in anger, but unlike Infantry, Armor, and the Medics, artillerymen had no badge that announced that fact to the world. Colonel Martinelli did not know exactly why that was, but it bothered him.

"Concentrate, Jack," Lieutenant Colonel Lowell offered helpfully. "Keep your cheek on the stock."

The sonofabitch is doing that to psych me, Colonel Martinelli decided with absolute accuracy. He glowered at Lowell.

"Your shooting is a little off," Lieutenant Colonel Lowell said understandingly, sympathetically. "Maybe you're trying too hard, Jack. Think of flowing water or something."

"Thank you," Colonel Martinelli said, forcing a smile onto his face.

He pretended to examine the action of the Browning, to give his temper a moment or so to cool down.

"Something wrong with the gun?" Lieutenant Colonel Lowell asked with concern.

"I think there's a pellet in there somewhere," Martinelli said.

"Need some help?" Lowell asked.

"I think it's all right now, thank you," Martinelli said. *You're*

*a wise-ass, Lowell. You antagonize people. Your fucking every-
thing in a skirt isn't the only reason you were a major so long.*

Lieutenant Colonel Lowell had been both one of the young-
est majors in the army and, until he had finally been promoted,
one of the most senior. He was, Martinelli thought, one of the
brightest officers he had ever known, and—if Major General
Paul Jiggs, the post commander, was to be believed—an absolutely superb combat commander. But his career had alter-
nated periods of outstanding service with episodes of outstanding
stupidity. Perhaps he was so rich that consistency did not matter
to him. At any rate, he had been teetering at the edge of
involuntary separation, having been twice passed over for promotion, when his promotion to light bird came through. And
it was the White House, not the Pentagon, that sent that promotion to the Senate for confirmation, the Pentagon then being
more than indifferent to the continuation of then Major Lowell's
army career.

After Lowell's admittedly gallant and courageous rescue of
Felter and a number of others during the Bay of Pigs catastrophe, General E. Z. Black, Commander in Chief, Pacific, had
written the President, personally urging that Lowell be promoted and retained. The President, who had a soft spot in his
heart for brave and brilliant eccentrics, complied, and Lowell's
career was saved yet one more time. Lowell had his defenders,
such as generals Black and Jiggs and even Jack Martinelli, as
well as his detractors.

But at times like this, Craig Lowell, Jack Martinelli fumed,
was a flaming pain in the ass.

Martinelli seated two shells in his Browning, snapped the
action shut, and checked to see the safety was off. He loaded
his own ammunition, since he was convinced that he made
better shot shells than he could buy; but today that was doing
him no good. And yet, why everything was going wrong was
beyond him. Maybe he had gotten oil on the primers, or the
powder had absorbed moisture, or some other disaster, like the
safety being on, had caused him to miss. Breaking these targets,
with Lowell on his back, was very important, but they just
were not breaking.

He touched the butt of his shotgun to his hip.

"Pull!"

Behind him the referee, the master sergeant in charge of the range, pressed a button on a handheld control. An electrical impulse was sent to both houses, and solenoids on the target throwers in the high house and low house were simultaneously activated, releasing powerful springs that threw the targets into the air.

Martinelli snapped the Browning to his shoulder and aimed at the target thrown from the high house. He aimed just under it and fired.

The circular target wobbled—he had come *that* close—but continued on its path.

Martinelli heard Lowell making a *tsk-tsk* sound of sympathy while he aimed at the target approaching from the low house. Of all the targets in a round of skeet, this was probably the easiest shot. You could practically reach up and hit it with the muzzle. He fired again, and again the target seemed to wobble, to hesitate, and then went on its path.

"Tough, Jack," Lowell said with absolutely transparent false sympathy. "You dropped both of them. What did the flight surgeon have to say about your eyes last time around?"

Martinelli did not trust himself to speak.

Lowell stepped under the high house and almost immediately called "Pull." The action of his shotgun closed as he brought it to his shoulder.

There were two barks, and both targets dissolved into small gray-black clouds of dust right over the center marker.

Lowell turned to Martinelli and smiled benignly at him. "Maybe you're getting a little too old for this game, Jack," he said.

Martinelli glared at Lowell and then glanced at the grassy field beyond the low house where the unbroken targets from the high house had landed. And then he stared in that direction. He could see half a dozen unbroken clay targets, nearly vertical in the tall grass. They were glistening, reflecting the bright fall sun. Clay pigeons are made of stamped pitch.

They normally break on impact, and they damned well don't glisten in the sunlight!

Martinelli thrust his shotgun into Lowell's hand.

"Don't go anywhere, Lowell!" he said, and then he ran across the range toward the unbroken targets.

"Sergeant," he heard Lowell ask, "do you get the feeling the colonel suspects that something is amiss?"

The range sergeant chuckled.

Martinelli picked up an unbroken target. It was painted white, and stamped WINCHESTER-WESTERN, but it wasn't a clay target. It was an ashtray—an advertising giveaway stamped out of aluminum, made in the shape of a target.

"You sonofabitch!" Martinelli shouted, looking back at the line. Lowell was laughing. The master sergeant was trying very hard not to. Martinelli looked around for, and picked up, seven aluminum ashtrays.

And then, his anger vanishing as the humor of what had been done to him by Lowell and the trap boys came to him (this had taken some preparation; it wasn't just a spur-of-the-moment funny idea), he began to chuckle. Shaking his head, balancing the stack of ashtrays in his hand, trying very hard to appear angry, he walked back to the high house.

A staff car pulled into the parking lot and stopped beside Martinelli's Buick station wagon. When the passenger got out of the front seat, he saw the solid gold cord on the overseas hat, and the two silver stars of a major general pinned to the front of it.

Did that sonofabitch actually invite Paul Jiggs out here to watch him make an ass of me? Anger returned.

Martinelli saluted when he walked up to Jiggs, who was standing with Lowell. Technically you weren't supposed to salute in civilian clothing, but a general officer was a general officer.

"Did he actually invite you out here to witness this?" Martinelli asked.

"Witness what, Jack?" Jiggs asked.

"The bastard's had me shooting at aluminum targets," Martinelli said.

"Claiming the protection of the thirty-first Article of War," Lowell said, "I decline to comment on the grounds that it may tend to incriminate me."

"Well, you got me good," Martinelli said. "But from now on, you will never be able to sleep soundly, and you're going to spend a lot of time looking over your shoulder."

"I called out to the board," General Jiggs said, "and your

secretary told me—reluctantly, I might add—that you two were doing your required exercise. I knew what that meant, so I came here."

"Is something up?" Martinelli asked.

"Primarily it gave me an excuse to get out of the office. I thought maybe there'd be a spare gun."

"Sure," Lowell said. "I've got a 12-bore in the car."

"Get the business out of the way first," General Jiggs said. "Lowell has been asked to be a pallbearer at a funeral. If there's no reason he can't—and it would have to be a pretty solid reason—I'd like to see him go."

"I can't think of anything, can you, Craig?" Martinelli asked.

"No, sir," Lowell said.

"That's good, because the request came from Felter," Jiggs said. "Which is the same thing as saying the White House."

"Who died?"

"A naval officer, a Commander Edward B. Eaglebury," General Jiggs said.

"Friend of yours, Lowell?" Martinelli asked.

"Yes, sir," Lowell said simply.

There was more to this than he was being told, Martinelli realized, and he also realized that he had probably been told all he was going to be told.

"It looks like duty to me," Jiggs said. "Maybe administrative leave. Lowell's being told to go. Not that he wouldn't want to, but this came pretty close to being an order."

"I'll have orders cut putting him on TDY,*" Martinelli said. "Where's he have to go?"

"Philadelphia," Jiggs said. "The funeral's tomorrow."

"Felter say how he got the body?" Lowell asked.

Jiggs gave him a cold look. He was talking about something that should not be talked about.

"Come on, Paul," Lowell said. "The Cubans know he's dead. They shot him."

"Felter didn't say. Probably through the Swiss."

"He was a good guy," Lowell said, and then: "I'll get you a gun."

---

*Temporary duty.

II

Philadelphia International Airport
1800 Hours, 29 November 1961

When Northeast Airlines Flight 208 discharged its Philadelphia passengers at gate three, Lieutenant Colonel Craig W. Lowell and First Lieutenant Thomas J. Ellis were waiting in the concourse. Lieutenant Ellis was wearing khaki trousers, an open-collared khaki shirt, and a zippered powder-blue quilted nylon ski jacket purchased an hour before in the men's shop in the lobby of the Bellevue Stratford hotel. He looked like a boy en route home from college. Colonel Lowell looked like an army officer. He looked, Ellis had thought, like the drawings hung on the wall of the uniform concessionaire's place of business in the PX at Bragg: "The Well Dressed Army Officer."

The uniform was of the highest quality material and superbly tailored. It had come from London, from an establishment that had been clothing British officers since before the American Revolution, and American officers—those few who could afford it—since World War I.

26

The orange-and-black embroidered insignia of the Army Aviation Center was sewn to the left sleeve of the tunic. The only other insignia were the silver oak leaves of his rank; the cavalry-sabers-superimposed-on-a-tank insignia of Armor; Army Aviator's wings with a star identifying a senior aviator; and above them a miniature (and unauthorized) Combat Infantry Badge with a star on its silver wreathed musket signifying the second award.

Colonel Lowell was tall, muscular, blond, mustached, and handsome, and in his uniform, complete with fur-felt cap with golden scrambled eggs of a field grade officer on the brim, he drew admiring glances from civilians in the terminal. Ellis felt like a slob beside him.

Four of the Northeast's Atlanta-boarded passengers who came into the terminal were also in uniform. They were Colonel Paul T. Hanrahan, who wore the crossed rifles of infantry. He was red-haired, ruddy-faced, and slightly built. Next came Lieutenant Colonel Rudolph G. MacMillan, another infantryman, stocky and round-faced; Major Philip Sheridan Parker IV, Armor, broad-shouldered, six foot three, two hundred and fifteen pounds, and very black; and Warrant Officer (Junior Grade) Stefan T. Wojinski, as pale as Parker was dark, barrel-chested, bullnecked, with two hundred and twenty pounds hung gracefully on a five-foot-eleven-inch frame.

Aside from the different insignia of rank, they were dressed identically in army-green uniforms. They all wore parachutist's insignia, and they all wore their trouser bottoms bloused around the tops of glistening paratrooper boots. They all wore Combat Infantry Badges. MacMillan and Parker wore Army Aviator's wings, MacMillan's with the wreathed star on top of a Master Aviator. They all wore a strip embroidered AIRBORNE sewn near the top of their tunic sleeves, and below that the embroidered insignia of Special Forces. And they all wore green berets.

Lowell walked up to Colonel Hanrahan and shook his hand.

"Yoo-hoo," he called over the colonel's shoulder to Major Parker. "Little girl, I'll take two boxes of the chocolate chip cookies and one of the vanilla wafers."

Major Parker shook his head, but he had to smile. When

his teeth were exposed against his very black skin, they seemed extraordinarily white.

"Oh, for God's sake, Craig," Colonel Hanrahan said angrily. He was having enough trouble about the Green Berets without having to take wise-ass ridicule from Craig W. Lowell.

Two days before, he had received a CONARC (Continental Army Command) directive. It had not come through normal distribution channels. Instead his copy had come addressed "Personal Attention of Col. Paul T. Hanrahan" in an envelope bearing the return address "Office of the Commanding General, Headquarters, Continental Army Command, Fort Monroe, Virginia." There was no accompanying letter. The return address had said all that had to be said. The CONARC directive forbade the wearing of "nonstandard headgear, to include foreign 'beret'- type headgear."

Hanrahan thought that Lieutenant General "Triple H" Howard was behind the directive. Not long before, he had defied Howard's local order banning the green berets by claiming that while the Special Warfare Center and School were on Fort Bragg, they were not subordinate to it. Howard did not have the authority the CONARC commander did over Special Forces.

Hanrahan hadn't told anyone of the CONARC order, not even Sergeant Major Taylor, who generally knew everything Hanrahan did. When he got back to Bragg, he would have to issue the order. But now he'd try to ignore it.

He thought it was perhaps fitting that the beret would sort of be buried with Lieutenant Commander Ed Eaglebury, a naval officer who had won the right to wear one and had jumped into Cuba as a Green Beret.

"I think you all look just splendid!" Lowell went on, undaunted. "I will sleep soundly tonight, knowing that the nation's defense is in your capable hands."

"He's been drinking," MacMillan said flatly.

"Naw," Wojinski said mockingly.

"How are you, Ski?" Lowell said to him, shaking his hand.

"Hello, Ellis," Colonel Hanrahan said. "I see that it took you no time at all to fall in with evil companions."

"Good evening, sir," Ellis said.

"And lucky for you that he has," Lowell said. "Since you are all famous for not being able to find your way out of a

closet, I have assumed logistic responsibility for this mission.
If you will all please get your luggage and follow me . . ."

"Meaning what?" Hanrahan asked.

"About the logistics?" Lowell asked. Hanrahan nodded. "I
have hotel rooms and wheels and the schedule. I have also
previously reconnoitered the area. I know where we're going."

"And you have been at the whiskey?"

"I *have* had a nip or two," Lowell said. "Widows and that
sort of thing depress me."

"I'm sorry you have been inconvenienced by all this," Hanrahan said sarcastically.

"I don't suppose you've heard from the Mouse?" Lowell
asked, ignoring the sarcasm.

Hanrahan shook his head. "Felter's not here?"

"No, and I get that 'I'll relay your message to Colonel Felter'
bullshit when I try to call the White House," Lowell said.

"Maybe he's driving up," Hanrahan said. "Maybe he brought
Sharon."

"Yeah, probably," Lowell said.

They were at the baggage carousel. A liveried chauffeur
trailed by a red cap walked up.

"Point out your luggage to these gentlemen," Lowell said,
"and give them the tags."

"Is he just dressed like that?" Hanrahan asked softly. "Or
does he have a long black car to go with that uniform?"

"Actually, it's maroon," Lowell said. "And there's no divider, so watch what you say." He saw the look in Hanrahan's
eyes. "It's not as expensive as you think, Paul, and it makes
a lot of sense to have a car that can hold us all and someone
to worry about it and run errands."

"Never look a gift jackass in the mouth, I always say,"
Hanrahan said.

He felt a little guilty. Lowell was probably right about the
car. Hanrahan, having never hired a chauffeured limousine,
had no idea what one cost. But it was probably less than it
would have been to hire two taxicabs, and with all their luggage
they would have had to hire two.

When they were all loaded in the limousine, Lowell announced that they were going to Old Original Bookbinder's
Restaurant. Ellis, however, would proceed to the hotel, where

he would "climb into a uniform, then join us at the restaurant. At Bookbinder's we will victual, and then we will all go out to Swarthmore and pay our respects to the family, and finally we will return to the hotel," Lowell said. "Are there any questions?"

"You seem to have everything under control, Colonel," Hanrahan said, paused, and added, "for once in your life."

"In case anyone gets lost," Lowell said, "and with MacMillan we always have to keep that in mind, we're in the Bellevue Stratford Hotel, in Penthouse B."

"Penthouse B?" Hanrahan asked dryly.

"They made me a deal," Lowell said. "You would be surprised, Paul, how seldom they have a chance to rent a suite like that. They're willing to bargain."

The penthouse, which was like a two-story house on the hotel roof, was the first penthouse Lieutenant Ellis had ever seen, except in the movies. The ride from the hotel to the airport, similarly, had been his first ride in a limousine. He'd heard the stories about Colonel Lowell being very rich, but until tonight, when Lowell had summoned him from the inexpensive room he had rented to the penthouse, it had seemed like so much bullshit. If a man had more money than he could spend, what was he doing in the army?

(Two)
The Presidential Apartments
The White House
Washington, D.C.
1815 Hours, 29 November 1961

The President raised his eyes from the noon-to-four-P.M. summary, and looked around for its author. Colonel Sanford T. Felter was on one of the scrambler telephones. The President waited until he was through and then called his name.

Felter walked over to him.

"Is everything laid on to go to Philadelphia?" he asked.

"Yes, sir."

"I've decided to do it," the President said. "What shall we have Salinger tell the Fourth Estate?"

Something close to a smile curled Felter's thin lips.

"That's not my area of specialization, sir," Felter said.

Pierre Salinger, the presidential press secretary, hearing his name, looked across the room at the President. The President beckoned to him.

"You will inform the gentlemen of the press that I will depart in ten minutes by helicopter for Camp David. Only Mr. Felter will go with me."

"You're going to Camp David? Why?"

"Actually, I'm going to Philadelphia," the President said. "But I don't want the press disrupting a funeral. Which they would."

"Jack," Salinger said, "is that smart?"

"I got him killed, Pierre," the President said. "The least I can do is tell his family I'm sorry. And spare them the press while he's being buried."

"What are you going to tell Johnson?"

"I presume the Secret Service knows where he is," the President said. "I can't see any reason why he has to hear about this. Don't tell him unless you have to. I will go from Philadelphia to Camp David. You can send a couple of pool photographers out there in the morning to take my picture getting on the helicopter."

(Three)
Old Original Bookbinder's Restaurant
Philadelphia, Pennsylvania
1835 Hours, 29 November 1961

They were given a table on the second floor. Walking to it, they passed a glass case in which live lobsters crawled.

"When the waiter comes, he will lie to you," Lowell announced as they sat down. "He will offer the confidential information that most people think smaller lobsters are tastier. That's simply not so."

The waiter did just that.

"Bring us the five largest lobsters in the tank," Lowell said. "And steamed clams all around. And beer for everybody."

"We'll need separate checks, waiter," Hanrahan said. He didn't think that it mattered to Lowell that he had more money than God and thus could easily afford grabbing checks, but mooching was mooching, and Hanrahan was determined to pay his own way.

"Yes, sir," the waiter said.

Lowell looked at Hanrahan, smiled and shook his head.

The beer was served immediately.

"Do me a favor, Craig," Hanrahan said. "Don't needle Ellis."

"I hadn't intended to," Lowell said.

"I think that business with the body on the boat was more of a strain than he's letting on."

"Oh," Lowell said. "I wondered why he's been so flaky."

"Okay," Hanrahan said.

"Why the hell did you send him? I could just have easily gone."

"Felter said send him," Hanrahan said.

"He told me the Cubans tried to sell us the wrong body," Lowell said.

Two heads at the adjacent table turned. Lowell smiled politely at them. They smiled back, sure that they hadn't heard correctly. Hanrahan shook his head.

Lieutenant Ellis, now in uniform, arrived as the waiter was serving the steamed clams.

"Bring the lieutenant a beer," Lowell said.

The waiter looked at Ellis.

"I'll have to see some proof he's twenty-one," the waiter said.

Lowell took his water glass and poured it on the floor. Then he filled it with beer from a bottle. He set it in front of Ellis.

"Now bring *me* a beer, please, and quickly," Lowell said icily, "for I become very difficult and cause unpleasant scenes when I think an officer of the United States Army has been insulted by an unwashed plate jockey."

The maître d', sensing trouble, hurried to the table.

"Is everything all right, Colonel Lowell?"

"We need a round of beer and another waiter," Lowell said. "Aside from that, everything's fine."

More heads had turned. The maître d'hôtel made a quick decision.

"Of course," he said. "Immediately."

"That's a good fellow," Lowell said. He picked up his beer glass.

"Mud in your eye, Lieutenant Ellis," he said.

"Fuck *him*!" Warrant Officer (Junior Grade) Wojinski said.

Embarrassed, but touched that Lowell had come so ferociously to his aid, Ellis took a sip of the beer. Then he put the glass down and gingerly removed the hot cheesecloth that covered his clams. He looked at them suspiciously. He was going to have to eat them, he understood. And the lobster that was going to follow. It would be the first time he had eaten either.

What this was, he thought as he watched MacMillan fork a clam, dip it in melted butter, and then pop it in his mouth, was field training at Elgin Air Base all over again. High class but the same thing. Eating strange food because the alternatives were going hungry and looking like a jackass in front of the others.

That made him think of Edward B. Eaglebury, whom they were going to bury tomorrow. Eaglebury, wearing the stripes of an army sergeant first class, had been a member of Ellis's "A" Team (Training) 59-23 at Eglin. It wasn't until after they had returned to Bragg, after they had spent all that time in Eglin's swamps, finally reduced to killing and eating a wild hog, that he had learned Eaglebury was an Annapolis graduate and a lieutenant commander in the navy.

"You seem dubious about the clams, Ellis," Lowell said to him.

"I never had any before, Colonel," Ellis said. He forked a clam, dipped it, and put it in his mouth. It wasn't as bad as he thought it would be. Strange but not slimy. He had been afraid it would be slimy.

"I thought all of you Green Berets were trained in eating exotic foods," Lowell asked innocently. "Snakes, lizards, that sort of thing."

"Shut up, Lowell," MacMillan said. "Lay off the Green Beret remarks."

"Oh, I am *heartily* sorry, Colonel MacMillan," Lowell said mockingly. "It's just that I am simply *intrigued* by all the stories I hear about those of you who wear the girl scout hats."

"Well, you won't have to be intrigued much longer," MacMillan said. "Those sonsofbitches at CONARC just outlawed them."

"How did you hear about that?" Hanrahan asked.

"I got friends up there," Mac said. "I was going to tell you just as soon as I had a minute alone with you."

"I found out two days ago," Hanrahan said. "They sent me a copy of the directive first class."

"Can they make it stick?" Mac asked.

"I'll have to issue the order when we get back," Hanrahan said.

"Can Felter help?" Mac asked.

"No," Hanrahan said simply.

"Shit!" Ellis said, more loudly than he intended.

"I didn't know that, of course," Lowell said. "I was just kidding."

"Oh, fuck you, Lowell!" MacMillan said.

He was far more angry at the loss of the green berets than at him, Lowell realized.

"Watch your tongue, Mac," Hanrahan snapped.

"The reason the pride of Mauch Chunk feels he can talk to me in that obscene and ungentlemanly way, Ellis," Lowell said lightly, "is that he has been privileged to know me since I was a PFC."

" 'Privileged' ?" MacMillan said incredulously.

"All right, then: 'honored,' " Lowell said agreeably.

"He was a lousy PFC, Ellis," MacMillan said.

The awkward moment, Lowell hoped, had passed.

"I was very young and impressionable," he said. "And I trusted MacMillan when he approached me and told me that he was going to make me an officer, and I would get more pay and nicer uniforms, and people would salute me and call me 'sir.' So I went along with him. And the next thing I know, I'm on a mountaintop in Greece, and they've lost my pay records. It's three degrees colder than at the north pole, and there are no American uniforms, so I'm wearing British battle dress, which is made from rejected horse blankets, and people are shooting at me."

Hanrahan laughed.

"MacMillan, meanwhile, covering his ass as always, has gone back to the States," Lowell went on. "So you will understand why, whenever he says something to me, I put one hand on my wallet and the other on the family jewels."

"Ellis," Hanrahan said. "That is known as disinformation.

A complex web of lies built upon a fragile foundation of truth."

"It's *all* true," Lowell insisted. "Don't revise history."

"I was advisor to a Greek mountain division, Ellis," Hanrahan said. "And I requested experienced tank officers in the grade of captain and above. What they sent me was Lowell, who was eighteen years old and a second lieutenant, and who had never been inside a tank. That much, at least, is true."

"It's all true," Lowell repeated. "There I was, shivering in my horse-blanket uniform, eighteen years old, and the colonel, here, was making a daily speech about how the entire fate of western civilization as we know it was resting on my shoulders."

"Mr. Wojinski told me about you in Greece, Colonel," Ellis said.

"Wojinski lies," Lowell said, nodding at the middle-aged warrant officer.

"How do you know what I told him, Duke?" Wojinski asked.

"The thing to remember about Colonel Lowell, Ellis," Major Parker said, "is that he is insane. If you keep that in mind, everything else he does falls into place."

"*I'm* insane? I'm surrounded by people who eat snakes, jump out of perfectly functioning airplanes, and wear girl scout hats, and *I'm* insane?"

"There he goes with that hat shit again," MacMillan said, and then stopped as two waiters appeared with trays of steaming lobsters.

"So far as the hat is concerned, Craig," Colonel Hanrahan said, "we brought one for you."

"I don't understand," Lowell said.

"You will wear it tomorrow," Hanrahan said. It was clearly an order.

"May I ask why?" Lowell asked. It was a subordinate asking a question of a superior, not a challenge.

"Because Lieutenant Commander Eaglebury was killed as a Green Beret, and will be carried to his grave by Green Berets. This will probably be the last ceremony in which people will wear green berets. Indulge me; we Irish are emotional and love symbolism."

"I am not, Colonel, a Green Beret," Lowell said softly.

"Just wear the hat, Craig, and don't argue with me," Han-

rahan said angrily, and then softened. "But you are. You've
commanded foreign troops in combat. You're as entitled as
Felter and me."

"Yes, sir," Lowell said. He looked thoughtful a moment,
then shrugged.

He looked over at Mac MacMillan.

"You don't eat the red part, Mac," he said. "Open it up and
eat what's inside."

"Fuck you, Lowell," Lieutenant Colonel MacMillan said.

Colonel Paul T. Hanrahan was on the curb outside Bookbinder's, about to enter the maroon limousine, before he thought
of the check.

"We didn't pay the bill," he said, looking at Lowell.

"The bill has been taken care of, Colonel," Lowell said.

He remembered that during the flap about Ellis's beer, the
headwaiter had called Lowell by name.

"You fixed it with the headwaiter," Hanrahan accused.

"Would the colonel enter the vehicle, please?" Lowell said.
"The colonel is blocking the sidewalk."

"Damn you, Craig," Hanrahan said, and got in the limousine.

(Four)
Company "C," First Battalion
Eleventh Infantry Regiment
U.S. Army Basic Training Center
Fort Jackson, South Carolina
2105 Hours, 29 November 1961

Company "C" occupied four two-story wooden barracks
built in 1941 to last five years. Two barracks faced the other
two across an open area, itself about as long as a barrack. To
one side were two one-story frame buildings. One housed the
orderly room, the mailroom, and the arms room. the other the
supply room.

Company "C" consisted of four platoons, each of forty men.
Each platoon had a barracks, the Third Platoon occupying one
of the barracks closest to the orderly room and supply-room

buildings. Each platoon consisted of four squads, each of ten men. The third and fourth squads of the Third Platoon occupied the second floor of the Third Platoon's barracks. At the top of the stairway were two private rooms. These were occupied by the acting squad leaders of the two platoons. The other basic trainees' bunks and equipment were in the squad bay, nine trainees on each side.

The interior of the barracks was open frame work. To the two-by-four stud beside each bed, a shelf had been nailed. The shelf supported the trainee's helmets, protective, steel; their liners, helmet; and their caps, service, brimmed. The shelf support studs had been drilled, and lengths of pipe had been inserted in the holes. The trainees hung their uniforms from the pipes: overcoat; raincoat; field jacket; tunic # 1 (with trousers inside); tunic # 2; shirts khaki, #1 through #3, fatigue jacket # 1 (with fatigue trousers inside); fatigue jacket # 2. Beside fatigue jacket # 2 was hung bath towel # 1 (on a wire hanger) with facecloth #1 on top of bath towel #1, centered. Each trainee kept beneath the left side of his bed near the aisle his two pairs of Boots, combat, his pair of Shoes, Low Quarter, and his shower clogs, the toes lined up so as to be directly below the left frame of the bunk. His laundry bag was tied to the end of his bunk, immediately to the left of the name plate hanging from the center of the bunk's frame.

Bath towel #2, facecloth #2, and other items (undershirts, men's, cotton, w/sleeves; underdrawers, men's, cotton, w/snap fasteners; socks, men's, wool, cushion-sole; and so on) were kept in a prescribed order in the locker at the foot of each bunk.

The arrangement of clothing and footlockers was subject to inspection at any time, and in the seven and one half weeks the men of "C-One-Eleven" had been in basic training, they had learned to store their gear neatly and according to regulation.

Regulation forbade the use of bunks between the hours of 0355 (when first call was sounded, via a phonograph record played over the PA system) and 2055 hours, when Lights Out was sounded. On this particular night, for some reason, Lights Out had not been sounded, although it was ten minutes after the schedule called for it. Because the trainees had been taught to do nothing unless expressly ordered to, they had not felt free to remove the blanket placed in the prescribed manner over the pillows and get into their bunks.

Some of them lay on the floor beside the bunks; some of them sat on their foot lockers; and others were gathered around the red-painted #10 cans, the "butt cans" nailed to pillars along the aisle between the two rows of bunks.

To a man, they were wondering whether Staff Sergeant Douglas B. Foster, their platoon sergeant, was actually going to do what he threatened to do. What he had threatened to do was knock some of the smart-ass out of Recruit (E-1) Geoffrey Craig II.

Like most other men in his family (his father being the notable exception), Geoffrey Craig II was tall, blond, lithe like a tennis player, pleasant-faced, and blue-eyed. Like forty percent of the other trainees, he was a draftee, involuntarily summoned by his friends and neighbors to military service for two years' active duty, to be followed by either three years in the active reserve or National Guard, or five years in the inactive reserve.

Like twenty-five percent of the other draftees, Recruit Craig had two or more years of college, in his case Princeton. He was the first Craig in six generations who had not attended Harvard College in Cambridge, Massachusetts. In the opinion of Porter Craig ('38), his father, Harvard had been devoured by the Jews and the Communists. He had expressed his displeasure with the takeover by no longer responding to the semi-annual plea for funds and by enrolling his two sons in Princeton, to which he now sent the not unsubstantial financial contribution he had formerly sent to Harvard.

Porter Craig, Sr., had not yet made up his mind what to do about St. Mark's School, from which he, his father, and his grandfather had graduated. St. Marks had fallen into something like the same crap at Harvard, encouraging kids who had no real business at St. Mark's to enroll. But the difference, Porter Craig, Sr., had been informed, was that the "recruited" students were recruited on the basis of test scores alone, and not because they belonged to some racial or ethnic minority. That was one thing. What Harvard was doing was something else: scouring the slums and the South for "disadvantaged" people to bring to Cambridge.

Recruit Geoffrey Craig had been summoned to military service following the completion of his junior year at Princeton, after the university had informed his draft board that he had failed to maintain a satisfactory academic average. His father was less concerned than he pretended to be about Geoff's grades, having graduated with a C minus average himself. Thus, after appropriate huffing and puffing, he had sent Geoff to Europe for the summer with instructions to give serious thought to his future. At the time, both had hoped that even though Geoff lost his "academic deferment," he would not be called up. They weren't taking everybody for the draft.

But his faceless friends and neighbors, after due consideration of the pool of young men available to them, had decided that the defense of the country required the military service of Geoffrey Craig II, and Geoff had had to come home from Salzburg and report to the Armed Forces Induction Center in Lower Manhattan for a preinduction physical.

What private hopes both of them had that the doctors would discover some disqualifying physical condition were not realized. Geoff was pronounced to be in perfect physical condition and was informed that he should settle his personal affairs and await the actual call to service.

On the appointed day and at the appointed hour, Geoffrey Craig II, more than a little hung over, had taken a cab to the Armed Forces Induction Center, had toyed with and discarded the notion that he should tell the army shrink that he was a closet faggot, and shortly after noon on a crisp afternoon in early September had taken one step forward, raised his hand, and solemnly sworn that he would defend the Constitution of the United States against all enemies, foreign and domestic, and that he would obey the orders of the officers and noncommissioned officers appointed over him.

He and sixty-six other young men, most of them draftees, had been taken by bus to Fort Dix, New Jersey, where they were given a series of inoculations designed to protect them from disease; had the Articles of War read to them by a commissioned officer; were given short haircuts; uniforms; and were subjected to a battery of tests to determine their suitability for various military occupational specialties and training.

Recruit Craig was summoned to an interview with a sergeant representing the Army Security Agency. His education, the sergeant told him, together with the really fine scores he had made on the Army General Classification Test (AGCT), qualified him for the Army Security Agency. After basic training, if he so chose, he would be given classified special training and assigned to duties having to do with the security of army communications.

Geoff had heard all about the Army Security Agency from a guy he had known at Princeton. Stripped of the bullshit, what they taught you was Morse code, and what you did for eight hours a day was sit at a typewriter and transcribe intercepted radio messages. The former ASA man Geoff had met at Princeton had told him that it was probably the worst fucking job in the fucking army.

Geoff told the sergeant he didn't think he'd be interested in that, and remained immune to the blandishments and threats that followed. The sergeant, who was having trouble making his quota, made good his threat concerning what would happen to Recruit Craig if he refused the golden opportunity offered him. He would be handed a fucking rifle and spend his two years running up and down hills and sleeping on the ground.

Recruit Craig was ordered from Fort Dix, New Jersey, to Fort Jackson, South Carolina, for basic training and for individual training leading to the award of Military Occupational Specialty 745, "Light Weapons Infantryman."

Recruit Craig met Staff Sergeant Douglas B. Foster the moment he stepped off the bus at Fort Jackson. Foster was thirty, a well-built, rather short man who had been in the army thirteen years. He had enlisted in the army after failing his junior year at Westwego High School in Louisiana. He had been a private in Germany when the Korean War broke out. Two years later he had been sent to Korea, where he served with the Forty-fifth Infantry Division, which was part of the Oklahoma National Guard.

Although he ultimately rose to sergeant with the Forty-fifth Division, his assignment there had not been a happy one. Fully eighty percent of the officers and men were either national guardsmen or reservists, who held the regular army in varying degrees of scorn. Foster reacted by regarding everyone not a member of the regular army with equal scorn. He still disliked draftees and Yankees, and held in even greater contempt Yankee draftees who had gone to college and thought their shit didn't stink.

On his return from Korea, Sergeant Foster had served with the First Infantry Division ("The Big Red One") at Fort Riley, Kansas, as a squad leader in Company "F" of the Eighteenth Infantry Regiment. There he had met and married a Manhattan, Kansas, girl six months before their first child, a girl, was born. And a month after he had been promoted to staff sergeant, in 1960, a second girl was born to them. It was difficult to make it on a staff sergeant's pay. If there was anything Staff Sergeant Foster disliked more than a draftee Yankee college boy, it was a rich draftee Yankee college boy.

Because he had heard that promotions came quick there, Staff Sergeant Foster had applied and been accepted for duty as a basic training instructor shortly after Lisbeth Marie was born. His hopes proved to be unfounded up till now. Foster had been at Fort Jackson for twenty months and had not been promoted. He had run ten cycles of trainees through the program without a nice nod in his direction from his superiors.

The very first time they had met, Recruit Craig and Staff Sergeant Foster had not liked each other. Craig had looked Foster in the eye, directly, as he learned that men did.

"I'll look at you, soldier," Staff Sergeant Foster had said to Recruit Craig, "but when I want you to look at me, I'll tell you!"

"Yes, sir."

"You don't say 'sir' to sergeants, soldier!"

"Yes, Sergeant."

"You look like a wise-ass to me, soldier," Foster said. "Are you a wise-ass?"

"I try not to be, Sergeant, in my present circumstances."

The only thing that Recruit Craig managed to do in basic training that met the standards of Staff Sergeant Foster was superior firing with the U.S. rifle, M 1. That was judged by the number of holes in or near the bull's-eye and was not a matter of opinion.

On the other hand, Recruit Craig was unable to meet Staff Sergeant Foster's standards of a clean rifle, and it was necessary for him to clean his weapon an average of four times each day of the live-fire training program. Neither could he seem to give his boots and shoes a luster that met the sergeant's approval. Nor draw the blankets of his bunk tight enough so that a quarter bounced on it would rise high enough to satisfy the sergeant. The sergeant, to express his displeasure, would then overturn the bunk.

When Staff Sergeant Foster was alone with his platoon, he referred to Recruit Craig as "Recruit Asshole" or simply "Asshole."

Recruit Asshole came to the conclusion that Staff Sergeant Foster was trying to provoke him into doing something foolish, like belting him in the mouth, and vowed that he would control himself. Basic training would eventually be over and he would leave. It couldn't possibly be as bad as this elsewhere in the army.

If he had correctly understood the mumbling second lieutenant who had read the Articles of War aloud to them, doing violence to a noncommissioned officer in the execution of his office was "punishable by death or such other punishment as a court-martial shall decide." Recruit Asshole didn't think they would actually punish him by death, but he probably would find himself in the stockade. And time spent in the stockade would not count against the one year, nine months, and however many days it was he had remaining to serve.

That morning, the press of his other duties had kept the platoon leader, a second lieutenant three months out of Officer Candidate School, from personally conducting the daily inspection of the barracks. Staff Sergeant Foster had conducted the inspection.

Recruit Asshole's bunk was sloppily made, and the bunk was turned over. Recruit Asshole's facecloth was hung crookedly on his bath towel and was thrown to the floor.

And then Staff Sergeant Foster found the buttonhole on Recruit Asshole's left hip pocket to be frayed. He ripped the button off and then faced Recruit Asshole.

"You think it would help you remember that buttons are to be sewed on good if you ate it, Asshole?"

"I doubt it, Sergeant."

"Eat it, Asshole!"

"I respectfully decline, Sergeant."

"That's an order, Asshole!"

"I believe it to be an unlawful order, Sergeant."

"You're refusing to obey an order?"

"I am respectfully declining to obey an order I believe to be unlawful, Sergeant."

"You don't like me, do you, Asshole?"

Recruit Asshole said nothing.

"I ast you a question, Asshole!"

"No, Sergeant, I don't like you," Recruit Asshole said.

"Just what *do* you think of me, Asshole?"

When Recruit Asshole said nothing, Staff Sergeant Foster repeated: "I ast you a question, Asshole!"

"I think you're a semiliterate cretin with psychological problems," Recruit Asshole replied.

Staff Sergeant Foster knew what *semiliterate* meant, and what *psychological problems* meant, but he was goddamned if he'd ask Asshole what *cretin* meant.

"Then why don't you do something about it, Asshole? You a fairy, or what?"

"I'm not a fool, Sergeant," Recruit Asshole said, saying more than he knew he should be saying, but unable to stop himself. "I would like to knock you on your ass, but I'm not going to pay for the privilege by going to the stockade for it."

"Is that all that's stopping you, Asshole?" Staff Sergeant Foster rose eagerly to the challenge. "Then I'll tell you what: Tonight, you and me will just step outside the barracks, and I'll take my jacket off, and then it'll between us. Man-to-Asshole. You want to try that?"

"I can think of nothing I would like better," Recruit Asshole heard himself say.

He regretted it during the balance of the day. It was a no-win situation.

At 2107 hours Staff Sergeant Foster appeared at the head of the stairs.

"Attention in the squad bay!" one of the trainees called, and every one jumped to attention.

"Recruit Craig," Staff Sergeant Foster called out cordially, "could I see you outside a moment?"

Recruit Craig walked down the aisle between the bunks to the staircase.

When he was at the head of the staircase, Staff Sergeant Foster snapped off the lights in the squad bay.

"Hit the sack, the rest of you," he said.

The trainees did as they were ordered, but no one slept. They knew what was about to happen.

There was some talk of going to the adjacent company and calling the platoon leader at his quarters. It was generally agreed that Staff Sergeant Foster was going to do more than knock the shit out of Craig; he was liable to hurt him really bad. Everyone agreed that somebody should call the lieutenant and tell him, but no one was willing to volunteer to do it themselves.

Ten minutes later it sounded like someone was falling up the steps. One brave soul got out of his bunk, took his flashlight, and went quickly down the aisle.

It was Recruit Asshole. He looked awful. He was bleeding from the mouth; his nose was bleeding and crooked, as if broken; and he was holding his right wrist in his left hand.

"I think I broke it," he said as he was helped to his bunk.

"You hit him, huh?"

"Hit him? I hope I killed the sonofabitch!"

Ten minutes later there was the sound of a siren, soon followed by flashing red lights. A brave trainee went to the window and reported that there was an ambulance outside.

Five minutes after that, the lieutenant came into the squad bay and turned on the lights and told Recruit Craig that he was under arrest.

Five minutes after that, two military policemen came into the squad bay and put handcuffs on Recruit Asshole and marched him down the aisle and down the stairs and put him in the back of their jeep and drove off with him.

(Five)
204 Wallingford Road
Swarthmore, Pennsylvania
2045 Hours, 29 November 1961

When the soldiers came in, Dianne Eaglebury, who was

nineteen years old, five feet seven, and honey blond, was sitting beside her mother and her sister-in-law on a couch against the wall of the living room.

In the center of the room was her brother's flag-covered casket. It was closed and sealed, and there was something unreal in the notion that Ed was in there, dead, and that she would never see him again. When her father had telephoned her at the Tri-Delt House at Duke, where she was a sophomore, to tell her the bad news, she had wept. Earlier a team of officers from the navy had gone to Ed's quarters at the Anacostia Naval Air Station to tell his wife, Suzanne, that Ed had been killed in the Bay of Pigs invasion and that "recovery of the remains was unlikely." Suzanne had called Ed's father, and he had called Dianne soon after.

She'd wept then and again that night, alone in her bed; and she'd wept when she'd come home for the memorial service at St. James' Church. But she had not wept since they had been informed by the navy that the remains had been recovered; nor when she went with her father and the people from the funeral director's to the Philadelphia Naval Shipyard to meet the submarine with the casket; nor here in the house. She wondered why she had not.

Ed was to be buried with full military honors, and Dianne wondered about that again when she saw the soldiers. Why didn't they say "naval honors"? Ed was a sailor, a naval officer. And what was the army doing here?

They hadn't been able to get any details about how Ed had been killed—just some formal business about it being "in the line of duty in connection with activities near Cuba." Dianne's father had pressed the captain who had taken them to the naval shipyard for details, but the captain said that he just didn't have any details to offer. He seemed genuinely sorry that he didn't, but Dianne's father was hurt and angry and had jumped all over him.

"I lose my only son, and nobody knows how it happened? God*damn* it!"

One of the soldiers was black. He was a very large man, Dianne saw. He stood alongside a tall stunningly handsome blond officer while three of the others, presumably Catholics, went to the prie-dieu that had been placed by the casket for

Ed's Catholic friends. One of these three Dianne recognized. She had seen him at the naval shipyard. She had thought then, and still thought now, that he didn't look old enough to be an officer. Nevertheless he had lieutenant's bars on his uniform, so he must be. All of the soldiers held something green in their left hands, and after a moment Dianne realized they were hats, French berets. She had never seen soldiers wearing berets, and wondered about that too.

While the three Catholics were saying their prayers by Ed's casket, Dianne's father came into the room from the dining room, where a buffet and bar had been set up. Dianne could tell from his flushed face that he had had more than a few drinks.

The handsome colonel led the way to the Eagleburys. As the young officer neared, Dianne saw that he was even younger than she had at first thought. Maybe, she thought, he was somebody's son. But she dismissed that when she saw they were all wearing the same kind of uniform.

"Hello, Suzanne," the colonel said to the widow.

"Hello, Craig," Suzanne said. "It was good of you to come. Dad, this is Colonel Lowell. He and Ed were friends."

"Colonel," Ed Eaglebury's father said to Lowell.

"Good evening, sir," Lowell said.

"And this is Ed's mother and his sister," Suzanne said. "My parents are around here someplace."

Lowell shook the offered hands.

"May I introduce these gentlemen?" he asked.

"Please do," Mr. Eaglebury said.

"Colonel Hanrahan," Lowell said, "Lieutenant Colonel MacMillan, Major Parker, Warrant Officer Wojinski, and Lieutenant Ellis."

"You're Lieutenant Ellis?" Suzanne Eaglebury said in surprise. "You were in Florida with my husband?"

"Yes, ma'am," Ellis said. He was visibly uncomfortable.

"My husband described you, Lieutenant, as 'tough as nails.' I expected someone a hundred pounds heavier, ten years older, who chews spikes."

Dianne's attention was diverted by someone new entering the room. A neatly dressed man in a business suit walked in, carrying a floral display on a metal stand. He crossed the room

and placed the display right in front of the casket, thus con-
cealing the two displays behind it. Then he turned and left the
room.

"Honey," Dianne's father said, a touch of annoyance in his
voice, "see what that's all about."

Dianne walked to the flowers, bent over them, and took the
card from an envelope wired to the stand.

While she was doing this, a tall man entered the room and
moved quickly toward the casket. He made the sign of the cross
and then dropped to his knees at the prie-dieu.

I wonder who he is, Dianne wondered. *He looks just like
Kennedy.*

She dropped her eyes to the card in her hand. There was a
gold-embossed National Seal and an engraved legend:

THE PRESIDENT

and

Mrs. John Fitzgerald Kennedy

She looked at the man on his knees, and for a moment their
eyes met. And then the President rose and walked to where
the soldiers and other Eagleburys were clustered. There was
no question it was Kennedy; the soldiers had come to attention,
and there was a buzz of whispers. As Dianne walked after him
she saw two men standing by the door. The Secret Service. A
small, wiry, balding man in a not–very–well-fitting suit came
to the door and was passed inside by the Secret Service.

". . . was a brave man, Mrs. Eaglebury," Dianne heard the
last part of the sentence, "and his death was not in vain."

"We are honored that you could come, Mr. President,"
Suzanne said.

"It is my privilege," the President said.

"Mr. President," Dianne's father said, "I would like to know
how my son died."

Dianne wondered if her father would have had the courage
to say that to the President of the United States if he weren't
half plastered. She decided that he would have.

The President seemed to consider that for a moment before
replying.

"Is there somewhere private?" he asked.

"There's a butler's pantry off the dining room," Mr. Eaglebury said.

The President looked over his shoulder and spoke to the small man in the ill-fitting suit.

"Felter, ask whichever of these gentlemen may have the information Mr. Eaglebury wants to come with us, will you, please?"

"Yes, Mr. President," Felter said.

Dianne was surprised to see there were two more Secret Service men inside the dining room. When they saw where Dianne's father was headed, followed by the President, they sped across the room and went into the butler's pantry ahead of them.

The President turned and looked at Dianne.

"I'm John Kennedy," he said, and offered his hand.

"This is Ed's sister, Dianne," Dianne's mother said.

"I'm very sorry about your brother, Miss Eaglebury," he said.

Felter came in the room, followed by the handsome colonel and the very young lieutenant.

"Colonel Hanrahan and Lieutenant Ellis, Mr. President," Felter said.

"Thank you, Felter," the President said. "These officers were intimately involved with Commander Eaglebury in the mission during which he gave his life. Colonel Hanrahan is commanding officer of the Special Warfare School; Lieutenant Ellis was commanding officer of the Special Forces team with which Commander Eaglebury infiltrated into Cuba. Will you take over, Hanrahan?"

Hanrahan looked hesitant. So Felter began the story.

"The mission was duofold," he said. "Lieutenant Ellis's 'A' Team was charged with establishing a radio direction finder on the ground, which would permit aircraft to locate themselves in relation to the invasion site. Commander Eaglebury had an even higher priority covert mission, and went in with Ellis's team in the uniform of an army sergeant."

"What was that 'even higher priority mission'?" Mr. Eaglebury asked.

Felter looked at the President.

"Tell him, Felter," the President said. "*I* decide who has the 'need to know.'"

"Commander Eaglebury believed that the Russians were constructing missile sites on Cuba," Felter said. "It was his intention to bring back proof that they were."

"The initial phase of the mission was successful," Colonel Hanrahan said. "That is, the parachute drop."

"My husband parachuted into Cuba?"

"Yes, ma'am," Hanrahan said.

"And you, too, Ellis?" Suzanne Eaglebury asked.

"Yes, ma'am," Ellis said.

Dianne looked at him in disbelief. He was a boy.

"And then what happened?" Suzanne asked. Hanrahan raised his palm toward Ellis.

"When we were in place, he went off wherever he was going," Ellis said.

"But he didn't make it," Mr. Eaglebury said.

"He got the proof—photographs is what I'm saying," Hanrahan said. "According to plan, he cached duplicates and tried to make it back to Ellis."

"But didn't make it?" Mr. Eaglebury pursued.

"No, sir," the President said. "He was captured and summarily executed."

"Without a trial?" Commander Eaglebury's mother asked.

"And for nothing," his father said.

"No, sir, not for nothing," the President said. "The mission was continued by Colonel Felter."

"Who?" Mr. Eaglebury asked.

"This Colonel Felter," the President said, pointing, "parachuted into Cuba and picked up the duplicate film, took some more of his own, and made it back to Ellis. They ultimately made their way to the coast, where they were picked up by Colonel Lowell and flown home."

"The Russians have missiles in Cuba?" Dianne's father asked. "What are we doing about it?"

"The matter is under consideration," the President said. "No decision has yet been made."

Mr. Eaglebury looked at the President.

"'Under consideration,'" he quoted bitterly.

"Commander Eaglebury has been posthumously awarded

the Distinguished Service Cross," the President said. "But I'm afraid under the circumstances there can be no public announcement."

"The DSC?" Mr. Eaglebury asked. "For what? For getting killed?"

"No," the President said. "For dedication to his country above and beyond the call of duty. Your son, Mr. Eaglebury, considered it his duty, at the risk of his life, to prove the President of the United States wrong. I really didn't think the Russians would do what your son believed they were doing."

"I didn't vote for you, Mr. President," Mr. Eaglebury said. "For some reason I think I should tell you that."

"I don't think Ed Eaglebury voted for me," the President said. "But when I took office, I became his commander in chief, and he chose to serve me with a dedication that ultimately cost him his life. That's distinguished service, I think, Mr. Eaglebury. He earned that medal."

The President and Mr. Eaglebury locked eyes for a moment.

"It was very good of you to come here, Mr. President," Mr. Eaglebury said. "We're grateful to you. And thank you for telling us what happened."

"I'm sorry I couldn't come earlier and that I can't stay longer," the President said. He glanced over his shoulder. "Felter!"

Felter handed him an oblong box.

"I thought," the President said, "that tonight might be the wrong time for this. But I finally decided that one day, Mrs. Eaglebury, Ed's sons might like to know you received this from the hand of the President."

He opened the box and handed it to Suzanne.

When she looked down at the medal in the box, there was a sob in her throat, but she fought it down, found her voice, and forced a smile.

"I think this belongs on the pillow," she said, "with Ed's other decorations."

It took the President a moment to understand what she meant.

"Yes," he said, "I think it does." He put out his hand, and Suzanne gave the box back to him. He took the medal from the box and handed the box back to her.

Then he led them all out the butler's pantry, through the

dining room, and into the living room, where he walked to the casket. When he was sure they were all standing beside him, the President pinned the Distinguished Service Cross to a blue pillow, which rested on the flag on the casket beside Lieutenant Commander Edward B. Eaglebury's brimmed cap, his sword, and his other military decorations. He pinned it immediately below Eaglebury's gold naval aviator's wings and his silver army parachutist's qualification badge. Then he shook the hands of the Eaglebury family, nodded at the officers, and walked quickly away from the casket and out of the room.

III

(One)
Camp David, Maryland
0715 Hours, 30 November 1961

The marine guard found Lieutenant Colonel Sanford T. Felter in the communications cabin.

"Sir," he said, and waited for Felter to look up from the IBM typewriter at the commo officer's desk. Then he went on: "The President asks that you join him, sir."

"I'll be right there," Felter said, and returned his concentration to the typewriter. He typed rapidly for another two minutes, then tore the sheet of paper with the TOP SECRET *(Presidential)* letterhead from the machine, folded it, stuffed it in an envelope, and stood up.

He followed the marine guard to the presidential cabin. The Secret Service man on duty outside opened the door for him.

"He was just looking for you," he said as Felter passed by him.

The President was sitting at a small table by a window, looking out on the mountains. A light snow had fallen during the night, and the snow looked very white in the early-morning light.

"Sorry to have kept you waiting, sir," Felter said, and handed him the envelope.

"Your breakfast was getting cold," the President said. "That's all." Then he said, "I ordered you ham and eggs."

"Ham and eggs are fine, Mr. President," Felter said. "Thank you."

He sat down at the table and opened a napkin and put it on his lap. A white-jacketed navy steward poured coffee into his cup, and Felter nodded his thanks.

The President read the summary and handed it back to Felter.

"That'll be all, thank you," he said to the steward.

Felter cut a piece of ham and broke the yolk of an egg with it.

"I was very impressed with that young Green Beret lieutenant yesterday," the President said.

"Lieutenant Ellis," Felter said. "Very interesting young man. His mother is Puerto Rican. He grew up in Spanish Harlem. If I may correct you, Mr. President, the proper term is *Special Forces*."

"I thought they . . . you . . . liked to be called Green Berets."

"That's become moot, Mr. President. The CONARC commander has seen fit to forbid the wearing of 'foreign-type' headgear."

"Is that was is known as a 'subtle appeal to higher authority,' Felter?" the President asked.

"The decision has apparently been made that Special Forces properly belong to the Airborne family, Mr. President, and should dress accordingly."

"When I was in the P T boats, Sandy, we used to take the stiffeners out of our hats, and we'd soak the gold braid strap in seawater so it would corrode. We didn't want anybody mistaking us for battleship sailors. And every time an admiral would see us, he would message our commander, ordering him to ensure that his officers dressed like naval officers. We would of course comply with that order. Sometimes for as long as a week."

"I don't wish to press the point, Mr. President," Felter said. "But . . . ?"

"The green berets are a symbol of independence."

"You think Special Forces should be independent of Airborne? Sort of supersoldiers?"

"I think they would be of more value if they were not considered as just one more Airborne asset, Mr. President."

"Max Taylor wants to send a flock of airplanes and about five thousand 'advisors' to Indochina. Are you aware of that?"

"I was not," Felter said. "But I'm not surprised."

"What do you think?"

"I wouldn't presume to comment on General Taylor's recommendations, sir."

"What do you think, Felter?" the President said.

"General Taylor is the best man you could have sent to Indochina, Mr. President. His military credentials are impeccable. He is, additionally, a scholar. Whatever recommendations he has made should be considered very carefully."

"President Truman sent American troops to Greece to advise the Greek army. They succeeded in keeping the Communists out of Greece. You were there. Why did that work?"

"Because, by and large, we sent highly qualified, highly motivated people to Greece. Colonel Hanrahan is a good example. He had been in Greece during the war. He knew and liked the Greeks. And they liked him. There was also a strong religious element in Greece. The people thought of the Communists as godless. The people believed they were defending their church as well as their country."

"Would the same kind of operation work in Indochina?"

"The Communists were defeated in Greece, Mr. President. They learn from their mistakes. In Indochina they will use the religious feelings of the population to their advantage. They will pit the Buddhists and members of other Asiatic religions against the Roman Catholics and against each other. They will also be able to paint American forces as colonists. They used that tactic successfully against the French."

"You were at Dien Bien Phu, weren't you?"

"Yes, sir. President Eisenhower sent me over there shortly before it fell."

"In one sentence, how do you assess the Viet Minh?"

"As a formidable opponent, sir."

"And how do you think our senior officers regard them?"

Felter was obviously reluctant to say what he had on his mind.

"Go on, Felter," the President said.

"They make two mistakes, sir: They do not hold the French army in very high regard, and infer from that that our army can accomplish things the French could not."

"The French haven't won any wars lately," the President said dryly. "That feeling is understandable."

"The Troisième Regiment Parachutiste of the Foreign Legion, which fell at Dien Bien Phu, was as good a regiment as any I've ever seen, Mr. President."

"You said *two* mistakes."

"They believe the Viet Minh to be a rabble of ignorant natives equipped with scavenged World War II small arms who will collapse as soon as they are faced with modern, well-equipped forces."

"Well, then, presuming we have to do something about them, what do you recommend?"

"General Taylor is far better qualified to answer a question like that than I am, Mr. President."

"I've already asked him; now I'm asking you."

"I would try to repeat what we did in Greece, Mr. President, rather than attempt to overwhelm the Viet Minh with conventional forces."

"Do you think that will work?"

"No, sir, I do not," Felter said. "I don't think we should go into Indochina."

"Neither, for your private information," the President said, "does General Taylor." When there was no response from Felter, he went on. "I'm going to send the airplanes, and I'm going to send advisors. But I haven't made up my mind yet what to call them. It's been proposed that these five thousand troops masquerade as flood-control engineers. I may end up calling them what they are, however."

There came the sound of helicopter rotor blades thrashing through the air.

"Ah, Pierre and the gentlemen of the Fourth Estate," the President said.

"With your permission, sir, I'll leave you to get ready for them," Felter said.

"Sandy, I want to go have a look at the Green Berets," the President said, "at Fort Bragg. And soon. Will you come up with some sort of itinerary?"

"Yes, sir."

"Maybe we can decorate Lieutenant Ellis or something."

"Yes, sir."

(Two)
Station Hospital
Fort Jackson, South Carolina
0815 Hours, 30 November 1961

Recruit Geoffrey Craig was transported to the emergency room of the station hospital in a patrol car, an olive-drab Chevrolet four-door sedan whose hood and trunk lid had been painted white and on whose roof were a siren and a flashing red light.

He was dressed in fatigues. A large *P* had been stenciled on the back of the fatigue jacket, and smaller *P*'s had been stenciled to the trouser legs above the knees.

In addition to the two military policemen assigned to the patrol car, Craig was accompanied by and handcuffed to a large military police sergeant. It was normal procedure to restrain a prisoner by handcuffing his hands together behind him, but Recruit Craig's right hand and wrist were so swollen that the Smith & Wesson cuffs would not close around the wrist.

Earlier, at 0430 hours, the prisoner had called the attention of the NCO in charge of the detention facility to his painfully swollen hand and wrist. The NCO in charge of the detention facility had reported the matter to the desk sergeant, who told the NCO that the prisoner would have to wait until the stockade medic came on duty at 0715 hours—unless it looked like the bastard was going to croak or bleed to death or something.

After examining him, the medical technician assigned to the post stockade said that the prisoner would have to go to the hospital. It looked like he had broken the wrist and probably a couple of fingers. This fact was reported to the stockade commander, and the decision was made that since the prisoner was in no immediate danger, moving him to the hospital would have to wait "until they were finished charging him." In the meantime he suggested that the medic give the prisoner a couple of APCs.

An APC was a small white pill, a nonprescription analgesic, so called because it contained aspirin, paregoric, and codeine. Enlisted medics had the authority to dispense APCs as they saw fit.

At 0805 the prisoner was brought from the detention cell, a small room with wire mesh over the windows, to the officer of the stockade commander in the Stockade Administration Building. He was there informed by the commanding officer of Company "C," First Battalion, Eleventh Infantry Regiment (Training), that he was being held pending investigation of certain charges made against him.

He was advised that, under the provisions of the thirty-first Article of War, he did not have to answer any questions; that he had the right to have an officer learned in the law present to advise him during questioning; and that anything he said could and would be used against him in a court-martial. He was asked if he understood that.

"Yes, sir."

"Well, then, Craig?"

"I think I'd better talk to a lawyer, sir."

"In other words, you refuse to answer any questions?"

"Yes, sir."

"In that case, Recruit Craig, it is my duty to inform you that I have conducted an initial investigation into the charges made against you and have decided to bring the facts of the case as I understand them before a board of officers with the recommendation that you be charged with assault upon a noncommissioned officer in the execution of his office. Do you understand what I'm saying to you?"

"Yes, sir."

"I have further decided that, in view of the violent nature of the charges made against you, it is in the best interests of the service to order you confined pending disposition of the charges made against you. Do you understand that?"

"Yes, sir."

"I inform you further that I am presently investigating other charges made against you, and that other charges may be brought against you. Do you understand that?"

"Yes, sir."

"I now serve you with the charges I am making against you," the captain said. "You will read them, and if you have

any questions, I will try to answer them. Then you will sign
your name, which signifies only that you understand the charges,
not that you acknowledge committing any offense. Is that clear
to you?"

"Yes, sir."

When it was obvious that Recruit Craig could not manage
the charge sheet with his one good hand, he was permitted to
sit down, and the folder was laid before him on the stockade
commander's desk. When the folder was opened in front of
him, he saw, in the brief moment before it was snatched away,
the typewritten speech his company commander had given him.
He'd wondered about that—wondered if the captain had previously memorized all that legal business, or whether he had
memorized it this morning before he'd come to the stockade.

Since the charges that he had "assaulted Staff Sergeant
Douglas B. Foster, RA 14 234 303, Company 'A' 11th Infantry
Regiment (Training), a noncommissioned officer in the execution of his office" were already typed out, it was pretty clear
he had made the right decision in refusing to answer questions.
The decision to court-martial him had apparently already been
made.

"I can't use my hand, sir," Recruit Craig said. "How do I
sign this?"

"Use your left hand," his company commander said.

After his interview with his company commander, Recruit
Craig was taken from the Stockade Administrative Building
into the stockade proper. This was a collection of twelve two-
story barracks and administrative buildings. These were surrounded by two barbed-wire fences, ten feet apart. The space
between the fences was filled with expanded coils of barbed
wire, called concertina. There were guard towers at each corner
of the stockade compound, to which flood lights capable of
illuminating the area were mounted.

The normal in-processing procedure began with the prisoner
being ordered to strip and shower. Following this, he was issued
prisoner fatigues (with *P*'s painted on them), given a haircut,
and fingerprinted and photographed. He was next given the
"Orientation Lecture for Newly Confined Prisoners." In the
case of Recruit Craig, since he was obviously unable either to
bathe himself or to have his fingerprints taken with his hand

swollen the way it was, it was decided that all the processing he would receive was the issuance of fatigues and the haircut. He could finish his in-processing when they'd done whatever they were going to do about his hand and wrist.

In due course, it was time to send him to the hospital. In the station hospital a medic directed Craig and his guards to a small cubicle and pulled a white drape closed after they had entered it.

Two minutes later a portly, balding, gray-haired man wearing a medical smock came into the room. There was a name-plate pinned to the smock, giving his name (J. W. Caen, M.D.) but no rank, although he was wearing a uniform shirt and trousers beneath the light green medical smock.

"Take the handcuffs off, Sergeant," the doctor said. "And wait outside."

The sergeant freed Craig's hand, and then stepped back against the white curtain.

The doctor gently pulled Craig's swollen hand away from his chest. Then he looked up.

"I said wait outside."

"I'm not supposed to leave the prisoner," the sergeant said.

"Get out, Sergeant," the doctor said flatly.

The sergeant hesitated a moment and then left.

"There's no question there's broken bones," the doctor said, conversationally. "We'll take an X-ray and see how many."

He probed Craig's chest with his fingers. Craig winced and yelped.

"We'll X-ray your ribs too," the doctor said. Then he looked into Craig's eyes. "You're not thinking of doing something else stupid, are you? Like running away?"

"No, sir," Craig said.

The doctor looked into his eyes for a moment. Then turned and whipped the white curtain away.

"You can run along, Sergeant," he said. "I'm admitting this man."

"I'll have to accompany him to the prison ward, sir," the sergeant said, "and have them sign for him."

"That won't be necessary," the doctor said. "I've just assumed responsibility for him."

"I'm sorry, sir, you can't do that," the sergeant said.

"Sergeant," the doctor said, "I command this hospital. You don't tell me what I can or cannot do. It works the other way around. I've just given you an order to leave."

"May I call the Provost Marshal's office, sir?"

"You can call anybody you want," the doctor said. He took Craig's arm and led him out of the emergency room.

The sergeant looked for a moment as if he wanted to follow them, but instead went to a telephone hanging on the wall.

After three minutes in a maze of corridors, they came to the X-ray suite. A medic came more or less to attention.

"Son, run down to the PN ward, tell them to set up a room, and bring back some pajamas, a bathrobe, and slippers, will you, please?" the doctor said.

"Yes, sir," the medic said.

"Hand, *hands*, first, I think," Dr. Caen said. "Then your ribs. Can you hold your hand and wrist flat against this thing?"

He pointed to a grayish plate on an X-ray machine.

"Yes, sir."

"PN stands for psychoneurosis," Dr. Caen said. "Otherwise known as the loony bin. Anybody who belts a sergeant is more than likely crazy. And you'll be more comfortable there than in the prison ward."

"I don't think I'm crazy, sir."

"I never met a loony who did," the doctor said.

He gently arranged Craig's swollen wrist where he wanted it, adjusted the X-ray equipment, then stepped behind a barrier. The equipment made a whirring noise and, a moment later, another. Dr. Caen reappeared, arranged the other hand where he wanted it, and repeated the process.

"I'm a bone man," he said, "and I've been looking since I was a resident for an X-ray technician who can take decent pictures. I feel like Diogenes."

Craig chuckled.

"You know who Diogenes is, do you?" he asked, then: "Hold it!"

"Yes, sir," Craig said, when the doctor reappeared.

"College boy?"

"Yes, sir."

"Draftee?"

"Yes, sir."

"Your ass in the frying pan; you know that, I suppose."

"Yes, sir."

The medic returned, carrying white pajamas, a purple bathrobe, and white cloth slippers.

"Put the pajama bottoms on," the doctor said, "and then climb up on the table. You need help with your boots?"

"I think I can manage, sir," Craig said.

"Help him," the doctor ordered, "and then soup the film."

"Yes, sir."

When he lay on the X-ray table, there was a sharp pain in Craig's chest, and when he complied with the doctor's order to roll over, he felt another so sharp that he grunted.

"The sergeant got in a couple of licks of his own, I see," the doctor said.

"He got the first lick in," Craig said. "The minute I stepped out the door, the sonofabitch belted me in the ribs."

"Is that the way it happened?" the doctor said.

"Yes, sir."

"Who taught you to fight?" the doctor asked.

"I was on the boxing team in school," Craig said.

"Well, you did a job on the sergeant, if that's any solace," Dr. Caen said. "I was up half the night working on him. You broke his nose and his jaw—in several places. It was a hell of a wiring job. He'll be taking liquids for a month."

When there was no response, Dr. Caen said, "I don't detect any signs of regret."

"I regret that I'm going to be court-martialed," Craig said.

"You got any money?"

"Yes, sir."

"They'll send you a defense counsel in a day or two. Tell him you want a civilian attorney. It's your right. Insist on it."

"I didn't know that," Craig said. "Thank you, sir."

"They're probably going to find you guilty anyway," Dr. Caen said. "'Pour l'encouragement des autres.' You know what that means?"

"To encourage the others," Craig said. "Yes, sir."

"But a civilian lawyer worthy of the name can get them to make all kinds of procedural errors that will get your conviction thrown out on appeal. You probably won't be in the stockade more than a couple of months."

"It doesn't matter that I didn't start it?"

"No," Dr. Caen said. "I don't think it will."

"I appreciate the advice, Doctor," Craig said. "You've been very kind. Thank you."

"About once a cycle, one of Staff Sergeant Douglas's trainees shows up over here," Dr. Caen said, "with various bruises, contusions, and fractures suffered 'taking a fall down the stairs' or 'slipping in the shower.' I didn't feel all that sympathetic to him when they carried him in here last night."

(Three)
204 Wallingford Road
Swarthmore, Pennsylvania
0830 Hours, 30 November 1961

Dianne Eaglebury was coming down the stairs when the door chime went off. She answered the door herself.

Colonel Hanrahan and the boy soldier were standing on the porch. Outside she saw a maroon Cadillac limousine backing out of the driveway.

"Good morning," Hanrahan said. "I thought it might be a good idea if Ellis and I came now, in case we are needed. The others will be along later."

"Please come in," she said.

They were both in uniform, a blue uniform Dianne could not remember ever having seen before. Lieutenant Ellis apparently did not have any medals to wear, for his tunic was bare; but Colonel Hanrahan's chest was heavy with his medals. For this occasion he wore the full-size medals, not just the narrow, inch-long ribbons. Dianne recognized the Distinguished Service Cross among them, the only one she could identify.

Ellis smiled shyly at her.

"Have you had breakfast?" she said. "I was just about to have them make something for me."

"We've had breakfast," Hanrahan said. "Thank you just the same."

"How about some coffee?" Dianne pursued.

"I'll have some coffee, thank you," Ellis said.

She led them to the dining room via the hallway rather than

through the living room, where Ed's casket was.

"The others should start arriving shortly," Dianne said. "My parents are still asleep, I suppose."

Neither said anything.

"There's some nice bacon," Dianne said. "Are you sure you won't reconsider having breakfast? Bacon and eggs?"

"If it wouldn't be any trouble," Ellis said.

"Not at all," she said. "Colonel?"

"Not for me, thank you," Hanrahan said. "But I will have some coffee."

Dianne went through the butler's pantry into the kitchen and ordered breakfast. The door chime went off as she was returning, and again she went to answer it.

It was a navy captain, and he had two other naval officers with him.

"Come in," Dianne said. "The army's already here."

"They are?"

"Two of them," Dianne said. "Would you like some coffee?"

"That's very kind of you," the captain said. "I need to have a word with the army."

Dianne led them into the dining room and offered them breakfast, which they refused. But coffee was accepted all around, so she went in the kitchen to get more cups and saucers.

When she returned, the navy captain had opened his briefcase on the dining-room table and was watching Colonel Hanrahan read a stapled-together sheath of papers.

The captain said, "The honorary pallbearers, Colonel—I'm sure the protocol is the same in the army—will walk immediately behind the remains, which will be carried by Commander Eaglebury's academy classmates. All but one. One of them is a Pensacola classmate."

Colonel Hanrahan looked at the captain and then at Dianne, who got the feeling that he wished she were not there.

"Warrant Officer Wojinski, Lieutenant Colonel Lowell, Lieutenant Ellis, and I will be among the pallbearers, Captain," Colonel Hanrahan said.

"I beg your pardon?"

"I said that half of the pallbearers will be soldiers," Hanrahan said.

"I'm afraid that's out of the question, Colonel," the captain said. "The admiral has personally approved these plans."

"What admiral is that?" Hanrahan asked.

"Rear Admiral Foster, whose flag flies at the Philadelphia Naval Shipyard."

"How did he become involved?" Hanrahan asked.

"I don't quite understand your attitude, Colonel," the captain said. "You're aware, I presume, of the President's personal interest in the funeral?"

Hanrahan nodded.

"When the admiral learned of the presidential interest, he naturally took a personal interest," the captain said. "And, to reiterate, he has approved this scenario. Any changes would have to come from him."

"I hope I don't have to carry this any further," Hanrahan said, "but it has been decided by a higher headquarters than the Philadelphia Naval Shipyard that Special Forces personnel will be among the pallbearers. I think we're embarrassing Miss Eaglebury with this, Captain."

"I don't know what you're arguing about," Dianne said, "but I think both my father and my sister expect Colonel Hanrahan and Lieutenant Ellis to be pallbearers."

"I understand your feelings, Miss Eaglebury," the captain said, "but it's not quite that simple. There's a good deal of naval tradition involved here. And, to reiterate, these plans have been approved by the admiral."

"This has gone quite far enough," Hanrahan said icily. "Commander Eaglebury was serving as a Green Beret when he died. And Green Berets will carry him to his grave."

"I understand your sentiments, of course," the captain said, "but the plan has been approved by the admiral—and that, I'm afraid, is it."

"He's my brother," Diane heard herself saying, "and the soldiers will help carry his casket!"

The captain looked very uneasy at that.

"Are you speaking for Mrs. Eaglebury?" he asked.

"Do you want me to go get her?" Dianne asked. She was close to tears, she realized.

"Your wishes, of course, are our first consideration," the captain said, "but I will have to discuss this with the admiral."

"You do that," Hanrahan snapped.

"Is there anything else to which the army objects?" the captain asked.

"Aside from insisting that the people I mentioned serve as pallbearers," Hanrahan said, "your plans, Captain, are fine."

The captain left the room as a maid served breakfast.

"I'm very sorry about that, Miss Eaglebury," Hanrahan said.

"Don't worry about it," she said. "I'm glad you insisted."

The truth was, she hadn't liked the captain from the moment she'd first met him.

"Thanks for your help," Ellis said. "The alternative was throwing that clown in a snowbank."

"Ellis!" Hanrahan snapped, but when Dianne looked at him, she saw he was smiling. She thought it over and decided that Lieutenant Ellis was entirely capable of picking the captain up and throwing him in a snowbank.

Suzanne Eaglebury came into the dining room a moment later. No one said anything to her about the argument.

An hour or so later, when Dianne again opened the front door, this time to admit the Reverend Helmsley, she saw Lieutenant Ellis sitting, despite the chill, on the railing of the porch. She gave in to the impulse and got him a cup of coffee and carried it to him.

"I thought you could use this," she said.

"Thank you," he said.

"What are you doing out here? Aren't you cold?"

"This is what is known as 'staying out of the line of fire,'" he said. "When lieutenants are around colonels, the colonel's generally find something for the lieutenants to do."

"Can I ask you something personal?" she heard herself saying, and then blurted out the rest of it. "Aren't you kind of young to be an officer?"

"I'm twenty," he said.

"Then you must have graduated from college very young," she said.

"I didn't go to college," he said.

She wondered if she had embarrassed him. She had presumed that to be an army officer, you had to go to college. The open areas at Duke were often full of young men marching around in their Reserve Officer Training Corps uniforms.

"Oh," Dianne said lamely.

"I got my commission from OCS," Ellis said. "Officer Candidate School. I joined the army to be a cook."

"A cook?"

"That was a mistake," he said. "So I went to OCS."

"Oh," she said.

"I guess you're in college?" he asked.

"Yes," she said. "At Duke. It's in North Carolina."

"I know," he said. "I'm stationed at Fort Bragg, North Carolina."

"You'll have to come see me sometime," she said.

"Well, maybe," he said uncomfortably.

She fled then, aware that she must have sounded like an idiot. She wondered what there was about Lieutenant Ellis that flustered her so.

Two hours later Lieutenant Commander Edward Eaglebury was laid to his final rest. He was carried to his gravesite by officer pallbearers, half army officers, half navy. A Marine Corps firing squad fired the traditional three volleys over the open grave, and a moment later five navy fighter aircraft, jets from the Willow Grove Naval Air Station, flashed low over the cemetery. One spot was missing in their formation, signifying the fallen flier. Directly overhead they cut in their afterburners and soared with an enormous roar out of sight. A sailor played taps.

Dianne Eaglebury saw Lieutenant Tom Ellis climb in a maroon limousine with the other army officers, but they did not appear again at the house. So she didn't get another chance to speak to him.

(Four)
Quarters #33
Fort Bragg, North Carolina
1830 Hours, 30 November 1961

Funerals always reminded Paul Hanrahan that, according to the laws of probability, he was actuarially unlikely. His body was not decomposing in either a mattress cover or a GI casket, and his soul was not suffering the eternal torments of the damned. He was still alive and kicking, in a position to watch his children mature and, more urgently, to give his wife a little squeeze on the ass as a signal of his carnal intentions.

Which he did, immediately upon walking into his quarters. He and MacMillan, Wojinski, and Ellis had arrived ten minutes before at Pope Air Force Base. Roxy MacMillan had left one of their cars for Mac at Pope, and Mac had given him a lift to the two-story brick house on "Colonel's Row" on the main post of Fort Bragg.

"The children!" Patricia hissed in his ear as he pulled her to him. For some reason she was dressed up. The dress exposed the very pleasing swell of her breasts. Despite four children and twenty years of marriage, Patricia Hanrahan had a fine body.

"Send them out to play in the street," he said. That was a joke. The children were too old to be sent out to play.

"*We're* going out to play," Patricia said, moving out of his reach, but hanging on to his hand.

"What?" he asked levelly.

What he wanted was to get out of his uniform, into slacks and a sweater, and make himself a very large, very cold martini. Just one, for more than one martini made him act the horse's ass. But one. He was entitled to that. Afterward he just wanted to have supper and then sit down and watch television until such time as he could entice Patricia to the nuptial couch. He did not want to go out.

That explained why she was dressed up, of course. He was more than a little annoyed that she had committed them to go someplace. The function of a husband, he thought angrily, was to provide for a wife and their children. There was nothing in the marriage vows that said anything at all about the husband being obliged to amuse the wife socially.

"With the general," Patricia said.

"What?" he asked, and then, when he was sure she was serious: "With what general?"

"*The* general," Patricia said. There were half a dozen general officers at Fort Bragg, but only one was referred to as "the general": Lieutenant General H. H. "Triple H" Howard, Commanding General, United States XVIII Airborne Corps and Fort Bragg.

Technically, Colonel Paul T. Hanrahan was not subordinate

to General Howard. The U.S. Army Special Warfare Center
and School was a Class II Activity of the Deputy Chief of Staff
for Operations, Department of the Army. Hanrahan took his
orders from DCSOPS, and his efficiency reports were written
by the Vice-Deputy Chief of Staff for Operations and endorsed
by DCSOPS himself. He had nothing whatever, officially, to
do with General Howard when General Howard was wearing
his XVIII Airborne Corps commander's hat. When he was
wearing his Commanding General, Fort Bragg, hat, General
Howard was responsible for providing logistical and administrative support to the Special Warfare Center. He provided
barracks and general court-martial authority, pay, rations,
ammunition and POL (petroleum, oil and lubricants) and
maintenance facilities for Special Warfare's hardware, from
typewriters to pistols to aircraft.

Hanrahan had never met General Howard until he had come
to Fort Bragg to assume command of the Special Warfare
Center and School. Hanrahan had not been General Howard's
choice for the assignment, and there was serious disagreement
between them on the role of Special Forces with regard to the
"Airborne family" and within the army. Their relationship had
been strained and formal.

"Howard?" he asked.

"He called himself," Patricia said.

That, too, was very unusual. Official contact between them
had been either written or via one of XVIII Airborne Corps'
general officers or full colonels. There had been virtually no
unofficial, semiofficial, or social personal contact between them.
General Howard did not have the power to banish Hanrahan
from his post, but he did not have to talk to him and be reminded
that he did not have the authority to issue orders to him.

"What, exactly, did he say?" Hanrahan asked.

"He said that he had just received word from Pope that you
were in a civilian airplane. . . . Where is Craig Lowell, by the
way? I thought he was going to spend the night?"

"When he checked in with Bragg, Jiggs told him to come
home," Hanrahan answered impatiently. "Get on with it, honey."

"He said you were an hour out, and that if we didn't have
anything planned for tonight, he would like us to have dinner
with him. At the Club. Civvies. At 1900."

"I wonder what the hell this is all about?" Hanrahan asked.

"It's half past six, Paul," she said.

A personal invitation from the commanding general, XVIII Airborne Corps and Fort Bragg, to dinner was a command, not an invitation, and Patricia had known this.

Instead of going into the kitchen to make a stiff martini, Paul Hanrahan went up the stairs to the second floor of his quarters, unbuttoning his tunic and pulling his necktie as he went.

When he came out of the bathroom from his shower, he was naked. He was a wiry man and not very hairy. The skin at his neck and on his arms was permanently tanned; the rest of his body was pale.

Patricia was sitting at her vanity, putting lipstick on. Their eyes met in the mirror.

"You know what I'd really like to do," he said.

"Well, don't drink too much at dinner and maybe you can," she said.

A glen plaid suit was laid out on the bed. When they had been in Saigon, French Indochina, he had sent Patricia to Hong Kong with two thousand dollars' worth of traveler's checks, to spend as she wished.

She had spent more than half of the money on Paul. In a Chinese tailor's in Kowloon, she bought him five suits, three sport coats, a dozen shirts, and a half-dozen pairs of slacks. It was more than selflessness on her part; it was prudence. They both believed he would soon be a civilian. He was then a lieutenant colonel who honestly considered his chances of promotion to be nil. Failing promotion, Paul would have been involuntarily retired at the completion of twenty years' service.

The clothes had been intended for his civilian wardrobe. With four kids to put through college, he could not live on his pension. Thus he would have had to get a job.

On their way home from Asia, all these fears were dispelled, however, after Paul was called from the airplane at Honolulu so that the pertinent points of a Department of an amended Army general order could be read to him: "So much of paragraph 34 as reads 'Lt. Col. Paul T. Hanrahan' is amended to read 'Colonel, Signal Corps, Detailed Infantry' and so much of subject paragraph as reads 'will report to USASWS&C

for duty' is amended to read 'will assume command of USASWS&C.'"

He still hadn't worn two of the suits. He didn't have that much need to wear civilian suits, and when he did get to wear one, he liked the one Patricia had laid out for him. The glen plaid was the nicest suit he had ever owned. He looked like a successful civilian in it, he thought, not an officer in civvies.

They drove to Main Club, a brick building, and parked in one of the slots reserved for full bull colonels.

They went to the Main Club so seldom that the hostess at the entrance to the main dining room didn't know who he was.

"Have you a reservation?" she asked.

"Colonel Hanrahan," he said. "I'm to join General Howard."

"Oh," she said. "The general's not here, but I'll take you to his table."

The general's table was in a corner by a window, separated from other tables by a distance sufficient to prevent conversation there from being overheard. It was set for only four, which was another surprise. Paul would have guessed that there would be half a dozen colonels and their ladies.

A waiter immediately appeared. He could practically taste the martini, but forced the urge down.

"Patricia?"

"A glass of white wine, please," Patricia said.

"Twice," Hanrahan ordered.

Lieutenant General H. H. and Mrs. Howard appeared as the wine was being served. The general was in uniform. Hanrahan stood up.

"Paul," Howard said, "I believe you have met my wife?"

"Yes, sir," Hanrahan said. "Good evening, Mrs. Howard."

"Colonel," Mrs. Howard said, and smiled at Patricia. "Hello, Pat," she said. "I want you to know I had as much notice about this as you did."

"Thirty seconds less," General Howard said.

"We had nothing planned, Jeanne," Patricia said. "This is very nice."

"I got hung up," General Howard said. "I figured it would be better to come in uniform than it would be go home and change and be even later."

A waiter hovered at his shoulder.

"Well, the Hanrahans are drinking wine, so why don't you bring us a bottle of whatever that is?" the general ordered.

"Yes, sir," the waiter said.

"How was the funeral?" General Howard asked.

"Now, there's a conversation-stopper if I ever heard one," Mrs. Howard said.

Her husband looked at her curiously and then chuckled.

Hanrahan decided that the mystery of the invitation had been solved. The fight he had had with the navy over who was going to carry Eaglebury's casket had already been relayed to Howard.

"I insisted," Hanrahan said, "that Green Berets serve as pallbearers. There was some discussion about that, but I won."

"Good for you," Howard said, surprising Hanrahan. "He died as a Green Beret, even if he was a sailor."

"The conversation is going from awful to unspeakable," Mrs. Howard said.

"This is, as I'm sure Paul has suspected, sort of a working dinner," General Howard said.

The waiter appeared with the wine. They went through the bottle-opening and cork-sniffing ritual, and then the waiter handed them menus.

"And, General, if I may remind you, it's lobster night."

Howard closed his menu immediately. "That settles that for me," he said.

Once a month the club had lobster air-freighted from Maine. It was supposed to be by reservation only, but there were always a dozen or so extras, and first call on them was one of the privileges of rank for General Howard.

Patricia closed her menu. It was lobster all around, with steamed clams for an appetizer.

"We always swear we'll come for the lobster," Patricia said, "and then we never do."

"That's my line," Jeanne Howard said.

"Paul," General Howard said, out of the blue: "I want you to know that I had nothing to do with that 'no foreign-type headgear' CONARC directive."

That literally left Hanrahan speechless.

"What's that?" Patricia asked, and immediately looked as if she was sorry she had spoken.

"CONARC's banned the berets," Hanrahan said.

He wondered if that was why he had been invited to dinner.

"While I don't like them," Howard said, "and continue to think they make you look like Frenchmen, I have decided that if they were important to you, I should mind my own business."

"Well, thank you anyway, General," Hanrahan said.

"I have also had occasion recently," Howard said, "to re-think my attitude toward Special Forces generally."

"And did you reach a different conclusion, General?" Hanrahan asked.

"Let me put it this way," Howard said, "which is just about how it was put to me: If nothing else, you represent a pool of some thousands of officers and noncoms who could form the cadre of another Airborne division if it should be necessary to activate one."

"That's true, of course, General," Hanrahan said, "but that's not what we're training to do."

"And at best, you just might be on to something," General Howard said.

Hanrahan felt his temper rising, but he couldn't quite put his finger on what precisely was making him angry. General Howard was being less disparaging about Special Forces than he normally was.

"I made these same points this afternoon, when I came back from Washington," General Howard said. "To General Harke. I do not believe I managed to make a convert of him."

Major General Kenneth L. Harke, formerly the commander of Eighty-second Airborne Division, had recently been assigned as Chief of Staff of XVIII Airborne Corps. It was generally believed that he was being groomed to take over the corps when "Triple H" Howard was promoted or transferred.

"May I ask, General, how the subject came up?" Hanrahan asked.

"For all practical purposes, General Harke will be running XVIII Airborne Corps for the next six months or so," General Howard said. "I was trying to make him aware of how I think he should do that."

"You're being transferred, General?" Hanrahan asked.

"Yesterday, I was asked to come to Washington," Howard said. "This morning, I met with the Secretary of the Army, the Chief of Staff, and DCSOPS. The Secretary of Defense is not satisfied with proposals submitted to him vis-à-vis the future of army aviation. He apparently met with the Chief of Staff; Brigadier General Bob Bellmon, the Director of Army Aviation; and a lieutenant colonel named Lowell, whom I believe you know."

"Yes, sir," Hanrahan said. "Lowell is an old friend."

"The Secretary of Defense apparently feels he must choose whether to put army aviation out of business or to expand it exponentially," Howard said. "He 'suggested' to the Secretary of the Army that General Bellmon submit a revised proposal, something on the order of a wish list, and gave him fifteen days to do it. It was delivered 20 October. There has already been a response indicating that General Bellmon has again failed to grasp the magnitude of the expansion the Secretary of Defense has in mind. So another proposal has been requested. I have been directed to oversee the preparation of the second proposal."

"Fascinating," Hanrahan thought aloud.

"In order, obviously, that I will be able to understand the problems of aviation better, the Secretary of Defense has waived the proscription against senior officers being trained as aviators."

"What?" Jeanne Howard asked, incredulously.

"While Bellmon is having another shot at the 'Army of the Seventies Aviation Estimates,'" General Howard said, "I will go to Fort Rucker and learn how to fly."

"That's absurd," Jeanne Howard said. "You're too old."

"Be that as it may," he replied, obviously annoyed with her, "the point of this conversation is not my decrepitude but the fact that I will frequently be away from the post. General Harke will be in command in my absence."

"I understand, sir," Hanrahan said. Howard had warned him that Harke was another anti–Special Forces senior officer. Most senior conventional Airborne officers were. And the reason Howard had Paul and Patricia to dinner was also pretty clear. It would be known to every senior officer on the post by noon the next day that the general and the Green Beret colonel and their wives had shared a social meal at the club. That would suggest that Triple H Howard held Hanrahan in higher esteem than was generally believed.

Hanrahan thought that was a very nice thing, indeed, for Triple H Howard to have done.

"As you well know, Paul," Howard went on, "you cannot leave an officer in charge and then second-guess his every decision. But on the other hand, since I will not be relieved of command of either the post or the corps, I want you to feel free to come to me—*I expect you to come to me*—with any problems you might have that General Harke may not understand."

That meant two things: that Harke was really going to go after him and Special Forces, apparently with the blessing of the CONARC commander; and that Howard was offering, at least to some degree, to protect Hanrahan personally, and Special Forces generally, from Harke.

"Thank you very much, General," Hanrahan said. "I'll try not to bother you."

"Honey," Jeanne Howard said, laying her hand on her husband's, "you're not really going to try to learn how to fly?"

"Does anyone else detect a certain doubt in her mind that I'm not up to it?" General Howard asked. "Or am I wrong?"

"You're fifty-one years old!" she said.

"I will not, because I am a very nice fellow, respond in kind," General Howard said, "with a recitation of your vital statistics."

The steamed clams were delivered.

"Tell me, Paul," General Howard said, "expert that you are on exotic food: Do these work the same way oysters do?"

"I intend to put it to the test," Hanrahan said.

"Tonight?"

"There is no time like the present, General," Hanrahan said.

"You're a pair of dirty old men!" Jeanne Howard said, loud enough to turn heads throughout the dining room.

IV

(One)
The Farm
Fairfax, Virginia
1645 Hours, 10 December 1961

"Take a quick shower," Barbara Bellmon ordered Brigadier General Robert F. Bellmon the moment he walked in the door. "I talked to Jeanne, and it's black tie."

"Why?" he asked. Bellmon was a man on the very near side of fifty, medium-sized, losing some hair, and in the process of growing jowls. His wife was slender and freckled. Although only a year separated them, she looked much younger.

"Because I felt like it," she said.

"Why?" he repeated, already starting to unbutton his tunic. "It's only a play."

"Because I always feel *je-ne-sais-quoi* when I have to wear my mink with my dungarees."

He laughed at her. The mink she'd paid for herself. She had believed that Kodak was going to take a drop when no one else did, and against the advice of her broker, she'd put her money where her mouth was. Kodak had dropped nine and three-eighths, and she had a mink.

And not many occasions to wear it, he thought as he climbed the stairs to their second-floor bedroom, except at times like this. Although he was not thrilled with this one—he wasn't much on stage plays—what the hell; if it pleased Barbara, he could go along cheerfully.

The bedroom was furnished in a style he thought of as Fu Manchu Modern. There had been a tour in Japan between War II and Korea, and they'd bought this furniture there. It wasn't really Japanese (the bed had a headboard and a footboard, lacquered and carved; the Japanese slept on the floor), but it obviously wasn't western.

The farmhouse was furnished in a wide range of styles. Just about everybody who had lived here had added something or other brought home from foreign tours somewhere.

The Farm had been in the Waterford (Barbara's) family for four generations. Brigadier General (later Lieutenant General) Porterman K. Waterford, Sr., upon his appointment to that rank and assignment as Deputy Chief of Cavalry, War Department, had bought it before War I. He had decided that it made much more sense to take some cash he had accumulated and buy a Virginia farm than it did to settle for some landless brownstone in the District of Columbia.

He correctly believed that he would one day be appointed Chief of Cavalry and major general, which meant that he would at that time be expected to live in the quarters set aside at Fort Meyer for the officer holding that appointment. He had seen those quarters and did not wish to live in them.

So he bought The Farm, a six-room fieldstone house and 120 acres. He added two rooms to the house and was able to finance the whole operation with his fifty percent of the proceeds from renting the land to a local farmer.

When he retired and left Washington, he did not sell The Farm; he rented it to his successor, who was similarly disenchanted with the quarters provided at Fort Meyer. Six years after that, Lieutenant Colonel (later Major General) James D. Waterford was assigned to the War Department, and remained on and off in Washington for fifteen years. During his time at The Farm, he added another two rooms and a kitchen to the building, and acquired an adjacent farm of 360 acres.

His son, Porterman K. Waterford II (ultimately major general), lived at The Farm three times during his military career, during which periods another 640 acres of farmland were added to the holding and four more rooms were built onto the farmhouse.

Under Major General (then Colonel) Porterman K. Waterford II, the somewhat unimaginatively titled Virginia Farm, Inc., was set up under the laws of Delaware. Stock was issued to various members of the family, officers were elected, and thereafter, with scrupulous attention to the rules of the Internal Revenue Service, The Farm was operated as a business.

Whenever the Waterford men, or the husbands of the Waterford women, happened to be stationed in Washington (which was virtually inevitable two or three times in an officer's career), they were permitted to live on The Farm, paying the corporation a rent equal to his army housing allowance. If there were two such men in Washington at the same time, the rules of seniority prevailed. On several occasions two families of young officers occupied The Farm at the same time, which had made it necessary to construct a second kitchen so there would be no conflict over that. Later the family had a second house built, "the guest house," in which lived the junior officer and his family.

The resident was required to manage The Farm during his residence, advised by whoever rented the farmland. This made it legal under IRS rules for The Farm, Inc., to furnish the manager an automobile in addition to the station wagon and the jeeps and other vehicles already property of The Farm.

The Farm now contained 1,240 acres of land. There were sixteen rooms in the farmhouse and seven in the guest house. Outside were a swimming pool, two tennis courts, and a skeet and trap range. If they got what they hoped to get for their share of this year's corn and soybeans, Brigadier General and Mrs. Bellmon were seriously considering bulldozing a dirt landing strip and building a simple hanger.

The Farm manager's vehicle was a Cadillac Fleetwood sedan, eight months old, and bore none of the military decals that festooned the Buick coupe and Ford station wagon that General Bellmon drove to work at the Pentagon. The Cadillac rarely went "officially" to the District. Officers, even brigadier generals, are as reluctant to be seen driving Cadillac Fleetwood automobiles as they are for their wives to be seen in full-length mink coats.

Neither was there anything so indiscreet as a sign to assist visitors to find The Farm. Instead, an ancient mule-drawn plow had been retrieved from one of the barns, sandblasted to remove the rust, painted black, and installed on a fieldstone pillar.

First-time visitors were instructed to "turn off the country road when you come to the black plow, and drive 1.5 miles. It's the first house you'll come to, an old fieldstone thing behind a stone fence."

Tonight they were going to the theater and then to dinner as the guests of Lieutenant Colonel Craig W. Lowell. Lowell, who was in Washington on TDY, working for Brigadier General Bill Roberts, had been a guest at The Farm for the weekend. Barbara had mentioned then in passing that she had been unable to get tickets for a touring Broadway-cast performance of a show she wanted to see. She had been not only frustrated but angry: Thirty minutes after she'd read the advertisement in the Washington *Post* she tried to buy tickets and was told nothing was available.

Shortly before noon on Monday, Craig Lowell had telephoned The Farm with the announcement that if she and Bob were free, he had "fallen into" tickets for the play for Wednesday night. Whether Craig was repaying their hospitality or showing he was very fond of Barbara Bellmon, it didn't matter. Barbara was going to get to wear her mink, go to the theater, and afterward have dinner.

Barbara drove the Fleetwood. She was a good driver, she liked to drive, and Bob had already made one round trip to the Potomac that day. They crossed the Fourteenth Street Bridge, drove past the White House, and circled Lafayette Square.

"You'll never find a place to park," General Bellmon said. "You're going to have to go to that parking garage."

"Watch this," she said, pulling up before the marquee of the Hay Adams Hotel.

The uniformed doorman hurried around the front of the car.

"General Bellmon," Barbara said, "as guests of Colonel Lowell. Will you take care of the car, please?"

"Certainly, madam," he said, and raised his hand over his head and snapped his fingers. A bellboy appeared and waited for Barbara to step out from behind the wheel.

As they walked across the lobby to the elevator Bellmon took his wife's arm and whispered in her ear, "Have you been here before? You seem to have everything pretty well organized?"

"I should tell you I have been carrying on with Craig every afternoon," she said, "but you'd be liable to believe it. He told me what to do."

He had not told her which way to go when they got off the elevator, and they had a long walk before they found the door with 623 on it.

Lowell, in a dinner jacket, answered the knock. He embraced Barbara enthusiastically, and she responded in kind, primarily because they both knew it annoyed General Bellmon.

"Looking the gift horse in the mouth," General Bellmon said, "I'd like to know how you managed to get tickets to this thing."

"Where there's a will, there's a way, General," Lowell said. "Set your heart on something and go after it."

He was not talking about theater tickets, Bellmon thought. He was up to something. Whenever Lowell called him "General," alarm bells rang.

Bill and Jeanne—Brigadier General and Mrs. William R. Roberts—were in the sitting room of the suite. They had obviously just arrived. The women smiled at each other; they were not the kissing kind. The men shook hands.

"This is very nice," Barbara said, looking around the suite.

"It's comfortable," Lowell said. "And there's an office over here." He led her to a room off the sitting room. It *was* an office, Barbara was surprised to see—a real, functional gray metal desk and IBM electric typewriter–type office, not a portable typewriter on a writing desk. It was complete, she saw, to a multiline telephone, a dictating device, and even a large combination-lock safe.

"Very nice," Barbara repeated.

"It's a good place to work," he said.

There was another knock at the door, and Barbara wondered who else's hospitality Craig Lowell was repaying. It was, instead, a waiter pushing a cart loaded with silver-domed dishes.

The waiter uncovered the dishes one by one with great flair.

Barbara saw that Craig was as pleased and surprised by what was offered as she was. There was, she thought, an explanation for that. Lowell's order for the hors d'oeuvres had probably been simplicity itself.

"I'm having a few people in for a drink. Would you send up something we can munch on?"

He probably had in mind chunks of cheddar, crackers, and peanuts. What the hotel delivered was oysters and clams, shrimp, ham, caviar, smoked salmon, and tiny sandwiches holding various combinations of the meat and fish. There was a wedge of Brie and a half-moon of Stilton. And two silver coolers, each with a large bottle of champagne.

"That's nice, isn't it?" Lowell said innocently. "I ordered the wine. There's booze, of course, but if I have two drinks, I'm sound asleep by act two."

"I thought we were going to have dinner afterward," Bill Roberts said.

"We are," Lowell said. He turned to the waiter. "Is that all the wine?"

"There's half a dozen bottles in all, Colonel," the waiter said.

"Well, that ought to be enough," Lowell said. "We can serve ourselves, thank you."

He handed the waiter a folded bill.

Barbara saw her husband shaking her head at the hors d'oeuvres. Like her, he had been estimating what the display had cost. Unlike her, he was sure it was simply another example of Lowell throwing his money in people's faces. Barbara thought differently. Lowell didn't look at money as other people did. He literally came into more money, month after month, than he could spend. When he was around his subordinates or people he didn't know, he was careful not to wave it around (his uniforms and automobiles and the airplane being obvious exceptions); but here and now, in what he believed was the company of his friends, his only concern was whether they would be pleased with what he offered. He had not a thought about the cost, she was convinced. There were people in the offices of Craig, Powell, Kenyon and Dawes charged with verifying and then paying Craig Lowell's personal bills. He never even saw them.

Lowell opened the champagne and filled glasses. As he was passing them out, there was another knock at the door. Barbara was closest to it and opened it.

A small, dark-haired, large-eyed woman was standing in the corridor.

"Sandy can't come," Sharon Felter announced.

"Well, at least *you*'re here," Barbara said.

Lowell walked quickly to Sharon Felter and handed her a glass of champagne.

"Am I late?" Sharon asked. "I had to wait for the baby-sitter."

"Not at all," Lowell said. "We just opened the grape, and I am about to propose the first toast."

The others looked at him curiously.

"To the Eagle flights," Lowell said, "and those who shall fly them."

Barbara had never heard of the Eagle flights. She glanced at her husband, and then at Bill Roberts. From their stiff faces it was evident they didn't like the subject coming up.

"And a question, gentlemen," Lowell said. "How come I'm here, shuffling paper? And not an Eagle flier myself?"

"Christ," Bill Roberts said. "That's classified, Craig. Don't you know that?"

"And here's three Kremlin moles if I ever saw any," Lowell said, nodding at the women. "Sharon even speaks Russian."

"It's classified, Craig," Roberts repeated.

"This place is probably more secure than the Situation Room in the White House," Lowell said. "Full of clever little gadgets that detect monitoring devices."

"Your participation in the Eagle flight program was considered, Craig," Bob Bellmon said, "and decided against. And I think we should change the subject."

"What's the Eagle flight program?" Barbara asked.

"We're sending aircraft and three hundred pilots to Vietnam," Lowell told her. "And I am not on the list."

"That was a flagrant breech of security," Bellmon said. "Do you realize that?"

"Come on, Bob," Lowell said. "Don't evade the issue by starting that."

Bellmon glowered at him.

"That major of yours, what's-his-name? Brokenhammer?" Lowell said to Bill Roberts. "The one who's always sucking on a noisy pipe?"

"Brochhammer," General Roberts corrected him automatically.

"Brochhammer, then. There's no reason he can't do what you've got me doing. He can do it better."

Roberts did not reply.

"Phil Parker's going," Lowell said.

"You saw the list?" Bellmon asked.

"Sure, I saw the list," Lowell said.

"I'd love to know who showed it to you," Bellmon said angrily.

"Somebody who was as surprised as I am that I'm not on it," Lowell said.

"I told you the decision has been made," Bellmon said.

"I think I'm entitled to an explanation," Lowell said.

"What gives you that idea?" Bellmon said. "'Entitled'!"

Barbara was now alarmed. The situation was on the edge of getting out of control.

"Craig," General Roberts said, "if it will bring this awkward situation to an end, I'll give you an explanation."

"Okay," Lowell said.

"There is reason to believe that both you and Jim Brochhammer are very shortly going to be involved in something in which the both of you can make a greater contribution than you could flying in Indochina."

"Doing what?" Lowell asked. "Shuffling more paper?"

Roberts was about to reply when there was the sound of a key in the door.

Roberts stopped, mouth open and looked at the door.

A stocky, well-dressed man in his forties pushed the door open. He was having trouble getting the key out of the lock, and it was a moment before he realized there were people in the room. A look of annoyance flickered across his face, quickly replaced by a forced smile.

He was Porter Craig, Craig Lowell's cousin, the chairman of the board and chief executive officer of Craig, Powell, Kenyon and Dawes, 13 Wall Street.

"Good evening," he said.

"Your timing, Porter," Craig Lowell said sharply, "is superb."

"I would say, Colonel," General Bellmon said, "that he got here just in time. Hello, Porter."

"Did I interrupt anything?"

"Did you ever," Barbara said.

"Come in and choke yourself on a toothpick, Porter," Lowell said.

"Where the hell have you been?" Porter Craig asked as he absently went to the man and woman and shook their hands.

Lowell didn't reply.

"When I finally found where you were supposed to be in the Pentagon, they said you were at home; so I called here, and there was never an answer."

"That may be because I disconnected the phone," Lowell said. "I was working here."

"Is it connected now?" Porter Craig asked, alarmed. "I've got calls in to both senators, and they'll call me here."

"It's connected," Lowell said. "What's going on?"

"The army has Geoff in jail at Fort Jackson," Porter Craig said.

"That was quick," Lowell said, amused. "He's only been in two months."

"It's not funny, goddamn you," Porter said. "He's facing twenty years in Leavenworth."

"What did he do?" Barbara Bellmon asked.

She got a withering look from her husband. She understood it. He was afraid that he would become involved in whatever difficulty Geoffrey Craig was in at Fort Jackson. Porter Craig did not understand the army: A general officer could not intercede on behalf of an enlisted man.

"There's half a dozen charges," Porter said, "the significant one being assault on a noncommissioned officer."

"He slugged a sergeant," Lowell translated. "I didn't think he had it in him."

"Craig!" Sharon said.

"I had to call Dorothy's doctor for her," Porter Craig said. "She's hysterical."

"You shouldn't have told her," Craig Lowell said. "You're pretty hysterical yourself. It was obviously contagious."

"Goddamn, if it was your son . . . !" Porter Craig said.

"Have a little champagne," Lowell said. "Better yet, have a drink. Calm down and then start at the beginning."

"I don't want a goddamned drink!" Porter Craig said.

"Have one anyway," Lowell said, and went to a bar and returned with a glass half full of Scotch. "Drink it, Porter," he said. "If you want to help Geoff, you're going to have to calm down. You've already done one damned dumb thing."

Porter took a swallow of the whiskey.

"What was that?"

"If you want the brass at Jackson to stick it in Geoff, have your senators put their two cents in," Lowell said. "I hope you haven't been able to get through to them."

Porter Craig shook his head. "One of them is 'unavailable at the moment.' I suppose that means he's fallen down drunk again. And the other one is going to dinner and then some goddamned play. My secretary is trying to run them down."

"Well, if she does find them, and they call here, tell them you just wanted to say hello," Lowell said.

"Did you hear what I said? Geoff's facing twenty years in prison."

"Tell me how you heard about all this? Did Geoff call up and tell you all this?"

"Geoff hasn't said a word," Porter Craig said. "And when I called down there, they wouldn't even let me talk to him."

"What do you know for sure," Lowell asked, "and how do you know it?"

"Geoff wrote a check to a lawyer down there. Fifteen hundred dollars," Porter Craig said. "They thought it was unusual and showed it to me. So I tried to call Geoff, and I got some sergeant on the line who told me he was 'confined' and that I couldn't talk to him. And then I got the runaround and wound up talking to some lieutenant colonel, who said that he couldn't discuss the case with me. Finally I called the lawyer, who's from Columbia, and he gave me the runaround. But finally he told me what was going on. At that point I tried to call you, but you had unplugged the telephone."

Barbara felt sorry for him.

"Perhaps it's not as bad as it looks," she said.

"There's one way to find out," Lowell said. He sat down

on the couch and pulled the telephone on the coffee table to him.

"What are you doing?" General Bellmon asked.

"I'm calling Jackson," Lowell said as he dialed for the operator.

Porter Craig sat beside him.

"I think maybe we should call this evening off," General Bellmon said softly to General Roberts.

"Don't be silly," Lowell said. "*You* didn't slug a sergeant. Eat an oyster or something; this won't take long."

Barbara Bellmon went to the table, placed half a dozen of the tiny sandwiches on a plate, and carried them to Porter Craig. He shook his head.

"You haven't had anything to eat," she said. "And you've had the whiskey."

"Bring me a couple of those, will you, please?" Lowell said. And then to the telephone: "Fort Jackson, South Carolina, station to station," he said.

"I'm not sure that's a good idea," Bob Bellmon said.

"Nobody asked you," Barbara said to him. They locked eyes for a moment, and then he shrugged and went to the buffet and helped himself to cherrystone clams.

"Post stockade, please," Lowell said. . . . "Put the duty officer on, please, Sergeant," he said. . . . "Lieutenant, this is Colonel Lowell. You have a prisoner in there named Craig, Geoffrey, II. What's he charged with? . . . Of course, you can tell me, Lieutenant. It's not classified information. . . . Thank you, Lieutenant."

He hung the telephone up.

"He is to be tried before a general court on several charges," he said, as much to Bellmon and Roberts as to Porter Craig, "the most significant of which is that he committed an assault upon a noncommissioned officer in the execution of his office."

"A general court?" General Roberts asked. There are three levels of army courts-martial: summary, special, and general. General courts-martial are those empowered to impose the most severe penalties.

"They're apparently trying to sock it to him," Lowell said. He heard what he said. "No pun intended."

"What does that mean?"

"It means I better go down there," Lowell said.

"Craig . . ." Roberts began, and then stopped.

"Duty first, General," Lowell said. "I know."

"I . . . uh . . . don't like—"

"'Aircraft Procurement Projections Through Fiscal 1965,'" Lowell said, "classified secret, in quintuplicate, are in my safe."

"You're finished?" Roberts asked, genuinely surprised.

"And you didn't believe me, did you, when I said I could work more efficiently here?"

"I'm surprised," Roberts said. Even as a rush-rush job, he had not expected the report for another three or four days.

"I'm sorry," Lowell said.

"What?"

"If I had known my paper-shuffling skill would keep me from flying like an eagle, General, I would have been far, far less dedicated."

"You're thinking of going there tonight?" Bellmon asked. It was more of an accusation.

"If I'm there first thing in the morning," Lowell said. "I can be back here by 1300, maybe a little later. That will give your Major Brokenhammer all morning to find fault with 'Projections Through '65.'"

"*Broch*hammer," Roberts corrected him again automatically.

"You've been drinking," Bellmon said. "You shouldn't fly."

"I'll get a pilot from Butler Aviation," Lowell said. "There's always somebody over there who wants to pick up the time." He looked at Porter Craig.

"You'll get the bill for that, Porter. And you can ride out to the airport with me and catch the shuttle back to New York."

"Thank you, Craig," Porter said.

"Before you get all wet-eyed, Porter," Lowell said, "if Geoff is guilty as charged, he's probably going to go to jail. And I won't do anything about that. What I'll do is go down there and make sure he's not being crapped on. But that's all I'll do."

"He's just a kid, for Christ's sake, Craig."

"When he came in the army, they read him the rules," Lowell said. "High on the list of no-no's is beating up your sergeant."

"How do you know he did that?"

"The lieutenant on the phone just now said 'Oh, that's the wise-ass who put his sergeant in the hospital with a broken jaw.'"

"If that's the case," Porter Craig said loyally, "he must have had his reasons."

"I'm sure he thinks he does," Lowell said. "But what I'm afraid of is that his reasons won't wash. The only excuse that counts is self-defense."

He walked out of the room and into the office, returning a minute or so later with a briefcase.

"Here's the fiscal '65 projections, Bill," he said, handing them to Roberts.

"What am I supposed to do with them?"

"You don't really want this grounded eagle to answer that, General, do you?" Lowell replied. "If I did, Bellmon would have me in the stockade with Cousin Geoff."

Jeanne Roberts tittered. Barbara Bellmon chuckled. Their husbands glowered at them.

Porter Craig looked confused.

Barbara Bellmon walked to the buffet and picked up the magnum of champagne. "Champagne, anyone?" she cheerfully inquired.

(Two)
Near Durham, North Carolina
0415 Hours, 11 December 1961

The farmer who owned the field they were standing and waiting in offered Lieutenant Tom Ellis a quart mason jar containing a clear liquid. The farmer had served with the 325th Glider Infantry Regiment of the Eighty-second Airborne Division during War II. He now was sixty pounds heavier than he had been in 1945, and much balder.

"Clears the sinuses," he said. "Made it myself."

"Thank you," Lieutenant Ellis said politely, and took a swallow, prepared for a burning sensation.

It was not nearly as bad as he expected. His experience with "white lightning" was limited, and what he'd had before had seared his throat and seized his brain like the punishment of the damned. This was pretty good stuff, and he said so.

"You can make better than you can buy," the farmer told him. "The secret is cleanliness. Stainless-steel retort, copper pipes, and cleanliness. And then you have to age it. That's more than a year old."

"Very good," Lieutenant Ellis said.

They were standing next to Lieutenant Ellis's automobile. It was a Jaguar XK-120, which five days before had been the property of a captain of the 505th Parachute Infantry who had placed entirely too much faith in three queens. Lieutenant Ellis held a king-high straight.

Ellis had, as a gentleman, given the captain three days to come up with the thousand dollars the captain had used as a symbol of his faith in three queens (pledging equity in the Jaguar in lieu of cash); and when the cash itself turned out to not be forthcoming, the captain and Ellis had gone to the Fort Bragg branch of the First National Bank of Fayetteville and sorted the situation out. The captain then drove away from the bank at the wheel of what until then had been Lieutenant Ellis's car, an MG TD. And Lieutenant Ellis and the bank now owned just about equal parts of the Jaguar XK-120.

The drive from Fort Bragg to Durham the previous afternoon had been very pleasant in the Jaguar, although it drank considerably more high-test gasoline than the MG consumed of regular. Since his mission to Durham was official, a jeep had been reserved for his use. But he had two missions in Durham, one official and one personal, and he needed for that one personal wheels, so the jeep sat in the motor pool at Bragg.

On his arrival, per his instructions, he had made contact with "the host"—the farmer—and the host had insisted that he come for dinner. The host had a large family, but two of his sons were put together, so that Lieutenant Ellis could sleep in their bed.

There were large lithographs of Jesus Christ hung on various walls in the farmhouse, and a lengthy grace was offered before an enormous meal. After dinner a scrapbook was brought out, and the host traced his World War II service with the Eighty-second from North Africa to Berlin. The first Kodak Baby Brownie photographs were sort of fuzzy, but in North Africa the host had liberated a Leica camera, and thereafter they were actually of high technical and gradually improving artistic quality.

At 0345 the next morning, Lieutenant Ellis was awakened by the Host's dog, a large short-haired brown and black animal that enthusiastically licked Ellis's face.

"Half an hour until they drop 'em," the Host announced happily from the door a few seconds later.

Ellis quickly showered and shaved and dressed in fatigues. He would dearly have liked a cup of coffee, but the Host announced they would have breakfast after the drop.

In the field the host handed the quart of white lightning back to Ellis, who politely took another swallow.

"I put a couple of quarts in the trunk," the Host said. "You can take it with you."

"You don't have to do that," Ellis said.

"Hell, I want to," the Host said.

Faintly, far off, Ellis heard the sound of an aircraft engine.

"Hell, that ain't them," the Host announced. "That's a pair of little bitty one-engine airplanes."

Ellis urgently searched the sky for the aircraft the Host had found so quickly. He found them finally, approaching from the Southeast. Two Beavers. It was them.

"They're Beavers," Ellis explained to the Host. "One engine, but they carry five people."

"In those little bitty airplanes?"

"They're bigger than they look," Ellis said.

"I'll be damned," the Host said. He took another pull at the white lightning and handed it to Ellis.

"I really don't need any more of this," Ellis said.

"Hell, boy, my motto is 'Get all you can while you can.'"

Ellis was aware that a warm glow in his stomach was spreading throughout his body. And he was aware that it was getting pretty close to the time for the drop.

He opened the door and reached into the back of the Jaguar. The Host's dog, which was sitting upright there, felt like licking his face. Ellis pushed the dog out of the way and picked up an Angry Nine, more formally known as the Army-Navy Ground Radio Communications Set, Model 9, or AN/GRC-9.

He pulled out of the car, leaned against the hood, turned the radio on, and put the headset to his ear.

Just in time.

"If you're down there and awake, Ellis, they just went out the door!" the voice of one of the pilots came metallically over the radio.

"Roger," Ellis said to the microphone, and then pointed up at the aircraft. The Host let his dog out of the car. The dog immediately raised his leg and decorated the Jaguar's lovely yellow lacquer near the rear right wheel.

"I don't see anything," the Host said. But then: "I'll be damned, there they are!"

A line of parachutes had opened in the early-morning sky. Ellis counted them. Eleven. Nine personnel chutes and two small cargo chutes.

"Now we sit here and hope nobody goes into the trees and breaks his leg," Ellis said. He devoutly hoped that would not happen. If somebody got hurt, it would be necessary to arrange for an ambulance, and then to accompany him to a local hospital, to notify Bragg, and to fill out a voluminous report. That would take most of the day, and he had something more important to do.

He waited impatiently and with growing concern for several minutes until the Angry Nine finally spoke: "Mother Hen, Mother Hen, this is Chick Leader. Over."

"Go ahead, Chick Leader, this is Mother Hen," Ellis said to the handset.

"Chick Team on the ground, intact, at 0418 hours."

"Roger Chick Leader, try to stay out of jail. Mother Hen out."

He turned off the Angry Nine, bent the antenna under its fasteners, and put it in the back of the Jaguar.

If there was an emergency from now on, if some member of the team was injured, or if someone went to jail—arrest by diligent and curious civilian law-enforcement authorities was entirely possible—each member of the team had a telephone number to call at Bragg. Ellis, meanwhile, would furnish the training coordinator at Bragg with a number where he could be reached. If there was trouble, Bragg would call that number, and he would do whatever had to be done.

With that exception, there would be no further communication between him and the team until their little exercise was over. Which meant that he would have all day, all night, all

day tomorrow, and all of tomorrow night more or less to himself.

"You want another little taste of this?" the Host asked as
he climbed into the Jaguar.

"If I had another little taste of that," Ellis said, "you would
have to get back to your house by yourself."

The Host chuckled and took a healthy swallow.

When they got to the farmhouse, the Host's wife was putting
breakfast on the table. Ellis ate everything put in front of him:
pancakes, sausage, eggs, and a large slice of ham swimming
in salty gravy. He washed all this down with tomato juice and
three cups of coffee.

"If you don't have anything to do until they finish running
around in the boonies," the Host said, "you're welcome to stick
around here."

"I've got to go into Durham," Ellis said. "Thanks anyway."

"Then you're welcome to come back anytime, on duty or
off," the Host said. "It's been real nice having you here, Lieutenant."

"That's nice of you," Ellis said. He reached in his pocket
and came out with a small box wrapped in white paper.

"Colonel Hanrahan asked me to give you this, Mr. Ford,"
Ellis said, and handed it to him.

"I told you, my name is Les," the Host said. He tore open
the paper and opened the box. "Well, I'll be damned"—he
beamed—"ain't that something!"

The box contained a Zippo lighter. It was engraved on one
side with glider/parachutist's wings (a representation of a glider
superimposed on standard parachutist's wings) and the legend
Lester H. Ford, T/Sgt., 325th Glider Infantry 1942–45, and
on the other with the Special Forces insignia (two arrows cross-
ing a vertical commando knife, and the legend *De Oppresso
Liber*) and the words *From His Friends in Special Forces,
1961.*

The lighter had cost $1.25, and the engraving another three
dollars. Lester Ellis held it in his hands like the Koh-i-noor
diamond.

"I'll be damned," he said again, and handed it to his wife.

"That's *real* nice," she said. "And you put it someplace
where you won't lose it."

She handed it to one of her sons.

"And Colonel Hanrahan said to be sure to tell you that whenever you can find the time to come to Bragg, he'd like to show you what we've got there."

"I just might do that," Lester Ford said. "By God, I will do it, first chance I get."

His third son handed the Zippo back to him. There was a thumb smudge on the shiny chrome. He polished it away with a paper napkin.

"You thank your colonel for me," he said. "And tell him anytime I can help, just say how."

"We appreciate your cooperation, Mr. Ford."

"Les, damn it! Anytime. What the hell, once a paratrooper, always a paratrooper. And it's no trouble having them use this place as a drop zone. Hell, I like to watch 'em jump."

(Three)
Office of the Professor of Military Science
Department of Military Science
Duke University
Durham, North Carolina
0825 Hours, 11 December 1961

The professor of military science was listed in the Duke catalog as Colonel G. F. Wells, Artillery, B.S., USMA; M.S., Cal Tech; Ph.D., University of California. He was a large florid-faced man who wore his hair closely cropped. His tunic bore ribbons signifying World War II service in Europe as well as service in Korea, and the insignia indicating two or more years of service on the army general staff was pinned to his tunic pocket.

He was annoyed when he looked up from his desk and saw the young man in the tweed sport coat, open-collared white shirt, and gray flannel slacks standing at his open door. It meant that his secretary, again, had not shown up for work on time, and it meant that he was going to have to counsel another young man about how it was in his own interests to remain in the Reserve Officer Training Corps program. He was sure that's what the young man wanted. Everybody in the program was supposed to be in uniform at the gym, and this young buck was in civilian clothes. And you couldn't drop out of ROTC unless you had an "interview" with the PMS&T.

Colonel Wells was tempted to run the little bastard off until tomorrow, when he wouldn't be as busy as he was now; but he knew that was not the way to deal with young men who wished to drop out of the ROTC program because it interfered with their social life.

He fixed a smile on his face.

"Come on in, son," he said. "You wanted to see me?"

"Yes, sir."

"How come you're not in uniform?" Colonel Wells asked as he offered his hand and waved the young man into the chair beside his desk.

"I thought it would be better if I wore civvies, sir," the young man said. "I'd be less conspicuous."

What the hell kind of an answer is that?

"We don't often have a chance for training like this," Colonel Wells said. "I sort of like to see everybody participate."

"I'm glad to hear that, sir," the young man said. "I hope we can make it worth your effort."

Colonel Wells was baffled by that response too.

"I'm afraid I've forgotten your name, son."

"I'm Lieutenant Ellis, sir," Ellis said, and when he saw the look of confusion on the colonel's face, added: "From the Special Warfare School at Bragg, sir?"

"Jesus, I thought you were one of my ROTC kids," Colonel Wells thought aloud, and then added: "The reason for my confusion, Lieutenant, is when we set this exercise up with your Colonel MacMillan, he told me that the training officer he was sending was a real fireball who had taken one of your teams into Cuba."

Ellis looked uncomfortable.

"No offense intended, Lieutenant. We're glad to have you. It's just that I expected someone a little older."

"I took an 'A' Team into Cuba, Colonel," Ellis said.

Now Colonel Wells looked uncomfortable. He decided to get off the subject.

"I've scheduled a meeting for my officers for half past eight," he said. "They're probably waiting for us. It's right down the hall."

"Yes, sir," Ellis said.

Some one called "Attention" when Colonel Wells entered the room, and he immediately responded: "Keep your seats."

There was a large library table, around which sat half a dozen officers. Two movable corkboards were set up at the front. On one a scale map on the Duke campus was thumb-tacked, and a map of the surrounding area on another. Little flags were stuck at various points on both maps.

"Gentlemen," Colonel Wells said, "this is Lieutenant Ellis of the Special Warfare School. He is wearing civilian clothing to avoid calling attention to himself."

Ellis had the feeling that none of the officers in the room was very impressed with him. He didn't think much of them, either, he realized.

"Lieutenant, would you give us your game plan?" Colonel Wells said, and sat down.

Ellis went to the map of the surrounding area and looked for a pointer. When he couldn't find one, he used his finger.

"At 0415 an 'A' Team was dropped here," he said. "The team consists of a captain, a lieutenant, three master sergeants, one sergeant first class, two staff sergeants, and one buck sergeant. They have their small arms, a combat load of blanks for the small arms, one mortar, one machine gun, one rocket launcher—with blank and/or inert ammo for them—three days' rations, three Angry Nine radios, six hundred pounds of sim-ulated Composition Two explosive in one-pound blocks, two detonating devices, and one hundred inert fuses. They were searched before they left Bragg, and they have neither iden-tification nor money. Their mission is to come here and blow up your water tower, your power generating plant, these two bridges, and this building. Your mission, as I understand it, is to stop them."

"Lieutenant, did you say six hundred pounds of phony C-2?" a major asked.

"Yes, sir."

"That's seventy-five pounds a man, plus their other gear," the major said.

"Yes, sir."

"How the hell can they carry that much weight?"

"It's not going to be easy, sir," Ellis said.

"They're going to look very strange standing by the side of

the road, trying to hitch a ride," another officer said, and the others laughed.

"I don't think they'll try to do that, sir," Ellis said. "Colonel MacMillan has come to an unofficial arrangement with the North Carolina Highway Patrol. They will report spotting the team."

"What's in it for the highway patrol?" someone asked.

"A bottle of whiskey for each confirmed spotting. The way that rule works, when the problem is later critiqued, half of the men spotted will be presumed killed if they are spotted. And whatever they might have done after having been spotted will be played with that in mind."

"What about the sherriff's deputies?" someone asked.

"That's between the highway patrol and the deputies," Ellis said.

"What are the rules of engagement between our people and yours?"

"If we attack, because of the element of surprise, we have a four-to-one advantage. In other words, if two of my people attack eight of yours, yours are dead. If we attack with the machine gun or the mortar, we have a ten-to-one advantage. With both, a fifteen-to-one advantage."

"And the rocket launcher?"

"There are six rounds for the rocket launcher. One hit with a round on the water tower will take it out; two hits are required for a bridge abutment. There's paint, in lieu of explosive, in the nose of the rocket."

"You're going to shoot paint at the water tower? The university's going to love that."

"I understand that Colonel Wells and Colonel MacMillan have agreed that we'll clean up the mess if you kill us, and that you'll clean it up if we succeed," Ellis said.

"We could just surround the objectives," an officer said. "Hell, I've got 160 cadets."

"However you do it is up to you, sir," Ellis said.

"Where are your people now?"

"All I know, sir, is that they dropped on Mr. Ford's farm at 0415. They could be anywhere," Ellis said. He looked at Colonel Wells. "That's all I have, sir."

"There's just one thing I have," Colonel Wells said. "To

put our cadets in the right frame of mind to play this game seriously, before you send them out to protect the campus, I want you to make sure they all understand what happens to them if they are killed or captured. I have made arrangements with the Athletic Department to borrow the stadium for the rest of the weekend. Casualties will be taken to the stadium, where they will spend the rest of the weekend in pup tents and be fed with ten-in-one rations. Signs will be posted around the campus, inviting the curious to come look at the prisoners."

There was laughter at that.

"And remind them that the losers get to scrape off the paint too," Colonel Wells said. "That will be all, gentlemen. Get out there and save Duke from Lieutenant Ellis's barbaric hordes."

(Four)
Post Stockade
Fort Jackson, South Carolina
0830 Hours, 11 December 1961

The shoulder insignia of the Military District of Washington was worn by officers and men assigned to the Pentagon and to other army units in and near the District of Columbia. It shows two swords crossed over the Washington Monument. Lieutenant Colonel Craig W. Lowell—and a large number of other officers and enlisted men—privately thought of it as the insignia of the "Chairborne Brigade." There were two swords, because the Chairborne Brigade required duplicate copies of everything, and they were unsheathed because the Quartermaster Corps had sent the sheaths to Alaska; the Washington Monument was pictured because without an unmistakable pictograph, the warriors of the Chairborne Brigade would not only be ignorant of what they were doing, they would otherwise not know where they were doing it.

After a satisfactory period of service in Washington on the General Staff of the Army, field-grade officers are awarded the General Staff Corps Badge, a gold and enamel device worn on the right breast pocket of the tunic. Lieutenant Colonel Craig L. Lowell was known to believe the award had been created to give a medal to warriors who otherwise would not get one. One qualified for it by serving two years in the Pentagon without becoming hopelessly lost in the corridors more than twice; by not contracting a social disease; and by having one's name spelled correctly in the Department of Defense telephone directory. Considering the Pentagon, these were notable achievements.

On his relief from assignment to the Pentagon, however, then Major Craig W. Lowell had "neglected" to remove the MDW shoulder insignia from one of his uniform tunics. He had likewise not added the General Staff Corps Badge to his informal (in a stainless-steel soap container from a long-discarded shaving set) collection of odd insignia he had once worn, but had left it pinned to the tunic with the MDW shoulder insignia.

Officers wearing such insignia could generally prowl the corridors of the Pentagon without interference. No one paid much attention to majors or lieutenant colonels in the Pentagon anyway, and one so bedecked simply vanished in the horde.

He had been wearing the tunic with the MDW patch and the GSC Badge in his present TDY assignment: doing the hurry-up revisions of aircraft requirements for Bob Bellmon—and ultimately for the Secretary of Defense. More attention is paid in the Pentagon to somebody with the badge and the MDW patch *(the guy has been here two years and possibly knows his way around)* than to an officer wearing the insignia of the Army Aviation Center *(the guy's on TDY; before I do what he wants me to do, he'll have gone home; so why bother?)*.

Before he got in the Hertz Ford and rode out to Fort Jackson, Lowell put on the tunic with the MDW patch and the GSC Badge in the motel in Columbia. He was very much aware that many people in the army—those who have never been to the Pentagon—regard officers assigned to the Pentagon as the military equivalent of divine messenger. When they are not out prowling the boonies, they stand at the right hand of God, otherwise known as the Chief of Staff.

From their reactions when he walked into the administrative office of the Fort Jackson stockade, Lowell decided that neither the captain, the lieutenant, nor the sergeant first class had had much experience with light birds of the General Staff Corps.

The administrative office, in a frame building with exposed studs, was divided by a counter. There was a sign on the door outside that read *Knock, Remove Headgear and Wait for Permission to Enter.* NO EXCEPTIONS. Lowell pushed open the door and walked in. There was a VISITORS REGISTER HERE sign thumbtacked to the counter with a loose-leaf notebook not far from it.

He walked to the counter and placed on it his attaché case and cap with the scrambled eggs on the brim. Ignoring the GI ball-point pen on a chain, he took a pen from his pocket and signed the register: *Lt. Col. C. W. Lowell, DCSOPS.*

That wasn't exactly the truth, the whole truth, and nothing but the truth. It was true, however, that he was on TDY to Bob Bellmon. Brigadier General Bellmon was Director of Army Aviation, Officer of the Deputy Chief of Staff for Operations. That was close enough.

The sergeant first class walked over to him, smiling.

"Good morning, sir," he said.

Nice guy, Lowell decided. *I won't jump on his ass, the way I'd planned to.*

"Good morning, Sergeant," Lowell said, and smiled at him.

The lieutenant was something else. He was a cadaverous, no longer young first john wearing an MP's leather regalia, a leather Sam Brown belt, and an MP brassard. He was looking at Lowell with frank curiosity, having diverted his attention from the crossword puzzle in the newspaper.

"Lieutenant, haven't you been taught to rise when a senior officer enters the room?" Lowell inquired nastily.

The lieutenant popped to attention. The captain also rose, not quite as rapidly, and walked to the counter.

"How may I help you, Colonel?"

"That would depend on who you are and what you do," Lowell said.

"Sir," the MP captain said, finally getting the message, "Captain Foster, Deputy Confinement Officer, Post Stockade, sir."

He saluted. After a moment Lowell returned it.

"You may stand at ease, Captain," he said.

"How may I help the colonel, sir?" Captain Foster asked.

"You have a private soldier named Craig in here. I wish first to see his file, and then I wish to interview him. Have you a suitable place, something private, with a table and a couple of chairs?"

The captain, Lowell saw, was desperately trying to read what he had written in the visitor's register. With that in mind, Lowell had printed *DCSOPS* in large, clear letters.

"Sir, the files are not kept here," Captain Foster said.

"Where are they kept?"

"In the Provost Marshal's Office, sir."

"And where is that?"

"Right next door, sir."

"Sergeant," Lowell said, "would you please fetch it for me?"

The sergeant looked at the captain, who licked his lips nervously and looked at Lowell, who had raised his eyebrows, questioning delay in responding to his order.

"Tell them I sent you for it," the captain said, and the sergeant lifted a portion of the counter, slipped through it, and went out the door.

"It won't take him a minute, sir," the captain said. He looked like he was about to ask a question.

"How many men have you confined here?" Lowell asked quickly. Over the captain's shoulder he saw the cadaverous lieutenant still standing at rigid attention.

"Two hundred seventeen, sir," the captain said.

"Lieutenant, you may sit down and get on with your duties," Lowell said.

The lieutenant hastily folded his newspaper, dropped it in the wastebasket, and took something from his desk drawer. He then began to study it with rapt fascination.

"How many pretrial?"

The captain had to think about that.

"Fifty-one, sir."

"And how many are confined in hospital?"

"I don't have that off the top of my head, sir," Captain Foster said. "I'll get it for you."

Lowell nodded.

Take your time, Captain. I need time to dream up other appropriate questions to ask.

The captain was still frantically searching for the right list when the sergeant returned, carrying a manila folder.

"Thank you," Lowell said to him, taking the file. He raised his voice slightly. "Get that information for me at your convenience, Captain," he said. "Now I would like the table and chair I requested, so I can read this. And then please send for the soldier in question."

"Would the colonel like to use the confinement officer's office, sir?"

"I would rather not," Lowell said. "Just a room and a table and two chairs will be fine."

"Yes, sir. Will you come with me, please, sir?"

He showed Lowell to a small cubicle, obviously where the officer of the day slept at night.

Lowell walked in, laid the file on the small table, and looked at Captain Foster.

"You have sent for the prisoner?"

"I'll do that right now, sir."

Lowell shut the door in his face. He sat down and opened the file.

There were five charges, the most serious of which was "Assault on a Noncommissioned Officer in the Execution of His Office." The convening authority, the post commander, approving the recommendation of the Board of Investigating Officers, had directed trial by general court-martial on all the charges and specifications.

A loudspeaker went off: "Attention on the parade ground. Attention on the parade ground. Confinee Craig to report to his barracks. Confinee Craig to report to his barracks. On the double."

V

The Coronado Beach Hotel
San Diego, California
0845 Hours, 11 December 1961

There were a number of temptations put into the path of a physician, Antoinette Parker, M.D., thought as she watched her husband get dressed, and high among them was a physician's virtually unquestioned access to any number of tranquilizing drugs. There was a plastic bottle of such a drug in her purse. Dr. Emory Stacey III, a colleague at Fayetteville, North Carolina, General Hospital, had given it to her a few days earlier.

Dr. Stacey, like Dr. Parker, was a board-certified radiologist. They had become professionally acquainted shortly after Dr. Parker had found employment as what the army called, in its quaint way, a "contract surgeon" at the Fort Bragg hospital. They had quickly become friends, and this friendship bloomed even though Dr. Stacey was a white North Carolinian male who referred to his wife as "the little woman" and who believed the election of John Fitzgerald Kennedy was a national catastrophe of about fifteen on the Richter scale, while Dr. Parker was a black very professional female from Massachusetts who believed that Richard Nixon posed the greatest threat to the republic since Benedict Arnold and who was not at all reluctant to say so.

For her part, Toni did not find Dr. Stacey sexually attractive, and she was sure that as a southern gentleman he would no more make a pass at a black woman than he would join the Abyssinian Baptist Church. Their friendship was thus initially based on mutual respect. Professionally they were head and shoulders over their peers, and that had immediately become apparent to both of them.

They saw themselves in the company of all-too-enthusiastic cutters, who saw carcinoma in every dark smudge of a film and considered it their joyous duty to exorcise the evil with a knife. Compensation for their selfless service to mankind naturally came quickly from the friendly folks at Blue Cross/Blue Shield.

Emory Stacey and Toni Parker believed surgery to be the last resort, and they found in each other allies of great value when surgery was being debated by the medical staffs of the two hospitals with which they were affiliated. Stacey had come out of Tulane and the Ochsner Clinic in New Orleans, and had done his residency at the Mayo Clinic. Parker had come out of Harvard and Massachusetts General. Their opinions could not be easily disregarded, and the cutters were often denied the chance to wield their knives.

Later they had become friends. They were both married to and in love with difficult people. Difficult, however, in very different ways. Jo-Ellen Stacey was a tall, good-looking southern belle with the brains of a gnat. Philip Sheridan Parker IV was a highly intelligent, well-educated, extremely capable man who was absolutely convinced that it was graven on stone tablets that he was destined to be a soldier, as his father, grandfather, and great-grandfather had been before him.

In time Emory Stacey learned, though not from Toni, that Phil Parker, who had earned a battlefield promotion to captain in Korea, had also not long afterward been court-martialed there. He had been charged—*and* acquitted—of having shot down a cowardly officer who had refused to fight. Legally the accusation was to have been expunged from army records on the return of a not-guilty verdict. But he remained by reputation the cold-blooded coon who had blown away some poor battle-weary first john and gotten away with it.

Philip Sheriden Parker IV later trusted the army when he was told that he was not promoted to major when he should have been because somehow the army had lost his records, and as a result his name had not been put before a promotion board. Dr. Toni Parker did not believe that explanation for a second. (The promotion eventually came through.)

Toni Parker learned, though not from Emory Stacey, that Jo-Ellen Stacey had had an affair with both her pediatrician and the pilot who had tried, and failed, to teach her to fly an airplane. Emory was not too embarrassed to talk about his wife to Toni, however. He had to talk to somebody, after all, and Toni was smart, sophisticated, discreet, and sexually unavailable. What Emory told Toni about Jo-Ellen was that she was dumb. Plain dumb. Not bad, just dumb. When she ran out of things to say to a man, she pulled her panties down.

And they continued to be married, Emory and Jo-Ellen, Toni and Phil, and there were children; yet, neither Emory nor Toni could imagine a normal married life with their lawful spouses. Still, it was nice to have somebody to talk to.

"He's going to Indochina for a year," Toni Parker told Emory Stacey not long before Phil—well, abandoned her yet one more time. "He thinks they have finally recognized his potential."

"What's he going to do in Indochina?"

"Fly airplanes. Kill people. Who knows?"

"You can't talk him out of going?"

"No more than Pavlov could make the dogs stop salivating once he rang the bell," she said. "He has heard the bugle blow and is pawing the ground."

"When's he going?"

"Right away. Everybody else in the army gets three, four months' notice. He sails from San Diego on December eleventh."

"By ship?"

"By aircraft carrier," she said. "That's a big secret, by the way. Don't tell anybody. The military is absolutely convinced that if they stamp *Top Secret* on somebody's orders, that will make an aircraft carrier loaded with army airplanes and helicopters invisible."

"You're going to stay here?"

"Sure," she said. "What else? I'm an officer's wife, and officers' wives smile bravely and put candles in their windows and wait for their men to come home."

Their eyes met, and he shrugged in sympathy.

"I know a fellow," Emory Stacey said. "He'll be helpful about a house."

"What?"

"Don't you have to give up your quarters when he leaves?" Stacey asked.

"Oh, that's nice of you, Emory," she said, understanding what he had offered: to use his influence to get a black woman and her kids into a decent house.

"Not at all," he said.

"Our quarters are my quarters," she said. "I hold the assimilated grade of colonel. They're really desperate for physicians, and they provide quarters. Assimilated colonels don't get to live on Colonel's Row, but they do get quarters. I'll stay on the post. I don't want to put the kids in one of your schools."

"No," he agreed.

"I'll have to ask you to cover for me for a week at the hospital though," she said.

"Sure," he said. "You're going to California with him?"

"With a stop at Valhalla," she said.

"Valhalla?"

"That's not fair of me," she said. "Phil and I are going to stop off to see his parents—that's Colonel Philip Sheridan Parker III, Retired. They have a house outside the gate of Fort Riley. That's not fair, either. They have a very nice house on 160 acres outside Manhattan, Kansas. The colonel raises horses. He was a cavalryman. But it is sort of Valhalla, or at least the Valhalla Museum. All the souvenirs all the Parker soldiers—and there have been a lot of them—have brought home from their wars. It's a sacred ritual, like Japanese ancestor worship, to go there and be reminded of Phil's noble, soldierly heritage. There is even a symbol like a ceremonial sword, an enormous Colt revolver, that Phil's grandfather carried in World War I."

"An old six-shooter?"

"Not the cowboy gun, but an old revolver. The colonel carried it in World War II, and Phil carried it in Korea. When Paul Hanrahan told Phil he was going to Indochina, he took it to pieces and cleaned it. Not that it needed cleaning, but that *is* the ritual."

Dr. Stacey chuckled.

"And while his daddy was taking it apart and putting it back together, little Phil stood quietly behind him, eyes wide, watching, just dreaming of the day when he can be a soldier."

"Don't get sore at me, Toni," Stacey said, "but I sort of understand that."

"That's because you're a male chauvinist," she said.

"You knew that," he said. "Is there anything I can do, Toni?"

"Come to the party," Toni said. "Prepared to tranquilize a hysterical wife."

"Whose party?"

"Mine, of course. An officer's wife has a ritual party for a husband going away. Everybody gets drunk and worships Mars with a ritual bloody steak."

When Emory and Jo-Ellen came to Quarters Six, Hospital Area, for the party, Emory slipped a bottle into Toni's hand. He had taken her at her word. There were enough tranquilizers in the bottle to put the officer corps of the Eighty-second Airborne Division into a happy stupor.

She had yet to take one, although there had been great temptation at the farm outside Manhattan, when, with tears in their eyes, the kids had waved good-bye to them. She was also tempted the day before when Phil had had to go to the navy base to check in and had left her alone in the hotel. Toni had really wanted to be either drunk or tranquilized then.

She did not do either, though. Phil didn't like her when she had too much to drink, and she didn't want him to go away remembering her that way, so that was out. But so were the pills. She was afraid of drugs, medical efficacy aside. She had seen too many women, Jo-Ellen Stacey among them, riding around on cloud nine.

So she'd gone to the pool and swam to work the emotional

poisons out of her system before Phil came back from the navy base. When she went up their room, there was an enormous floral display standing in front of the dresser. It was in the shape of a horseshoe, and it carried a legend, *Bon Voyage!,* in gold letters on a purple ribbon. She didn't have to open the card to know that it was from Craig Lowell. Lowell sent flowers on every occasion—always too many, too garish.

Lowell, whom Toni Parker regarded as another lost soul, was Phil's best friend. They had met at Fort Knox long ago as second lieutenants, and Phil believed Lowell's testimony in his behalf was the reason he had been acquitted at his court-martial. Lowell had been Phil's best man at their wedding. The flowers made her think of that and consider that she very possibly was on the next to the last day of her time with the man she had married. Soldiers got killed in wars, and her husband, goddamn him, insisted on being a soldier.

She had not taken a pill then, either. If these were to be their last hours she wanted to remember them in detail, not through a chemical fog.

As Phil tied his tie, Toni jumped out of bed.

"I'm going with you to the dock."

He turned and looked at her.

"I thought we talked that through," he said. "The dock will be loaded with sailors' wives."

"And at least one soldier's wife," Toni said.

"It's not smart," he said.

"Maybe not," she said, "but I'm going."

"Okay," he said.

My God, she thought, *he's pleased. He really is pleased. He wants me to go with him. And I almost lay here on my tail and didn't go.*

There was a marine guard at the gate to the navy base. He started to wave them through with a crisp salute, but then held his hand out.

Toni thought she understood that. He had first seen the officer's insignia, the gold major's leaves, on Phil's epaulets. Then he had seen, certainly, the color of the major's skin.

"Good morning, sir," he said, and leaned down to look in the window, looking at both of them carefully. "Your destination, sir?"

"The USNS *Card*," Phil said.

"Thank you, sir," the MP said, and waved them through.

She had never seen an aircraft carrier up close before. This one, Phil had told her, wasn't even a full-sized one. It was a World War II carrier taken out of mothballs and converted into an aircraft ferry. It wasn't even officially a navy ship, but crewed by civilians and called USNS for *U.S. Naval Ship* rather than USS, which stood for *United States Ship*. Toni didn't pretend to understand the convoluted military logic behind that.

From a distance she could see the flight deck. It was jammed with helicopters and airplanes. She knew what they were. Piasecki H-21 "Flying Bananas," with a rotor at each end. DeHavilland of Canada L20 "Beavers" and the larger version of the Beaver, the U1A "Otter." There were Mohawks aboard, too, but they were being carried internally, Phil had told her. The twin turboprop Grumman reconnaissance aircraft were a deep secret within the larger deception involved in sending army airplanes to Indochina.

Even though *Card* was a small vessel, close up it was so large, it was overwhelming. When Phil stopped the car at a marine MP's hand signal on the dock, Toni could not see anything but the carrier's enormous expanse of gray steel.

"You're going aboard, sir?" the marine asked.

"Yes," Phil said.

"You'd better hurry, sir. They've already begun to take in the lines."

With a little bit of luck, it'll leave without him.

"Thank you," Phil said.

He took off his brimmed cap and handed it to Toni.

"Take care of that for me, will you?" he said. He opened his attaché case, which contained, among other things, the ceremonial Colt revolver, and took out a green beret.

"I thought they were outlawed," she said.

"CONARC directives apply only in the States," he said, setting the beret in place on his head. He twisted the rearview mirror of the Econo-Rent Ford to examine himself.

They're like little boys with those hats. Little boys dressing up to go play war.

"If I have neglected to mention this," Phil said, "I love you. Take care of yourself."

He leaned over and kissed her, very tenderly, on the lips, then quickly stepped out of the car. He stuck his attaché case under his arm and then pulled his two suitcases from the backseat.

Their eyes met and he smiled. Then he straightened up, kicked the door shut, and marched down the pier in the shadow of the enormous gray bulk above him.

Two soldiers in green berets came running to him and relieved him of the suitcases. He turned and looked at her for a moment, waved, and walked farther down the pier.

Toni jumped out of the car and walked after him.

There was an open door, as large as a house, in the side of the ship, with a wide stairway leading into it. She thought she caught a glimpse of him at the top, but she wasn't sure.

She stood on the pier looking up at the ship.

A crane pulled the wide stairs away from the door in the ship.

A navy band began to play "So Long, It's Been Good to Know You."

She sensed, rather than saw, that the carrier was moving.

She walked backward away from it, and gradually the deck came in sight. It was possible now to see people up there, army officers among them, looking down at the pier, but she didn't see Phil.

It took a long time for the USNS *Card* to begin to move, and the band changed tunes. They played "She Wore a Yellow Ribbon." That was an old Cavalry tune she had learned from Colonel Philip S. Parker III. The navy was playing it for the army. That was nice, she thought.

She did not see Phil again, although she searched the USNS *Card* until it was too far away to make out faces.

Now she would have one of those goddamn pills, she thought.

She went back to the rented Ford, sat behind the wheel, and ran her fingers over the scrambled eggs on the brim of Phil's hat. Then she pulled the pill vial from her purse and took a pill from it. She stared at it a moment, then left the car and walked to a fifty-five gallon trash barrel on the pier and threw the pill and the bottle into it.

• • •

(Two)
Post Stockade
Fort Jackson, South Carolina
0845 Hours, 11 December 1961

The day had begun for Confinee Craig at 0345 hours. The lights had been turned on, and a half-second later the corporal in charge of the barracks had blown his whistle.

Confinee Craig was on the second floor of the barracks, along with a number of other confinees. A confinee was not a prisoner; a confinee was awaiting trial. A prisoner had been found guilty at his court-martial. For that reason prisoners were separated from confinees. And following the principle of American jurisprudence that individuals are presumed innocent until proven guilty in a competent court of law, confinees were not denied the privileges taken from prisoners. Confinees, for example, were permitted to salute. Prisoners were denied that privilege.

Confinees were also allowed the privilege of military training, although Geoffrey Craig had been unable to detect any difference whatever between "confinee military training" and "prisoner retraining." Both consisted primarily of close-order drill, calesthenics, and the preparation of field sanitary facilities. That meant digging a latrine in the morning and then filling it back up in the afternoon.

When the lights went on and the whistle blew, the confinees had leaped out of their beds, ripped from the beds the blankets and mattress covers issued in lieu of sheets, and thrown them to the floor—mattress covers to the left, blankets to the right. Pillows were not available for issue.

They then stood to attention at the foot of their bunks for "confinee count," which was conducted by the barracks corporal. As he walked past each confinee, the confinee sang out his last name, his first name, his middle initial, and the last four digits of his serial number.

Confinees were required to be wearing at that time T-shirts, shorts, and socks, men's, woolen, cushion-sole.

Once confinee count was completed, the trainees had forty-five minutes to shower, shave, dress, make up their bunks (less mattress covers), and wash the mattress covers and the uniform they had worn the previous day. A good soldier takes pride in his personal cleanliness. The clothing and mattress covers were washed by taking them to the latrine and scrubbing them with a brush and GI soap on the concrete floor. The washed uniforms, underwear, and mattress covers were then taken outside and hung, in the prescribed manner, on a wire clothesline to dry.

Inasmuch as Confinee Craig's hand was in a cast, the daily laundry ritual posed something of a problem for the barracks corporal. This dilemma was resolved by the appointment of a roster of fellow detainees, one of whom each day would be responsible for washing Confinee Craig's laundry in addition to his own. Because Confinee Craig was perfectly capable of taking the laundry down when it was dry and of making his bed as required, these tasks he did on his own.

The confinees' uniform of the day was fatigues (stenciled with *P*'s in the designated places), cartridge belts, canteens, first-aid packets, and helmet, steel, protective. It was the same uniform prisoners wore, except that prisoners were denied the privilege of soldier's headgear. They wore instead caps, fatigue, with brim reversed, which made them look like German soldiers in the movie *All Quiet on the Western Front*.

Prisoners wore their cartridge belts upside down with the flaps hanging open, signifying that they had lost the privilege of bearing arms.

Roll call was held at 0430, and differed from confinee count in that it was held outdoors.

The confinees were then marched to breakfast. Confinees were given the standard ration, which was spooned onto each confinee's stainless-steel compartmented tray. Confinees were required to eat everything on their trays.

At 0505 the day's training began: First came forty-five minutes of calisthenics, followed by a ten-minute break, followed by an hour of close-order drill, a ten-minute break, and another hour of close-order drill.

At 0800, training in techniques of field sanitary procedures began. Again Confinee Craig's hand in a cast posed a problem for the noncommissioned officer in charge of training. Since he could not in fairness be excluded from the training, Craig was required to stand at the end of the latrine being dug and to count aloud the number of shovelfuls of dirt taken from the hole.

It was unfortunate that some dirt spilled on the spot where he had to stand in order to make an accurate count. Much of this dirt, predictably, fell onto his boots. By the time the field sanitation facility had been dug to the required depth, his boots were just about completely covered.

When the loudspeakers blared Craig's name, he had just announced the removal of shovelful number 128.

The call was probably a summons to the hospital, he thought, for the every-other-day examination of his hand. He didn't believe that the hand required all that much examination, and there was always a wait for most of the morning, and it was humiliating standing there in the emergency room with an MP guard, but that was considerably less unpleasant than standing at the end of a field sanitation facility in the process of excavation, having your boots buried in dirt.

The barracks corporal waited patiently for Craig to replace his muddy boots and trousers with clean items suitable for an appearance at the administration building. Confinee Craig had yet been unable to learn to tie his bootlaces with one hand, but he had grown rather adept at stuffing the loose ends beneath the crisscrossed laces so the ends wouldn't drag on the ground.

The barracks corporal ordered him to proceed to the administration building gate. Confinees always moved at double time. When Craig reached the rear door of the building he double-timed in place until the barracks corporal caught up to him and ordered him to halt.

When the barracks corporal knocked at the door, it was opened by the confinement sergeant.

"What the hell took you so goddamned long?" the sergeant barked at the barracks corporal. Then, to Confinee Craig, he said, "I will knock at the door. When we are told to enter, I will enter. You will follow me. When I stop, you will stop one pace behind me. When I render the hand salute, you will render the hand salute."

"Yes, Sergeant," Confinee Craig said.

When the confinement sergeant knocked at the door, a voice said, "Come in."

The confinement sergeant and Confinee Craig marched into the room and stopped.

"Sir, Confinee Craig is present, sir," the confinement sergeant said, and saluted.

"Thank you, Sergeant," the officer said. "I'll call you when I need you."

"Sir, confinees are to be accompanied at all times."

"I won't tell you again, Sergeant," Lowell said. "You are dismissed."

The sergeant saluted again, about-faced, and marched out of the office.

"Hello, Geoff," Lowell said.

"What do I call you, under the circumstances?" Geoff asked.

"'Colonel' or 'sir' will do nicely," Lowell said.

"How did you hear about this?" Geoff asked, and remembered after a moment to add "sir."

"The check you wrote to the lawyer was called to your father's attention," Lowell said. "He brought it to mine."

"I'm sorry he found out," Geoff said.

"You're in no position to antagonize me, Geoff. I told you to call me 'sir.'"

"Yes, sir," Geoff said.

"You do have, I hope, some idea of the magnitude of the jam you're in?"

"Yes, sir."

For the first time Geoff saw Craig Lowell as an officer. For as long as he could remember, he had known his cousin was in the army. But he had rarely seen him, and never before in a uniform. He wasn't exactly an expert on the army's doodads, but he recognized some of the things pinned to Craig Lowell's uniform: the pilot's wings, the Combat Infantry Badge, and the Purple Heart medal, with the little gadgets that indicated his kin had suffered wounds on a number of occasions. And there was row after row of ribbons, more than Geoff remembered seeing on most of the officers he had seen here.

The lieutenant colonel's silver oak leaves he recognized. His kin did not rank as high as the regimental commander, but he outranked the battalion commander, the bastard who had put him in here and who was probably going to send him to prison.

"What happened to your hand?" Lowell asked.

"It's broken in several places, Colonel," Geoff said.

"Apparently you've had adequate treatment for it."

"Yes, sir."

"Are you in pain?"

"No, sir."

"Why did you beat up the sergeant? Beat up, as opposed to punch."

"I lost my temper, sir."

"What did he say to you that made you lose your temper?"

"He didn't say anything; he hit me."

"'He hit me, sir.'"

"He hit me, sir."

"Any witnesses?"

"No, sir."

"You would be expected to accuse the sergeant of landing the first blow," Lowell said. "Why do you think he did that?"

"Because the ignorant bastard thought he could get away with it," Geoff said.

"Geoff, it is also a violation of the Uniform Code of Military Justice, 1948, to refer to a noncommissioned officer in disrespectful and/or obscene terminology," Lowell said. "The next time I hear you do it, I'll charge you with it. Do I make my point?"

"Yes, sir. May I ask what it is you're doing here, Colonel?"

"When your mother heard that you're about to go to the Federal Penitentiary at Leavenworth, she grew hysterical to the point where your father felt it necessary to summon a physician. Your father reacted to this by telephoning our senators. Fortunately, I was able to turn off the senators."

"Excuse me, sir, I don't know what you mean by that."

"When it became known to the members of your courtmartial that there was what is known as 'congressional interest' in your case, they would feel honor-bound to throw the book at you," Lowell said. "We're not at war, so they couldn't sentence you to death. But in peacetime, what you're charged with is punishable by life imprisonment. What that really means is that you would probably pull six months at Leavenworth. At that point you would be offered a chance at rehabilitation—that is presuming good behavior, of course. That's sort of basic training, extending over a period of six months, right in Leavenworth. Presuming successful completion of that, you would be offered the chance to enlist for three years, and your offense would be expunged from the records."

"They only drafted me for two," Geoff said.

Lowell decided to forgive the omission of the term *sir*.

"If you were not selected for rehabilitation, or declined it, you would probably come up for consideration for parole toward the end of your fifth year of confinement," he went on conversationally. "Your status would be that of a paroled felon, which means that you could not have a seat on the stock exchange or for that matter own a shotgun or get a driver's license. After several years on probation, depending on who was in office, we could probably get you a pardon, and you could resume your normal life."

Geoff said nothing.

"Now, your attorney has promised you that the army always makes enough mistakes so that he can get the conviction reversed on error," Lowell said. "Well, cousin, you can treat his promise as bullshit."

Geoff looked at him in genuine surprise.

"I talked to that sonofabitch last night," Lowell said. "I was disappointed in you. I thought that by now you would have learned that the primary motivation of lawyers is not justice but money. You never feed a bird dog before you take him hunting, and you never pay a lawyer before he's done what you're hiring him to do."

"He demanded a retainer," Geoff said, and remembered to add "sir."

"He smelled money," Lowell said. "He doesn't have any idea how much, but he figured that if there was a colonel in the family, there was probably another fifteen hundred to be had. He asked me for it. I fired him, of course."

"You had no right to do that!" Geoff said.

"See if you can get this into your stupid head, Geoff," Lowell said. "You are in no position to tell me what I have any right to do. I am very fond of your mother. I will do what I can for you because of what I feel for her."

"Yes, sir."

"That corn-pone shyster did not tell you that the Judge Advocate takes very particular care not to make any technical mistakes when the local legal civilian hotshot appears on the scene. And contrary to what you might think, all lawyers in the army are not stupid."

Geoff was white in the face.

"Cousin Craig," he said, "what the hell am I going to do?"

"Now we're down to 'Cousin Craig,' are we?" Lowell asked. "I suppose that's an improvement over a surly 'sir.'"

"I didn't mean to sound surly, sir."

"You will be defended at your court-martial by the army lawyer appointed to defend you," Lowell said. "He will try to get you off on your self-defense plea. I don't think he will get away with that, but he'll try. I'll come down here just before the trial and suggest to him that we paint you in court as a spoiled rich kid to whom the army posed such a culture shock that you lost control. I will suggest to him that he plead with the court that because you were pushed beyond your limits, a lengthy sentence would not be in the public interest.

"When your trial is over and goes through the local review process, we will get letters from your priest, the headmaster at St. Mark's, and whoever else your father can beg them from, saying what a saintly character you are. That may induce the commanding general here to cut a couple of years off your sentence. The more we can get off, the better."

"Oh, Jesus!" Geoff Craig said.

"And at that point, we'll call in some competent lawyers experienced in this sort of thing, and we'll appeal your sentence all the way up to the Court of Military Appeals. With a little bit of luck, we'll have you out in eighteen months or two years."

"Two years?" Geoff Craig asked.

"That's presuming you don't get in any more trouble in the stockade," Lowell said. "You had better be the ideal prisoner."

"Two years!" Geoff Craig repeated.

"Be happy if it's only two years," Lowell said.

"But all I did was defend myself!"

"So you say," Lowell said. "But you're going to have to convince the court of that, and my estimate of your chances of doing that range from very slight to none."

He stood up and went to the door and knocked on it.

"Take your punishment like a man, Geoff," Craig Lowell said. "You did it, and you're going to have to pay for it."

He nodded curtly at Confinee Craig and walked out of the room.

• • •

(Three)
Station Hospital
Fort Jackson, South Carolina
0940 Hours, 11 December 1961

"Base, this is One-Seven," the military police sergeant said into the microphone of his Motorola police radio.

"Go, One-Seven," the military police dispatcher replied.

"I think we got that Hertz rent-a-car MP Five is looking for. It's parked at the hospital."

"Is the subject in it?"

"Negative, negative."

"You're sure it's the car?"

"Affirmative, affirmative. We checked it out. It's unlocked, and the rental papers are on the driver's seat. The name checks out, but it doesn't say anything about him being an officer. Same name, but it says he's vice-chairman of the board of some company."

"Hold on, One-Seven," the military police dispatcher said. There was a delay of several minutes.

"One-Seven, Base."

"Go ahead, Base."

"MP Five is en route to join you. If subject tries to leave the hospital, you are to detain him until MP Five arrives on the scene."

"Understand MP Five is en route?"

"That is affirmative, affirmative."

"Roger, Base," the MP sergeant said.

MP Five, who was the Deputy Provost Marshal, arrived in the hospital parking lot at the wheel of the Provost Marshal's staff car (though PROVOST MARSHAL rather than MILITARY PO-LICE was painted on the trunk and doors, it was otherwise identical to an MP patrol car) just as Lieutenant Colonel C. W. Lowell came out of the hospital entrance and started toward his car.

MP Five, Major J. William Hasper, Jr., MPC, was a roly-poly little man of thirty-five with a carefully tended pencil-line mustache. With the exception of white MP leggings, he was wearing MP accouterments.

"One moment, please!" he called out as he opened his door and Craig Lowell opened his.

He walked quickly to Lowell.

"May I see some identification, please?" he demanded.

"Doesn't anyone at Fort Jackson salute or say 'sir'?" Lowell asked.

The MP major considered that a moment, and repeated: "May I see some identification please?"

"You salute me, Major, and call me 'sir,' and I will show you my identification," Lowell said. "And then you will show me yours, because I want to make note of the name of an MP major who displays such an appalling lack of military courtesy."

MP Five lost his temper.

He gestured angrily toward the two MPs who were standing beside Patrol Car 17, and they came over at a trot.

Trained by long habit, the MP sergeant saluted. Lowell returned it crisply.

"Good morning, Sergeant," he said. He looked at the Major. "Your men display fine military courtesy, Major."

"Now I'll see your identification, if you please," MP Five said.

Lowell made no move to comply.

"Sergeant!" MP Five snapped.

"Sir," the sergeant said, "may I see some identification, please?"

"Certainly," Lowell said, and handed him his AGO card.

The MP sergeant looked at it, looked at Lowell, and then handed it to MP Five.

MP Five paled.

"Colonel, there's apparently been some sort of misunderstanding," he said.

"Now that you know who *I* am, may I see *your* AGO card, please?" Lowell asked.

Red-faced, the major produced it. Lowell took a notebook, wrote down the name, and then handed the AGO card back.

"Now I would like an explanation of this extraordinary episode," Lowell said.

"Colonel, would you wait here for just a minute, please?" MP Five said.

"If you wish," Lowell said.

MP Five trotted to his car and spoke on the radio. Then he came back.

"Colonel," he said, "Colonel Sauer's compliments, and would you please follow me to Colonel Sauer's office?"

"Who is Colonel Sauer?"

"Colonel Sauer commands the Eleventh Infantry Regiment, sir."

"What an extraordinary coincidence," Lowell said. "Just the man I was going to see."

(Four)
Headquarters
Eleventh Infantry Regiment (Training)
Fort Jackson, South Carolina
1005 Hours, 10 December 1961

Colonel Fritz J. Sauer, Infantry, was short, barrel-chested, and crew-cutted. He was wearing fatigues. They had been tailored to his body and were stiff with starch. Sewn above the breast pocket were embroidered representations of the Combat Infantry Badge (Second Award) and senior parachutist's wings with two stars. The circled *A* of Third Army was sewn to his left sleeve at the shoulder, and the Indian head of the Second Infantry Division to the shoulder of the right sleeve. Regulations permitted the wearing on that sleeve of the shoulder insignia of the division with which the individual had served in combat.

Colonel Sauer had the choice of wearing the insignia of the Second Infantry, a battalion of which he had commanded in Korea; the Eighty-second Airborne Division, a platoon and a company of which he had commanded in War II; and the Ninety-sixth Infantry Division, a company and a battalion of which he had commanded in War II. This move from the Eighty-second came about after he'd caught a couple of Schmiesser rounds in the leg at Anzio. He had to be reassigned when he got out of the hospital and couldn't pass the jump physical.

Colonel Sauer had been around the army awhile, and although he was fully aware that the Eleventh Infantry Regiment

(Training) was neither the Sixteenth Infantry Regiment of the First Division, or the 505th of the Eighty-second, it was a regiment of the United States Army, and he was the regimental commander, and he didn't have to put up with some chair-warming sonofabitch of a Pentagon flyboy nosing around in his affairs without even the simple goddamn courtesy of coming to the regiment and announcing his business. It was Colonel Fritz J. Sauer's intention to burn the ass of this sonofabitch as it probably had never been burned before.

"Colonel," his adjutant announced over the intercom, "Major Hasper is here with Lieutenant Colonel Lowell."

"Ask Colonel Lowell to come in, please," Colonel Sauer said.

There was a knock at the door.

"Come in," Colonel Sauer ordered.

The fat little shit from the Provost Marshal marched into the office, followed by a tall, mustachioed officer in Class As.

The MP major saluted but said nothing.

The tall mustachioed officer, who had his brimmed cap under his left arm, crisply saluted and held it.

"Sir, Lieutenant Colonel Lowell, C. W., reporting to Colonel Sauer as directed, sir."

Colonel Sauer's adjutant, who had suggested that it would be a good idea to have a couple of witnesses, slipped into the office accompanied by the S-2. They were both captains.

Lieutenant Colonel Lowell, Colonel Sauer saw, was indeed a Pentagon flyboy with the aviator's wings and the GSC badge pinned to his tunic. But there were other things pinned to his tunic too. There was a Combat Infantry Badge with the star of a second award. A Distinguished Service Cross. A Distinguished Service Medal. A Silver Star. A Bronze Star with a couple of *V*'s, meaning more than one award: for valor, not for just being there. And a Purple Heart with several oak leaf clusters. And there were a bunch of foreign decorations, of which Colonel Sauer recognized only the Korean Tae Guk and the Korean Presidential Unit Citation, both of which he was entitled to wear himself.

Colonel Sauer returned the salute; Lowell completed his, and remained at attention, looking six inches over Colonel Sauer's head. Colonel Sauer was somewhat annoyed with Major Hasper, who took it upon himself to assume the position of "At Ease."

"You may stand at ease," Colonel Sauer said.

Lowell shifted position.

"I hope you don't mind," Sauer said, "the means I used to fetch you here."

"Not at all, sir," Lowell said.

"There seems to be some question of your identity," Sauer said.

"Would the colonel like to see my AGO card, sir?"

"I have seen Colonel Lowell's identification, sir," Major Hasper volunteered.

"Then the question would seem to be what your mission is here, Colonel," Sauer said.

"Sir, I had hoped the colonel would grant me an interview in private, sir," Lowell said.

Sauer considered that a moment.

"That will be all, gentlemen, thank you," he said.

Major Hasper, who looked disappointed, saluted, did an about-face, and marched out of the room. The adjutant and S-2 followed him.

"Please have a seat, Colonel," Sauer said. "Can I offer you some coffee? After which, I would like an explanation of what the hell's going on."

"Thank you, sir, and yes, sir, I would like some coffee."

Colonel Sauer ordered coffee and then took a box of cigars from his desk and offered it to Lowell.

"Thank you, sir," Lowell said, and took one. He unwrapped it, sniffed it, pinched it gently along its length, and bit the end off. By that time Sauer had his own cigar unwrapped. Lowell extended a lighter. Sauer had never seen one like it before. It was European, he decided. And gold. Not gold-plated. Gold.

"Nice lighter," Sauer said.

"Thank you, sir," Lowell said. "It was a Christmas present from my father-in-law."

The sergeant major delivered two china cups of coffee.

"I'll get the cream and sugar," he said.

"Not for me, thank you, Sergeant Major," Lowell said.

When the sergeant major had left, closing the door behind him, Colonel Sauer said, "You are a very courteous man,

Colonel. I am therefore curious why you didn't have the courtesy to stop by and talk to me before you started nosing around in my affairs."

"I can only offer my apologies for that inexcusable breech of courtesy, sir, and hope the colonel will accept them."

"What is the interest of DCSOPS in my regiment, to get to the point?" Sauer said.

"So far as I know, sir, only that you continue to maintain the pipeline of trainees," Lowell said.

"Then what are you doing here?"

"I'm interested in the case of Recruit Craig, sir."

"Why?"

"There are several reasons, sir. One of them being that he is my second cousin."

"Oh," Sauer said. "He asked you to come?"

"No, sir. And when I left him this morning, I suspect that he was very sorry that I had come."

"Why would he feel that way?"

"Because I left him believing that he is going to spend the next several years behind bars," Lowell said. "Following which he will have the status of a convicted felon."

"That's just about what's going to happen to him, Colonel, I'm sorry to say."

"With respect, sir, I must disagree," Lowell said.

"I understand you read his file," Colonel Sauer said.

"Yes, sir."

"I recommended that he be tried," Sauer said.

"I must presume, sir, that you did so because you were not fully aware of the facts."

"Colonel, if you think you can come down here and wave that GSC badge in my face and get that young man off, you've got another thing coming."

"I am here, sir, because the alternative to my coming was a delegation from the offices of two United States senators."

"You're saying he's got political influence?"

"His father is a very wealthy and very influential man. If I may be permitted the use of the vernacular, sir, when Geoff's father says 'Shit' to the junior senator from Connecticut and the senior senator from New York, they squat and make grunting noises."

Despite his best efforts to the contrary, Colonel Sauer could not keep from smiling. Under other circumstances, he thought, he would like this Lieutenant Colonel Lowell.

"You're not suggesting, are you, Colonel, that I would be in any way influenced by congressional pressure?"

"I told Geoff, sir, that if the court heard about any political influence being brought to bear, they would throw the book at him."

"In that case, Colonel," Sauer said, "what are you doing here?"

"I'm a soldier, sir," Lowell said. "At the risk of sounding presumptuous, I am here to piss on an ember before it can flare up and cause a fire."

"I'm not sure I understand that. If it means what I think it does, I don't like it."

"What I mean to say, Colonel," Lowell said, "is that if that boy goes before a general court, he's going to walk out free."

"I heard he hired a civilian lawyer," Sauer said. "It won't do him any good."

"I fired the civilian lawyer," Lowell said. "I don't want to take any chances that I don't have to."

"Meaning what?"

"That I devoutly hope the Staff Judge Advocate, if it gets that far, will assign his newest, least-experienced, six-months-out-of-law-school first john to defend Geoff."

"That I don't understand," Colonel Sauer said.

"May I speak freely, sir?"

"Go ahead," Sauer said.

"The first defense witness will be the post surgeon. He will testify that there has been a pattern of trainees from Staff Sergeant Foster's platoon requiring serious medical attention. There have been quite a few falls, statistically speaking, down stairs and in showers. This will be documented by hospital records. Then there will be a series of witnesses, other trainees, who will testify that they heard Staff Sergeant Foster announce his intention to kick the shit out of Geoff. Up until now, these trainees have been frightened into silence by the company commander. He will, however, be summoned as a hostile witness and unless he chooses to swear falsely under oath, he will testify that he threatened the trainees into silence, not only in this incident, but in the ones which preceded it."

"Those are pretty serious charges, Colonel."

"Yes, sir, I'm afraid they are."

Goddamn him, Sauer thought. *He's right about this.*

A wave of anger at his adjutant swept through him. The sonofabitch had told him he'd checked out the facts. Then he turned the anger inside. It was his responsibility to check the facts. He had signed the charges.

"I'll look into this, Lowell," he said. "And if what you allege is true, I'll have your nephew, or whatever he is, out of the stockade, and some other people in it."

"May I continue to speak freely, sir?"

"Go ahead."

"I respectfully suggest, sir, that Staff Sergeant Foster has learned an important lesson: Never pick on anybody who's going to break your jaw. I am really less annoyed at him than I am at the company commander. He should have relieved Staff Sergeant Foster the first time he had an idea that he was beating up the trainees. I had a great big guy in my company one time who used to take people in the bushes and talk to them. But that was educational; it wasn't sport."

Colonel Sauer had in his own mind a bull of a Polish coal miner from Pennsylvania, a platoon sergeant, whose conversations in the bushes with a series of paratroopers had done much to improve the company's discipline. But he hadn't broken any bones and then charged the guy he had talked to with assault because he had gotten a punch in himself.

"I suggest, sir, that court-martialing Foster or his company commander would do the army no good. There are other ways to deal with people like that."

There were, Colonel Sauer agreed, and he knew most of them.

"And what do I do with your nephew? Call him in here and tell him 'Sorry about all this'?"

"He's my second cousin," Lowell said, "and I would hate to have him (a) spend the balance of his service hating the army, and (b) convinced that all he has to do the next time he slugs somebody is call his cousin, the colonel, who will make things right."

Sauer nodded and waited for Lowell to go on.

"Slugging people, sir, is something that all kinds of people do, not only enlisted men. I have heard stories that a very distinguished lieutenant colonel took offense at the attention another colonel was trying to pay his wife and punched him off an officer's club balcony."

"Apropos of nothing whatever, Colonel," Colonel Sauer asked, "do you happen to know a Lieutenant Colonel Rudolph G. MacMillan?"

"I have the privilege of the colonel's acquaintance, sir," Lowell said. "The officer I'm referring to, who shall be of course nameless—"

"Of course," Sauer interrupted.

"—should have, of course, been punished for this offense. But it was decided, I understand at the very highest level—"

"Do you happen to know General E. Z. Black, Colonel?"

"Yes, sir, I have that privilege."

"I thought you might," Sauer said. He was now grinning.

"—that the best interests of the army would be served by sending this unnamed pugnacious officer to Special Forces at Forg Bragg, where he could expend his excess energy running around in the woods, eating snakes."

Colonel Sauer chuckled. "Do you think, Colonel, that your first cousin once removed would be interested in a transfer to Special Forces?"

"I think, sir, he would probably prefer to remain in the stockade. But I think that if he was properly counseled, sir, he might suddenly view it as a great opportunity to better his country, sir."

"What about the paperwork?" Colonel Sauer asked.

"I think they can have anybody they want," Lowell said. "A friend of mine volunteered and went to Bragg over the howling objections of his commanding officer."

"Why don't we call Mac and find out?" Colonel Sauer said. He pushed the lever on his intercom. "Sergeant," he ordered, "put a call through to Lieutenant Colonel MacMillan at Special Forces in Bragg." He sipped his coffee and then smiled at Lowell. "I've known Mac since he was pathfinder platoon sergeant in the 508," he said.

The sergeant major knocked and put his head in the door.

"Sir, I have the sergeant major on the horn. Colonel MacMillan is not available."

"May I?" Lowell asked, and reached for the telephone. "Sergeant Taylor, this is Colonel Lowell. How are you? Where's Colonel Mac?"

Lowell held the telephone away from his ear so that Colonel Sauer could hear.

"Over at Pope with the colonel, Colonel. The President's coming in at 1100, and they're all going ape shit."

"How would a recruit in basic training get into Special Forces?" Lowell asked.

"That would be a little rough, sir. You're supposed to be jump-qualified. And we don't take hardly any privates."

"But there are exceptions?"

"There's always exceptions, Colonel," Sergeant Major Taylor said. "People that come highly recommended or have some kind of special skill."

"You were at Anzio with the 508, weren't you, Taylor? Do you remember an officer named Sauer?"

"Yes, sir. Captain Sauer. He caught it a couple of days before I did."

"Colonel Sauer has a young man, pretty good with his fists, that he thinks would be happy in Special Forces."

"Well, that's a good recommendation," Taylor said. "What we could do, Colonel, if Colonel Mac agrees, is arrange to transfer him here, and then we send him to jump school. I can probably get Colonel Mac on the jeep radio if you want to talk to him."

"Give it a shot, will you?"

"Hold on, Colonel," Taylor said. "And I'll need the name, rank, serial number, and unit, too, Colonel."

Colonel Sauer got up from his desk, went to the door, and told his sergeant major he needed Craig's serial number and full name.

"Hat Five, this is Hatrack," Taylor's voice came over the phone.

"Hatrack, Hat Five," came the reply.

"Colonel Mac around there? Important telephone call."

"Hold on."

"Colonel MacMillan is busy. This is Colonel Hanrahan. Can I help?"

"Good morning, Paul," Lowell said.

"Christ, what do you want, Craig? The President's fifteen minutes out. Can it wait?"

"All you have to do is say yes," Lowell said. "Taylor's on the line."

"Yes to what? What are you up to, Craig?"

"I've been beating the bushes, dredging up bodies for you."

"Why is it that I am suddenly suspicious, Craig? Does this body have a name?"

"Geoffrey Craig," Lowell said.

"What's his claim to fame?" Hanrahan asked. "What's his rank?"

"He's just like Mac. Goes around punching people. He just broke his sergeant's jaw"—he paused—"after provocation. The sergeant got in the first blow."

"No, I don't want him. Absolutely not. What is this?"

"It's important to me," Lowell said.

There was a pause.

"What's the story, Craig?"

"Do me the favor, Paul, please," Lowell said.

There was another long pause.

"Damn you, Craig," Hanrahan said, then: "Oh, shit. Okay. Do what he wants, Taylor. Good-bye, Craig."

"Hat Five, clear," Taylor said, then: "What *is* the story, Colonel?"

"Just take this kid and turn him into your ordinary run-of-the-mill snake-eating killer, Taylor," Lowell said. "Yours not to reason why, et cetera, et cetera."

"Let me have the name, serial number, and organization, Colonel," Taylor said.

VI

(One)
Pope Air Force Base
Fort Bragg, North Carolina
1100 Hours, 11 December 1961

The Commander in Chief's visit to Pope Air Force Base and Fort Bragg, North Carolina, was not a simple, casual affair. This being the case, two days earlier a plane had arrived containing representatives of the President's staff and several senior Secret Service agents. These people made arrangements for communications and reviewed the proposed itinerary for security and press considerations.

Seven other aircraft, the last of them a chartered Piedmont Airlines Plane bearing the brighter lights of the Washington press corps, arrived at various times before *Air Force One*, the Presidential aircraft, made a low gentle approach over the Fort Bragg reservation and touched down at precisely 10:59:45, fifteen seconds ahead of schedule.

The President and his party deplaned and were greeted at the foot of the stairway by Lieutenant General H. H. Howard, U.S. Army, commanding general XVIII Airborne Corps and

Fort Bragg, and by Major General Stanley O. Zarwich, USAF, Commanding General, Pope Air Force Base.

The senior officers were introduced to the President. The roster (prepared by Major General Kenneth L. Harke, U.S. Army, who was for all practical purposes commanding Bragg in the frequent absences of Lieutenant General Howard) included the commanding general and deputy commanding general of the Eighty-second Airborne Division; the deputy commander of Pope Air Force Base; the XVIII Airborne Corps artillery commander; the Eighty-second Division artillery commander; and the commanding general of the Eighth Support Brigade; all the general officers, army and air force, stationed at Fort Bragg and Pope Air Force Base; and, with two exceptions, the officers who commanded the major troop units. The exceptions were the commander of the station hospital, a full colonel, and the commandant of the U.S. Army Special Warfare School and Center, also a full colonel.

Colonel Hanrahan was not, after all, a general officer, General Harke reasoned. Furthermore, he had been informed by CONARC that it was entirely likely that the President would take the opportunity of his visit to announce that the Fifth Special Forces Group was to be redesignated the Fifth Airborne Combat Team, assigned to the Eighty-second Division. It would be awkward for Colonel Hanrahan to be part of the official party if that was indeed the President's intention.

Following the introduction of the general officers, the President got into a specially prepared jeep of the Eighty-second Airborne Division. It was outfitted with chrome sirens and flashing lights; white covers had been placed over its canvas cushions; the national colors and presidential flag flew from special mounts on the fenders; and there was an arrangement of specially welded bars that would permit the President, the Vice-Chief of Staff, and Lieutenant General H. H. Howard to stand up as the jeep slowly made its way down the ranks of the "alert regiment" to take that salute.

Each regiment of the Eighty-second Airborne Division, in rotation, served one month on alert. The alert regiment was prepared to leave Fort Bragg for any destination in the world within three hours. At this time the 502nd Parachute Infantry was the alert regiment, and they (and their supporting artillery and technical services units) did not stand down from alert status because of the visit of the Commander in Chief.

They were in fatigues and steel helmets, their loaded trucks lined up on parking ramps at Pope, waiting the order to enplane.

As appropriate for an official visit by the Commander in Chief, all the other troop units, with one conspicuous exception, were in Class A uniforms. They would carry their rifles at right shoulder arms during the march past. (The alert regiment would carry theirs slung over their shoulders.)

The exception was the Fifth Special Forces Group, which had shown up at Pope in fatigues and fatigue caps. Major General Harke was absolutely sure this was a final act of insubordination on the part of Colonel Hanrahan. Hanrahan was as usual being a guardhouse lawyer about his relationship with Fort Bragg and XVIII Airborne Corps. He was a Class II activity of DCSOPS, he was always quick to point out, and therefore not subject to the desires of the Fort Bragg and XVIII Airborne Corps. He had flatly refused to get his troops out of their girl scout hats until ordered to do so by CONARC.

It should have been perfectly clear to Hanrahan that Major General Harke believed that his troops should be in Class A uniforms. If there had been time, General Harke would have ordered them back onto their trucks to change into the proper uniform.

But they hadn't even begun to show up until half past ten (the other troops had begun to arrive at 0730; the last of them were in place at 0930), and there simply hadn't been time for Harke to order them back to Smoke Bomb Hill to get in the proper uniform.

Technically, Harke had fumed privately, they were AWOL (Absent With Out Leave, being defined as not being in the proper place, at the proper time, *in the proper uniform*). It had also bothered Harke to see that it was a rare sleeve indeed in the Fifth Special Forces Group that did not bear the chevrons of at least a staff sergeant. That was something he intended to correct personally just as soon as the First SF Group was redesignated as a Combat Team and placed under XVIII Airborne Corps. He would see all those excess sergeants assigned where needed in the division and put to work earning their pay as sergeants, instead of drawing sergeants' pay for doing what a private first class should be doing.

They could call it an "A" Team or anything else they wanted to, but as far as General Harke was concerned, nine men was a squad, and there should be a sergeant as a squad leader, not a captain, and a corporal assistant squad leader and seven privates or specialists, not a second officer and seven noncommissioned officers.

After the President and the two senior generals climbed into the jeep, General Harke led the rest of the party to the reviewing stand. As he did this he saw in the front passenger seat of the jeep immediately behind the presidential jeep the Warrant Officer with the Bag. The Bag contained the codes the President would need to order a nuclear attack. The Bag Man never got more than fifteen seconds from the President. In the passenger seat of the second jeep behind the presidential jeep was a diminutive lieutenant colonel whom General Harke knew only by reputation. He was—not very common for a Jew—a West Pointer; but he was not much of a soldier, in General Harke's opinion. First under Eisenhower, and now under Kennedy, he had been appointed the President's Personal Liaison Officer to the Intelligence Community. So that he could deal with his military superiors, he had been officially named a Counselor to the President.

In reality, as far as General Harke was concerned, he was nothing more than a paper-shuffler, an infantry officer who had been almost entirely with one ragtag organization or another in Greece and Korea. The little Jew had taken the time to go to parachute school and Ranger school solely in order to pin the wings and the embroidered strip to his uniform.

And to put the cap on his gall, today he was showing up at Fort Bragg, home of the Airborne, wearing parachute wings, jump boots, and a Ranger patch—and a goddamned green beret.

General Harke hoped that the Vice-Chief of Staff would say something to him about it, preferably within the hearing of the President.

The jeeps, having completed the trooping of the line of the

alert regiment, crossed the concrete taxiway and deposited the President, the Vice-Chief of Staff, and the Fort Bragg and XVIII Airborne Corps commander before the reviewing stand.

The drums and bugles played the ruffles and flourishes prescribed by regulation to pay honor to the Commander in Chief. This was followed by the twenty-one-gun salute regulations prescribed to honor the President of the United States. General Harke noticed that one of the charges had gotten damp. The report was somewhat hollow-sounding, and a lump of unexploded powder flew out of the howitzer's mouth to land, burning, on grass between the parking ramp and a runway. The grass ignited.

The possibility had been planned for. A three-quarter-ton truck with a crew to man a grass-fire–extinguishing apparatus appeared and extinguished the blaze.

The Eighty-second Airborne Division marched past the reviewing stand, playing appropriate airs. One of these, "Anchors Aweigh," was in consideration of the President's service as a naval officer during World War II. The band then marched into position directly in front of the reviewing stand, where they would play during the march past.

The President, trailed by the Vice-Chief of Staff, the Adjutant General, and that goddamned Lieutenant Colonel Felter in his green beret, took a few steps forward to a battery of microphones set up in front of the reviewing stand.

The colors followed them, the national flag, the presidential flag, the Eighty-second Division flag, and the red (and one blue) flags of the general officers present. The color bearers formed a rank behind the President and the others.

"Colonel Paul T. Hanrahan, front and center!" the Adjutant General ordered.

Major General Harke was surprised at that, but then he thought he understood. It had been a battle to put Special Forces where it belonged; for Special Forces had had more friends that it had any right to have, including that goddamned Jew with the President's ear. They were going to give Hanrahan a medal, the Legion of Merit, probably, or possibly even the Distinguished Service Medal, although that was normally reserved for general officers but sometimes awarded to especially deserving colonels. They would tend to make the redesignation of the Fifth Special Forces Group into a proper Airborne unit more palatable.

Far down the parking ramp, the solitary figure of Colonel Paul T. Hanrahan appeared. He was in fatigues. He didn't even have the common decency to stiffen the crown of his fatigue cap with cardboard to give it a military appearance. Except for the silver eagle pinned to it, it was identical to the field cap worn by private soldiers riding garbage trucks.

It took some time for Hanrahan to march all the way from the rear of the line of the march, where the Fifth Special Forces Group was positioned, to the reviewing stand. And the band, after four choruses of an appropriate air, went silent.

There was only the tick of a drummer striking his stick against the metal rim of his drum. General Harke was not sure if the drummer was doing that on order to help Hanrahan march in a military manner, or whether it was his own idea. Harke wished he were not doing it.

Hanrahan made a one-man column right, stopped ten feet from the presidential party, and saluted.

"Colonel Hanrahan, Paul T., reporting as ordered, sir."

The Vice-Chief of Staff, the Adjutant General, and Lieutenant Colonel Felter saluted in return.

"Attention to orders," the Adjutant General read. "Headquarters, Department of the Army, Washington, D.C., eleven December, one-nine-six-one. General Orders number three one zero. Paragraph one. By direction of the President, with the advice and consent of the U.S. Senate, Paul T. Hanrahan, Colonel, Signal Corps, Detail, Infantry, is promoted Brigadier General, with date of rank eleven December one-nine-six-one. For the Chief Staff. J. Eastman Fuller, Major General, the Adjutant General."

"Congratulations, General Hanrahan," the President said. "Felter!"

Lieutenant Colonel Felter stepped forward and handed the President two silver stars. The President pinned one to each of Hanrahan's collar points.

"Congratulations again, General," the President repeated.

"Thank you, sir," Hanrahan said.

"I have the feeling this came as a surprise," the President said.

"An absolute surprise, sir," Hanrahan said.

"May I be permitted to observe, General, that I don't think very much of that cap of yours?" the President asked, smiling.

"I'm not very fond of it, either, Mr. President."

"Colonel Felter has something you might like better, General," the President said.

"Mr. Wojinski!" the little man bellowed in a surprisingly loud voice.

From the side of the reviewing stand, two soldiers in fatigues appeared. One was Sergeant Major Taylor, the other Warrant Officer (Junior Grade) Wojinski. Sergeant Major Taylor carried a pole on which flew the silver-starred red flag of a brigadier general. He took a position beside the other general officer's flags. WOJG Wojinski marched out to General Hanrahan, his massive hands crossed in front of him. They held a green beret. A silver star was pinned to the Special Forces flash.

"Now that's more like it," the President said.

Hanrahan put the beret on.

Wojinski removed his fatigue cap delicately and let it fall to the ground. He reached in his fatigue shirt and came out with his beret and put it on. He saluted the President and marched off.

From far down the parking ramp, there came a roar of men's voices.

Ten minutes later, when the Fifth Special Forces Group, at the tail end of the march-past troop units, passed the reviewing stand, they were all wearing green berets.

The President looked at Brigadier General Hanrahan. Tears were running down Brigadier General Hanrahan's cheeks.

(Two)
Headquarters, Eleventh Infantry Regiment (Training)
Fort Jackson, South Carolina
1305 Hours, 11 December 1961

"Sir, Confinee Craig is present, sir," Colonel Sauer's sergeant major said, saluting as he stopped four feet from the colonel's desk.

Confinee Craig, two feet behind him, also saluted.

"I am not returning your salute, Craig, because you are

under charges and not entitled to the privilege of a salute," Colonel Sauer said.

"Sorry, sir."

"You will speak only when directed to speak," Colonel Sauer said.

"Yes, sir."

"Leave me with this piece of garbage, Sergeant Major."

Colonel Sauer stared at Confinee Craig coldly for a full minute before he spoke.

Nice-looking kid, he thought. *Well set up. Looks intelligent.*

"Earlier today, Craig, I went through a very distasteful scene because of you," he said. "I cannot remember being so embarrassed."

Geoff looked at him and then away.

"A very distinguished officer came to see me," Colonel Sauer said. "An officer who wears the nation's second highest decoration, and many others. And he was embarrassed and ashamed to come to me."

Confinee Craig looked miserable.

"He came to beg for you," Sauer said. "Or not for you. I think he holds you in the same contempt that I do. But for your mother. He told me your mother is under doctor's care because of the mess you're in."

Confinee Craig looked even more miserable.

"Do you have any idea how humiliating it is for an officer like Colonel Lowell to have it become common knowledge that his cousin is in the stockade, charged with assault upon a noncommissioned officer, like some scum from the slums?"

There was no reply.

"I asked you a question!"

"I only hit that sergeant after he hit me," Geoff Craig said.

"I didn't bring you in here to argue with you! I asked you a question!"

"I'm sorry, sir, that Colonel Lowell has been embarrassed by my actions."

"You damned well better be! I felt sorry for him, an officer like that, having to come and beg for the likes of you!"

That's enough, Colonel Sauer decided. *Any more and I'll have him throwing up on the carpet.*

"Well, I didn't have the heart to refuse him. Against my better judgment, I'm going to give you a chance to pay for what you did without either further humiliating a fine officer or putting your mother in the hospital. Not that I think you'll do anything with it but something stupid again and be right back in some other stockade, waiting to be tried."

"Another chance, sir?"

"I personally don't think you're man enough to do it. I personally think you're nothing but a spoiled, over-privileged punk. If it wasn't for Colonel Lowell, I'd happily send you off to the federal prison at Leavenworth. But I think, if the circumstances were reversed, that he would do the same thing for me. So I am going to send you to Fort Bragg; and from there you are going to Fort Benning for parachute training. When you finish that—if you're man enough to finish that— you will return to Fort Bragg and go through Special Forces training. It is the toughest training in the world, and I will be personally surprised if you can make it. But if you do, your actions here will be wiped from the books. If you don't, you will spend the rest of your military service as a cook's helper in the most remote place that can be found to send you."

"Yes, sir."

"That's all? You can't even say 'Thank you, sir'?"

"Thank you, sir."

"Sergeant Major!"

"Yes, sir."

"Take this piece of garbage out of my sight. Put him in a Class A uniform. Take him to the airport. There will be a ticket to Fayetteville, N.C., waiting for him at the Piedmont counter."

"Yes, sir," the sergeant major said. He took Geoff Craig's arm and led him out of the office.

Colonel Lowell came out of Colonel Sauer's lavatory.

"You think that was necessary, Lowell?" Sauer asked. "I felt like I was pulling the wings off a fly."

"Yes, sir, I think it was," Lowell said. "Thank you."

"Why Special Forces? Have you got something nasty planned for him at Bragg?"

"Oh, I think Snake-Eating 101 will be nasty enough in itself, Colonel," Lowell said. "The truth of the matter is—and I wouldn't want Mac to hear me say it—in a perverse way and from a distance, I rather admire what Hanrahan is doing down there."

"You obviously know Hanrahan well enough to call in a

favor," Colonel Sauer said. It was a question.

"I served under him in Greece," Lowell said. "I think he's right."

"I'm not sure I agree with the theory of elite troops," Sauer said.

"That depends on the definition of elite troops," Lowell said. "If that means super troopers, trained to the *n*th degree, who are then sent in as assault troops and damn the casualties, neither do I."

"Then, what are they?"

"Hanrahan objects to tying the Rangers in as part of the Special Forces heritage," Lowell explained. "The Rangers were trained to accomplish the most difficult missions without regard to costs. He says he's training his people to stay alive, so that when he's finished training them, the army has too much invested in them to have them get blown away while charging up hills through a Willy Peter* barrage, shouting 'Follow me!'"

"Follow me!" is the motto of the Infantry School. But Colonel Sauer decided that an officer wearing four Purple Hearts, the Distinguished Service Cross, and the Combat Infantry Badge (Second Award) was entitled to make light of it if he so chose. As a matter of fact, Sauer had often thought that the function of a junior officer or noncom leading troops in combat was not to get out on the point himself. He would be quickly blown away there, leaving his troops leaderless. His job was to keep himself alive so that he would be in the position to make the painful choice of which of his troops was to assume the point and probably get himself killed.

"Then what are they supposed to do?"

"Train and command indigenous forces," Lowell said. "The equation is simple: For every indigenous troop bearing arms for his country, one less American has to pick up a weapon. One of Hanrahan's 'A' Teams can train and operate a couple of companies of native troops. When they're in that role. Their other role, as guerrillas—blowing up bridges, cutting communications—can tie up an awful lot of enemy troops just running around trying to find them. I stand in that thin line of soldiers who think Hanrahan is right and everybody else is wrong."

---

*White phosphorus.

"I'm a little surprised to hear you say that," Sauer said. "The word I get from people I know at Bragg is that those green hats they wear went to their heads. They think they're better than everybody else."

"They are," Lowell said. "But that's past tense with the Green Berets. They lost that fight. CONARC forbade the wearing of 'foreign-type' headgear."

"I hadn't heard that," Sauer said. "You think CONARC was wrong?"

"Yes, I do. And I think CONARC is wrong in the next step in their screw Special Forces program."

"Which is . . . ?"

"They want to convert the Fifth Special Forces Group into the Fifth Airborne Regimental Combat Team and assign it to XVIII Airborne Corps. When I talked to him before lunch, Hanrahan said the President was about to arrive at Bragg. What I'm afraid of is that the President came there to make the announcement."

"Why would he do that?"

"Airborne just lost a very serious pitch to take over Army Aviation. I think they're going to be thrown a consolation bone called Special Forces."

"Is that why you're not down there in a green beret? You found out they're going to lose the battle?"

"I have an unfortunate reputation in the army," Lowell said. "I am one hell of a paper pusher. That being the case, I might as well shuffle paper in comfort rather than in a swamp, eating snakes."

Colonel Sauer sensed the bitterness and understood it. Once an officer acquired a reputation as a "good staff man," that's what the army assigned him to do. Napoleon said his army moved on its stomach. The U.S. Army had solved that problem, but only at the price of acquiring another problem. The U.S. Army moved on a sea of paper, and people who could shuffle that paper skillfully were in short supply and great demand. Whether or not they liked it, they were given desks rather than battalions and regiments.

"Speaking of which," Lowell went on, "I was due in Sodom on Potomac thirty minutes ago."

"You going to be in hot water?" Sauer asked.

"My general will be so relieved that you didn't throw me

in the stockade for putting my nose in where it didn't belong,
I doubt he'll say anything to me for being late," Lowell said.
"And I'm grateful to you, sir, for what you did. Thank you."

Offering his hand, Sauer said, "I will, Colonel Lowell, deal
with the situation here in such a manner that I doubt there will
be a reoccurrence." And then, as Lowell walked out the door,
Colonel Sauer called after him. "Say hello to Mac when you
see him, will you?"

"Yes, sir," Lowell said. "I'll do that."

"Charley," Colonel Sauer said to his adjutant. "Cut orders
relieving the company commander of 'C' Company. Have the
exec assume command for the time being. Transfer the first
sergeant and the field first out by 1500 this afternoon, and
replace them. I will not entertain protests from the first battalion
commander. Have the first battalion commander and the ex—
company commander report to me at 0730 tomorrow. Let them
squirm overnight about what I'm going to do to them."

"Yes, sir," the adjutant said crisply.

"And when you're not doing anything tonight, Charley,"
Colonel Sauer said, "I want you to write a little essay for me.
Say, a thousand words."

"An essay, sir?"

"Your subject, Charley, is 'The Importance of Providing
the Commander with Accurate Facts on Which He Will Base
His Decisions.' I somehow have acquired the feeling that you're
not as up on that as you should be."

(Three)
The Delta Delta Delta House
Duke University
1530 Hours, 11 December 1961

There was absolutely no question whatever in Dianne Eaglebury's mind that she was being followed around by a weirdo.
She had first had the feeling when she had gone to French 202
at nine o'clock. She'd felt eyes on her, which had made her
very uncomfortable, and she'd had fleeting glances of a man
who jumped out of sight the moment she turned around.

In French 202 she managed to convince herself that her
imagination was running off with her. And the proof of that

seemed to come when no one was waiting for her when French was over.

But it started again at lunch. She had gone to the cafeteria for a ham sandwich and a bowl of Jell-O and a glass of milk, and she'd felt the eyes on her again. This time she had quick glances at a vaguely familiar face, a guy wearing a tweed coat.

When she came out of Political Science 440: City States of Italy and started back to the Tri-Delt house, she sensed again that she was being followed. This time, by spinning suddenly around, she saw the vaguely familiar young man in the tweed coat again, this time at the wheel of a Jaguar. (She didn't know anybody who owned a Jaguar.) If he wanted to talk to her, why didn't he just walk up and talk?

When she spun around again, the yellow Jaguar was nowhere in sight. He had seen her looking at him, she realized, and that had frightened him off. When she got to the Tri-Delt house, she pretended to drop a book. While picking it up, she looked up and down the street. But there was no young man in a tweed jacket or a Jaguar convertible visible.

Where had she seen him before?

She settled on the mixer she had been talked into going to at the Delta Kappa Epsilon house. Dekes were weird, especially when they were drinking, and they prided themselves on how much they drank. That's what it was.

She went to her room, spent half an hour making her City States of Italy notes legible enough to read when exam time came up, and then went down to the living room to look for a newspaper.

The yellow Jag was parked down the street in front of the Sigma Delta Chi house. There was somebody behind the wheel.

Dianne had enough. Whoever it was, drunk or not, he had no right to follow her around. The Dekes had a reputation for letting things get out of hand. And a reputation for meanness. She didn't want to have to keep looking over her shoulder to see if she was being followed. Or maybe getting grabbed and thrown into a car and kidnaped. Not really kidnaped. It would be some elaborate Deke joke.

She found Mrs. Hawkins, the house mother, in her office off the kitchen and told her what was going on. Mrs. Hawkins went to the front door and peered out from behind the curtains.

Satisfied that Dianne was telling the truth, she called campus security on the telephone and told them she would appreciate it if they would run off the young man in a yellow Jaguar who was annoying one of her girls.

Once it was done, Dianne felt miserable. She didn't want to get anybody in trouble. She just wanted to be left alone. She then talked herself into thinking that she had done the right thing. She didn't *know* that it was innocent; for all she knew, he could be a rapist. Or worse.

She went upstairs, headed for her room, but at the top of the landing she changed her mind and walked down the corridor to Louise Pfister's room, which looked out onto the street. Louise, wearing nothing but panties with a hole in the side, was washing her hair in her sink. This was against the rules, since hair clogged the drains of the little sinks, but stuff like rules never bothered Louise.

"What do you want?" Louise snapped.

"I want to look out your window a minute," Dianne said.

"Look out your own window," Louise said. Soap got in her eyes. "Shit!" she cried out, and put her head in the sink again. Dianne looked out the window.

She saw a campus security Ford come up the street and then suddenly pull to the curb in front of the Jaguar. Two campus policemen got out, went to the car, and ordered the driver out. One of them spun him around and gave him a shove hard enough to send him sprawling toward the car. He threw his arms out against the car roof and stopped himself.

The driver turned his head to say something to one of the policemen, and for the first time Dianne got a really good look at his face.

I know him!

One of the policemen ducked his head in the car and came out with a funny-looking object.

"Oh, *my God!*" Dianne said aloud and raced out of Louise Pfister's room, down the stairs, out the front door, and down the street.

"It's all right," she said. "I know him. This is all a terrible mistake!"

"Who are you?" a policeman asked her.

"I'm the girl he's been bothering," she said, instantly aware that was a really dumb thing to say. "But it's all right. He's a friend of mine."

The policeman shook his head at her and returned his attention to Tom Ellis.

"What are you doing with an army radio?"

"I'm an army officer," Tom Ellis said. He took his wallet out and showed his AGO card.

"I know he is," Dianne said.

The policeman handed the AGO card to the other policeman.

"That looks legitimate," he said.

"What's he doing with an army radio in his car?"

"If you'll call Colonel Wells, he can explain everything," Ellis said.

Dianne had seen boys blush before, but never this red, and never for so long.

One of the policemen went to the police car and got on the radio. Dianne wanted to smile at Tom Ellis, but he wouldn't look at her.

The policeman came back in a minute.

"Colonel Wells is down at the stadium," he said. "We'll go there and ask him about this. You follow us. We have your license number, and we'll keep the radio until we talk to the colonel."

Ellis nodded.

The policemen, one of them carrying the radio, went to their car and got in. Ellis, without looking at Dianne, got behind the wheel of the Jaguar. He started the engine and waited for the policemen to get their car moving.

He's leaving! If he leaves, he will not come back!

Dianne ran around the front of the Jaguar and then climbed in beside him.

He turned and looked at her, and then away, and then back.

He has beautiful eyes, she thought. *So sad.*

"I'm going with you," she said.

"I thought about coming here since you told me you were here," Tom Ellis said. "But when I got here, I just didn't have the balls."

They were moving now.

He suddenly banged his fist on the steering wheel.

" '*Balls,*' " he quoted himself, furious with himself. "Shit!"

He shoved the gearshift angrily into high.

Dianne put her hand over his, then pulled it away from the gearshift knob and held it in both of hers.

"It's all right, Tom," she said. "Take it easy."

He looked over at her.

"There's something you should know about me," he said.

"What's that?"

"I have this tremendous ability to make an ass of myself."

She laughed.

"You actually came all the way up here to see me?" she asked. "I'm flattered."

"Well, actually," he said, "I came up here to blow up your water tower."

"Well," she said, giggling, "whatever, I'm glad you're here."

I am, she thought, with considerable surprise. *I really am very glad to see him.*

(Four)
William B. Hartsfield Atlanta International Airport
Atlanta, Georgia
1830 Hours, 11 December 1961

It wasn't until he got off the airplane and found himself in the terminal that Geoff Craig really believed the nightmare was coming to an end, that he wasn't going to wake up and find himself back in the stockade.

But the night and the sounds and the smells of the airport made it all real. He was not going to be court-martialed, not going to be taken in handcuffs to the federal prison at Leavenworth, Kansas. He didn't know what was coming next, but it was beyond belief that it could be worse than what he had left.

Tucked under his arm, he had a square eleven-by-fourteen-inch heavy manila folder, sealed shut, that contained his service record. The sergeant major who had driven him to the airport and marched him past the MPs on duty there had told him that he doubted he would be stopped and asked for his orders in Atlanta while he was changing planes, but if that happened, he was to tell the MPs that he was traveling "VOCG," which meant "Verbal Order, Commanding General," and if they didn't believe that, to call, collect, the number written on the paper tape sealing his service-record envelope.

When he got to Atlanta, the sergeant major told him, he was to retrieve his duffel bag and take it to the Piedmont ticket counter. There had not been time to confirm his Atlanta–Fayetteville reservation, and therefore his duffel bag could not be checked through to Fayetteville. There would probably be a reservation waiting for him at the Piedmont ticket counter, but if there was not, he was to get the first available seat to Fayetteville. When he got to Fayetteville, he was to look for a sign—there would almost certainly be one—giving a telephone number to call for transportation from the Fayetteville airport to Fort Bragg. He was to tell whoever answered the telephone that he was reporting to the Special Warfare Center—not Fort Bragg, nor the XVIII Airborne Corps, nor the 82nd Airborne Division; get that straight—and they would arrange transportation for him.

The sergeant major had waited with him until the boarding call was given, and then he had surprised Geoff Craig by offering his hand.

"Let me tell you something, kid," he said. "Not all the sergeants in the army are like the bastard who crapped on you. Off the record, I'm glad you broke his goddamn jaw."

Geoff had been so surprised that he couldn't think of anything to say.

"Good luck, Craig. Keep your mouth shut and your eyes and ears open," the sergeant major had said.

And then Geoff had boarded the airplane, and it was like coming home from Mars. The flight wasn't long enough for a meal, but a stewardess served a snack, a sandwich, cheese and crackers, and an apple. And she asked if he would like a cocktail.

The temptation to order a drink was nearly overwhelming, but he knew it was a court-martial offense (the phrase had an immediate, awesome meaning now) to drink on duty, and he was afraid that traveling on orders the way he was would be considered duty, so he didn't take one.

By the time he got to Atlanta, he regretted that decision. Most of the passengers on the airplane were soldiers, privates, noncoms, and officers, and most of them had had at least two drinks. They would not all be risking the stockade by taking a drink, he reasoned. He realized what was starting to happen to him. He was beginning to think like a human being again, not like a trainee or a confinee.

Just as soon as he arranged for a seat to Fayetteville, he would have a drink. Christ knows, he was entitled to one. He hadn't had a drink since the night before he had taken a cab downtown to the Armed Forces Induction Center—two million years ago.

First things first. He had to reclaim his duffel bag.

There were twenty-five or more duffel bags on the luggage carousel, all identical except for the names stenciled onto the sides. It was some time before Geoff could reach out with his good hand and pull his off the merry-go-round and onto the floor.

He looked around for a skycap. None was in sight. He would have to move the damned thing himself. There were two options: He could try to stagger through the terminal with the bag hanging from its strap on his shoulder, or he could drag it along the marble floor. He opted for that. He was aware that he looked a mess anyway.

When they had arrested him, someone had taken all of his possessions from their prescribed place and jammed them into the duffel bag, which had then been taken to the supply room and stored. His tunic and trousers were badly crushed, and so was his brimmed cap. It was entirely possible, he thought, that whoever had packed his things for him had taken special pains to crease beyond repair the leather brim of his cap.

He started down the corridor to the Piedmont ticket counter. Two MPs appeared in the line of traffic. Geoff's heart stopped when they looked at him.

As the ferocious-looking sergeant came close to him, he smiled.

"And where did you have your hand that it wasn't welcome?" he inquired, while the other MP laughed. And they kept walking.

Geoff looked over his shoulder as they continued down the corridor.

"I giff you a hand wid dat," a heavily accented voice said at his shoulder. "Dragging it on duh groundt, you shouldn't."

Startled, Geoff snapped his head around and found himself looking at a very large young man in uniform. He was everything that he was not, Geoff thought instantly. His uniform was impeccable. He was a PFC, and pinned to the breast pocket of his tunic were the qualification badges he had earned in basic training. Geoff had qualified with his weapon, and had been awarded a simple Iron Cross (which he had thought a little odd, for the U.S. Army), signifying that he was a Rifle Marksman. This PFC had the Expert Medal (the marksman's Iron Cross, surrounded by a wreath and with the representation of a bull's-eye superimposed on it). Beneath it hung a ladder of specifications: rifle, pistol, grenade, automatic rifle, submachine gun, machine gun.

An Annie Oakley in pants, Geoff thought, and then he realized that was unkind. The guy was trying to be nice.

"I'm going to the Piedmont counter," Geoff said.

"Ids over dare," the PFC said. "I vus dare. I carry id over dere for you."

"Thank you," Geoff said. What he would do now, he decided, was buy the Good Samaritan a drink. That would be the decent thing to do, and it would also give him a little company. What was the accent? he wondered.

Piedmont told him he had a seat on Flight 119, departing at 8:15, arriving in Fayetteville at 9:05, and to please be ready to board the aircraft at 8:00.

"Let me buy us a drink," Geoff said to the Good Samaritan.

"I godda ged back," the Good Samaritan said. "I god somebody."

"I would be happy to buy him a drink, too," Geoff said.

"I godda ged back. Tank you chust duh same. Maybe I see you on duh airplane. Vee going to Fort Bragg too."

"Well, thank you very much," Geoff said.

"You uniform's a mess," the Good Samaritan said. "You know dat?"

And then he walked away.

German, Geoff decided. He had an accent very much like Fräu What-was-her-name, who had been his governess one summer at Agonquit.

Well, he had tried.

He turned back to the man at the Piedmont counter.

"Where's the Admiral's Club?" he asked.

The clerk raised his eyebrows.

"Take the escalator to the second floor," he said. "Turn right. Room 220."

When Geoff pushed open the otherwise unmarked door to Room 220, an attractive young woman in a stewardesslike uniform rose from behind a desk to bar his way.

"I'm sorry," she said firmly, but smiling. "This is a private club."

"Yes, I know," Geoff said. He fished the card authorizing access to the Admiral's Club from his wallet and showed it to her. It was issued by the airline to certain favored people, such as those who traveled first class a great deal, and to some more favored, such as those with an intimate knowledge of the airline's financial affairs, like Porter Craig, chairman of the board of Craig, Powell, Kenyon and Dawes, who had arranged for the financing of the airline's last twenty additions to its fleet of aircraft. Geoff's version of the card was the one with the color coding that meant that no bill would be rendered for drinks or anything else the Admiral's Club had to offer.

"I'm on Piedmont 119 at 8:15," Geoff said. "If I fall asleep, make sure I make it."

"We'll have you on it, sir," she said.

"Thank you," Geoff said, and walked around the barrier into the club. A second hostess greeted him. She seemed a little surprised to see a private soldier (he was now a private, the sergeant major had told him, and his records would indicate that he had satisfactorily completed basic training) in a mussed uniform, but he had passed the Keeper of the Portals, and must be presumed to be a bona fide guest.

"There's a chair here," she said. "And a table there. Would you like something to eat?"

"Yes, indeed," Geoff said. "What are my options?"

"I think the open-faced steak sandwich is very nice," she said.

"Please," he said. "Medium rare, and a bottle of Tuborg."

She sat him down and returned in a moment with *The Wall Street Journal* and the Atlanta *Constitution* and, a moment after that, with a bottle of Tuborg beer and a stemmed glass.

He opened *The Wall Street Journal* to the rear pages and found what he was looking for, a small advertisement:

(This announcement appears as a matter of record only.)

>   *$139,000,000*
>   *Limited Partnership Interests*
>   *Izamatzu Steamship Company Ltd.*
>   *A Steamship Holding Company*
>   *We Assisted in Placing These Limited*
>   *Partnership Interests*
>   *Craig, Powell, Kenyon and Dawes*
>   *11 Wall Street and Worldwide*

It didn't matter what the advertisement said, just that it was there in the *WSJ*. There was generally at least one such announcement a week. Craig, Powell, Kenyon and Dawes was still out there, loaning money to the Japs and whoever else of sound financial standing was willing to pay them a percentage off the top of the gross figure. And he was in the Admiral's Club having a Danish beer and about to have a steak sandwich, and not in the Fort Jackson stockade, about to scrub the floor with a toothbrush. All was right with the world.

But then, as he sipped the cold beer, he realized that not everything was in its place. His mother in New York was, because of him, taking pills and making life for his father and the help hell. He should have thought of calling home right away.

There were telephones in here, but he didn't think he should pick one of them up and startle the business community with his greeting. "Hi, Mom! I'm out jail."

He would have this beer and another one, and then he would walk down to one of the phone booths in the terminal, a real phone booth, not a fiberglass clamshell mounted on the wall.

He saw the hostess who had taken his order lean over to take someone else's. Not very far, but enough for her skirt to lift in the back. Taking in that glimpse of her slip, he realized that it had been one day longer since he had dipped his wick than it had been since he had had a beer.

He wondered if there was anything that could be done to remedy that sad situation at Fort Bragg.

The steak sandwich was delivered, and he ordered another beer to drink with it; and then, aware he was doing his duty, he got up from the table and walked out of the Admiral's Club and took the elevator to the main concourse.

VII

(One)
Main Concourse
William B. Hartsfield Atlanta International Airport
Atlanta, Georgia
2015 Hours, 11 December 1961

"The Craig Residence," Finley's usually plummy voice came somewhat tinnily over the line.

"I have a collect call for anyone from Geoffrey Craig. Will you accept charges?"

"Yes, of course," Finley said. Geoff had a mental picture of him sitting in his overstuffed chair in the kitchen, television on, feet on a leather hassock.

"Hello, Finley," Geoff said.

"We have been rather concerned about you," Finley said.

"I'm out of jail, Finley," Geoff said.

"Your parents will be enormously relieved to hear that," Finley said. "Presuming of course, you left with the permission of the appropriate authorities."

Geoff heard a buzz on the line and then his father's voice.

"Mister Geoffrey is on the line, sir," the Craig's butler said.

"Geoff?"

"Hi, Dad," Geoff said.

"Where are you?"

"In the Atlanta airport."

"What are you doing there?" There was alarm in his father's voice.

"On my way to Fort Bragg. I'm out of the stockade."

"Thank God!"

"Cousin Craig had a lot to do with it, I think," Geoff said. "He was at Fort Jackson this morning."

"I know," Porter Craig said. "He called here. He . . . led me to believe you would be . . . confined . . . for some time."

Why, that sonofabitch! Geoff thought. *He certainly knew before he left Colonel Sauer whether or not Sauer was going to turn me loose. He was sticking it in the old man for some reason. Why?*

"Well, I'm out."

"Now what?"

"I've been reassigned to Fort Bragg," Geoff said.

"To do what?"

"I don't know yet."

That's a white lie. This is not the time to tell him I'm going to be a paratrooper and God only knows what else.

"Is Mother there?"

"She's resting," Porter Craig said. "I don't think we should disturb her."

"No," Geoff said. Resting translated as tranquilized into a zombie.

"Are you all right, Geoff?" his father asked.

"Fine," Geoff said. "I just had a steak sandwich and a beer."

"You all right for money?"

"Yes, thank you."

"Is there anything I can do for you?"

"Not a thing," Geoff said. "I'm fine."

"Is there any chance that you could come home anytime soon?"

"I'll be better able to answer that after I get to Fort Bragg."

"Have you an address there?"

"Not yet," Geoff said. "I'll send it, or call, when I know."

"Call," his father said. "Call collect."

"Don't I always?"

"I'll tell your mother you called when she gets up."

"Please."

"Well," his father said.

"Dad, I have to catch my plane," Geoff said.

"I understand. Geoff . . . take care of yourself."

"Good-bye, Dad."

He hung the phone in its cradle and exhaled audibly, then started back to the Admiral's Club.

There was a small waiting room opening off the corridor, six rows of fiberglass chairs. He saw the Good Samaritan in it. He was at the back of the room, sitting with a young blond woman. They were sitting sideways on the fiberglass chairs, doing something on a chair that separated them. In a moment he saw what it was. They had a loaf of bread and a couple of packages of plastic-wrapped luncheon meat, and she was making sandwiches for them. As Geoff watched, the Good Samaritan took a bite from a sandwich.

Geoff thought that was an extraordinary thing to do in an airport, and wondered why they just didn't go to a restaurant or one of the hamburger—hot dog counters scattered around. But then it came to him: They didn't go to a restaurant because airport restaurants were expensive, and they hadn't gone to a hot dog counter because they couldn't afford even that.

This made Geoff very uncomfortable. He averted his eyes and picked up his step, hoping that the Good Samaritan had not seen him.

When he returned to the Admiral's Club, two soldiers in uniform were there. A middle-aged major general was sitting with a lieutenant, who looked to be about as old as Geoff. So far as the major general was concerned, Geoff was invisible. The lieutenant at first appeared surprised to see a private soldier in the Admiral's Club, but when he noticed the mussed uniform, he, too, seemed unable to see Geoff.

When the hostess came, Geoff ordered an Old Bushmill's Irish whiskey with just a little ice and not much water, picked up a copy of *Time*, and read that until the hostess came back and told him they had just announced his flight.

● ● ●

(Two)

When Geoff got on the plane, the Good Samaritan and the young blond woman were in the second row of seats behind the plastic divider that separated first class from coach.

The Good Samaritan was in the aisle seat, the blond woman beside him. The window seat was empty.

"I zaved you a zeat," the Good Samaritan said. He crawled past the young woman, freeing the aisle seat for Geoff.

"Thank you," Geoff said.

"Dis Ursula," the Good Samaritan said. "I'm Karl-Heinz. Karl-Heinz Wagner, like the composer."

The young woman shyly offered her hand. *She acts as if she's afraid of me,* Geoff thought. *Or ashamed. Or maybe she's just shy.* Her hand was soft and seemed fragile.

Karl-Heinz Wagner's hand was firm and calloused.

"Geoff Craig," Geoff said.

"I saw you walk past in the airport," Karl-Heinz said. "I tried to catch up with you, we had sandwiches, but you was gone."

"I didn't see you," Geoff lied.

"It takes forty-five minutes to Fayetteville," Karl-Heinz offered. "Not long. I asked."

"No," Geoff said.

Karl-Heinz disapproved of the slackness in Ursula's seat belt. When he tightened it for her, his cuff rose and Geoff noticed his wristwatch. It was ugly—an oblong with rounded edges—and battered, and it was on a cheap artificial leather strap.

Karl-Heinz and his wife were obviously very poor. There had been some obviously very poor people in Company "C," but that hadn't made him uncomfortable. Karl-Heinz and his wife, though, made him uncomfortable. He didn't feel superior, he thought. It was nothing like that. Just sorry for them.

The plane left the terminal and taxied to a taxiway. There were two parallel taxiways. The other was lined with airliners.

"Look at that!" Karl-Heinz said. "So many airplanes. This is the busiest airport in the world, not just the Free World. Did you know that?"

"I think I heard that," Geoff said.

A stewardess leaned over them.

"I'm taking drink orders while we wait to take off."

"Please, let me buy you a drink," Geoff said. "I owe you for carrying my bag."

"I'll carry it in Fayetteville too," Karl-Heinz said practically. "If you want to do that. I don't have the money to buy back."

"Don't worry about it," Geoff said. "What'll you have?"

"What will you have?"

"Do you have any Tuborg?" Geoff asked, and the stewardess shook her head no. "Heineken?"

"Yes, sir."

"I'm going to have a beer," Geoff said.

"Me too," Karl-Heinz said. "Thank you."

"And what will you have?" Geoff asked Mrs. Wagner.

"Nothing, thank you," she said, barely audibly.

Karl-Heinz said something to her in German. Geoff couldn't make a word for word translation, but he understood it. It was a phrase he had often heard from Fräu What-was-her-name, a rough translation of which was "Take it, it's good for you."

"Please bring three beers," Karl-Heinz said to the stewardess.

Mrs. Wagner seemed embarrassed.

The beers were served as they were coming out of their climb. Karl-Heinz poured some in his glass, looked at it a long second, and took a swallow.

"That's good," he said, and raised his glass. "Prosit!"

"Prosit!" Mrs. Wagner said ritually. Shyly.

"Mud in your eye," Geoff returned the toast.

"'Mud in your eye,'" Karl-Heinz quoted and laughed. Then he looked at his beer bottle and laughed again.

"What a wonderful country!" he said.

"Excuse me?"

"The beer is European, right?" he said. "It says *Holland*. It comes all the way from Europe, and a private soldier is unhappy because it isn't the kind of beer he wants."

"*Was hast du gesagt?*" Mrs. Wagner asked, and Karl-Heinz repeated in German his observation that it was proof of what a wonderful country it was that a private soldier had to settle for an imported beer.

Geoff was genuinely surprised at how much he could understand Karl-Heinz's German. He had obviously learned more from Fräu What-was-her-name than he had thought he had. *Dietrich*—Hannelore Dietrich. She came clearly into his mind's eye. A large, comfortable woman who had worn her blond hair parted in the middle and drawn into a bun at her neck. She had always smelled slightly of caraway seeds.

And she had tried to teach him how to speak German. He wished now that he had paid more attention to her.

When she finished her beer, Mrs. Wagner asked her husband softly about a *toilette*. Obviously, Geoff decided, she did not have much experience with airplanes. Karl-Heinz looked around and found the sign and directed her to the rear of the cabin. Geoff stood in the aisle to let her pass. She seemed embarrassed, he thought, as if going to take a leak was somehow shameful.

When she came back, at the moment he stood to let her by, the airplane ran into what the pilot would call "a little mild turbulence," and she lost her footing and fell onto him. She knocked him back in his seat as her breasts collided with his hand.

Geoff Craig was instantly made aware that Mrs. Wagner was not wearing a brassiere under her gray, rather ugly suit and high-necked blouse. The softness of her breast pushing heavily against his face instantly aroused him and as instantly shamed him. Not only was she somebody's wife, but there was something about this female that was uncommonly wholesome and vulnerable. Her embarrassment embarrassed him.

Her husband made things worse by softly calling her a clumsy ox.

She finally found her footing and got into her seat. Her face was dark red, and she kept her face averted from Geoff during the rest of the flight.

Karl-Heinz declined the offer of a second beer, and Geoff was unwilling to drink alone.

(Three)

Inside the terminal at Fayetteville, there was the sign the sergeant major at Fort Jackson had told him to look for. But when they went to the baggage carousel to claim their luggage there was something else.

There was a sergeant wearing a green beret, a pleasant-looking young man in fatigues, holding up a sign on which U.S. ARMY SPECIAL WARFARE CENTER had been neatly lettered in the prescribed Army fashion. Stuck to the bottom of the sign was an automobile bumper sticker, one Geoff had seen on cars in Princeton: "HI, THERE! I'M YOU'RE WELCOME WAGON LADY!"

Karl-Heinz Wagner headed right for the green beret sergeant, and so did three rather swarthy senior noncoms, a first sergeant, a master sergeant, and a sergeant first class. They were wearing the Big Red One insignia of the First Infantry Division, as well as regimental crests on the epaulets of their tunics, and some sort of colored ropes hanging from the epaulets down over their arms.

"On behalf of the commanding general, gentlemen," the sergeant said drolly to the noncoms, "welcome, welcome to the U.S. Army Special Warfare School. If you will exit this building by the door to my immediate right, you will find a carryall with the rear door open and a corporal asleep at the wheel. Please deposit your luggage in said vehicle and I will join you shortly, just as soon as I am sure I have all my rabbits in the net."

The sergeants chuckled, and turned to the carousel to find their luggage.

Karl-Heinz Wagner walked to the sergeant and came to attention.

The sergeant was obviously amused.

"You need not stand to attention, my good man," he said. "Kissing my hand will suffice."

"Sergeant, I have my sister with me," Karl-Heinz Wagner said.

Sister! For some reason Geoff's heart jumped.

"I must find a place for her to stay," Karl-Heinz said.

"There's the guest house at the post," the sergeant said. "She can stay there for three days. Buck and a half a night."

"Is it permitted for her to ride in the army vehicle?"

"No," the sergeant said matter-of-factly, "but on the other hand, it's a hell of a long walk to the post. Load her up. Put her in the backseat. We will infiltrate her past the MPs."

That was a damned decent way for the sergeant to act, Geoff Craig instantly decided.

The sergeant looked at him.

"And are you, too, coming with us?"

"I'm traveling VOCG to the Special Warfare Center, Sergeant," Craig said.

"Then you must be the famous Private G. Craig," the sergeant said. "The rabbit I was told to ensure I netted."

"Yes, Sergeant," Craig said.

"If you will be so good as to hold up my sign, Private G. Craig," the sergeant said, "I will carry your duffel bag to the vehicle."

He handed the sign to Craig. Then he went to the carousel and waited for Geoff's duffel bag to appear. He snatched it from the carousel, lifted it easily to his shoulder, and walked out the door.

He returned in a moment and took two battered tin suitcases from Ursula Wagner. Geoff was absolutely certain that the two suitcases, plus the third, slightly larger one PFC Karl-Heinz carried in one hand, contained everything they owned.

The three of them went outside for a couple of minutes. Then the sergeant reappeared.

"Yoo-hoo!" he called. "Standard bearer! You can come now!"

Geoff walked quickly to the door, which the sergeant held open for him.

"How's the hand?" the sergeant asked.

"Fine."

"Damn!" the sergeant said.

The vehicle was a GMC carryall, a closed panel delivery truck that had been equipped with windows and seats and a rack on the roof. The sergeant took the pole and sign from Geoff and handed it to a corporal, who lashed it beside the suitcases and other luggage.

"You get in the backseat," the sergeant ordered. As Geoff was squeezing past the center seat, which held two of the swarthy First Division sergeants, the sergeant said, "I don't think they'll stop us, but even if they do, don't panic. They'll just be harassing me for the trip ticket. When I give the word, miss, you just duck down and put your head in your brother's lap until I tell you it's okay."

It was a twenty-minute ride to the main gate at Fort Bragg.

"Bragg Boulevard" was lined with motels and hamburger joints and honky-tonks. Very much aware of the innocent pressure of Ursula Wagner's thigh against his, Geoff Craig decided that once he was given any free time at all, his first priority was to correct his lackanookie condition. There was only one rational explanation why this shy, timid female, who had shown absolutely no interest in him as a man, should have produced his painful erection except that he had been denied sexual release for two whole months.

He had a moment's panic when the sergeant called out for her to duck. If she made a mistake, she would put her head in his lap, which would more than likely cause him to groan loudly and have sticky spots on his underpants.

Ursula put her head in her brother's lap, but her movement shifted her rear end so that it pressed against Geoff's legs. He thought of the *Titanic* sinking, and of a dog being run over, and finally of Staff Sergeant Foster. That seemed to put things under control.

"Okay," the sergeant said when they were rolling again. "We have successfully infiltrated. You can sit up now, miss."

Quite by accident, when Ursula sat up, she shifted herself into position with her right hand. The proof that she knew she had set it right down in his wang came when she audibly sucked in her breath and flung back her hand as if it had landed on a hot stove.

"Barring violent objection," the sergeant said, "we'll take the lady by the guest house before we go to Smoke Bomb Hill."

The two sergeants in the seat in front of them had a brief conversation in Spanish.

Jesus, where am I headed? The tower of Babel?

The Enlisted Guest House turned out to be a collection of four barracks. The term meant nothing to Geoff, but it was reasonable to presume that it was a place provided by the army for wives of enlisted men to stay until they could find someplace else to live.

The corporal driving the van and the sergeant got out of the carryall. Ursula and Karl-Heinz crawled over Geoff to get out. She took great pains to keep her body from touching his.

"It was nice to have met you, Ursula," Geoff said. "I hope to see you again."

"Auf Wiedersehen," she said, barely audibly.

The sergeant and the corporal helped Karl-Heinz and Ursula with their tin suitcases, and they went inside the building with them.

The three Spanish-speaking sergeants carried on what sounded like an excited conversation until the sergeant and Karl-Heinz reappeared. They then clammed up.

The U.S. Army Special Warfare Center and School did not look much unlike the Eleventh Infantry Regiment (Training) at Fort Jackson. It was a collection of wooden buildings, most of them two-story barracks built in the early 1940's. The buildings looked tired.

The carryall stopped before a one story building identified by a sign painted on a four-by-eight sheet of plywood as Head-quarters, Fifth Special Forces Group.

Everybody got out of the carryall and followed the sergeant into the building. There were several noncoms and an officer in the room. The noncoms played liar's poker while the officer watched.

The officer smiled when he saw them coming in the door.

A master sergeant stood up, jammed a fistful of folded dollar bills into his pocket, and pleasantly asked for orders and service records.

The first sergeant from the First Division handed him a stack of service record envelopes and a sheath of orders. Karl-Heinz Wagner handed him his service record and sheath of orders. Geoff Craig handed over his service record and began the rehearsed speech.

"I'm traveling VOCG—"

"Ah," the sergeant interrupted him, smiling. "Private Craig. Sergeant Dempster has been waiting for you."

Geoff naturally interpreted that to mean that they knew all about him, and *all* meant that he had been released on sort of probation from the stockade. Whatever happened next was going to be humiliating. He had had six, seven hours of freedom, and now it was all going to start all over again.

"Gentlemen," the lieutenant said, "I'm Lieutenant Martin. On behalf of the center commander, Colonel Paul—"

He was interrupted by cries of "Shame!" "My God!" "Heresy!" and "Bite your *tongue*!"

"As you were," Lieutenant Martin went on. "On behalf of the Center Commander, *Brigadier General* Paul T. Hanrahan—" He was interrupted again, this time with applause and cries of "Try to remember that!" "Write that down, Lieutenant!" and "That's *much* better!"

Laughing, Lieutenant Martin went on: "—welcome to the U.S. Special Warfare Center. We're glad to have you with us. First things first: Have you eaten?"

Everybody chorused "Yes, sir."

"That will doubtless cheer the cook who waited up for you no end," Lieutenant Martin said. "Next question: Did all your luggage manage to arrive, or are we going to have to go back to the airport for it later?"

There was a chorus of "All here, sir."

"Splendid," Lieutenant Martin said. "This is your schedule. You noncoms go in the transient BNCOQ right across the street." He handed each of them a key. "You can settle who gets which room among yourselves. Just make sure you put your name on the door. Reveille goes at 0700. You don't have to stand it. The mess serves from 0715. Take the morning to get settled—this applies to you two, too," Lieutenant Martin said, turning to Geoff and Karl-Heinz—"which means, really, taking care of your personal business. Official business, like getting paid, that sort of thing, we'll take care of starting at 1300. You come here at 1300 tomorrow. Get rid of your old insignia. In your case, Sergeant, that means swapping those first-soldier stripes for master sergeant's stripes."

"By tomorrow, sir?"

"By 1300 tomorrow, Sergeant," Lieutenant Martin said. "There's a PX tailor shop down the street. Everybody is to show up in starched fatigues, with the patch—which the PX tailor shop will happily sell you—at 1300."

He turned to Karl-Heinz Wagner.

"You go to the orderly room at the end of the second row of barracks across the street. They'll show you where your bunk is. You will stand reveille."

PFC Karl-Heinz Wagner snapped to attention.

"Yes, sir," he barked.

Geoff thought he looked as if he were going to click his heels.

"And then you come back here and fetch Private Craig," Lieutenant Martin said.

"Yes, sir," Karl-Heinz barked again.

"We have heard about your hand, Private Craig," Lieutenant Martin said. "You could say that Sergeant Dempster has been eagerly anticipating your arrival. Isn't that so, Sergeant Dempster?"

"I am merely doing my duty, sir," Sergeant Dempster, a ruddy-faced, heavy-faced master sergeant said, straight-faced, "as God has given me the light to see that duty."

He turned and looked at Geoff.

"How is your hand, my boy?"

"My hand's fine," Geoff said.

"Damn," Dempster said. "I dared hope, considering that absolutely disgusting cast that there would be complications worthy of my attention."

"My hand's fine," Geoff repeated.

Lieutenant Martin spotted PFC Karl-Heinz Wagner, still standing rigidly at attention.

"You can go, son."

"Sir, will the lieutenant permit me to wait for Private Craig?"

"It's likely to be a sight that will turn your stomach, Wagner," Lieutenant Martin said. "I am personally washing my hands of the whole idea."

Wagner didn't understand that.

"Sir, I think I help him carry duffel bag."

"If you promise not to throw up on the floor, you may stay," Lieutenant Martin said.

"Yes, sir, thank you, sir," Karl-Heinz said.

"Private Craig," one of the other sergeants said, "when the commanding general of Fort Jackson was kind enough to TWX us the information that you were about to grace Special Forces with your talents, whatever in hell they might be, he also mentioned that your right digital extremity would more than likely require medical attention."

"Which, of course, thrilled Sergeant Dempster," another sergeant said.

"The good news, Private Craig," the sergeant said, "is that Master Sergeant Dempster is an honor graduate of the Special Forces Medical Course at Fort Sam, and the bad news is that he graduated last week."

"Since which time, he has been stalking around with glazed eyes, praying for an accident," Lieutenant Martin said. "He therefore regards you as a gift from heaven."

"My hand's fine, sir," Geoff said uneasily.

"You can't possibly know that," Master Sergeant Dempster said. "That sort of professional medical opinion can be issued only by someone like myself, who has been certified by the army as capable of performing any medical procedure short of opening the cranial cavity."

"He can also cure the clap," one of the sergeants said.

"Indeed, I can," Master Sergeant Dempster said. "And a good thing for you I can. Now, if you'll just come this way, Private Craig, we'll have a look at that hand."

This is obviously a joke, Geoff decided. *I am the butt of some elaborate practical joke.*

He allowed Master Sergeant Dempster to lead him to a desk.

"Sergeant Fitts," Dempster said, "would you be kind enough to hand me my doctor tools, please?"

"I would be honored," Sergeant Fitts said, and a moment later laid a large rolled up bundle of canvas on the desk. Dempster unrolled it. It contained an imposing array of bona fide surgical tools.

"I don't think we'll be needing the amputation saw," Dempster said, "but it's nice to know it's there if something goes wrong."

He sat down at the desk and took Geoff's cast in his hand. He was now dead serious, Geoff saw, and that alarmed him more than the bantering had.

Dempster, one by one, manipulated Geoff's fingers.

"If that causes pain, speak up," he said.

It felt strange, but there was no pain.

"No pain?" Dempster asked.

"No."

"And if the Jackson TWX is to be believed, this somewhat sloppy cast has been in place for ten days?"

"Yes," Geoff said. "The doctor said it would be on there for ten days to two weeks."

"The most recent medical literature with which I am familiar," Master Sergeant Dempster said, "suggests that in a healthy young male, keeping a cast in place—and thus immobilizing the bones of the hand—is contraindicated once the bones have had a week to ten days. Atrophy of muscle tissues sets in. Stiffness in joints develops. It is therefore my decision to free you of this filthy cast, Craig." He pulled the surgical tools toward him and took out what looked like a tool to build model airplanes.

"You sure you know what you're doing, Dempster?" the lieutenant asked.

"You weren't listening when I said the army says I can do everything but brain surgery," Dempster said.

"The kid only needs one hand anyway," one of the sergeants said.

Dempster put the tool, a sharp little saw on a stainless-steel handle, to Geoff's cast and began to saw. He was surprisingly gentle, Geoff thought. He wished that he had been in a position to demand the services of a physician, not an enlisted medic; but under the circumstances, he had not dared that.

Very quickly, the cast was sawed in half, so that the portion over the fingers could be pulled off the fingers. Then the part of the cast that circled the heel of the hand was sawed and snapped and taken off.

His hand, Geoff thought, looked awful. The skin was white and unhealthy-looking. Master Sergeant Dempster again gently manipulated the fingers. There was no pain. He pushed a heavy glass bottle, once an inkwell and now full of paper clips, to Geoff.

"Pick that up," he ordered.

Geoff picked it up.

Master Sergeant Dempster stood up and bowed.

"My very first solo patient," he said. "I am overwhelmed with the emotion of it all."

"To hell with your emotions; is his hand going to be all right?" Lieutenant Martin asked.

"I prescribe exercise," Dempster said. "Get a ball and squeeze it, Craig. Not your own, you understand. The kind they hit with racquets. And you may consider yourself medically excused from doing push-ups until further notice."

Geoff looked at Lieutenant Martin, who smiled at him and shrugged.

"If it starts to hurt, Craig," he said, "go on sick call."

"'Oh, ye of little faith'!" Master Sergeant Dempster said.

Then he turned to Craig. "Would you like to have the cast? As a souvenir?"

"No, thank you," Geoff said quickly. It would be a souvenir of the Fort Jackson stockade.

"In this case, I'll take it. I will send it off to the baby-shoe people and have it bronzed."

"You have made his day, Craig," Lieutenant Martin said, laughing.

"May I go now, sir?"

"Yes, sure."

"Do foolish things, Craig," one of the sergeants said. "Take chances. Get hit by a truck. Fall in the shower. Dempster will be waiting."

PFC Karl-Heinz Wagner staggered under the weight of both duffel bags, but refused to let Geoff try to carry his.

When they got to the orderly room, a corporal led them to a barracks. There were only six bunks on the entire floor. Three of them were made up.

"Where can we get sheets and blankets?" Wagner asked.

"You don't like the ones I put on those bunks with my very own hands?" the corporal replied.

This was not going to be like Fort Jackson, Geoff decided. This place was almost like the real world.

Karl-Heinz Wagner went immediately to work unpacking his duffel bag. The clothing he took from it was hardly mussed at all. He hung it carefully in a wall locker, and put his already folded underwear and his already-rolled socks in the footlocker. Geoff watched, wondering if he was just the Compleat PFC or someone afflicted with compulsive neatness.

Geoff opened his duffel bag and shook everything he owned out on the floor. Everything he owned needed laundering or dry cleaning. The lieutenant had said there was a PX tailor shop. One of the great privileges the trainees of Company "C" had been promised, after they finished basic training and had begun advanced individual training, was access to the laundry and dry cleaners. Until that time they would wash their own clothing. Geoff took from the bag a set of fatigues, his field jacket, and a pair of combat boots, and hung them in the wall locker. Next he took a set of underwear and a pair of wool cushion-sole socks from the bag and laid these on the bunk.

Then he found a towel and his toilet kit and sat them on his footlocker. Then he stuffed everything else back in the bag. In the morning he would put everything else into the care of the PX tailor shop.

He took a shower. It was the first time that his left armpit had been washed in eleven days; it reeked accordingly. What few showers he had had in the past ten days he'd taken with his right hand held high over his head.

The shower was a delightful experience with what seemed to be unlimited hot water. When he went back to his bunk, wearing his damp towel around his waist, Karl-Heinz Wagner was already in his bunk, lying in what Geoff thought was a military manner. He was on his back, the blankets were drawn up to his chin, and he was supporting his head on both hands.

"I take bath in morning," Karl-Heinz offered. "Shave in shower. Saves time."

"You really eat this stuff up, don't you?" Geoff asked.

"I am a soldier," Karl-Heinz Wagner said simply.

"You're German, aren't you?" Geoff asked, slightly hesitant that it was question he should not have asked.

"Dresdener," Karl-Heinz said. "I was born and schooled in Dresden."

Dresden, Geoff recalled, was in East Germany.

"How did you get here?" Geoff asked curiously.

Karl-Heinz turned his head enough to look at him.

"Is only one way to get out," he said matter-of-factly, his tone implying that he thought everyone should know that. "Over the wall."

Geoff had seen the newsreels of the Berlin Wall, and an image came to his mind's eye of an East German hanging dead from a fence of barbed wire, blood dripping from multiple bullet wounds.

"Wasn't that risky?"

"Yes, it was risky," Karl-Heinz said.

"How did you do it?"

Karl-Heinz moved his head again to look at Geoff, and Geoff knew he was making up his mind whether or not to tell him.

"They are always improving wall," he said. "They take down weak section and put up strong section. When they do this, they take up mines and move big barriers out of way. I find out where they do this. I go to motor pool and tell them to load truck with cement bags."

"I don't understand that," Geoff said.

"I go to motor pool and tell them to load truck with cement bags," Karl-Heinz repeated. "Great big Czech truck, *Skoda*, like American six-by-six, but with diesel motor."

"How did you get them to do that?"

"Oh," Karl-Heinz said, as if for the first time understanding Geoff's confusion. "I was *Oberleutnant* of Pioneers. Same as first lieutenant. In DDR army, when *Oberleutnant* says load truck, soldiers load truck."

"Then what?"

"Then I take guns away from them," Karl-Heinz said. "And I tell them what I am going to do, and ask if anybody wants to go with us. . . ."

"Ursula was with you?"

"I got to take her with me," Karl-Heinz said. "She's my sister. We don't have nobody else."

"Oh," Geoff said softly.

"So nobody wants to go with us. What they do, for the soldiers, is make sure the ones close to the wall have families. So I lock them up and drive truck myself."

"Where was Ursula?"

"In back of truck. Bullets won't go through cement."

"And you crashed through the wall?"

"*Ja*," Karl-Heinz said simply. "We was lucky. We made it."

"And now you joined the American army as a private?"

"*Ja*," Karl-Heinz said.

"There was nothing else you could have done?" Geoff asked.

"I am soldier," Karl-Heinz said. "Since I am fifteen, I am soldier. My father was soldier, killed in Russia. A soldier is what we do."

"But as a private?" Geoff wondered aloud.

"When I finish this school, I am sergeant," Karl-Heinz said. The surprise was evident on Geoff's face. "You didn't know that?" Karl-Heinz asked. "When you finish training, they make you sergeant?"

"No," Geoff said. That was the first time he had heard that.

"Then I am sergeant," Karl-Heinz said. "When I am soldier two years, I can apply to be citizen. When I am citizen, I go to officer school. I will be officer again."

"You volunteered for Special Forces so you could get a quick promotion?" Geoff said.

"That's nice, but not the reason. I come Special Forces so I can kill Communists."

He means that, Geoff realized. *He is dead serious. He wants to kill people.* It gave him a little chill.

"Why you come Special Forces?" Karl-Heinz asked.

"That's quite a story," Geoff said after a pause.

"You don't want to talk about it," Karl-Heinz said. "Okay. I go to sleep now."

He rolled over on his side.

Geoff looked at the back of his neck.

Jesus H. Christ! he thought. I am actually in a bunk beside a man who used to be an officer in the East German army, who escaped with his sister by crashing through the Berlin Wall in a stolen truck, and whose announced purpose in life is to kill Communists.

It took Geoff longer to go to sleep than he thought it would. And then he dreamed. Ursula was rubbing her breast against his face again. The difference in his dream from what had happened in the airplane was that she was naked. And she moved her breast so that he could get the nipple in his mouth. When he kissed it, he woke up in his bunk with the accumulated seminal fluid of two months abstinence in his shorts.

He got up and took another shower, and as he walked back to his bunk, past the sleeping PFC Karl-Heinz Wagner, he had two thoughts: Karl-Heinz Wagner was the first friend he had made in the army; and PFC Karl-Heinz Wagner would not hesitate to slit his throat if he tried to do awake what he had done to Ursula in his dream.

(Four)
Room C-232
The Holiday Inn
Durham, North Carolina
2230 Hours, 11 December 1961

Lieutenant Thomas Ellis was asleep on his back, with his mouth open and his legs spread, and this triggered in Dianne Eaglebury several emotions she had not previously experienced. One of them was anger: *How dare he fall asleep!*

Another was sort of a detached anatomical curiosity. His thing looked about as long as his thumb—and about as threatening. Yet, five minutes, three minutes (how long had it been?) before, it had been at least four times that size and as stiff as a board. And in her.

The first time had not hurt her nearly as much as she had been led to believe it would, and it had produced in her physical and emotional reactions that she had heard a lot about.

She was now a woman, she thought: no longer a virgin.

My God! What was I thinking of?

She was not only a woman; she was a somewhat lewd and shameless woman who had decided to ask this boy to make love to her in the middle of the afternoon, in the bright sunlight, without so much as a sip of alcohol to blame it on.

It was worse than that. She had decided that she was going to let him be *The First One* while he was still acting The Perfect Gentleman. He was not displaying the slightest hint that he would like to get her into a horizontal position, rip off her clothes and do wicked and forbidden things to her innocent body. She had, in other words, none too subtly let him know what she wanted.

She had touched his hand, and his arm, and let her breasts rub against his arm, and looked into his eyes, and done everything but take off her clothes and throw him a bump and grind.

And, God forgive me, that was thrilling!

She corrected herself. Maybe it hadn't been a bump and a grind, but she had certainly rubbed her middle against his middle and kept it there even after his thing had grown stiff.

They had been dancing. Old-fashioned dancing in a new place on Jefferson Avenue that played old big-band records and records of Frank Sinatra singing romantic songs, and where it was so dark, you couldn't see your hand in front of your face.

Going there had been her idea. After they'd had dinner.

He smelled like a man. She had never before paid any particular attention to how a boy—a *man*—smelled, unless he was sweaty and needed a shower. But when he put his arms around her and she felt his hand on her back, she had smelled him. She couldn't describe the smell, but it did things to her. It made her want to put her face in his neck and smell more of him. It made her want to rest against him, to feel the hardness of his chest against her own softness.

They hadn't had anything to drink in the Stardust Ballroom. Tom said he was sort of on duty and didn't want Colonel What's-his-name to smell alcohol on his breath if "something happened." She hadn't wanted anything to drink because she understood that she was crazy enough as it was on Coca-Cola.

And they'd only stayed for one Coke. Two dances. The first dance was the one when she hadn't pulled her middle away from his stiff thing in maidenly modesty. And in the second dance she had removed any question of the first time being innocent by rubbing her middle against his the minute he put his arms around her.

They went out and got in his Jaguar, and he turned to her and looked at her. And kissed her. And she had her tongue in his mouth the minute their lips touched. And pressed herself against him as hard as she could.

And he hadn't said a word while he drove her to his motel.

At the motel she felt strange—not like a dream, but like she was watching somebody else getting out of a car and walking up a noisy steel stairway to an outside corridor, and going into a motel room. It had even been unreal when she looked around the room, saw that there was an open canvas suitcase on the other double bed, saw him locking the door, saw him coming toward her and putting his arms around her again.

There had been a moment's panic when she felt his hand under her skirt and his fingers under her underpants, the very first time anyone except Dr. Gladys Eisenberg had ever touched her there. But she was by then too far gone, and the next thing she knew, she was on the bed with her skirt and slip and panties off and he was putting it in her.

She still had her sweater on. And her brassiere. He was still wearing his shirt and undershirt and socks.

He woke up. His eyes opened and he looked up at her.

"Jesus!" he said.

She averted her eyes.

Now she felt shamed and humiliated. She wanted to cry.

"Are you all right?" he asked.

She nodded her head, averting it from him. Her eyes were closed.

"Why did you do it with me?" Tom Ellis asked. "The first time, I mean?"

He had to ask the one question that was absolutely the worst question he could possibly ask.

She shook her head.

"Jesus!" he said.

She wished the floor would suddenly open up and swallow the entire damned motel room.

He put his hand on her back. She squirmed away from the contact.

"If I had known," Tom announced, half apologetically, half righteously, "I wouldn't have done it."

He is letting me know that I seduced him, Dianne thought, and then realized that was ridiculous. Virgins don't go around seducing men. Except *she* had.

His hand touched her again, lower down. She stiffened but did not jump away.

The telephone rang.

"Oh, my God!" Dianne said.

He chuckled, and she turned and glowered at him.

"Jesus Christ," he said, wonderingly, "you're beautiful!"

"Yeah," she said bitterly.

The telephone rang again.

"Answer it, for God's sake!" Dianne said.

With a sudden movement, and with such strength that she could not resist, he reached up and pulled her down against him. Her face was against his chest, and she could feel his heart beating as he stretched out and picked up the telephone.

"Lieutenant Ellis," he said.

She felt his hand move under her sweater and the balls of his fingers caressingly, possessively, run over her backbone.

He laughed. "I'm very glad to hear that, sir," he said to the telephone.

She relaxed her torso against his, marveling again at how hard his chest was.

"Yes, sir, I'd love to see it," he said. "I'll leave right away, sir. Thank you for calling."

If he was leaving, that meant she would have to get up.

Dianne didn't like that. She wanted to stay right where she was forever.

He stretched again as he replaced the telephone in its cradle, and then he lay down again. She felt him tugging at her sweater. What he was doing, she realized, was pulling it and her bra up, so that her breast would be naked where it pressed against him.

"Oh, my!" he said, when they had finished what they wanted.

"You went to sleep," she accused.

"Did I?" He sounded surprised.

"You did," she said.

"I'm awake now," he said, and then he chuckled. "All over."

He took her hand and pushed it to his crotch. She balled her fist.

The nerve of him! How dare he do that!

But she let it touch her hand. It was hard again. She opened her eyes and raised her head just enough to look down there. It was standing up, sort of curving in her direction. Her balled fist opened and closed around it.

"You must think I'm a slut," she said.

"I think maybe I'm in love with you," Tom said.

"Oh, you shouldn't have said that!" she said.

"Probably not," he agreed.

Why did you have to say that?

"I have to go," he said.

"Where? Who was that?"

"We have blown up the water tower," he said.

"You said that before," she said, with one part of her mind. "What are you talking about?"

The other part was thinking that if she just rolled over a little on him, she could stick it in her. There had been a dirty movie at the house, and there had been a scene of a girl sitting on a man. It was the first time Dianne had ever considered it possible to do it that way.

"My 'A' Team is destroying your campus," he said, laughing.

She really didn't hear what he had to say.

She rolled over on him and put him in.

"Jesus!" he said.

"You like that?"

"Oh, God, yes!"

She moved up and down on him. It was wild. She was sore, but that didn't seem to matter.

"Take your sweater off," he said. "I want to look."

She pulled her sweater off, and the brassiere. She looked down at him and at her breasts, and then glanced and saw her reflection in the mirror over the washbasin in the bathroom.

She felt the trembling, and the tremors, and the shortness of breath starting all over again.

She heard him saying something and forced herself to pay attention.

"I love you," he said.

"Me too . . . me too . . . me too," she said and then the convulsions came over her and she collapsed on him, and she thought that would be the end of it, but he gently turned her over and kept at it, and as if from a distance, far off, she heard her voice calling his name over and over.

(Five)
The Delta Delta Delta House
Duke University
Durham, North Carolina
0825 Hours, 12 December 1961

Dianne saw the Jaguar pull up in front of the house, but she could not force herself to go down to face him.

It was daylight now, and a new day, and the craziness had left her. Last night it seemed like a splendid idea to have breakfast with Tom. Now it seemed like a lousy one. She wished that she would never have to see him again in her life— ever.

"The army is here for you," one of her sisters said. Dianne looked at her but said nothing. "Some guy from ROTC. He's on the porch."

"Thank you," Dianne said. She picked up her books and went into the foyer.

He was dressed in work clothes. Last night he had worn a regular uniform. She had thought he looked very nice in his uniform. She thought he looked very nice now.

"Sorry to keep you waiting," she said.

She had planned to say that something had come up, and she just couldn't have breakfast with him. He would go away, and she could avoid, somehow, seeing him again.

"It's okay," he said, and he pulled the storm door outward and held it open for her.

If he tries to kiss me, I don't know what I'll do.

He didn't try to kiss her, or even to touch her. He just walked beside her to the car. He didn't even hold the door for her.

He drove off the campus.

"Where are we going?" she asked in alarm. "I meant the cafeteria!"

"There's a steak place down here a little ways," he said. "The team is there."

"Steak. At eight o'clock in the morning?"

"They serve breakfast," he said. "You can have eggs or whatever."

"Oh," she said. There was nothing she could do but go.

Inside Western Sizzling Family Steak House nine soldiers were eating breakfast around three tables pushed together. Each of the soldiers was eating a very rare steak.

Two of the soldiers were officers; one was a captain.

"These are the guys who blew up the campus last night," Tom introduced her. "This is Dianne Eaglebury."

They politely shook her hand.

"How did a nice girl like you wind up knowing a disreputable character like this one?" the captain asked as soon as she sat down.

"My brother was a Green Beret," she said. "Or the next thing to one."

The reply had come without her thinking about it.

"'The next thing to one'?" he asked, politely curious.

"He was in the navy, but he trained with Tom," she said.

Screw her sisters, she thought angrily. Screw what people at Duke thought. Screw what anybody thought.

"He bought it in Cuba," Tom said levelly.

"I'm sorry . . ." the captain said.

"It's all right," Dianne said. "It explains how come I know this disreputable character."

She reached over and caught Tom's hand and squeezed it.

They heard the *fluckata-fluckata-fluckata* sound of a helicopter ten minutes later.

"Our transportation has arrived," the captain said.

The "A" Team had an army truck, on the door of which was taped an ROTC recruiting poster, and they drove it back to the football stadium. Dianne was supposed to be in class, but that didn't seem to matter. She hadn't used all her cuts, and she didn't want to leave Tom.

Tom parked the Jaguar outside the stadium. The truck drove inside. Cadets were being shown the helicopter as the "A" Team loaded its gear aboard when she and Tom walked up to it. He knew the pilot.

"The general's compliments, Lieutenant Ellis," the pilot said. "And would you present yourself at your earliest opportunity?"

"What general?"

"Brigadier General Paul T. Hanrahan," the pilot said.

"No shit? They made him a general?"

"And you will notice the berets," the pilot said. "We got those back too."

"Jesus, that's great," Tom said. And then he asked, "He really sent for me?"

"Yeah. Taylor called and said I was to bring you back."

"I drove up here," Ellis said.

"Let one of these guys drive the jeep back," the pilot said.

"My *Jaguar*?" Ellis asked incredulously. "No way." He thought of something else. "I haven't checked out of the motel. I wasn't going back until tomorrow."

"My heart bleeds for you," the pilot said.

Tom turned to Dianne. He put the Jaguar keys in her hand, reached in his pocket, and came up with money.

"Check me out of the motel, will you?" he asked. "And I'll call when I know what's up."

"Sure," she said.

He did that very possessively, she thought. *As if I belong to him, and he has the right to expect me to take care of him.*

"Anytime you're ready, driver," the "A" Team captain called from the helicopter door, "we are."

Tom kissed her. The kiss, to applause from the "A" Team, was possessive. He stood in the door of the helicopter as it rose from the football field, not waving, not even smiling, just looking at her.

And then the helicopter was gone, soaring over the end of the stadium, and she was standing there with his keys and three twenty-dollar bills in her hand, while the guys in ROTC looked at her.

I should be furious at him, she thought.

But I am not.

The entirely pleasant thing to consider—scary but pleasant—is that I do, in a way, sort of belong to him. Which means that he, sort of belongs to me.

She smiled as dazzlingly as she could at the guys in ROTC who knew who she was, and then wiggled her rear as she walked off the football field and out to Tom's car, swinging his keys in her hand.

VIII

(One)
Office of the Commanding General
U.S. Army Special Warfare Center
Fort Bragg, North Carolina
1115 Hours, 12 December 1961

"Lieutenant Ellis reporting as ordered, sir," Tom Ellis said, saluting before Hanrahan's desk.

"If you had added 'to the commanding general,'" Hanrahan said, "you would have earned three Brownie points, Tom," Hanrahan said.

"I was about to ask if I could offer congratulations, General," Ellis said.

"Oh, how I like the sound of that," Hanrahan said. "And I see you got the word about the berets."

"The pilot told me, sir," Ellis said.

"Let this be a lesson to you, Lieutenant," Hanrahan said. "Virtue is its own reward."

"I think most of us are as happy about your star as you are, sir," Tom said, and then corrected himself: *"General."*

"I understand the Duke University water tower has developed a leak," Hanrahan said.

"Yes, sir, but—"

"Which occurred while you were out spreading goodwill among the natives."

"Yes, sir. But—"

"And a very comely native it was you were spreading goodwill upon, according to Colonel Wells. You apparently lost no time in reconnoitering the area."

"It was Dianne Eaglebury, sir. Commander Eaglebury's sister?"

"Oh, yes. You took notes in Philadelphia, obviously."

"She told me she was at Duke, sir, and suggested I come to see her."

Hanrahan smiled at him.

"Colonel Wells tells me that the engineer says he can fix the water tank."

"He told me it can be caulked, sir."

"Have you got his name?"

"Yes, sir."

"Make sure he and Colonel Wells get one of our famous 'From His Friends in Special Forces' Zippos, Tom."

"Yes, sir. But I thought Sergeant Taylor—"

"The sergeant major took care of little odds and ends like that for me when I was a lowly colonel," Hanrahan interrupted. "But now that I am a general officer, I am entitled to have a commissioned officer in the grade of either captain or lieutenant robbing dogs for me. Can you guess who I have chosen for that awesome responsibility?"

"General," Tom said uncomfortably.

"Do I detect something short of uncontrollable enthusiasm?"

"General, you need somebody who knows how to do something like that. One of the trade-school types. I'm a dogfaced soldier out of OCS. I don't know anything about what an aide has to do."

Ellis's objection had occurred to General Hanrahan within an hour of his getting his star, as they lunched with the President at the officer's open mess. He had considered what he needed in an aide-de-camp very carefully. He really needed an aide steeped in the fine points of protocol and military courtesy, someone with a grasp of the army beyond command of an "A" Team, someone who would know how to help his general make his way through the minefields of the social side of the army. Someone, he now thought wryly, who does not openly refer to graduates of the United States Military Academy as "trade-school types."

But there were several good arguments in favor of appointing this boy-faced lieutenant as his aide-de-camp. For one thing, Hanrahan was determined that none of his people should get the idea that the West Point Protective Association had a chapter in Special Forces. If there was to be a fraternity of officers taking care of each other, it would be made up of officers who wore the green beret. Despite their permission to wear berets, despite his promotion, it was still Special Forces against the rest of the army.

That war had already started. It had started while the President was still at Bragg. There had been an innocent remark at lunch, a crack about Hanrahan being now entitled to an aide, and a not-so-innocent remark from Major General Kenneth L. Harke, who was running XVIII Airborne Corps while Triple H Howard was off doing whatever he was doing: "What the General really needs is a commandant for the school. He needs somebody to take some of that weight off his shoulders."

"He's right, Paul," Triple H Howard had agreed.

"I'll name Mac commandant," Hanrahan had said.

"Mac isn't senior enough," General Harke said.

"No, he's not," Howard had agreed.

"We'll send you somebody, General," the Vice-Chief of Staff said. "I think General Harke is right. You can only spread yourself so thin."

They had really been enthusiastic to make sure he didn't spread himself too thin, that he had the help he needed: a colonel serving as commandant of the Special Warfare School to take the weight off his shoulders.

He had been informed that morning that Colonel Roland T. Miner, G-4 (Supply), 82nd Airborne Division, would report to him for duty as commandant of the Special Warfare School. Colonel Miner was an artillery officer (Special Forces had no artillery) and was a member in good standing of the Airborne family. He was known to feel that Special Forces was a waste of assets, and Hanrahan had heard his name mentioned as the man most likely to be appointed to assume command of the Fifth Airborne Regimental Combat Team (the redesignated Fifth Special Forces Group) when that happened and Hanrahan got his marching orders. Hanrahan had also heard that Colonel Miner, a strict disciplinarian, was considered just the man to shape up Hanrahan's ragtag army of misfits and ne'er-do-wells and turn them back into decent paratroopers.

There were two compelling arguments for naming Lieutenant Tom Ellis aide-de-camp to the commanding general of the Special Warfare Center. The first was his loyalty, which was to Hanrahan personally. The second was that he deserved it. His performance in Cuba, had that been an official war, would have earned him at least a Silver Star, and possibly a Distinguished Service Cross, *and* a battlefield promotion to captain. It had not been an official war, and he had got neither medal nor promotion. All he'd gotten out of that was a remark on his efficiency report that he "had demonstrated, under combat conditions, not only great personal valor, but leadership far beyond that expected of an officer of his age and experience."

That was good, of course, but when the captain's promotion board sat, there was bound to be some chair-warming sonofabitch on it who would point out that the officer in question had only a high school education, and neither professional education nor experience beyond commanding—no matter how well—a smaller than platoon-sized unit.

What Hanrahan intended to do when (as Lieutenant Ellis's *immediate* superior) he wrote his next efficiency report was to make him sound like a combination of Von Clausewitz and Georgie Patton the Elder. "In the undersigned's personal observation, this officer has demonstrated a grasp of material and concepts one would expect from an officer of far superior rank and experience. He has demonstrated, time and again, his talent as a staff officer. I recommend him without qualification for rapid promotion, having no doubt whatever that he could not only assume command of a company, but serve with distinction as a staff officer at divisional or higher level."

It would take that much bullshit to get him the captain's railroad tracks his performance had already earned him. It bothered Hanrahan's sense of right and wrong, and of honor, to have to play the game; but he hadn't written the rules, and he and Ellis were in the game, and it would not be fair to Ellis, or ultimately to the army, to describe him honestly as "a smart, tough young man who has the ability to lead men and more than his share of courage" and see him lose the promotion he deserved to another officer whose rating officer had been so pleased with the lieutenant's performance in inventorying the supply room that his efficiency report made him out to be a logistical and tactical genius.

And finally, Paul Hanrahan was comfortable around Tom Ellis. If he practically had to adopt some young officer into his family, he wanted somebody he liked. And whom Pat and the kids liked.

"If you don't want the job, Tom," General Hanrahan said, "because you don't want to be a dog robber, that's okay. But if you're worried about whether or not you can handle it, I'm a better judge of that than you are. And I'd like to have you."

"If you'll point out the dogs to me, General, I'll get their bones for you," Ellis said.

"Sergeant Major!" Hanrahan called.

Sergeant Major Taylor came into the office.

"Yes, sir?"

"He took the job," Hanrahan said.

"May I presume to offer my congratulations to you, Lieutenant Ellis, sir, on your elevation to the upper echelons of command?" Taylor asked.

"Screw you, Taylor," Ellis said.

"And I just made a special trip to the PX for you!" Taylor said, feigning a hurt pout. He handed Ellis a small piece of cardboard onto which were pinned the insignia of an aide-de-camp to a brigadier general, a shield with one star. "They were a buck a half," he said. "But the rope was $21.95."

(As a badge of office aides-de-camp to general officers wear a golden cord hanging from the tunic epaulet over their upper arm.)

"Twenty-one ninety-five!"

"That comes to $23.45," Taylor said, "if you please."

"Close the door, Taylor," Hanrahan said. "I'll pay for that stuff."

"I'll pay for it, sir," Ellis said.

"The first and great commandment for an aide-de-camp, Tom," Hanrahan said, "is 'Don't argue with the general.'"

"Yes, sir," Ellis said. "Thank you, General."

"Pin the pin on," Hanrahan said. "The appointment is official as of now."

"Yes, sir," Ellis said, and started to unpin his infantry rifles from his fatigue jacket collar.

"Let me do it," Taylor said, and went to him.

"First the social business," Hanrahan said. "Mrs. Hanrahan and I will receive the officers and their ladies for cocktails tomorrow at five. You're in charge, Tom, and your orders are that my wife is not to exhaust herself doing it herself. Check with Mrs. MacMillan and tell her what I said."

"Yes, sir."

"You will arrange to have beer delivered to the mess halls, two bottles per man, to be served with the evening meal tomorrow with my compliments," Hanrahan said.

"For everybody?" Ellis asked, surprised. Two bottles of beer for every enlisted man in the group and school was going to cost a bundle.

"For everybody," Hanrahan said. "This is probably my last promotion, and I'm going to do it right."

Ellis glanced at Taylor, who had put his finger in front of his lips, telling him to shut up.

"Yes, sir," Ellis said.

"We have three personnel problems to discuss, and this discussion is not to go outside this room," Hanrahan said.

Sergeant Major Taylor and Lieutenant Ellis looked at him curiously.

"We are about to be joined by Colonel Roland T. Miner, who will be commandant of the school," Hanrahan said.

Ellis had never heard of him. Sergeant Major Taylor obviously had. He frowned and shook his head.

"It has been put to me that Colonel Miner's assignment as commandant will take the weight of the school off my shoulder," Hanrahan said. "With that in mind, I intend to see that none of the responsibility for the group, or the center, falls on Colonel Miner's shoulders."

"Yes, sir," Sergeant Major Taylor said.

"Colonel Miner will doubtless feel it his duty to familiarize himself with the activities of the group and the center. Inasmuch as you are privy, Taylor, to all the classified activities—and you shortly will be, Tom—I wish to take this opportunity to remind you both, in the strongest possible terms, that possession of a Top Secret security clearance does not of itself grant anyone access to anything without a Need to Know. Do I have to go over that again?"

"No, sir," they chorused.

"I will decide what Colonel Miner needs to know to perform his duties," Hanrahan said. "I will not delegate that authority."

"Yes, sir," they chorused again.

"You, Tom, can play the dumb lieutenant who hasn't been told anything. But it won't be easy—it will be impossible—Taylor, for you to play the dumb sergeant. It is natural to presume that you have access to everything. I can only hope that you can handle this. I'll back you up, if I have to tell you that, but I am relying on you to see that nobody has access to any classified material without the Need to Know."

"I understand, sir," Taylor said. "Damn it, I knew things were going too smoothly."

"There's no such thing as total victory, Sergeant Major," Hanrahan said.

"Is he bringing his chicken with him, General?"

"I'm sure he is," Hanrahan said. "I will do what I can to see that it is fenced in, so the fowl's feces will drop only where it belongs, but I want you to keep your eyes open in case the chicken escapes."

"Yes, sir," Taylor said.

"The other two personnel problems are at the other end of the rank structure," Hanrahan said. "I'll bring you up to date on the first one, Ellis. Taylor's already aware of it. We were joined last night by a Private Geoffrey Craig. He came to us from the post stockade at Fort Jackson, South Carolina, with his hand in a cast. He broke his hand when he broke his basic-training sergeant's jaw."

Hanrahan saw the surprise on Ellis's face. Enlisted man accepted by Special Forces were invariably superior-quality troops, ninety-five percent of them already noncoms.

"Private Craig was recommended to me personally by Colonel Lowell," Hanrahan said. "Now, we are all fond of Colonel

Lowell, and some of us, as you know, Ellis, more fond than others. I daresay that if Colonel Lowell called and asked you for a favor, Ellis, you would do your best to grant it."

"Yes, sir," Ellis said. There was emotion in his voice.

Not too many months ago, Ellis had been with his "A" Team on the beach of the Bahai de Cochinos on Cuba's Southern Coast. Sure that in no more than an hour or two he would be captured, he had been debating the merits of suicide, wondering if he could make himself do it. He had been absolutely convinced it was either putting his .45 in his mouth or undergoing unspeakable treatment at the hands of Castro's patriots. At that moment Craig Lowell had landed in the water at the controls of an old amphibian. It didn't matter that Lowell was not looking for them but for his buddy, Colonel Felter; there had been room on the *Catalina* for the whole team. Lowell had saved their ass too. Ellis considered that he owed him.

"I was happy to grant Lowell's request," Hanrahan said. "But I have known Colonel Lowell since he was a second lieutenant, and I wondered about his sudden touching concern for this private soldier who had just broken his sergeant's jaw. Sergeant Major Taylor made a few discreet inquiries at Fort Jackson, and the mystery was solved. Private Craig is Colonel Lowell's cousin."

"Oh," Ellis said.

Taylor chuckled.

"That poses the question 'Is Private Craig a chastened young man who, having recognized the errors of his ways, has straightened up and will fly right, or is he what his first sergeant at Jackson told Taylor he was—a wise-ass rich kid who thinks he's too good for the army and needed his teeth knocked down his throat?'"

"Why don't I talk to him and find out?" Ellis asked.

"I was going to call him in for a chat," Taylor said.

"If you awe me, Sergeant Major, imagine how you will terrify a kid fresh from the stockade," Ellis said.

"You're an officer," Taylor said.

"I'm also as old as he is," Ellis said. "If he is going to put the con on anybody, which is what we want to find out, he's much more likely to try it on me than you."

"Go ahead," Hanrahan chuckled. "Let's find out what we're dealing with. Where is he, Taylor?"

"They gave them the morning off to get settled. Probably in the barracks."

Hanrahan looked at his watch.

"You won't have time. Do it tonight. The other problem is a little stickier. We have a PFC in the same barracks. Very interesting young man. He was an *Oberleutnant* in the East German army. Crashed through the Berlin Wall in a truck and brought his sister with him. As soon as he got to the States, he enlisted. The CIC, for obvious reasons, has run quite an investigation on him."

"They think he's a plant?" Taylor asked.

"No. That question has been settled. He's who he says he is, and he did what he said he did. There were thirty-seven bullet holes in the truck he came through the wall in. And counterintelligence apparently has some interesting contacts on the other side of the wall. I just read the whole report. The problem with this guy is money. He and his sister are living on what we're paying him as a private. He made PFC as honor graduate in basic training."

"Jesus!" Taylor said.

"If he was going to be here, I could fix something," Hanrahan said. "Get her permission to stay in the Guest House for more than three days. Get her a job in the PX or someplace. But he's going to Benning for three weeks for jump school, and where he goes, she goes. The way they get the money for her ticket is by not buying any food."

"I got some friends at Benning," Sergeant Major Taylor said.

"Not me," Ellis said. "I was in OCS there."

"Well, see what you can come up with," Hanrahan said. "This guy is too proud to take a handout, from what I read. But I am very uncomfortable with one of my people—or his dependent—going hungry. According to the CIC, they're living on beans and rice and bologna. I won't have it. Come up with something."

● ● ●

(Two)

Private Geoffrey Craig was summoned to the orderly room by the intercom system.

He went at the run and was almost there when he saw an officer, a lieutenant. He stopped running, saluted, and walked past. When he was past, he would start running again. Or at least that was his intention. He didn't get past. The officer examined him closely as he went by, then called him by name.

"Craig?"

Geoff stopped and turned and came to attention.

"Yes, sir?"

"Come with me," Ellis said.

"Sir, I've been ordered to the orderly room," Geoff said.

"I ordered you to the orderly room," Tom Ellis said. He turned and walked to the side of the small frame orderly-room building. He got behind the wheel of a jeep and signaled for Geoff to get in.

Geoff was surprised. He had never seen an officer driving himself before.

"My name is Ellis," Tom said. "I'm the general's aide-de-camp."

"Yes, sir?"

"Because I am the general's aide-de-camp, I know about you," Ellis said. "*All* about you."

"Yes, sir," Geoff said.

"Let there, therefore, be no bullshit between us," Ellis said.

"Yes, sir," Geoff said.

Ellis, driving easily, took them out of the Smoke Bomb Hill area.

"We're going to Camp McCall," he said. "Do you know where it is? Do you know *what* it is?"

"No, sir."

"It's where we take officers and noncoms who are already pretty good soldiers and turn them into Green Berets. We get very few people right out of basic training, and you are the very first we have ever had straight from the stockade."

Geoff was very uneasy. He decided against saying anything.

"Turning good soldiers into Green Berets is both difficult and expensive," Ellis said. "There is a considerable doubt in several people's minds, including my own, that you are going to be worth the time and effort."

Geoff couldn't think of anything to reply to that either.

"Do you even know, for example, what a Green Beret is?"

"Not really," Geoff confessed. "I mean, I've seen the posters, but—"

"Didn't they teach you to say 'sir' in basic training?" Ellis asked, scornfully, but not angrily, a comment reflecting contempt for his training as a soldier, Geoff thought, rather than offense at his lack of military courtesy.

"Sorry, sir," he said.

They were on a two lane macadam highway now, passing through scraggly stands of pine. MAX SPEED 35 was stenciled to the jeep's dashboard. The speedometer needle was pointing to 55, almost off the speedometer.

"You don't like the army, do you?" Ellis asked.

"No, sir, I don't," Geoff said. He had been told no bullshit, so there was a no-bullshit answer.

"You think you were screwed by the draftboard?"

"By fate," Geoff said, and added, "sir."

"The fickle finger of fate, having fucked, moves on," Ellis said, and smiled, pleased with himself. "First, you get yourself drafted. Then you run into a nasty sergeant who puts you not only in the hospital with a broken hand but into the stockade. And then you wind up here, where you don't belong, expected to jump out of airplanes and do other things which make basic training look like girl scout camp by comparison. Is that about the way you see it?"

"Yes, sir, that's about it," Geoff said.

"Are you as rich as Colonel Lowell?" Ellis asked.

Jeff hesitated a second. "My father is," he said.

"You ever hear what Colonel Lowell did at the Bay of Pigs?"

"No, sir."

"When the whole thing came apart, after Kennedy didn't send in Naval Aviation to take out the Cuban tanks and they started kicking the shit out of the invasion force, it looked like a buddy of his—a colonel named Felter—was either dead or about to be dead. So Colonel Lowell, ignoring a direct order to mind his own business, went to get him. He hired an airplane,

an amphibian, and went down there and pulled his buddy off
the beach. Him and what was left of an 'A' Team."

"I didn't know that," Geoff said.

"Which explains why you're here," Ellis said.

"Excuse me?"

"The general figured he owed Colonel Lowell one," Ellis
said. "What the hell, Special Forces owed Colonel Lowell one
'A' Team that otherwise would have gone down the toilet.
Taking his punk in-law and trying to run him through Camp
McCall and make a man of him didn't seem to be too much
to ask, so here you are."

"That's very interesting," Geoff said. "I didn't know he'd
been involved in the Bay of Pigs."

"What's interesting, Craig, is *why* Colonel Lowell did what
he did," Ellis said. "That's about as interesting as what he's
doing in the army in the first place. You ever wonder about
that?"

"Yes," Geoff said. "I have."

"Well, the one thing Colonel Lowell is not is a goddamned
fool. He knew what he was getting into when he rented that
amphibian. The odds were pretty good that he would get blown
away without being able to do a damned thing for his buddy.
He knew that. But he went anyway. *Why?*"

Ellis looked at Geoffrey Craig, and then suddenly swerved
the jeep to avoid a pothole.

"You got a buddy you'd stick your neck out for that way?"
Ellis asked.

Geoff thought it over and shook his head no.

"You think your father has?" Ellis pursued.

"Probably not," Geoff said. He had never before even thought
of his father in a life-threatening situation.

"The next question you have to ask yourself is why Colonel
Lowell arranged to have you sent here," Ellis said. "It would
have been much easier to get you out of the stockade and into
some office, pushing a typewriter."

"Why did he?" Geoff asked.

"He's *your* cousin, you figure it out," Ellis said.

He didn't say another word for the balance of the twenty-
mile trip to Camp McCall.

There was an elaborate gateway to Fort Bragg; a stucco MP

guard shack; a billboard giving a map of the post; another billboard reading WELCOME TO FORT BRAGG, THE HOME OF AIR-BORNE; a statue of a parachutist; and huge representations of XVIII Airborne Corps and Eighty-Second Airborne Division shoulder patches.

At the entrance to Camp McCall there was just one battered sign painted on a four-by-eight sheet of plywood momentarily lit up by the jeep's headlights as they passed: CAMP MCCALL. U.S. MILITARY RESERVATION. NO TRESPASSING. And past the sign there was nothing but more Carolina clay and more stands of pine trees.

They finally came to a small clearing, and Ellis stopped the jeep. When he turned the headlights off, there was no other light. Ellis produced a flashlight.

"This is the rappelling tower," he announced, and shined the light on it.

It was built of enormous creosoted pilings, twice the size of telephone poles, bolted together and reinforced with rough timber. There was a storage shed at ground level and a deck on top. A stairway climbed five long flights to the platform. Two sides of the structure were covered with rough planking. The others were open.

Ellis went to the storage shed, unlocked a padlock, pulled open a door, and came out with huge coils of nylon rope. He draped one of them around his neck and handed the other to Geoff Craig, obviously intending for him to do the same thing.

"Truth time," Ellis said as he picked up shorter lengths of rope, two pairs of leather gloves, and two stainless steel oblong rings. "Watch your step as we go up."

Geoff was afraid of the tower, an embarrassing fear that increased as they climbed up, seemingly forever.

Finally they reached the top. There was no railing at the edges of the platform, which would have been frightening enough in the daytime. At night, with only Ellis's flashlight for light, it was terrifying. He felt a little dizzy and had a strong urge to sit right down where he was. If he was sitting down, falling off seemed less of a real possibility.

Ellis moved to the center of the deck, where there was some sort of railing. In a moment Geoff understood its purpose. It was where the rope was tied.

"It is sometimes necessary to descend steep places: buildings, mountains, or whatever," Ellis said. "This is a mountain climber's technique, which isn't nearly as dangerous as it looks."

Geoff said nothing, unable to accept what seemed obvious. Ellis was going off the side of this thing on a rope. There were two ropes. Ellis therefore expected him to go off the side too.

Ellis immediately proved this by dropping to his knees in front of Geoff and quickly making a sort of harness around his waist and between his legs with a short length of rope and the oblong stainless-steel ring. Then he handed Geoff the light.

"Shine it on me so you can see what I'm doing," he said. He quickly made a rope harness for himself.

"Now, the way you do this," Ellis said, "is wrap the descent rope around you like this. You control the rate of descent by friction. It's that simple."

"I don't think I like this," Geoff said.

"You don't think you like this, *sir,*" Ellis said. "I didn't think you would."

He went to the railing and tied his rope to it, explaining: "The way I'm tying this, once I'm on the ground all I have to do is jerk on it, and it'll come loose."

Geoff didn't say anything. He now felt both numb and dizzy.

Ellis took the rope from Geoff's shoulders and tied it to the rail. He then took Geoff's arm and led him dangerously close to the edge of the deck. He wrapped the rope around him and backed Geoff to the edge.

"You're tied to the rail," he said. "You can't fall. Give the rope a jerk."

Geoff pulled on the rope, and experienced enormous relief that he was indeed firmly attached to the railing.

"What happens now is we see if you have any balls," Ellis said. "I'm going down by the rope. You can go down by either the rope or the stairs. If you go down by the stairs, I'll have you reassigned tomorrow to Headquarters, Fort Bragg, as a clerk or jeep driver or whatever you can do, and no hard feelings. We'll just tell Colonel Lowell you didn't have what it takes. Few people do. He'll understand. If you come down by way of the rope, we will then open the subject of how we can help your buddy Wagner."

"What do you mean by that?" Geoff asked, curiosity overwhelming everything else.

"Well, the poor sonofabitch and his sister are living on beans and bologna, and Special Forces takes care of its own," Ellis said. "If you're going to be one of us, maybe you can help. If you're not, you can't."

Ellis shined the flashlight on his face and grinned broadly at Geoff.

"These things are supposed to be shockproof," he said. "Let's see."

He threw the flashlight up in the air and over the edge of the platform. It spun as it fell, and it took what seemed like a very long time to fall to the ground. Where it went out.

"That goes to show you, I suppose, that you can't trust what people tell you," Ellis said.

Geoff didn't reply. He waited for his eyes to adjust to the darkness. In a minute they did. He saw for the first time lights a quarter of a mile or so away, but Ellis was gone.

He considered his options. He could pull himself away from the edge and crawl to the center of the platform, untie the rope, and coil it, and then—very carefully—crawl to the edge of the platform, find the stairs, and very carefully climb down them.

And tomorrow he would be a clerk in some safe office. And this insanity would be over.

And Cousin Craig would hereafter know that he was a wimp. And he would not look too hot in Ursula's eyes, either, even if he had the balls to go see her.

"Oh, *shit!*" Geoff said, and stepped off into the darkness.

(Three)
Office of the Commanding General
U.S. Army Special Warfare Center
Fort Bragg, North Carolina
1530 Hours, 12 December 1961

General Hanrahan's aide-de-camp and sergeant major entered his office together.

"Colonel Miner is on the horn, asking to speak to the general," Taylor said.

"That's not why you two are grinning," Hanrahan said as he reached for the telephone.

Colonel Miner, it soon became clear, wanted to bring with

him his warrant officer, his administrative assistant. Hanrahan could see nothing wrong with that and was about to say sure when he saw Sergeant Major Taylor describing the outline of a female form with his hands.

"One moment, please, Colonel," Hanrahan said, and covered the mouthpiece with his hand.

"Female?" he asked. Taylor nodded. "You're sure?"

"The lady is a very attractive redhead," Taylor said. "I don't know where she got the warrant."

"Colonel, if your man is able to become Special Forces—qualified," Hanrahan said, "then certainly I'll arrange for his transfer."

Colonel Miner was indignant. He wanted his administrative assistant for administrative purposes. He didn't plan to have his administrative assistant, "with all respect, blowing up bridges or whatever else you people do."

"The rule is ironclad, I'm afraid," Hanrahan said. "Everyone here has to be first parachute-qualified, then go through the basic course." There was a pause. "Why, certainly it includes you, Miner," Hanrahan said. "Where did you get the idea that it wouldn't?"

Taylor and Ellis looked very pleased with themselves.

"I don't intend to debate this with you, Colonel," Hanrahan said, "but we can discuss it further, if you insist, when you're here for duty."

He hung the telephone up.

"I don't see why that was so funny," Hanrahan said, somewhat sharply.

"Sorry, sir," Taylor said, wiping the smile from his face.

"As a matter of fact, you should have told Colonel Miner that yourself," Hanrahan said.

"I did, sir," Taylor said. "The colonel called and told me to cut orders on his people. When she came on the line, I told his warrant officer as politely as I could that we don't have women, and she said 'We'll see about that' and hung up. He called back and asked me if I knew what an order was, and I told him yes, sir, that I did and that my orders were that I could cut transfer orders only on qualified people. It was then that he asked to speak to you, sir."

"We're off to a flying start, I see," Hanrahan said. "He

hasn't even reported in, and I'm already a bastard." And then he changed the subject: "And what have you done about ex-*Oberleutnant* Wagner's problem?"

"We have that under control, if not yet completely solved, sir," Taylor said. "And we have, so to speak, killed two birds with one stone."

"Who was the other bird?" Hanrahan asked. "Not the Craig boy?"

"Yes, sir," Ellis said.

Hanrahan made a "Come on" gesture with his hands.

"I ran him off the rappelling tower," Ellis said. "He's all right."

"You ran him off the rappelling tower?" Hanrahan asked, shaking his head. "At night?"

"I thought a little motivation was in order," Ellis said. "And it worked. He had no sooner hit the ground than he was asking if it was true he would make sergeant when he completes the course."

"I'm glad to hear that," Hanrahan said. "What about Wagner's problems?"

"I told Craig all about TPA.*"

"I don't understand that," Hanrahan said. "What about TPA?"

"I told him I would have his first sergeant approve TPA to jump school at Benning for him and Wagner. That means they would both get eight cents a mile and ration money in lieu of a plane ticket voucher and a meal ticket. Craig doesn't give a damn about the money, but that's not only a lot of money to Wagner, but he gets to take his sister along free. And without it looking like charity."

"He doesn't have a car, does he?" General Hanrahan asked.

"Private Craig is presently with the proprietor of Bragg Boulevard Motors," Ellis said, "who, after Sergeant Major Taylor telephoned him, was kind enough to drive out here to demonstrate a creampuff Volkswagen he happened to have for sale."

"You know this guy, Taylor?"

"Yes, sir. He retired out of here. I did a tour with him with the Seventh Group in Bavaria."

*Travel by private automobile.

"And will this creampuff Volkswagen make it to Benning?" Hanrahan asked.

"It went through Post Inspection a week before he took it on trade," Taylor said. "And I told him it had to make it to Benning and back."

"Well, that solves that," Hanrahan said. "I gather that Private Craig did not give you the urge to knock his teeth down his throat?"

"I think he's a good kid," Ellis said. "I had to pull the story of what happened to him out like a wisdom tooth, but once he told me, I believed him. The sergeant was going to knock him around for the hell of it, and he picked on the wrong guy. I knew a sergeant like that once."

"And did you break his jaw?" Hanrahan asked.

"I think he has since been very careful about who he calls a 'greasy spic,'" Ellis said.

"Well, to repeat," Hanrahan said, "another of life's little problems solved."

"There is one small problem, General," Taylor said.

"Which is?"

"Post Finance won't pay TPA and ration money in advance."

"Why not?"

"They say it's a post regulation: They've had bad experience with people getting the advance and then spending it on something else. I also think they don't like to pay it in advance because the advance is an estimate, and they have to do more paperwork when the travel is completed."

"You talked to the finance sergeant?" Hanrahan asked. Taylor nodded. "And the finance officer?"

"One of the assistants," Taylor said. "A major."

With one hand Hanrahan reached for his telephone and pulled it to him; with the other he opened his desk drawer for the post telephone directory.

"Six Two One One Nine," Taylor said.

Hanrahan dialed 62-119 and told the sergeant who answered that he was General Hanrahan, and if the finance officer wasn't tied up, he would like a word with him.

A clever sergeant first class from Group Signal had rigged General Hanrahan's telephone with an amplifier and a speaker, so that both ends of a telephone conversation could be heard all over his office when he threw the switch. He threw the switch.

"Good afternoon, General. How may I be of service?"

"Colonel, I know you're a busy man, and I hate to bother you," Hanrahan said.

"No bother at all, sir. How can I be of help?"

"You could save your time and mine, Colonel, if you could manage to convince your sergeant that when my sergeant major calls over there, he presumes that he's calling for me."

"Is there some sort of problem, General?"

"I don't know the details, because I don't want to take the time to learn them," Hanrahan said. "What I do know is that your sergeant told my sergeant major that something my sergeant major wants done—which is to say, something I want done—can't be done because it's against post regulations."

"I wish I had the details, sir, I could make a more intelligent response."

"I don't think you have the time, Colonel, any more than I do, to concern yourself with the details. You and I both know that post regulations concerning finance don't apply to the Special Warfare Center, that in effect you are my finance officer and thus charged with providing what finance services army regulations and I require."

"Yes, sir," the finance officer said.

"So far I have found those services perfectly adequate, Colonel," Hanrahan said.

"General, I'm sure this is a simple misunderstanding."

"On the part of your sergeant, you mean?"

"Yes, sir."

"Well, I have every confidence that you'll be able to straighten out any misunderstandings he has by the time my sergeant major calls back, and that hereafter neither you nor I will have to concern ourselves with the petty details of getting a couple of enlisted men a travel advance."

"Yes, sir," the finance officer said. "Thank you, General, for bringing this to my attention."

"If there's anything the Special Warfare Center can ever do for you, Colonel, give a holler."

"Thank you very much, General."

"Good afternoon, Colonel," Hanrahan said, and hung up.

"Wipe the smile off your face, Taylor," Hanrahan said. "You should have been able to handle that yourself."

"Sir," Taylor said, "I was just marveling at what an amazing difference one little word makes."

"What word?"

"'General,'" Taylor said.

Hanrahan considered that a moment. "You have been reading my mind, again, as a good sergeant major should," Hanrahan said. "Anything else?"

"One thing, sir. About the beer for the mess halls?" Taylor said.

"What's the problem there?"

"Sir, we just got the check from the PX. It's beer-bust time. I was about to suggest that instead of buying beer to celebrate your promotion, you might consider a cow roast."

"A what?"

"There's a couple of guys, Mexes—"

"Mexican-Americans, if you please, Sergeant Major," Ellis said. "Or we minority-group members will rise in rebellion."

"There's a couple of *Texans*," Taylor said, "in Dog Company who get whole cows and roast them over fires. We can't use the PX money for that—we have to spend that through the PX—but if the general was willing to spring for a couple of cows—"

"The word, I believe, is 'steers,'" Hanrahan said.

"—then we could use the PX check to buy beer, beans, and whatever else goes with it."

"Go ahead," Hanrahan said. "That seems like a good idea. You want the money now?"

"I'll get a bill, sir."

"Could I come?"

"Yes, sir, of course. I thought Sunday afternoon?"

"Fine," Hanrahan said.

"I'll get the word out, sir," Taylor said.

"That's it?" Hanrahan asked.

"Yes, sir," they chorused.

"You done good, you two," Hanrahan said. "Why does that worry me?"

They saluted and left the office.

They were both pleased with themselves. Lieutenant Ellis

had got Lowell's cousin off on the right foot and handled the problem of Wagner's poverty as neatly as it could have been done.

And by recruiting the two Mexes in Dog Company to roast their cows, Sergeant Major Taylor had frustrated General Hanrahan's foolish intention to spend a lot more money than he could afford by buying every sonofabitch in a green hat two beers. The Mexes would roast free (they normally charged $200) two cows and fix the other food, and Hanrahan would not have to cash in any war bonds or float a loan at the bank in order to throw a party for his troops to celebrate his promotion. Nor would he ever suspect what had happened.

These kinds of things, they believed, were what aides-de-camp and sergeants major were supposed to do.

(Four)
The Officer's Mess
Subic Bay Naval Station
Commonwealth of the Philippines
1730 Hours, 24 December 1961

If he stayed at the bar, Major Philip Sheridan Parker IV thought, he would certainly get drunk. He had just finished a twelve-minute telephone call with his family. He would have talked a great deal longer, even at $3.90 per minute, but from where he sat scrunched down in a phone booth, he was looking directly at a poster reminding one and all: OTHERS ARE WAITING!

Others were indeed waiting. All the army personnel on the *Card*, as well as most of her crew, had come ashore and headed for telephones. The lines were tied up. He had placed the call at 1445, and it hadn't come in until 1715. He had spent the time reading even more ancient copies of *Time, Life,* and *National Geographic* than were available on the carrier.

For no particular reason he chuckled and said "Jesus!"

"What did you say, Phil?" Major Jack Walsh asked.

"What I was thinking was that if I stay here, I am going to get drunk."

"Funny, that thought ran through my mind too," Walsh said, and signaled to the bartender for drinks. "Merry Christmas, Major Parker."

"I don't really want that, Jack," Phil said.

"When in Rome..." Walsh said. "The navy lives well, don't they?"

"Yes, indeed," Parker agreed. The club was elegant and luxurious. "I guess the reasoning is that they don't get to come on land very often. I don't like the navy."

"Try to keep it a secret until we get where we're going, will you?" Walsh kidded. "We have to get back on that thing."

"I meant, I don't think I'd like to be a sailor."

"I don't know," Walsh said. "They certainly treat their officers better than we get treated."

"There has be a reason for that," Parker said. "And I don't think it's the milk of human kindness."

"I don't think I would want to be a navy enlisted man," Walsh said thoughtfully. "Did you see the troop quarters?"

"I understand that compared to smaller boats—*ships*—these are the height of luxury," Parker said.

"I heard that," Walsh said.

"What I was really thinking a while back—while I was waiting for the damned call to go through—is that, Civil War aside, this is one of the few places where we really got our ass whipped. The Japs took this away from us."

"What's that got to do with the Civil War?"

"Both sides were American in the Civil War, Jack," Parker said. "Hadn't you heard?"

"Oh," Walsh said.

"Somebody, some soldier like us," Parker said, "had to blow this place up so the Japs couldn't use it, then wait around to be locked up. And not that long ago—twenty years."

"You're really full of the old Christmas spirit, aren't you?" Walsh asked. "Any other cheerful yuletide thoughts?"

"I'm going back to the ship before I do get full of Christmas spirit," Parker said. "You coming?"

"You haven't drunk your drink," Walsh said.

"You drink it. If I do, I will try to run them out of booze," Parker said, and pushed himself off the stool.

He walked to the wharf, where a boat was waiting to ferry people out to the USNS *Card*, which sat, brilliantly lit up, out in the harbor. Even at that distance, it was enormous. Parker had spent a lot of time roaming around the ship (when he was stopped by sailors and asked if they could be of help—translation: What the hell are you doing down here, Mac?—he pretended that he hadn't seen the signs restricting access to authorized personnel). It was so big as to be incomprehensible. If sailors thought differently than soldiers, that was understandable. They lived in different worlds.

The boat—it was called a barge—that carried him out to the USNS *Card* was divided into sections. In the back—aft—there was a cabin with plastic upholstered seats for officers. Up front—forward—exposed to the elements, there were wooden benches for sailors. Chief petty officers, the navy equivalent of army master sergeants, rode standing up in the back rather than up front with the other sailors. When they reached the ships, the officers would get off first, then the chief petty officers, then the sailors.

The navy was heavy with tradition, and by and large, Parker decided, it was a good thing. The army had little tradition, and Army Aviation and Special Forces had none that he could see. On the other hand his grandfather had retired as a full bull colonel, after command of a regiment, and it wasn't until after War II that the navy had finally allowed colored sailors to be more than mess stewards.

The army had an officer of the day, one of the warrant officer pilots, standing at the head of the ladder up the side. The ladder didn't reach all the way up the flight deck, only to a door on the hangar deck.

"You're back early, Major," the warrant said to him, tossing a casual salute and checking his name off on a clipboard roster.

"It was either come back now or come back later and be hoisted aboard in a sling," Parker said.

"I get off at 0600," the warrant said. "And then I have shore leave. What sort of trouble do you think I can get myself into from six o'clock on Christmas morning until 1600?"

"I'm sure you'll think of something," Parker said.

He went to the flight deck. A marine guard stopped him at the door. Because there had been several incidents of sailors taking souvenirs from the army aircraft (the instrument panel eight-day Waltham clocks were popular), and after a heated argument with the *Card*'s civilian captain, it had been decreed that only personnel with business with army airplanes would be allowed on the flight deck. There was a list of fifteen officers who were authorized to visit their airplanes whenever they wanted, and the marine guard was doing his duty. He not only checked to see that Major Parker's name was on the list, but insisted on checking Parker's ID card.

A difference in discipline, Parker thought. The marine guard was a black guy, and there was no question whatever in Parker's mind that the black marines were very much aware that there were four black army officers, one major, one captain, and two warrants. The marine guard knew that the very large black man with the major's leaves standing in the door was Major P. S. Parker. An army guard, black or white or brown, would have passed him without question. Not the marine. The marine did exactly what he was told to do.

Was this better, Parker wondered, or did it tend to make enlisted men hesitate to make their own decisions? There was an old army saw that said when in doubt, attack. He wondered if navy and marine enlisted men would attack when in doubt, or just stand there waiting for orders.

He made his way through the closely parked airplanes and helicopters to the bow of the ship, careful not to trip over the cables that tied the aircraft to the deck. The door in the side of the fuselage of a Piasecki H-21D was slightly ajar.

Was the ship's crew collecting souvenirs again? Or had it just been left ajar after the last of the twice-daily inspections? He opened it far enough so that it would close when he slammed it, then changed his mind and climbed aboard.

He made his way up the steeply slanting floor to the cockpit, and he started to slip into the pilot's seat. There was a small puddle of water on the deck, and he slipped on it, falling hard but harmlessly into the seat. The on-deck aircraft were hosed down twice a day with a fresh-water spray to keep the salt water off them, and this bird apparently leaked. Although he didn't think any real harm in that, he thought he would mention it to the maintenance chief in the morning.

This was his world, the cockpit of a chopper, and it was somehow comforting to sit where he was sitting. He sat there for ten minutes, and then got up and carefully made his way back onto the deck. He went back inside the ship and made his way to the wardroom and had a cup of coffee and two sugar-coated doughnuts. Finally he went to his stateroom.

He would not be able to sleep yet, he thought, so he opened the little safe built into the wall of the cabin and took out a report to study it.

He had taken it out for a very strange reason. He wanted to look at the signature block again. The report had been prepared eight months before, and Major Parker had been provided with only part of it: two copies, classifed Secret, of Inclosure 18. Inclosure 18 was entitled "An Appraisal of Special Aviation Requirements in the Event of the Deployment of Special Forces in the Highlands." In the signature block was "Craig W. Lowell, Major, Armor."

The report was probably very good, accurate, and thorough, for Lowell was very good at that sort of thing. But that wasn't the reason Phil Parker had taken it out. The truth of the matter was that he was lonely and homesick and even a little afraid, and Craig's signature in front of him made him feel a little less lonely, homesick, and afraid.

He wondered where Craig was spending Christmas Eve.

Between the silken thighs of some long-legged wench who would reek of expensive French perfume, he concluded.

That thought cheered him. He put the report back in the safe and went back to the wardroom. There was a warrant officer, a weird redheaded guy who hung around there, always looking for somebody to play chess. Playing chess seemed like a very good way to pass the evening.

IX

(One)
An Lac Shi
Kontum Province
Republic of South Vietnam
2325 Hours, 24 December 1961

For almost two years Captain Van Lee Duc, Commanding the Ninth Company, Fifty-third Regiment, People's Liberation Army, had had a working relationship with Song Lee Do, Mayor of An Lac Shi, a middle-sized village eleven miles west of Kontum.

Song Lee Do had ensured that his constituents had paid their taxes to the Provisional Government of the People's Liberation Army. The taxes were one bag in five of the village's rice stocks. These stocks included not only what the village's farmers had raised themselves but also what had come from the Agency for International Development in hundred-pound bags painted with the legend PRODUCT OF LOUISIANA, USA. Below the legend was the picture of a pair of hands shaking in partnership.

Similarly, the village of An Lac Shi, through the agency of

200

Mayor Song Lee Do, had contributed one pig in five to the cause of National Liberation; one chicken in five; one bunch of carrots in five; one head of cabbage in five; and so on. The burden had not been intolerable, Captain Van Lee Duc believed. It was the duty of every Vietnamese to make some sacrifice to the cause of national liberation. What he was asking of An Lac Shi was far less than other commanders were asking of other mayors of other similarly situated villages.

He had not, for example, demanded that cattle in the village be slaughtered to provide sustenance for his men. He agreed with the mayor that not only were the cattle necessary for the tilling of the rice paddies (which would make their slaughter the same thing as eating the seed rice), but that it would be wasteful. Without refrigeration, or other means of preserving the meat, a substantial portion of it would spoil and do no one any good.

Song Lee Do had also done as much as could be expected of any man in his position to explain to his villagers the necessity of cooperating with the provisional government. He had told them that when the People's Liberation Army had completed its task, they would no longer be required to pay taxes to the regime in Saigon. The fruits of their hard labor would no longer be taken from them to enrich the politicians and generals. When Vietnam was free, taxes would be returned to the people in the form of paved roads, so that shipping of their produce to Kontum would be easier; and to provide schools, medical care, and all the other good things that would come to the people once all Vietnam had become Socialist.

Song Lee Do had repeated to his people what Captain Van Lee Duc had told him: "The root of all of Vietnam's problems was colonialism. Colonialism put the property of the people in the hands of outsiders, who diverted the fruits of the peasants' and workers' labors from the good of the peasants and workers into their own pockets.

"When the French left, there remained evil people in Saigon, *Vietnamese* people, who had not seen to it that the workers and peasants got what was theirs, but who had instead simply assumed the roles of colonial, capitalist overseers themselves. They had been corrupted, infected, as animals or a crop sometimes became infected, and it was going to be necessary to remove these infections ruthlessly from the body of Vietnam in the same way it was necessary to sometimes plow under a bad crop, or use acid on an infection on the body of an animal.

"These corrupt Vietnamese would be killed, and what they had stolen from the people returned to the people."

That is what Number Nine Company of the Fifty-third Regiment of the People's Liberation Army was doing in the vicinity of An Lac Shi. And it was clearly not only the duty of the people of An Lac Shi, but in their own interest, to help Number Nine Company in any way they could.

Captain Van Lee Duc believed that Song Lee Do understood all this, because he cooperated. Not only were taxes paid when due, but the people of An Lac Shi gave beyond what he had demanded of them. When he came to collect the taxes, for instance, the villagers almost always had a meal for him and his men—and sometimes wine. They were very helpful in other ways, too, like digging tunnels in which rice and other food could be hidden from the eyes of the Saigon regime's officials.

And they sent their children running into the jungle to find one of Captain Van Lee Duc's men to tell him when another shipment for the Agency for International Development was supposed to arrive.

That truck could be then intercepted by Number Nine Company, the foodstuffs and whatever else they carried instantly converted to the use of the People's Liberation Army, the truck destroyed, and the soldiers of the Saigon regime's puppets killed.

The Saigon regime would then waste a good deal of time, money, and effort sending soldiers in jeeps and trucks and armored cars looking for Captain Van Lee Duc's soldiers. They would not find them. They would vent their anger at not finding them on the people, and would probably beat up half a dozen young men of the village.

Young men who had been beaten by soldiers of the Saigon regime often joined the People's Liberation Army.

Captain Van Lee Duc would not attack the soldiers sent to look for him. Nor would he attack the column of troops sent to guard the load of foodstuffs that would invariably be sent to replace the loads lost. The People's Liberation Army would get one-fifth of what was successfully delivered anyway. And if he was too greedy, the Saigon regime would decide that it was too risky to send any supplies at all.

He would probably send two or three soldiers to take a few shots at the convoy on its way back to Kontum. If that was done properly, a few Saigon soldiers would be killed or wounded, and their mates would waste time and ammunition shooting in all directions, long after his men were safely out of the way.

There was trouble now in An Lac Shi—not much, nothing that Captain Van Lee Duc could not handle, but trouble that had to be nipped in the bud before it took roots.

The priest of the Blessed Heart of Jesus Roman Catholic Church, Father Lo Patrick Sho, who had heretofore only concerned himself with the spiritual welfare of his flock, was now starting to interfere in the political affairs of the village. The Saigon regime had come to An Lac Shi three weeks before in three jeeps. One of the jeeps carried an American. The American wore a green beret, and he said that he would be coming back to the village on a regular schedule. The first thing he was going to do, he said, would be to treat the injured and sick. He would also arrange for the very sick to be taken to Kontum to the hospital. There would be no charge for his services, and he didn't even ask questions about units of the People's Liberation Army that might be in the area.

The villagers of An Lac Shi, of course, did not rush to get the free medical services. The first time the American Green Beret came to the village, he just sat there with Mayor Song Lee Do all afternoon, trying to make conversation in French. No villager went near him. Nor did a villager go near him on his second visit, three days later.

But the third time he came to An Lac Shi, Father Lo Patrick Sho brought a woman with a sick baby to see him. The baby had a very high fever, and the mother was willing to try anything, even an American soldier in a green beret.

The American gave the baby an injection, and gave the mother some other medicine in little bottles. After the American had gone away, Father Lo Patrick Sho made the mother give her baby the medicine. The baby lost its fever, stopped throwing up, and started suckling. The next time the American came, Father Lo Patrick Sho had two people for him to see, an old man whose jaw was large with a bad tooth, and a young woman who had an infection between her legs.

Captain Van Lee Duc spoke with Mayor Song Lee Do. He told him that he did not want the villagers to go to the American for help. This was not to the advantage of the People's Liberation Army, but more important, the pills and injections the American was giving them were really bad drugs, worse even than heroin, which would destroy their minds and make them slaves to the Saigon regime.

Mayor Song Lee Do did what Captain Van Lee Duc asked him to do, but the priest told the people just the opposite. Father Lo Patrick Sho said that the American was offering them help they could get nowhere else. The injections were not bad. The proof of that was the baby was now well. Consequently he was going to let the American use a room in the Blessed Heart of Jesus R.C. Church and was going to fix it up for him by whitewashing the walls and giving him a desk, a table, and some chairs.

Captain Van Lee Duc then went to see the priest personally. He didn't try to tell the priest that the American Green Beret was injecting a bad drug, because the priest was an educated man and knew better. But he told him that the real reason the American was in An Lac Shi was not to help the people, but to gain information about the People's Liberation Army, so that the Saigon regime could send soldiers and tanks and airplanes. He obviously could not permit that or anything else that would keep the People's Liberation Army from accomplishing its purpose.

Father Lo Patrick Sho told him that he knew nothing about politics, and wanted to know nothing about politics. He was the parish priest and it was his duty to get help for his parishioners from wherever he could. Before he had made the room available to the American, he went on to say, he had asked his bishop, who had said that as long as he did not take sides in the unpleasantness between the Saigon regime and the People's Liberation Army, he should do anything he felt would help his people.

When the people of the Blessed Heart of Jesus parish went to the church for midnight mass on Christmas Eve, they found Father Lo Patrick Sho, Mayor Song Lee Do, and four altar boys in the sanctuary between the communion rail and the altar.

The altar boys had been shot in the ear.

Father Lo Patrick Sho and Mayor Song Lee Do had had their throats cut and then had been emasculated.

Captain Van Lee Duc regretted the necessity of ordering that action, but he was under orders, too, and Colonel Hon Kwan of the Fifty-third Regiment had told him that nothing could be permitted to interfere with the ruthless rooting out of opposition by the People's Liberation Army.

(Two)
204 Wallingford Road
Swarthmore, Pennsylvania
1930 Hours, 24 December 1961

The chiming of the doorbell annoyed the hell out of Edward Eaglebury, Sr. Who the fuck would come calling on Christmas Eve without telephoning?

As he pushed himself out of his chair to take care of the damn thing, he decided that it was probably somebody collecting for some damned do-gooder cause. Starving Ethiopian Orphans or something. There had been a piece in the *Bulletin* about that. The fund raisers had found that people were extraordinarily generous on Christmas Eve, and teams of volunteer do-gooders were giving up their Christmas Eve to make the collecting rounds.

Edward Eaglebury, Sr., had nothing against charity, but he thought that it was outrageous that fund raisers should be working on Christmas Eve. He would give whomever the hell it was a dollar and wish him a quick Merry Christmas and close the door in his face.

Suzanne and the kids were with them tonight. Christmas Day they would go to her family. That meant that as soon as they finished trimming the tree, they would be exchanging gifts tonight instead of Christmas morning, as was the Eaglebury custom. Except for watching the kids when they got their presents, the truth was that Edward Eaglebury, Sr., didn't give a damn about Christmas.

And now some sonofabitch was at the door with his hand out.

It was a vaguely familiar young man.

Someone who was chasing Dianne and who was not willing to give up the chase simply because of a little thing like Christmas Eve. Why the hell wasn't the fucker home with his own family?

"Yes?" Edward Eaglebury, Sr., asked with less edge in his voice than he felt.

"Good evening, Mr. Eaglebury," the young man said. "Merry Christmas, sir."

"Merry Christmas to you," Mr. Eaglebury said. "What can I do for you?"

"I'd hoped to see Dianne, sir," the young man said.

"I don't wish to be rude, young man," Mr. Eaglebury said, "but we're celebrating Christmas Eve. It's—I don't know how to say it—just family."

"Oh," the young man said, obviously disappointed. "I'm sorry to have intruded, sir. I wonder if you would give her this?"

He thrust a small, Christmas-wrapped package at him.

Damn! If he knows her well enough to give her a present, she'd probably bought one for him. And I will be doing the wrong thing by sending him away.

"Just a moment," Edward Eaglebury, Sr., said. "I'll get her."

He felt something like Scrooge, shutting the door and leaving the kid standing in the cold on the porch, but he didn't want him inside, didn't want him intruding.

"One of your admirers is on the porch," he announced when he went into the living room.

"One of my what?" Dianne asked.

"You left him standing on the porch on Christmas Eve?" his wife asked.

He elected to respond to his daughter: "A young man bearing a gift," he said. "I forget his name."

Dianne walked to the door.

She'll be gone, too, in three or four years, Edward Eaglebury thought. *The boys are already after her. And then there will be just two of us in this house.*

She knew this one, too. She gave a little yelp when she saw him through the glass beside the door, and then she shouted his name: "Tom!" He could not recall any one of her boyfriends being named Tom.

She brought the kid into the living room. He should have known that she would do something like that.

"Everybody but Daddy remembers Tom, don't they?" Dianne asked.

"Of course," his wife said.

Suzanne, who had been on her knees by a box of Christmas-tree ornaments, scrambled to her feet. There was surprise and pleasure on her face.

"Oh, Tom!" she said. "How nice to see you!"

She went quickly to him, grabbed his arms and kissed his cheek.

Who the hell is he?

"Please forgive my husband, Lieutenant Ellis," his wife said, "when he is into the Christmas cheer, he turns into Scrooge. I apologize for his leaving you standing in the cold."

She went to him and gave him a hug.

My God, he's the young officer who was with Eddie! The one who brought his body back. What does he want here?

The answer to that was self-evident: Dianne. How the hell had he had time to get to know her? He wasn't here more than five, six hours all told. And now he shows up on Christmas Eve with a present for her.

"Oh, damn!" Dianne said when Ellis handed her the present. "I mailed you yours."

"What are you doing up in this neck of the woods?" Suzanne asked.

"My mother lives in New York," Tom said. "I'm on my way there now. I just stopped in to wish Dianne and all of you Merry Christmas."

"Well, I'm glad you did," Dianne's mother said. "Dianne, get him a glass of eggnog."

"You're going on to New York . . . City? . . . Tonight?" Suzanne asked.

"Yes," Tom Ellis said.

"And you drove from North Carolina?" she asked.

He nodded.

"You've apparently been seeing Dianne at Duke?" Mr. Eaglebury asked.

"Yes, sir," Tom said.

"He came there with an 'A' Team and blew up the campus," Dianne said. "They made a leak in the water tower."

"That's what you're doing, Tom?" Mr. Eaglebury asked. "Training young people? Like you trained Ed?"

"No, sir," Ellis said, and then thought it over. "No, sir, twice. Commander Eaglebury and I trained together. I was training the people I had at Duke. And I'm not doing that anymore."

"He's General Hanrahan's aide," Dianne said proudly as she handed him a cup of eggnog. "Daddy made that. Be careful."

"General Hanrahan?" Mr. Eaglebury asked. "Is he the fellow who was here for the funeral?"

"Yes, sir," Tom said. "He was promoted."

"If you're driving onto New York," Mrs. Eaglebury said, "that egg nog may not be such a good idea. Do you have to be there tonight? Could you stay over? We have more than enough room."

The fucker's going to accept. He's actually going to intrude on our family Christmas.

"I really have to go," Tom refused politely. "But thank you anyway."

"Anytime you're here, Tom," Mrs. Eaglebury said, "we'd love to have you."

"Thank you very much," he said. "I'll take a rain check."

"Are you hungry?" Dianne asked.

He shook his head.

"Don't be bashful, Tom," Mrs. Eaglebury said. "We have more food than we know what to do with."

"There was a McDonald's when I came off the interstate," he said. "I had coffee and a whatever they call the big one."

"That's indecent on Christmas Eve," Suzanne said. "You should have waited until you got here."

"I thought it would be quicker," Tom said. "I'm a little pressed for time." He looked at his watch. "I just wanted to say Merry Christmas."

You just wanted to see Dianne. Who do you think you're kidding?

"I'll walk you to your car," Dianne said.

"You'll catch your death of cold," Mr. Eaglebury said.

"Ed!" Mrs. Eaglebury said.

"Ed, what?"

"Ed, mind your own damned business," she said.

"It was nice to see you all," Tom said, and went to Suzanne and Mrs. Eaglebury, who kissed his cheek. He picked up Little Ed.

"He looks like the commander," he said.

"Doesn't he?" Suzanne agreed.

That's not really a compliment; you really didn't have to say that.

He shook Mr. Eaglebury's hand.

"It was nice to see you," Mr. Eaglebury said dutifully. "Sure you can't stay over?"

"Thank you, no, sir," Tom said.

A minute later Edward Eaglebury, Sr., pushed aside the curtain.

"He's kissing her," he announced.

"No!" Suzanne said in mock horror.

"I told you before," his wife said, "Ed, mind your own damned business."

"She's nineteen years old, she is my business."

"He's a very nice boy," Mrs. Eaglebury said.

"You think so?" he said. "I was wondering what she saw in him. He's sort of a runt, actually. And—"

"I know what she sees in him, Dad," Suzanne said. "What I saw in Ed. There's something special about people like that, people who do what they do."

"You're not suggesting there's anything serious going on between them, are you?"

"No, I think he came all the way out here because he had nothing better to do on Christmas Eve," Suzanne said. "Didn't you see the way she looked at him?"

"No," he said flatly. "I didn't see anything like that at all."

"What's wrong with him?" his wife asked. "He's nice, and he's pleasant, and he already has a career."

"Did I say anything was wrong with him?"

He looked out the window again. Ellis still hadn't left. He was still kissing Dianne.

"If she doesn't come in here in a minute, I'm going out and get her," he said.

"You'll do no such thing!" his wife said.

"What's wrong with him, Dad?" Suzanne said.

"I told Mother, there's nothing wrong with him," he said.

What's wrong with him is what you said, Suzanne. There's something special about people like that. You saw it in Ed, and you married him, and now you're a thirty-year-old widow with two kids. I'll see Dianne make the same mistake over my dead body.

(Three)

Tom Ellis parked the Jaguar on the Jersey side of the Lincoln Tunnel and took the bus to the Port Authority Bus Terminal on Forty-first Street. If he took the Jaguar home, he could count on losing the wheels and tires, and possibly the whole car. But it was Christmas Eve, and perhaps he was being too cynical. Perhaps, full of joyous yuletide season spirit and goodwill, the punks would only run a knife blade through the roof and down the fenders.

He had trouble with the cabbie. The cabbie said there was no way he was going "up there."

"You either take me 'up there' or down to the cop on the corner," Tom said. "The law says you have to take me."

"It's Christmas Eve, for Christ's sake! Give me a break!"

"I don't want to ride the subway up there on Christmas Eve," Tom said. "Give *me* a break. Do we go talk to the cop, or what?"

"Sonofabitch!" the cabbie said. "On Christmas Eve!"

But he put the hack in gear and did a U-turn and headed uptown.

Cars lined both sides of the street in front of the three-story brownstones in Spanish Harlem. The cabbie drove past the number Tom had given him and stopped instead at the far corner, before the plate-glass windows of a bar and grill. The cabbie was afraid that if he stopped where he was supposed to on the dark street, drug-soaked spics with flip-blade knives or guns would appear out of the darkness and relieve him of both his money and his life.

Tom took all the bills out of his wallet, paid the cabbie, and put the rest of the bills in his sock. Then he got out of the cab and started walking down the street to his mother's apartment. He was carrying a small blue canvas bag, the kind people carry gym clothes in. The cab was gone before he had taken a dozen steps.

He had gone twenty-five yards when he heard the footsteps behind him.

"Excuse me, sir," a voice asked with exaggerated courtesy.

Tom stopped and turned.

There were three of them. A tall, thin one with sunken eyes, a stocky one who looked nervous, and a little, wiry one, who looked both vaguely familiar and dangerous.

"Merry Christmas, sir," the tall thin one said. He was wearing a nylon zipper jacket and a too-small hat with the brim turned down all around. He was probably freezing his ass, Tom thought.

When Tom didn't reply, the tall thin one said, "You got a match, sir?"

Tom's hand came out of his pocket. There was a click as his switchblade opened.

"No, but if you want that cigarette cut in half, I'll be happy to do that for you," he said in Spanish.

Two switchblades and a length of chain were produced.

"You are not very friendly," the tall thin one said.

"No, I am not," Tom said.

"What have you got in the bag?"

"Let me tell you something, my friend," Tom said. "What I have in the bag is none of your business."

"What are you doing in this neighborhood?"

"My mother lives in 333," Tom said, "with her husband the policeman."

"I know this man," the little wiry one said. "He lived here."

"Then you know of my mother's husband the policeman," Tom said.

"He's not a policeman, he is a Transit Authority cop."

"But he has a gun, and if he should hear screaming, as if someone had their belly slit open, he would come with his gun."

"Who would have their belly slit?" the little wiry one asked.

"You," Tom said. "Maybe you and me, but you for sure, because you know who I am, and it is not nice to rob your neighbors on Christmas Eve."

The intentions and tactical capability of the enemy were being evaluated, Tom thought. The enemy was not what he at first appeared, a white alien, sure to be unarmed and unsure of himself on foreign territory. They had challenged instead an armed former native, who could be presumed to know the territory and who might not be worth the trouble that attempting to relieve him of his goods and money might provoke.

"We don't rob our neighbors," the tall thin one said, having on due deliberation reached his decision. "We just don't like strange people on our turf, you understand."

"I am a neutral passing through," Tom said.

"Yeah," the tall thin one said. "You know how it is, my man."

"Say Merry Christmas to your mother," the little wiry one said.

They turned and walked away with a swagger.

Tom's stomach hurt, and he was aware of a chill, clammy sweat. He folded the switchblade against his leg and put it back in his pocket, and walked down the street to 333.

His mother's husband opened the door. He was a tall and paunchy black man, a Puerto Rican.

"Well," he said in Spanish, "the lieutenant."

He stepped out of the door.

"Hello, Philip," Tom said. "How are you?"

Tom's mother was Philip's second wife. His first wife lived a couple of blocks away with their four children, on sixty percent of what the New York City Transit Authority paid Philip to ride the subways forty hours a week.

Tom's mother was Puerto Rican and white. Or at least, he thought, mostly white. His father had been another Transit Authority policeman, an Irishman, who had started beating up Tom's mother after they had been married long enough to produce him. He was now living in Staten Island with his second wife, an Irishwoman, and their three children. Tom's father saw in Tom shameful proof of the one great big mistake he had made in his life: marrying a spic. Tom had not seen his father in years.

Tom's mother's husband saw in Tom shameful proof that his wife was so dumb that she had married an Anglo. The Anglo, predictably, had thrown her out.

Two days after he had turned eighteen, his father being no longer required to pay child support, Tom had enlisted in the army. The recruiting sergeant had told him the army would send him to cooks and bakers school, where he would learn all there was to know about cooking and baking, so that when he got out of the army, he would have a trade. He also told him that the union had a special rule for veterans, so that he could get into the union.

When he had been at the reception center, they had made him take the Army General Classification Test twice. When they saw the scores he had made on it the first time, they thought it was either a mistake, or that he'd cheated, or that he had just been incredibly lucky just guessing where to put the pencil mark on the test form.

He hadn't understood what that meant then, but when he was in cooks and bakers school at Fort Lee, Virginia (Christ, what a mistake that was!), the company commander had called him in and said that he'd been going over his AGCT scores and that Tom was in Category I, thus qualifying him to apply for OCS. He hadn't really understood what OCS was, and the idea of becoming an officer was incredible, but he figured what the hell, it would get him out of the kitchen.

In OCS at Benning, his tactical officer had called him in and asked whether hs mother was a member of a Spanish Surnamed Hispanic Minority Group, and Tom told him she was. The tactical officer was a good guy, a little guy like Tom, who had explained that the army was leaning over backward to make sure that all the opportunities the army had to offer were made available without regard to race, creed, or national origin. And what that meant, his tac officer said, was that if Tom claimed status as a member of the Hispanic minority group, he could forget getting commissioned in the Quartermaster Corps and counting canteen cups and get a commission in a combat arm: infantry, artillery, or armor. He could also probably get jump school right out of OCS, which meant another $150 a month, and get himself assigned to the Eighty-second Airborne Division.

By then Tom had understood something of the army. If he was commissioned in the Quartermaster Corps, after having graduated from cooks and bakers school, there was a very good chance he would be assigned as an assistant mess officer in some huge consolidated mess, as officer in charge of condiments. He proclaimed himself to be a member of the Hispanic minority group and applied for a commission in infantry, for parachute school, and for initial assignment to the Eighty-second Airborne Division. His requests were favorably acted upon.

The night before Second Lieutenant Thomas Ellis, Infantry, left the parachute school at Fort Benning, Georgia, for the Eighty-second Airborne Division at Fort Bragg, North Carolina, there was a game of chance in the BOQ. Normally, Tom Ellis was a lucky poker player, and far more skilled than his boyish face would suggest. But that night he had lost his ass: all of his money, his watch, his ring, and his MG coupe.

Once he got to Bragg, he would be all right. He would be reimbursed for his Travel by Private Automobile. That and charging his meals at the officers' club would see him through to payday. The problem was how to get from Benning to Bragg. There was only one way: by standing by the side of the highway and sticking up his thumb.

He was quickly picked up by a tanned man in a Cadillac, who told him he was going right through Fayetteville. It's a long drive from Benning to Bragg, and they talked. He told the guy in the Cadillac that he was just out of OCS and jump school and on his way to Bragg. The guy in the Cadillac told him he'd been in the Eighty-second during the war. Tom told him what had happened in the poker game, which explained why he was hitchhiking.

Just outside Fayetteville the guy in the Cadillac pulled into a truck stop and said he would spring for dinner. Then he went to the john, and when he came back he was wearing a uniform with the silver oak leaves of a lieutenant colonel on the epaulets and a bunch of ribbons. It was the first time Tom had ever seen one of the ribbons, an inch and a half of blue with stars on it, but he knew what it was: the Medal of Honor.

Lieutenant Colonel Rudolph G. MacMillan pressed two hundred dollars upon Second Lieutenant Thomas Ellis and told him he wanted it back a hundred a month for the next two months. Colonel Mac said he was going to the Special Warfare School, where Ellis could find him on payday.

Lieutenant Ellis was assigned as a platoon leader in Dog Company, 502nd Parachute Infantry Regiment, with additional duty as mess officer, VD control officer, reenlistment officer, and minority affairs officer. He heard what the Special Warfare School was. It was where they trained the snake eaters. The snake eaters ran around in the jungle, eating snakes, sticking knives in people, and blowing things up. Snake eaters wore green berets, and for that reason were called Green Berets.

There was supposed to be very little chickenshit among the Green Berets, mainly because most of the enlisted men were sergeants, and because of their colonel, an Irishman named Hanrahan. It was also supposed to be very good duty for a junior officer, the catch being that you had to be one hell of an unusual junior officer to get into Special Forces. They did not want second johns right from jump school, but senior lieutenants and captains who had done their troop duty and been overseas, preferably during a war.

Lieutenant Ellis, who did not like being mess officer, VD control officer, reenlistment officer, and minority affairs officer in addition to his basic duty as platoon commander, decided that all Colonel Mac could tell him was no. It wouldn't do any harm to ask, and just as soon as he had Colonel Mac's two hundred bucks, he would go over there to give it to him and see if he could bring up the subject of his becoming a snake eater.

That fell in his lap. The first thing that happened was that when he was hoping to draw a seven to go with his three kings and a seven, he drew another king. The fourth king was worth Colonel Mac's two hundred, a wristwatch, and a substantial down payment on a red Ford convertible.

The second thing that happened was that when he drove the red rag-top Ford over to Smoke Bomb Hill and the Special Warfare Center, he found that Colonel Mac had a small problem on his hands.

As Tom handed him the two hundred, the first question Colonel Mac asked was "You sure you can afford this?"

"Yes, sir."

The second question was "What have they got you doing over there? VD control officer?"

"Yes, sir, and some other things too."

The third question was "You know some spics over there who're looking for a new job?"

"I don't quite understand the question, sir," Ellis said.

"You know what a spic is, don't you, Ellis? Pepper eaters? I've got to find a bunch of them. They have to be jumpers, and they have to speak spic."

Lieutenant Ellis's next reply was in Spanish.

"Where'd you learn to talk spic?" Colonel Mac had asked in surprise.

"Most of us spics speak spic, my colonel," Ellis said. "I was raised in Spanish Harlem. My mother's maiden name was Juanita de Torres."

"Jesus!" Colonel Mac said. "You sure don't look it. No offense, Ellis."

"None taken, sir."

"You want to come over here?"

"*Sí*, my colonel."

"Let's go see the colonel," Colonel Mac said.

The commandant of the Special Warfare Center and School, Colonel Paul T. Hanrahan, had not taken Ellis's word that he spoke Spanish. He had called in a sergeant and told him to find out how well the lieutenant spoke Spanish.

Three minutes later the sergeant reported that Ellis spoke a strange kind of Spanish, almost Castilian, although he was just as fluent in the Puerto Rican dialect.

"We had Spanish nuns in school," Ellis explained.

He had thought that he had a fair chance to be transferred to Special Forces. There was a chance, a good chance, that his company commander would not want to let him go. If his company commander didn't want to let him go, the regimental commander would go along with him. But maybe, Tom had thought, he could plead his case, maybe pull that member-of-Hispanic-minority bullshit and get them to let him go.

He was wrong about that. While he was still in Colonel Hanrahan's office, the colonel had picked up the phone and called the Eighty-second Airborne Division G-1 (Personnel Officer) and told him to cut orders transferring Second Lieutenant Tom Ellis from the 502nd Parachute Infantry Regiment to the Special Warfare Center. Tom moved in a Special Warfare Center BOQ that same afternoon.

Special Warfare had a "personnel priority." Hanrahan had been directed to recruit Spanish-speaking recruits from wherever he could find them. The Deputy Chief of Staff, Personnel, had been privy to President Eisenhower's decision to have the CIA send a force of exiled Cubans back to Cuba to take it back from Castro. Special Forces was to "cooperate" with the CIA in training and equipping the exiled Cubans. When DCSPERS directed Hanrahan to recruit Spanish speaking personnel, he at the same time issued a directive stating that personnel selected by Special Warfare, and who wished to volunteer for Special Forces duty, would immediately be made available for transfer, regardless of any other consideration.

Lieutenant Tom Ellis had not known of the "personnel priority" or of the reasons for it. They hadn't told him they wanted him to take an "A" Team into Cuba by parachute to set up a radio direction finder until he was just about finished with his Special Forces training, two weeks before he was to jump into the hills above the Bahai de Cochinos.

Tom's mother came into the corridor, yelped, and ran to him. While she hugged him, she asked why he hadn't let her know he was coming.

"I didn't know I could get away," Tom said.

He set the canvas bag on the kitchen table, unzipped it, and gave her her Christmas present. It was French perfume from the PX. He knew how much his mother liked perfume.

"I sent your presents off to the army," she said.

"It's all right."

Tom took a second package from the canvas bag and handed it to Philip.

"What's this?" Philip asked. The package was heavier than it looked, and Philip almost dropped it.

"Merry Christmas," Tom said.

"I didn't get you anything," Philip said.

"It's all right."

Philip weighed the heavy package in his hands. Curiosity got the better of him, and he set it down and tore the Christmas wrapping from it.

"What's this?"

"You're always complaining that they make you buy your own ammo to qualify," Tom said. "So I got you some."

The package contained eight boxes of what the army called "Cartridges, pistol, .38 Special, ball, 50 rounds per box."

Philip looked at him.

"They're not hot, Philip," Tom said, knowing what he was thinking.

"Where'd you get them?" Philip asked.

"In the PX," Tom said.

"They just sell these to anybody?" Philip asked. "No wonder every punk on Manhattan Island's got a gun."

"I'm an officer, Philip," Tom said.

He had, in fact, not bought the cartridges in the PX. He had gotten them from the armorer. He had gone there to get the general a couple of boxes of .45s. General Hanrahan liked to shoot the .45 pistol. He had one that was all tuned up, with adjustable sights. Tom had learned from him that cutting a playing card in half with a pistol bullet at twenty-five feet wasn't really so awesome if you considered that the .45 bullet was nearly a half an inch in diameter, which meant that if you came within an inch of the card, you hit it.

He had seen the .38s on the steel shelves in the armory, and thought of Philip bitching about having to buy his own ammo every six months to qualify with his service revolver. He thought that if he had to do what Philip did to make a living, he would be out on the range, practicing every spare moment, not bitching about having to qualify every six months and pay for his own ammo.

"What's with the .38s?" Tom had asked the warrant officer armorer.

"You want some? Help yourself, Lieutenant."

"Are they on the books?"

"Same as the .45s," the warrant had told him. "'Available for informal practice.' I got a ton of it. Nobody wants to shoot a .38."

"My stepfather's a cop in New York," Tom said. "They make them buy their own for practice and qualification."

"Lieutenant, if you wanted some of that .38, I don't think anybody would say a thing if you took it home to practice with your stepfather."

"Give me a couple of boxes, then."

"Couple, shit. You can't do any practicing with a lousy couple of boxes."

He had handed Tom as much as he could pick up with two hands—eight boxes.

Philip had one of the boxes open and was looking at one of the cartridges.

"I can't use this; it's armor-piercing," he said, holding up the cartridge, indicating the bullet, which was metal-plated. Philip seemed pleased, Tom thought, that he had found an excuse to refuse the gift.

"That's not armor-piercing," Tom said. "That's what they call 'gilding metal.' Like the .45."

"You're an expert on ammunition now, Lieutenant?"

"I know the difference between armor-piercing and ball," Tom said.

"And I know armor-piercing when I see it," Philip said.

"Okay, so it's armor-piercing. Go shoot up a tank with it."

He wasn't inside the door ten minutes, and they were at it already.

"I'm glad you're here," his mother said, obviously hoping to end the argument before it got out of hand. "Philip is going to 116th Street to see his children, so we can have a nice talk."

His stepfather wasn't determined to have a fight tonight. Sometimes he was.

"I was about to leave when you came," Philip said. "I got to see my kids, take them their presents, you understand?"

"Sure," Tom said.

He told himself there were a number of reasons why Philip didn't like him. For one thing, Tom was white. For another, Philip must know that he didn't make nearly as much money as a lieutenant on jump pay in the army did.

Screw it. What difference did it make?

Tom had an amusing thought. Philip really believed the .38 was armor-piercing. He was not going to take Tom's word that it was not. What he would more than likely do was big-deal it with the other cops, tell them he'd come into some army armor-piercing ammunition, and pass it out six rounds at a time. All over the subway system of the City of New York there would be cops carrying pistols loaded with what they thought was armor-piercing ammunition.

He had to get out of here, Tom realized. He had to come because it was Christmas and it was his mother. And he had to get out of here because she was his mother.

After Philip left, his mother told him about work. She worked downtown, off Third Avenue, in a loft where they sewed dresses. She had started years ago with the same firm, and she was now sort of a supervisor. What that meant was that she spoke both Spanish and English: The seamstresses were newcomers from Puerto Rico who spoke only Spanish, and Mr. Feldstein and the cutters and fitters didn't speak Spanish. So she told the Puerto Rican women what was expected of them.

Tom listened politely, not because he gave a damn about Field Fashions, but because if his mother wasn't talking about work, she would have nothing to talk about. She liked her job, which was a good thing, since sixty percent of Philip's pay went for child support, and they needed the money. She was happy married to Philip, and he was glad about that too.

But even if she was his mother, he didn't belong here. And just as obviously he didn't belong in Swarthmore either. The only place left was the army. He belonged to the army.

When Philip came back, just before one (he had more than likely taken his kids to midnight mass), Tom left. Philip called a cab for him so that he wouldn't have to walk the streets, trying to catch one. Philip told the cab company he was Officer Francissa. Otherwise the dispatcher wouldn't have sent a cab to that address. When the cab came, Tom asked him how much he would charge to take him to the other side of the George Washington Bridge, so that he wouldn't have to go through the bus terminal.

Cabdrivers had the right to refuse out-of-the-city fares, and even after Tom showed him his AGO card, this one refused to take him to the car park in Jersey.

He rode the bus back across the Hudson, brushed the snow off the Jaguar's windshield, and got the engine going. He would stop at the first motel he came to. Then, in the morning, he'd drive straight through to Bragg.

He had had some half-baked notion of maybe dropping in on Dianne again on the way home. He knew now that he couldn't do that. For Christ's sake, the thing with Dianne had been about as smart as his enlisting for cooks and bakers school. He would not, he knew, go to see her again when the holidays were over and she was back at Duke.

He knew what he would do. They were about to send some Berets to Vietnam, wherever the hell that was. He would tell the general he didn't like being a dog robber. He wanted a team to take to Vietnam.

• • •

(Four)
Building To 2007
The Infantry Center and School
Fort Benning, Georgia
1930 Hours, 24 December 1961

There had been hardly anybody at supper in Consolidated Mess Number 6, which served the Parachute School; but aside from having fewer mess trays, tableware, and coffee cups to wash, there was little difference in what was expected of the KPs from a day when the whole place was full of paratroopers-in-training.

The red tile floor of the kitchen, the stoves, and the work tables had to be scrubbed. And the floor of the mess hall itself, and the tables, and the coffee urns, and the steam table.

It was nearly seven before Private Geoffrey Craig, shivering in water and grease-soaked fatigues, got back to his barracks after fourteen and one half days of KP. He found a newspaper in a garbage can and balled it up, then stuffed it into his soaked combat boots so they would dry overnight. Then he stripped off his fatigues and shoved them under his bed, found clean underwear and his shower clogs, and went to the shower room for a long and hot shower.

There was a feeling, not exhilarating but satisfying, that coming off KP was sort of significant. He would not have to pull KP again at the Parachute School. He was two-thirds through the three week course. Which meant that the worst of that was over too.

The first week had been primarily muscle building and brain-washing. The muscle building hadn't bothered him much, except for push-ups, which had hurt his hand. The sit-ups hadn't bothered him at all, although some of the other trainees had thrown up from the strain on their muscles and stomachs. The duck walk had been a strain, but he had been able to handle it.

The brainwashing, the chickenshit, Karl-Heinz Wagner had told him with professional assurance, had a valid purpose. Presuming everyone did exactly what they were told, and did it instantly, there was really very little danger in parachute training. They had been teaching people to jump out of airplanes for twenty years, and by now they knew how to do it well and safely.

But things happened—accidents, mistakes, broken equipment. When that happened, the instructors knew how to handle it, presuming the trainee did exactly as he was told. According to Karl-Heinz Wagner, the chickenshit, the "Give me fifty" (push-ups) for the slightest violation of petty rules and regulations was designed so that the trainees would instantly and without question obey any order they were given.

The instructors, the "cadre," were without exception young men in splendid physical condition who performed their duties with enthusiasm. They dressed in rigidly starched fatigue uniforms and wore calf-high lace-up boots, jump boots, polished to an unbelievable shine. When the cadre was functioning at a high level of sadism, Geoff sometimes thought that he would like nothing more in the world than to immerse them all in a giant vat of used engine oil.

As far as the parachute school was concerned, there were two classes of people: trainees and cadre. The cadre was just as willing to scream at an officer trainee as they were at a private, although they seemed to treat the two field-grade officers in Geoff's training company with a modicum of respect: "I would be grateful, sir, if the major would get down and give me twenty-five, sir."

Before they had left Bragg for Benning, they had had a pep talk from the first sergeant.

"What we want you people to do at Benning is what they tell you to do, and with your mouths shut. Put up with whatever they throw at you. You'll only be there three weeks, and you have to get through jump school before you can start your training here. If they give you your weekends off, behave. Stay the hell away from Phoenix City, which is right across the river from Benning in Bragg. Falling out of an airplane, tied to a static line, which automatically opens your chute, does not pose any intellectual problem to anybody. When you get back here, we will teach you what parachute jumping is all about."

It had been a long trip from Bragg to Benning in the Volkswagen. Ursula had ridden in the back with their tin suitcases, while he and Karl-Heinz had shared the driving. Ursula apparently did not know how to drive, which dashed Geoff's hope that at some time during the trip he would be alone with her on the front seat.

Karl-Heinz insisted on buying the gasoline and the food. The food was sandwiches and hard-boiled eggs and milk packed by Ursula in a grocery bag. They would not accept his offer to spring for dinner. They could not afford to reciprocate.

Somewhat reluctantly, once they had gotten to Benning, Karl-Heinz borrowed the Volkswagen and drove it into Columbus, Georgia, to find a place for Ursula to stay. The sergeant who had told Geoff about TPA had told Karl-Heinz that the NCO club at Benning was always looking for waitresses, and if his sister needed a job, she should go see a Sergeant Whitman.

That had come to pass too. Every afternoon, after she had washed and starched Karl-Heinz's fatigues to a stiffness equal to the rigidity of the cadre's fatigues, Ursula took a bus from the furnished room and a half in Columbus out to the NCO club on the post and worked from 1600 to 2230 as a waitress in the dining room. She was paid $1.25 an hour, plus tips. Karl-Heinz didn't like the idea of her being alone at nearly midnight, so, insisting that he pay for the gas, he allowed Geoff to drive them to the NCO club and wait for her to come out.

She always looked tired, Geoff thought. *Goddamned* pretty, even in that stupid uniform, but tired. And even more beautiful when she smiled and showed off how much she had earned in tips on a good night.

Sometimes Karl-Heinz would get in the back, which meant Geoff would be alone with her in the front seat and could steal a look at her every once in a while. Sometimes she caught him looking at her, and then she flushed and modestly looked away.

Geoff cordially hated the Volkswagen, its sole redeeming feature being that it was so small that sometimes, when Ursula was in the front seat with him, her leg would accidentally brush against his. Otherwise it burned a lot of oil, and other things went wrong. Karl-Heinz was apparently an expert on Volkswagens—another one of his surprises.

There were Volkswagens in East Germany, imported from the capitalistic west for the use of senior East German officials. Karl-Heinz's commanding officer had owned one, and he and Karl-Heinz had rebuilt the motor when it began to burn oil.

Geoff, he said, was going to have to think about doing a ring-and-valve job on the Volkswagen before the problem developed into something serious.

It had taken the seed of what Karl-Heinz had said some time to bear fruit, but then it had all seemed clear. Karl-Heinz could fix engines. People who fixed engines were paid to do so. Karl-Heinz needed money. Ergo, Karl-Heinz should fix whatever he said was wrong with the engine and get money for doing so.

When they got back to Fort Bragg, maybe, Karl-Heinz said. The car would probably not break down before they got there. But Geoff was right: The car needed work. Therefore, since going back to Bragg in it was the highest priority, it should be saved for that purpose. They would no longer use it to take Ursula home each night from the NCO club. He would ride with her on the bus, and then come back out to the post.

The very first night that Karl-Heinz rode into Columbus on the bus with Ursula, the engine of the Volkswagen failed. It took Geoff fifteen minutes to find the engine oil drain plug on the bottom of the engine, and another five minutes and skinned knuckles to get the damned thing out. But only five laps around the parking lot before the engine seized. He'd tell Karl-Heinz it was vibration that did it.

Master Sergeant Martinez, the ex–first sergeant from the First Division (who, although neither of them suspected it, had been told by Sergeant Major Taylor to keep an eye on PFC Wagner and Private Craig), kindly dragged the Volkswagen into Columbus behind his Buick station wagon.

While Geoff had been on KP, Karl-Heinz had been installing a rebuilt engine from Sears, Roebuck. He had determined that exchanging the failed engine for a rebuilt one would be cheaper than rebuilding the one that had failed.

Karl-Heinz was charging Geoff ninety percent of what Sears, Roebuck wanted for installing the rebuilt engine, and was honest enough to tell Geoff that he was glad to have the work. He knew that Ursula was buying him a little Christmas present, and now he could buy her one. She was probably going to give Geoff a present, too, Karl-Heinz said.

Geoff had spent more time in the PX, selecting a present for Ursula, than he had ever previously spent selecting presents.

He finally settled on a one-of-a-kind portable FM radio. That way she could listen to good music. It cost $119.95. He also bought a "$10.95 reduced from $29.95, slightly damaged" electric can opener. He took both back to Building T-2007 where he spent twenty careful minutes with a razor blade and a can of lighter fluid moving the "$10.95 reduced from $29.95, slightly damaged" price sticker from the can opener to place on the radio where she would find it. He had thrown the can opener away.

In the morning, at 1115 hours, Karl-Heinz and Ursula Wagner would motor to the post to the mighty purr of the replacement engine. They would take Christmas dinner in the mess, where for eighty cents they would be served the army's ritual fourteen-course Christmas banquet—literally everything from soup to nuts, via roast turkey and baked ham. They would then take Private Craig into Columbus with them for "coffee and cake." There he would give Ursula the $10.95 FM radio and Karl-Heinz a Swiss army knife he had admired; and Ursula would give him whatever she was going to give him; and just maybe, carried away with the Christmas spirit, she might actually let him kiss her.

Dressed in clean underwear, smelling of Lifebuoy, Private Craig took the blanket off his pillow and slipped between the sheets. He rearranged his pillow and the blanket so that it would support his head and began to read *Time* magazine.

He sensed, a few minutes later, that somebody important, a cadreman or even an officer, had come to the second floor of Building T-2207. The conversations in the three small knots of people in the almost deserted squad bay died. There was an expectant, almost frightened hush. It had to be a cadreman, Geoff decided. No one had called "Attention." What did the sadistic sonofabitch want on Christmas Eve?

The visitor, wearing a camel's hair overcoat over his shoulders like an actor and a green Tyrolean hat with what looked like a shaving brush stuck in its band, looked around the room, found Geoff and sat down on the bunk beside him.

"Hello, there, young man," he said cheerfully. "Jumped out of any good airplanes lately?"

Geoff chuckled. "I haven't yet; that's next week."

"In bed a bit early, aren't you?"

"I've been on KP."

"So I have been informed."

"Am I supposed to leap to my feet under the circumstances?"

"No, just kissing my ring will suffice."

"And what do I call you, under *these* circumstances?"

"The circumstances being Christmas Eve, which has apparently escaped you, you may call me Cousin Craig."

"How did you know I was here?"

"I just spoke to your mother; my annual Christmas Eve next-of-kin telephone call. When I asked where you were, she said, tears choking her voice, that not only had the beastly army refused to let you off for Christmas, but it was denying her baby access to a telephone."

"Christ, I didn't call!" Geoff remembered.

"So I have been led to understand," Lowell said. "Put your clothes on; we'll get you on the horn."

Geoff pulled his legs out from under the blankets and started to put on fatigues.

"Have you got civilian clothes?" Lowell asked.

"No."

"It's permitted, you know," Lowell said.

"There hasn't been time to get any from home or to buy any here," Geoff said.

"Well, then, Class A's," Lowell said.

"Why, where are we going?"

"I thought I would take you away from all this," Lowell said dryly. "After we got to my motel and call your mother, we'll go down to Rucker. I can't offer a Christmas tree and roast turkey, but I thought you might settle for steaks and booze."

"I can't do that," Geoff said.

"Yes you can," Lowell said. "I've fixed it with the army."

"That's not what I mean," Geoff said. "I've made other plans."

Lowell looked at him and smiled.

"You say that with such determination that there must be a female involved," he said.

"Yes," Geoff said.

"Well, you can tell me all about her on the way to the motel," Lowell said. "I promised your mother I would put you on the phone."

When they went outside the barracks, a captain wearing an OD brassard and a sergeant were standing nervously beside a silver Volkswagen.

"Go sign out," Lowell ordered. "I'll wait."

As Geoff went to the orderly room door he heard the captain say "Good evening, sir."

"Merry Christmas," Lowell said.

"Is there some way I can help the general, sir?" the captain asked.

"I'm not the general," Lowell said. "He just loaned me his car. Actually, he loaned me his wife's car."

"Well, then, sir," the captain said, "is there some way I can help you, sir?"

"Well, I had planned to entertain that poor lonely soldier away from home at Christmas," Lowell said, "but he has already found some female to do that for him."

The captain chuckled. "You scared hell out of the sergeant, sir. He saw the bumper sticker and called me."

"I'm sorry about that, Captain," Lowell said. "Having to be on duty on Christmas Eve is bad enough without having a general sneaking around."

Geoff signed the sign-out book and came back out of the orderly room. He looked at the bumper. It bore both Fort Benning and Fort Rucker bumper stickers. The Rucker sticker was number six, the Benning number twenty-eight. Both stickers had the single star of a brigadier general.

When they were in the car, Geoff said, "I wondered what you were doing with a Volkswagen."

"Never look a gift Volkswagen in the trunk," Lowell said. "It belongs to a friend of mine, Bill Roberts."

"What are you doing here?" Geoff asked. "At Benning, I mean. You didn't come here because of me?"

"I'm shuffling paper," Lowell said. "Unfortunately, I'm very good at that."

"I don't know what that means," Geoff confessed.

"I am preparing a lengthy document, which will be signed by General Roberts and favorably endorsed, we hope, by General Howard, which will recommend to the Secretary of Defense how the army should use airplanes in the next war."

"Oh," Geoff said. "Why is that unfortunate?"

"Because those who write about it seldom get to do it,"

Lowell said. And then he went on quickly, as if anxious to change the subject: "When General Roberts went home for Christmas this afternoon, he left me the keys to his car."

"You're going to spend Christmas in a motel here?"

I feel sorry for him, Geoff realized. *He really wanted me to go with him, because he is going to be as alone on Christmas as he thought I was going to be.*

"No. I've got my airplane here. I'm going home myself. Home being Ozark, Alabama, outside Fort Rucker. I was going to take you with me and bring you back in time for duty on Thursday morning."

"I haven't thanked you for getting me out of the stockade," Geoff said, changing the subject.

"When they have you running around in the Florida swamps, eating snakes, you may wish you were back in the stockade," Lowell said.

"Why Special Forces? Why did you do that for me?" Geoff asked.

"For you or *to* you?"

"Either."

"Are you miserable in Special Forces, the lady aside?"

"No. So far it's been interesting."

"You want a straight answer to that question?"

"Please."

"For one thing, sounding like a guidance counselor at St. Mark's, I thought that getting through Special Forces training would make a man out of you," Lowell said.

"Or kill me in the process," Geoff said, chuckling.

"To coin a phrase, 'it separates the men from the boys,'" Lowell said. "And then I had a selfish interest."

"I don't know what you mean by that," Geoff said.

"There's an old saying; Kipling said something like it, which I forget. The modern version is 'Soldiers and dogs, keep off the grass.' Ten years from now, when you're in your office at 13 Wall Street and you read in the *WSJ* that our Senator is about to take the army off the gravy train, I want you to remember the good people you met when you were a soldier. Underpaid and overworked and literally prepared to lay down their lives. And, remembering them, I want you to get mad enough to call the sonofabitch up and really tell him where to head in."

"Is that what you do?"

"I get your father, kicking and screaming in protest, to do it for me," Lowell said. "They pay more attention to him than they do to me. I'm just one more soldier they want to keep off the grass."

"You really like the army, don't you?" Geoff said. "It's not what Dad says."

"What does Dad say?"

"That you just don't like banking."

"I don't like banking," Lowell said. "He's right about that."

"And you do like the army?"

"I'm not sure you'll understand this, Geoff," Lowell said.

"Try me."

"The toughest thing a decent man has to do in life is send another decent man somewhere where he's probably going to get killed," Lowell said. "That's called command. And the most satisfying thing a man can do in life is to be a commander."

"I don't think I understand that," Geoff confessed a moment later.

"I didn't think you would," Lowell said. "Tell me about the lady."

"Why?" Geoff said, unwilling to end the conversation. "Why is that satisfying?"

Lowell down geared the Volkswagen. They were approaching the Fort Benning Gate. The MP on duty, who had been casually waving cars through, saw the general officer's sticker, popped to rigid attention and saluted.

Lowell absentmindedly returned it.

"I don't know," Lowell said thoughtfully. "It's probably got something to do with the fact that we are far less removed from the savage than we like to think we are. All I know is once you experience it, you'll do anything to have it again."

"You've been a commander." It was more of a statement than a question.

"Once, when I was about your age, in Greece. And a couple of years later, in Korea."

"And that's it? That's why you put up with all this bullshit?"

"Tell me about the lady, Geoff," Lowell said. "We have exhausted the previous subject."

Geoff knew that he had somehow disappointed his cousin.

And he sensed that in saying what he had, Craig Lowell had opened a door that was rarely opened. Now that it was closed again, it would not soon be reopened.

He wished that he had been unable to understand.

"She's the sister of a friend of mine," Geoff said. "She's German."

"German German, or what?"

"German German," Geoff said. "They escaped from East Germany."

"And you're stuck on her?"

"I never felt this way before."

"It will go over like a lead balloon with your parents," Lowell said. "Can you handle that? Or isn't it that serious?"

"What's wrong with Germans?" Geoff snapped, and then remembered. "Your wife was German, wasn't she?"

"Yes, she was," Lowell said. "The family, with the possible exception of your mother, was united in the belief that Ilse, who was eighteen when I married her, was a conniving European slut who had latched on to a meal ticket."

"They'll jump in on Ursula, then. They don't have a pot to piss in."

"Does she know that you're . . . 'comfortable'?"

"No."

"One final profound philosophical observation as we approach the end of our journey," Lowell said, turning into a Ramada Inn. "One of the advantages someone like you has in being in the army as a private soldier is that you're likely to come in contact with a girl who will look at you as a private soldier, not as Craig, Powell, Kenyon and Dawes, Jr."

Geoff looked at him as he stopped the Volkswagen in front of a motel building.

"Yeah," he said.

"I keep this room all the time," Lowell said. "I'll give you a key."

"She's not that kind of a girl."

"All I said was, you can use it if you want to," Lowell said.

"When did your wife die?" Geoff asked.

"God was in his heaven, and all was right with the world," Lowell said. "I was commanding the task force that made the breakout from the Pusan perimeter. An hour before I was to link up with the people who had landed at Inchon, my battalion commander caught up with me in an L-4. I was convinced the sonofabitch was going to steal my glory. I was wrong. I got the glory and the DSC. What Jiggs wanted to see me about was a TWX he had just got from Germany. The TWX said that Ilse had been killed twenty-four hours before in an automobile accident."

"Jesus!"

"Grab what you can while you can, Geoff," Lowell said. "There's not much out there."

Geoff didn't reply.

"Do I get to meet her?" Lowell asked.

"Shit, I want you to," Geoff said. "But I think now would be a lousy time."

"I understand," Lowell said. "Let's go talk to Mommy. I've still got to go to Rucker tonight."

X

Miller Army Airfield
Fort Benning, Georgia
1905 Hours, 24 December 1961

Lowell parked Bill Roberts's wife's Volkswagen in a spot reserved for colonels' automobiles and then went into Base Operations. He gave the keys to the noncom on duty and told him that as far as he knew, General Roberts would be returning to Benning early Thursday morning.

Then he checked the weather. He had seen the jeep driver comfortably curled up on a cot with *Action Comics*, and decided it wouldn't hurt him to leave him there and walk to the aero commander. He thought wryly that he had nothing else to do anyhow.

The commander was parked some distance from Base Ops, in a parking ramp behind the hangars, where it wouldn't be quite so conspicuous among its olive-drab brothers. He had walked no farther than the end of the parking ramp in front of Base Ops, where the VIPs' airplanes and transient aircraft were parked, when he glanced at the line of aircraft and stopped short.

He was as much upset at what he would now have to do—chew ass, and rather intensely, on Christmas Eve—as at the violation itself. He turned and went back in Base Ops.

"Where's the aerodrome officer?" he asked.

"He's taking a nap, sir. Can I help you?"

"Wake him up," Lowell said.

"Yes, sir."

The aerodrome officer, a captain wearing the infantry center insignia, appeared, sleepy-eyed, a moment later.

"Can I help you?"

"There's an armed Mohawk on the line," Lowell said. "Who does it belong to?"

The aerodrome officer did not know who the guy in the Tyrolean hat was, and he was annoyed at having been roused from his nap.

"We don't talk about armed Mohawks," he said. "May I ask who you are?"

"I'm Colonel Lowell, and we don't park armed Mohawks on the transient ramp. I asked you who it belonged to, Captain."

"Sir, I don't know," the captain said. "But if it's important, Colonel, I'll see if I can find out."

"Get to it!" Lowell ordered sharply.

The captain was on the telephone when another captain in an International Distress Orange flight suit walked into Base Ops carrying a flight helmet and a Jepp case. An embroidered cartoon insignia of the Mohawk was sewn to the flight suit.

"Who the *hell* parked that Mohawk on the line?" he demanded angrily.

"Who are you?" Lowell asked.

The captain looked at him and after a moment recognized him.

"I'm Captain Witz, Colonel," he said. "I'm to take that Mohawk to Rucker. But I didn't expect to find it on the line."

"Neither did I," Lowell said. "Why is it going to Rucker?"

The captain visibly considered for a moment Colonel Lowell's Need to Know, and decided in the affirmative. He knew Lowell to be in the small group of brass in charge of what was going on.

"The story I get is that half of the black boxes are out, and that they gave up on fixing them here. Major Brochhammer's arranged to have SCATSA fix them tomorrow at Rucker. He told me to take it down there and make sure that it was fixed."

"Guns and all?" Lowell asked.

"I guess it was time, sir. It'd take three, four hours to get them off."

"When did all this happen?"

"Major Brochhammer called me about half an hour ago, sir."

"Taking you away from your family on Christmas Eve?" Lowell said.

"Yes, sir."

"If you'll loan me your orange rompers and your hat," Lowell said, "I'll take it to Rucker. I presume they expect it?"

"Yes, sir. I'm to taxi right to the SCATSA hangar, Colonel."

"I think I know what happened," Lowell said. "The people who couldn't fix it were anxious to get home on Christmas Eve. So instead of waiting for you to show up at the hangar, they had it pulled out here so they could lock the hangar up and go."

"That's probably it, sir," the captain agreed.

"We can't have that," Lowell said. "So before you go home, Captain, you will find out if that's what's really happened. If it is, you will call the sergeant—I think it's a warrant officer, come to think of it—out here, and really eat his ass out. We simply can't have the air force finding out what we're doing. That's really more important than whoever was in charge disobeying his orders."

"I understand, Colonel."

"If it turns out that he got permission from his commanding officer to do what he did, call Major Brochhammer and turn the incident over to him. And tonight. I want some ass chewed tonight."

"Yes, sir," the captain said.

"Beneath his friendly smile," Lowell said, "behind the smoke screen he sets up from that smoldering root he keeps in his mouth, Major Brochhammer can be one mean sonofabitch when aroused. I think he should be aroused tonight. To repeat myself, more is involved here than somebody taking off early because it's Christmas Eve. If the air force can prove we're putting guns on these things, we're in trouble."

"I wasn't aware the colonel was checked out in the Mohawk, sir," the captain said carefully.

"Captain," Lowell said with a smile, "I'll have you know I was co-pilot on the famous, very first acceptance test of the very first Mohawk. It was famous because Lieutenant Colonel Rudolph G. MacMillan, who was driving, got us as far as the threshold of the active before he set the brakes on fire. We had to be towed ingloriously back to the hangar."

"I'd heard about that, Colonel," the captain said, chuckling. "But I didn't know it was you with Mac."

He pulled the heavy plastic zipper that ran all the way down the front of the flight suit, and started pulling the suit off.

"Oh, to hell with it," Lowell said. "No one's going to see me in civvies on Christmas Eve. Just loan me your helmet and help me turn the airplane on." He turned to the aerodrome officer. "I presume there's an APU* in place?"

"No, sir," the aerodrome officer said. "No one asked for one."

"If you weren't napping, Captain," Lowell said, "you would have seen that Mohawk on your line and known that either a tractor or an APU would be required. Get one out there!"

"Yes, sir."

"What do we put on the manifest, sir, authorizing you to replace me?"

"I'll sign it," Lowell said. "I think everybody but Jim Brochhammer and I are gone. In that case, the rules of seniority probably put me in charge."

They walked out to the Mohawk. There were those who considered it an ugly airplane and those, Lowell included, who thought it was beautiful, in the sense that function is beauty. It was a no-nonsense, businesslike airplane, the first "real warplane" the army had ever had.

He was in large measure responsible for the army having it at all. When he was flying a desk in the Pentagon, he had been the money man in a conspiracy involving himself, Bill Roberts,

---

*Auxiliary power unit, a trailer mounted gasoline engine electric power generator, necessary to start aircraft engines.

then still a colonel, and Brigadier General Bob Bellmon.

Roberts and Bellmon had had the idea, and he had found the money in available funds. The other piece in the pie was the marine corps.

The marine corps had been authorized to look into a new observation airplane to replace the Cessna L19, a two-seater single-engined airplane. The navy pretty well left the marine corps alone when it wanted new equipment, exercising control through control of funds. And the marine corps was not restricted, as the army was, to a very limited aviation role. The marine corps was authorized fighters and fighter-bombers and had unquestioned right to twin-engined airplanes, if that was what they thought they needed and if they could get the money from the navy.

The marines had been concerned about "twin-engine reliability." They wanted an observation airplane that could continue to fly if one engine failed or was damaged by ground fire while the plane was directing artillery over enemy-held terrain. They had been looking at a Cessna idea. Cessna proposed to put two engines on a version of its single-engined civilian model 172.

It was a good idea. Instead of mounting an engine on each wing, which would have required beefing up the wings to take the strain and would have been enormously expensive, they planned to mount the second engine in the rear of the cabin, in line with the engine in front. There were several advantages to this: For one thing, it would be very easy and cheap to design and build two thin booms—which had only to be strong enough to support themselves—to replace the existing single tail and make room for the propeller arc of the second, rear-mounted engine.

Reinforcing the existing cabin to take the second engine would not be a major expense. And the airplane could be flown by anyone who could fly a single-engine airplane. With the engines in line in a "push-pull" configuration, all that happened when either one of the engines quit was that the airplane flew slower. When a wing-mounted engine quit, the plane immediately made a sharp turn toward the dead engine. Training pilots for this eventuality was both expensive and dangerous, for the only way to demonstrate the condition was to shut one of the engines down.

The army placed an order for half a dozen of the marines' push-pull Cessnas for test purposes and to put the air force to sleep. And after Colonel Bill Roberts and General Bob Bellmon had some discreet talks with some old friends in the marine corps, the Deputy Chief, Plans and Requirements Section (Fiscal), Aviation Maintenance Section, Office of the Deputy Chief of Staff for Logistics—an obscure office under the command of an anonymous major named C. W. Lowell—quietly made available to the marine corps almost nine million dollars of the funds available to his office.

Nine millions of dollars, in other words, that would have gone to purchase aviation fire trucks, avionic maintenance vans, hydraulic stands, tools, APUs, and the other paraphernalia of aircraft maintenance, went instead to the marines to fund a "Joint Project in Engineering Feasibility Studies for Twin-Engined Observation Aircraft."

Grumman Aircraft of Bethpage, Long island, longtime supplier to the navy and marines of fighter and utility aircraft for use from aircraft carriers, quickly came up with engineering drawings of a strange little airplane that looked like neither a fighter nor a utility airplane but contained features of both.

There were twin engines—not little gas-poppers but turboprops—of one-thousand-shaft horsepower each. They had been proved on Grumman utility aircraft long in use flying mail and passengers onto aircraft carriers. There were two sets, side by side, up in front of the engine. There was originally a single vertical stabilizer on the tail, but this didn't work out, and two additional vertical stabilizers were added.

Because the marine corps was not denied armed aircraft, provision was made in the wings and fuselage for "hard points" of sufficient strength to take machine guns and other weaponry.

The marine corps knew that the navy would never give them the money to buy aircraft like Mohawks for observation purposes or even, with weapons mounted, for use as close ground-support aircraft. But the marines also knew that if the army got the aircraft into production, should a war come, there would be no problem in ordering their own. In the meantime the army had made a gentleman's agreement to loan a number of Mohawks to the marines immediately on the opening of hostilities.

It had thus been in the marines' interest to keep the air force in the dark, too, and the marines are good at keeping secrets.

When the first Mohawks were delivered to the army, the army announced that they were unarmed electronic surveillance aircraft to study the battlefield with an array of radar and infrared sensing devices. A twin-engine aircraft was needed to carry all that electronic equipment.

That was true.

And it was also true that it would have cost an enormous amount of money to remove the weaponry-capable hard points from the wings and fuselage. The army assured the by now alarmed-that-the-army-camel's-nose-was-under-the-tent air force that they understood perfectly well that the Key West Agreement of 1948 specifically forbade them armed aircraft. The army promised to continue to abide by that agreement.

This was not true.

Roberts and Bellmon and some others believed that once the army got armed Mohawks into battle, the air force would look pretty silly beating its breast and pulling its hair and complaining that the army was breaking the rules. The army was actually shooting at the enemy, and they'd have to be ordered to stop.

The problem was to get the Mohawks into battle without letting the air force know they existed. And a kind warrant officer wanting to turn his troops loose because it was Christmas Eve could blow the whole thing.

Under an interservice agreement, air force planes routinely refueled at Miller Army Airfield, and their pilots routinely took a good look around to see what the army was up to. Any air force pilot, not just one sent to have a look, would have been fascinated to see one of the army's turboprop "reconnaissance" planes sitting in front of Base Ops, festooned with a rocket pod under one wing and a machine gun pod under the other.

Lowell walked around the plane doing the preflight as an APU in a jeep trailer was plugged into the airplane and fired up.

With his story that he had been co-pilot on the first acceptance test flight of the Mohawk, Lowell had given the Mohawk pilot the impression that he was highly experienced in the airplane. That was some distance from the truth. He had gone along with Mac that first time because all Mac had planned to do the first time was take it up, circle the field, and bring it down. It had been more a ceremony than a real test flight. The plane had just been delivered from Bethpage by a Grumman test pilot. It had performed flawlessly. Lowell's ceremonial ride was a bone tossed to a hungry dog: He would not get command of the OV-1 Observation Platoon (Provisional, Test) that was shortly to be formed, although he had done everything but wag his tail and beg for it. He would continue shuffling paper. Bellmon had told him pilots were a dime a dozen, but "staff men" of his caliber were one in fifty thousand.

His checkout and subsequent experience as a Mohawk rated aviator (a total of thirty-five hours) had been much of the same thing: "Check him out in it; make him feel he's part of the team."

He had never before actually flown a Mohawk solo, although on paper he had. It had all been done with great finesse: "We know you can fly it, so take Lieutenant So-and-so to Benning, drop him off, and pick up Captain So-and-so."

C. W. Lowell, Lieutenant Colonel, 25 hours total Mohawk time, pilot in command.

Lieutenant So-and-so, 250 hours total Mohawk time, "passenger."

He wasn't sure if they were concerned that he might bend the bird or that he would hurt himself while bending the bird. The Grumman line was rolling Mohawks out in a steady stream; the aviation school was turning out a steady stream of pilots. But "staff men of his caliber were one in fifty thousand."

He put the Mohawk pilot's flight helmet on, stood on the hood of the jeep, and climbed into the cockpit and plugged the helmet in.

He flicked on the main power buss and heard the gyros come to life. There were a number of red flags on the panel, and he examined each one carefully. With the exception of a malfunctioning ADF, all the problems were in the black boxes on their shelves in the fuselage. These had nothing to do with the engines, controls, or navigation aids of the airplane itself.

He looked down at the ground and gave a thumbs-up signal. The Mohawk pilot, who was manning a huge wheeled fire extinguisher, nodded.

Lowell reached for the Port Engine Prime control and worked it. Then he held down the Port Engine Start toggle switch. The engine started smoothly, and the blades began to whirl. He primed the starboard engine and pushed down the SRBD Engine Start switch.

The ground crewman disappeared from sight to pull the chocks from the wheels and then reappeared.

"Miller," Lowell said to the boom microphone, "Mohawk One-One-One at Base Ops for taxi and takeoff."

The tower operator came right back.

"One-One-One, you are cleared via Taxi One to the threshold of one-eight."

Lowell waved to the people on the ground and put his hand on the throttles, advanced them, and started taxiing.

He lowered the canopy in place when he came to the threshold of the runway.

"Miller, One-One-One on the threshold of one-eight. Request takeoff permission, VFR direct OZR."

"One-One-One is cleared for takeoff. There is no reported traffic in the local area. The winds are negligible, the altimeter is two-niner-niner-eight, the time is five to the hour."

Lowell turned the Mohawk onto the runway, locked the brakes, put the flaps all the way down, and ran up the engines.

"One-One-One rolling," he said, and took off the brakes.

The force of the acceleration pressed him hard against the seat. The airspeed needle hesitated, then sprang to life, indicating seventy. When it reached eighty, he eased back on the stick and felt it almost jump into the air. He pulled the gear and the flaps and farther back on the stick.

Fort Benning and Columbus dropped beneath him. There was enough light to see U.S. 431 below him to his left. He broke off the climb and dropped the nose. The altimeter was at 2,500 feet. The sonofabitch climbed like a rocket. He took it down to 750 feet and put the highway on his right.

The airspeed indicator had climbed to 350.

It was a pity, he thought, that at that speed he would be over Dothan in twenty minutes. It would be nice just to fly for a while.

Nap-of-the-earth flying was forbidden without specific authority.

"To hell with it," he said aloud, and pushed the nose down again.

The altimeter indicated less than one hundred feet, but he wasn't looking at it. He was looking out to make sure he didn't run into a power line—or over a cow.

Even at an indicated airspeed of 370 knots, he could see Christmas trees in some of the farmhouse windows.

(Two)
Quarters No. 1
The Army Aviation Center
Fort Rucker, Alabama
1230 Hours, 25 December 1961

Lowell turned the Mercedes off Colonel's Row and into the drive leading to Quarters No. 1. Colonel's Row at Fort Rucker looked more like Levittown than Colonel's Row at Bragg, Benning, or Knox. Dependent housing at Fort Rucker was new—construction was still going on—and the houses were frame, with a little brick facing in the front, one story; the only visual difference between the ranch houses on Colonel's Row and those on any street in a lower-middle-class housing development were the little signs on the lawns providing the occupant's name and rank.

Quarters No. 1 differed from the houses on Colonel's Row only in that it sat on a small knoll on an acre plot and was slightly larger than the colonels' houses.

Quarters No. 1 at Fort Knox was a substantial two-story brick colonial building, the sort of house a vice-president of Ford Motor Company would have. This one, Lowell thought, carrying a dozen roses in green florist's tissue up the narrow concrete walk to the front door, looked like the house of an assistant zone manager for some second-rate life insurance company.

The little sign on the lawn at the entrance to the drive read:
P. T. JIGGS, MAJOR GENERAL.

Jane Jiggs opened the door.

Lowell thrust the flowers at her.

"Merry Christmas, louse," she said.

"Louse?"

"I was sure it was Meissen china," she said. "And what did I get?"

"I'll get you china," he said.

"Oh, I'm only kidding," she said. "Come in. I'll make us a drink and we can watch the kids play with their toy."

"Where's Paul?"

"That's who I mean," she said. "You don't think he'd let the little kids play with that, do you? He and Davis are up to their ears in train parts."

She led him into the living room, where Major General Paul T. Jiggs, Lieutenant Jerome Davis, his aide-de-camp, and the Jiggs children were assembling an elaborate electric train set.

"Santa Claus is here, children," Jane Jiggs said. "Scotch, Craig?"

"Please," he said.

"Not meaning a word of what I have to say," Paul Jiggs said, "you really shouldn't have done this, Craig."

"I got a deal on it," Lowell said. "By which I mean my father-in-law bought the company. He apparently told somebody to send me a sample, and with Teutonic efficiency they sent one of everything they make." He stooped and picked up a locomotive. "Nice, isn't it?"

"Oh, *yeah!*" Paul T. Jiggs, Jr., thirteen, said in awe.

The men laughed.

"I just got off the horn to him," Lowell said. "General-leutnant von Greiffenberg, Retired, extends his best wishes to Major General Jiggs and family on Christmas and for the New Year."

"You repaid the compliment, I hope?" Jiggs asked.

"Sure," Lowell said.

"How's Peter-Paul?" Jane Jiggs asked.

"Like this one," Lowell said, touseling the hair of Paul Jiggs, Jr. "Except that he talks English like a limey."

"He was just fourteen?" Jane Jiggs asked as she handed him a drink.

"Last month," Lowell said. "And what interesting has been going on while I have been off, shuffling paper?" Lowell asked. It was evident he wanted to get off the subject of his son.

"Odd that you should mention that," Jiggs said, getting to his feet. "At nine this morning I had a most interesting telephone call from the staff duty officer. It seems the mayor of Eufaula, Alabama, had telephoned him last night, more than a little upset—'furious' was the word the SDO used—that one of our airplanes had buzzed his bucolic little town on Christmas Eve."

"No!"

"According to the staff duty officer, the mayor said that this maniac, whoever he was, came like the hammers of hell right down Main Street, twenty feet or so over the trees, scaring dogs and old ladies, and disappeared in the direction of Fort Rucker."

"Did His Honor happen to get a tail number?" Lowell asked.

"No," Jiggs said, "he did not."

"Then I guess you'll have some trouble finding out who did something like that, won't you?" Lowell said. "Pity. We can't have our people going around scaring dogs and old ladies, can we?"

"What the hell is the matter with you, Craig?" Jiggs asked. "How much Mohawk time do you have?"

"More than *thirty* hours," Lowell said. "We paper-shufflers are given first shot at flying the Mohawk."

"You really buzzed Eufaula, Uncle Craig? In a Mohawk?" Paul T. Jiggs, Jr., asked, delighted.

"Is that what I'm accused of?" Lowell asked innocently. "Of course not. I am a responsible field-grade paper-pusher–type officer who wouldn't dream of doing something like that. I might have been a little under fifteen hundred feet when I flew *down the river*, they're having electrical trouble with the Mohawk I was flying, and the altimeter might have been off. But twenty feet off the trees? Me?"

Lieutenant Davis chuckled.

General Jiggs gave him a dirty look.

"Davis," Lowell asked. "Did you know that I served under General Jiggs in Korea?"

"I believe I've heard something about that, sir."

"And have you heard that when he was nothing but a lowly lieutenant colonel, he posed for an obscene photograph?"

"Oh, God!" Jane Jiggs said.

Mary-Beth Davis, Lieutenant Davis's bride of four months, looked baffled.

"It's not as bad as it sounds," Jane Jiggs said to her.

"*I* think it's a *lot* worse than scaring dogs and old ladies,"

Lowell said. "Particularly for a West Pointer who, one presumes, is taught all about the conduct expected of an officer and gentleman."

"Show them the picture, Craig," Jiggs said.

"Paul!" Jane said.

"Dare I? They just got married," Lowell said. "Could she stand the shock? She probably has never seen one."

"We'll have to now," Jiggs said. "Otherwise Mary-Beth will think it's really obscene."

"As opposed to what?" Lowell asked innocently.

"Come with me, please, Mary-Beth," General Jiggs said.

Smiling uneasily, Mary-Beth Davis followed General Jiggs to a small room he had outfitted as a personal office. One wall was covered with photographs. One of the photographs showed a younger Paul Jiggs standing on the engine cover of an M-46 tank, relieving his bladder. He was shaking his fist at the photographer. It was clear that the photographer had called his name to get his attention and had snapped the photograph the instant Jiggs had seen his camera.

"I'm sorry you had to be exposed to something like this, Mrs. Davis," Lowell said unctuously.

"That's the Yalu," Jiggs said.

"What he was doing was what Patton the Elder did in the Rhine," Lowell said.

"I didn't expect to have it recorded for posterity," Jiggs said.

"But once it was, what the hell, hang it on the wall, right?" Lowell said.

"Who took the picture?" Lieutenant Davis asked.

"Do you have to ask?" Jiggs said.

"What's the 'Yalu'?" Mary-Beth Davis asked.

Lowell and Jiggs exchanged glances.

"It's the border between North Korea and China, honey," her husband, embarrassed, explained to her. "It was as far north as the army got in the war."

"Oh," she said.

"Another officer would have planted a flag," Lowell said. "But you see how General Jiggs chose to mark the spot."

Mary-Beth was aware that she had just revealed her ignorance of something that was important to her husband's boss.

She desperately searched her memory and came up with something.

"I was just a kid then," she said, "but that was when all the Americans had to retreat . . . through the mountains in a blizzard?"

"I like to think of it," Lowell said solemnly, "as advancing in the other direction."

"Jesus!" Jiggs said.

Mary-Beth was now genuinely impressed.

"You two were there?" she asked.

"Legends in our own time," Lowell said. "Me for my distinguished service and General Jiggs for . . . well, now you've seen the photo."

"How would you like to go back, Craig? For Auld Lang Syne?" General Jiggs asked.

Lowell looked at him.

"Somehow I don't think that's an idle question," he said.

"It's not," Jiggs said. "How would you like thirty days in Korea?"

"If I can have a tank battalion or an aviation battalion for the standard tour, I can be on a plane this afternoon," Lowell said. "But do I want to go to Korea for thirty days? No."

"It's for thirty days," Jiggs said, leading everybody out of the office. "That's not up for debate. But you're going for thirty days. The only question is where."

"Because I am suspected of livening things up in Eufaula?" Lowell asked. "Is the mayor that mad?"

Jiggs shook his head.

"Then what?" Lowell asked.

"Let's say that some people think you have been working too hard and that you need thirty days away from your typewriter to recharge your batteries."

"Who is 'some people'?"

"The Vice-Chief of Staff," Jiggs said.

"Paul, honest to Christ," Lowell said, "the only thing I have done that's half an inch out of line was last night. And I don't think the Vice-Chief of Staff has heard about that yet."

"The first proposal is on the Secretary of the Army's desk," Jiggs said. "Thursday, maybe, and no later than one January, it goes to McNamara."

"I know, I wrote it," Lowell said.

"Do you know that McNamara talked to Bill Roberts and Jim Brochhammer?"

"I heard that he did," Lowell said.

"That made a lot of people mad," Jiggs said. "The Secretary of Defense is supposed to get his advice from the Chairman of the Joint Chiefs of Staff, not from a buck general and a major."

"They didn't go to McNamara," Lowell said. "He sent for them."

"Right. And if he sends for you, which is considered very likely, the Secretary will be told, 'Sorry about that, he's out of the country.'"

"Christ!"

"What they especially don't want you to tell McNamara, Craig, is 'In the proposal *I* wrote, I had twice this many aircraft in the division: 450.'"

"Four fifty-nine," Lowell corrected automatically. Then he heard what Jiggs had said. "They didn't cut the aircraft in *half?*" he asked.

"The proposal sent to the Secretary of the Army calls for 289 total, including zero armed Mohawks and zero rocket-armed Hueys."

"And what's the reasoning?" Lowell asked icily.

"That we shouldn't be greedy, that it is better to ask for something we have a chance to get, something the air force can't protest violates the Key West Agreement, rather than ask for something we have virtually no chance to get."

"The old foot-in-the-door theory?" Lowell asked sarcastically.

"Sometimes called the old camel's-nose-under-the-tent-flap theory," Jiggs said. "It is believed we can always go back and ask for the rest later."

"When we go back, it will be to defend what we have been given, not to ask for anything more. In the second round we're going to lose, not gain. All this is going to do is increase the aircraft assigned to a division. That would have happened anyway, and it will not result in an air-mobile division, which is what I thought we were building."

"Oddly enough, I said something very much like that when

my opinion was asked," Jiggs said. "That was just before I was told that Jim Brochhammer is being sent to Panama for a month to look into tropical operations, and asked where did I want to send you for a month."

"Why don't I just go on leave," Lowell asked, "and happen to bump into McNamara in the locker room at Burning Tree?"

"You are not to go anywhere near Washington for the next thirty days," Jiggs said. "They thought of that too."

"McNamara wants more than recommendations on aircraft augmentation," Lowell said. "He wanted a new concept. We have one to give him."

"Hey," Jiggs said, "you're preaching to the converted. I'm telling you how it is at CONARC, DCSOPS, and with the Chief of Staff."

Lowell looked at him but said nothing.

"Where would you like to go, Craig?" Jiggs asked. "On leave to Germany to see Peter-Paul? Or to Korea on TDY? What about Indochina? You could probably do something useful there, see what support we should send the H-34 and Otter Companies. Parker could probably use some help with his Mohawks too."

"What about Parker's Mohawks? Have they been disarmed too?"

"I have no idea what you're talking about, Colonel," Jiggs said. "I am not privy to anything concerning the Twenty-third Special Warfare Aviation Department. They're under the operational control of the Defense Intelligence Agency."

The Defense Intelligence Agency was a creature of the Defense Department, staffed by personnel of the several armed services. It got some of its money from the CIA and some of it from presidential contingency funds. It did a good deal more than intercept radio and cable messages to and from Russian and Eastern Bloc nations, and it was not under the thumb of any of the individual services. If the Secretary of the Air Force or, for that matter, the Secretary of the Army tried to tell the four-star admiral who ran DIA that DIA's Armed Mohawks violated the spirit and the law of the 1948 Key West Interservice Agreement on Roles and Missions, he would be politely asked, "Mohawks? What's a Mohawk?"

If he persisted, he would be told, far less politely, that DIA answered to the Secretary of Defense and the Director of the CIA, and when either of those gentlemen wished to avail themselves of his opinion, they would send him a memorandum asking for it.

"Well, that's something, at least," Lowell said.

"I thought you knew, Craig," Jiggs said.

"I guess the Mouse fixed that," Lowell said. Then he said, "Parker's not due there until the ninth or tenth. Can I do both? Can I go to Europe on leave and then go on to Indochina?"

Jiggs nodded. "Davis'll have your orders by noon tomorrow."

"I've got to get back to Benning," Lowell said. "My airplane is there."

"I'll go with you myself," Jiggs said. "It will give a chairwarmer such as myself a chance to drive the Mohawk. And I think *I* can make it to Benning in a Mohawk without scaring hell out of the natives."

(Three)
Lufthansa Stadt Köln *(Flight 228)*
Over Massachusetts
2030 Hours, 28 December 1961

There were six rows of two seats on each side of the aisle of the first-class compartment of the Boeing 707. They were staggered. At the head of the left row of seats, there was a table with four chairs by it, installed for the convenience of businessmen wishing to work while en route; and there was a similar table at the rear of the right row of seats. There were only fourteen first-class passengers.

There were two kinds of first-class passengers: the regular kind, who had paid the first-class tariff and whom Lufthansa intended to make as comfortable as possible on the flight to Rhine-Main Airfield near Frankfurt am Main. The other kind were passengers who, in addition to paying the first-class tariff, were known to someone in the Lufthansa administrative apparatus as passengers who were to be treated just a bit more considerately than the other first-class passengers. They were identified to the air crew by a small slash mark on their boarding passes.

There were two slash marks on the boarding pass of the passenger named Lowell, C. W. His ticket had been charged to Craig, Powell, Kenyon and Dawes, a firm that spent a good deal of money with Lufthansa moving its executives (in first class) and its couriers (in tourist) around the world, and it was Lufthansa practice to put a slash mark on the boarding passes of any Craig, Powell, Kenyon and Dawes executive. It was also the Lufthansa administrative practice to compare the names of all first-class passengers against a company list of people to whom, for any number of reasons, the company wished to be especially hospitable. Lowell's name had come up on that list, too, with the notation that he was related to Generalleutnant Peter-Paul von Greiffenberg, Retired, who sat on Lufthansa's board of directors.

Two slashes.

When Mr. Lowell asked the senior cabin attendant if one of the tables was free, she told him it was, escorted him to it, told him they weren't full, and removed the armrest between the two seats at the table so that he could stretch out across both seats if he wished to nap.

And when they were off the ground, he was the first passenger she went to ask if he would like some champagne or a cocktail. She smiled very warmly at him—and not only because there had been two slash marks on his boarding pass. He was a very good-looking man, in finely tailored clothes, and there was no wedding ring on his hand. The odds against his being both unmarried and smitten with her charms to the point that he would take her away from all this were enormous, but hope springs eternal in a cabin attendant's breast.

In fluent, unaccented German he asked for a beer and salted almonds. When she brought these to him, he already had his briefcase on the table and had taken from it a number of folders imprinted *Craig, Powell, Kenyon and Dawes*.

"If you need anything," she said. "Just ring."

"Thank you," he said, and smiled at her.

He didn't mean to be nasty, she thought. But he didn't see her as a young and reasonably attractive woman. He saw her as an airborne waitress. Which, she decided, was pretty much the case. Most of the passes made at her were made by men who had wives and children at home. Very rarely did men from whom she would like a pass make one. They had better prospects than airborne waitresses.

She would have to settle—by way of making this flight interesting—for second best. Second best was two movie stars bound for the Berlin Film Festival. They had settled themselves in the left front of the cabin.

Brian Hayes, who looked older, smaller, and stranger (with thick-glassed horn-rimmed spectacles on his nose) than he did on the screen, sat at the table with a bald, pleasant-faced Italian, carefully reading some sort of legal document. Georgia Paige, who looked older than she did on the screen but still uncommonly beautiful, sat alone against the window in the third row of chairs, with her feet stretched out toward the aisle. She had a copy of *Time*, which she was reading through enormous red-framed glasses. She had a bottle of Coca-Cola on the fold-down shelf in front of her.

When she saw the cabin attendant, she sat up, pushed her glasses up into her hair, and motioned the cabin attendant over.

"Can I help you, Miss Paige?"

"The gentleman in the rear," Georgia Paige said.

"Yes, Miss Paige?"

"Is his name Lowell?"

"Yes it is," the cabin attendant said.

"Would you bring me a bottle of champagne and two glasses, please?"

"Certainly, Miss Paige," the cabin attendant said.

When she brought it and the cork proved difficult, Georgia Paige impatiently reached for it, extracted the cork with a grunt and practiced skill, and quickly poured the overflow into one of the glasses. She gulped this down quickly, jammed the cork into the neck of the bottle, and then stood up.

She walked down the aisle to the table in the rear of the first-class cabin and stood there until Lowell noticed her.

"Coffee, tea, or me?" she asked.

"Hello, Georgia," Lowell said.

"Would you like a little of the bubbly, since you're obviously disinterested in me?"

"I would love some bubbly," he said, and shoved the folders on the table into the briefcase.

She poured the champagne.

"Would you like me to sit here, so we can stare soulfully into each other's eyes? Or next to you, where we could play kneesy?" she asked.

"Whatever pleases you," he said.

She sat down next to him, sitting sideways on the chair, and touched her champagne glass to his.

"Long time no see," she said.

"To coin a phrase," he said.

"Weren't you going to talk to me?"

"I wasn't sure you would remember me," he said.

"Ha!"

"And I seem to recall that you are married to the gentleman in the spectacles," Lowell said.

"I am," she said, "but what has that to do with anything?"

"If I were married to you, I don't think I would like an . . . 'old friend' . . . like me rushing up with lechery in his eye."

"But you like women," Georgia said.

It was a moment before he responded.

"Why did you feel you had to tell me that?" he asked.

She poured more champagne in his glass.

"A couple of reasons," she said, shrugging. "Among them, I don't want you shoving his head in a fire bucket."

There was confusion on his face for a moment, and then he remembered.

"I'd forgotten about that," he said.

"I really think you had," she said, and laughed.

"I was under a certain emotional strain at the time," he said.

"Brian is very nice," she said. "I want you to behave yourself when you meet him."

"Am I going to meet him?"

"If I stay here, he'll come back. Not to be curious, but to be nice."

"I am older and wiser, Georgia," Lowell said. "Far less prone to violence."

"We are all older, damn it," she said.

"You have weathered the storm miraculously," he said.

"Flattery will get you everywhere," she said. "It's not true, but I love to hear it."

"You are a remarkably beautiful woman," he said. "Even more beautiful than I remembered."

"You did remember?"

"Oh, yes," he said. "Often."

"Do you know how long ago that was?" she asked, surprise in her voice.

"Ten years and two months," Lowell said. And then he laughed. "The tank is in a museum," he said.

"What?"

"The tank is in the Patton Museum at Fort Knox," he said. "I was there a while back and saw it."

She satisfied herself that he was serious, and then laughed herself.

"With a sign, no doubt, that says: 'In this tank, then on the front line, Major Craig Lowell screwed Georgia Paige, September whatever, 1951'?"

He had forgotten how her foul tongue sometimes offended him. He had been offended by the foul language of her director when he had visited her on her set in Los Angeles, and had shoved his head in a fire bucket. The act, he had later been informed, had rendered the director emotionally incapable of practicing his art and shut down the company for the day, and thus had cost Craig, Powell, Kenyon and Dawes somewhere in the neighborhood of forty thousand dollars.

He had forgotten, too, that she had achieved prominence by going around without a brassiere. He checked. She was wearing one now. She saw him looking.

"They are not yet pendulous, to answer your question," she said. "Not yet."

"I'm glad," he said.

"Why are you going to Germany? What do you do now?" she asked.

"I'm going to see my son," he said.

"God, I'd forgotten you had one," she said.

"He's fourteen. That's how long ago it was."

"He doesn't live with you?"

"With his grandfather," Lowell said. "I'm still a soldier."

"You're still a soldier?" she asked in surprise, and then, before he could reply, she asked: "What are you now? A general?"

"Colonel," he said. *"Lieutenant* colonel."

"I thought you'd certainly be at least a general by now," she said.

"So did I," he said.

"That sounded more bitter than 'Ha-ha,'" she said.

"A little of each," he said.

The cabin attendant came and laid two trays of hors d'oeuvres on the table.

"May I bring a menu?" she asked.

"And would you ask my husband to come back here?" Georgia said. "We'll eat with the colonel."

When she had gone, Georgia said: "I want you to meet him."

"I'm delighted," he said.

"No, you're not," Georgia said. "But you'll like him. He's nice. And he's understanding. I'm understanding, and he's understanding."

"I understand," he mocked.

"You bastard!" she laughed.

She picked up a bacon-wrapped oyster and popped it in her mouth.

"Did you order these special?" she asked. "Do you need oysters now? You're not as randy as you were when you were young?"

"Christ!" he said.

Brian Hayes came down the aisle and stood by the table. He had, Lowell thought, a gentle smile.

"Say hello to Craig Lowell," she said.

"Hello, Craig Lowell," Brian Hayes said.

His handshake, Lowell thought, was not quite John Wayne, but it wasn't exactly pansy. He did not look like a faggot, either.

"*Colonel* Craig Lowell," Georgia said.

"Oh," Brian Hayes said, making the connection. He smiled. "The man who *extinguished* Derek Nesbit in a fire bucket. I'm very happy to meet you, Colonel. How often, working with him, I have envied you."

"I told the stewardess we'd eat here," Georgia said. "Sit down."

"How nice," Brian Hayes said.

"Craig is going to see his son in Germany," Georgia said.

"I see," Brian Hayes said.

"I am trying to get him to abandon that noble duty and come to Berlin with us," Georgia said.

"Sounds like a marvelous idea," Brian Hayes said, after a moment.

He knows what she means, Lowell realized. *And he doesn't give a damn.*

"I don't think that will be possible," Lowell said. "I'll only be in Germany a week or ten days."

"Then you're going right back?" Georgia asked.

"Then I'm going on to the Orient," Lowell said.

"If you and your son, and if there is a Mrs. Lowell—"

"Is there?" Georgia asked.

Lowell shook his head.

"You never got married again?" she pursued.

"I came close once," he said.

"And . . . ?"

"She left me at the altar," Lowell said.

"Well, if you and your son could get to Berlin," Brian Hayes said, "we could get you credentials for the film festival. Or doesn't that sort of thing interest you?"

"I don't even know what a film festival is," Lowell said.

"It's a bribing contest," Brian Hayes said. "We all send films. And then we try to bribe the judges. The one who succeeds wins the prize. Since the prize sells tickets, votes cost accordingly. It's very profitable to be a judge."

Lowell chuckled. Georgia was right. He did like this man. He thought that he had sort of a rule: He did not screw the wives of men he liked. But did that apply here? Where the husband didn't care?

"I thought you were an actor, not a producer," Lowell said.

"You just said exactly the wrong thing," Georgia said.

"Sorry," Lowell said.

"I've produced the last three of her pictures," Brian Hayes said.

"I didn't know," Lowell said.

"And you didn't see the pictures either, did you?" Georgia challenged. His answer came on his face. "You sonofabitch!" she said.

"I don't have much time for the movies," Lowell said.

"What do you do in the army, Colonel?" Brian Hayes asked.

"I'm a paper-shuffler," Lowell said.

"I don't believe that," Georgia said. "You did something

famous in Korea, a task force or something that everybody talked about."

"That was, as we were just discussing, a very long time ago," Lowell said.

"I think, Colonel," Brian Hayes said, "we all, at one time or another, find ourselves shuffling paper."

That was a very kind thing to say, Lowell thought. *Kind and understanding. I will* not *screw your wife.*

After the filet mignon and the Camembert, both washed down with a half-dozen splits of a California Cabernet Sauvignon, they had a good deal of brandy before Mr. and Mrs. Brian Hayes finally went forward again.

Lowell got a pillow and a blanket from the stewardess, and made himself comfortable by propping the pillow in the corner between his seat and the aircraft wall.

He had a lewd and lascivious dream. He was in the hull of an M-46 tank on the military crest of Heartbreak Ridge. He had just shown Georgia his tank, and had started to hoist her up, so that she could climb out of the commander's cupola. But she wiggled out of his grasp and lowered herself back down, opening her khaki shirt as she did, so that he could get his mouth on her nipples.

He woke up and shook his head. He wanted to sit up, but there was some weight on him. The weight was Georgia Paige. She had thrown a blanket over them, and her hand was in his fly.

"They're playing backgammon," she said. She laughed deep in her throat, and resumed methodically pumping his organ. "You must be getting old. It took a long time to wake it up."

"For Christ's sake," he said. "Somebody'll see us!"

"That never bothered you before," she said. "When we finally climbed out of the tank and your GIs applauded, you took a bow."

Then she put her head in his lap, pulled the blanket over her head under the blanket, and finished what she had started.

(Four)
Rhine-Main Airfield
Frankfurt am Main, Germany
0950 Hours, 29 December 1961

Lufthansa's *Stadt Köln* made its approach to Rhine-Main over the city of Frankfurt am Main. Lowell stared intently out of the window and picked out the Ninety-seventh General Hospital on the edge of the city cemetery and then the curved I. G. Farben Building, which had been intentionally spared bombing in World War II and had served continuously since as an American headquarters, and finally the Hauptbahnhof.

Coming to Frankfurt was very much like coming home. The first time he had come to Frankfurt, he had been an eighteen-year-old private, a draftee. Six months after that, a brand-new and more-than-a-little-frightened second lieutenant, he had left Rhine-Main on a battered air corps C-47 for Greece. And he'd flown into Rhine-Main in an old three-tailed TWA Lockheed Constellation four months after that, his shirt back and sleeves stiff with the suppuration from the wounds he'd got in Greece to marry Ilse and to learn that she was pregnant.

And with brand-new major's leaves on his epaulets, a brand new Distinguished Service Cross in a blue box in his Valv-Pak, he'd been flown into Rhine-Main on a MATS flight, Tokyo–Rangoon–Calcutta–Cairo–Frankfurt, on an AAA priority authorized by the Supreme Commander, Allied Powers, himself. General of the Army Douglas MacArthur had wanted to do everything possible for a young officer who had suffered great personal tragedy literally at the moment when he had been displaying the "distinguished leadership and great personal valor" that had earned him the DSC. Lowell had arrived at Rhine-Main from Korea eighty hours from the moment Task Force Lowell had linked up with elements of X U.S. Corps near Suwon. And twenty-four hours after they had put Ilse into her crypt.

Her father had simply been unable to believe that any army would fly an officer halfway around the world just to attend his wife's funeral, so he had gone ahead with it.

"What's so fascinating?" Georgia Paige asked.

"Just looking around," Lowell said. "I used to fly in here a lot."

She raised her eyebrows in question.

"I was stationed here after I knew you," he explained.

The first-class passengers were debarked first and loaded onto large, wide-doored buses. The tourist-class passengers were debarked next. A large number were American soldiers, officers and enlisted men, and their dependents. He had not seen them before. He had just about missed the flight at Idlewild, and the curtain separating first-class from the cheap seats had already been drawn when he got on board.

They had been inside the terminal building no more than thirty seconds when the loudspeaker went off.

"Herr Oberst Lowell, bitte! Herr Oberst Lowell, bitte!"

Lowell raised his hand over his head and described a circle with his index finger.

A stocky blond-haired man in his late twenties walked quickly over to him, trailed by a man in a gray suit and brimmed cap.

"Colonel Lowell?" the man asked in German, and when Lowell nodded, went on: "General von Greiffenberg asked me to meet you, Colonel. If you'll give me your baggage stubs, we'll clear you through customs. The car is directly outside, if you'll be good enough to wait there."

"Thank you," Lowell said, handing over the baggage check stubs. "Where is the general?"

"He will return later today, Colonel, and join you in Marburg an der Lahn," the man said, avoiding a direct response.

"And my son?"

"I believe he is in Marburg, Colonel. If the colonel will excuse me, I will see to the colonel's luggage."

"Thank you," Lowell said.

The man bobbed his head and walked away.

"I'm impressed," Georgia said. "I didn't know that you were in that tight with the Gestapo."

"That's not funny, Georgia," Lowell said, more sharply than he intended.

"Sorry," she said, surprised at the intensity of his remark. "What was that all about?"

"My father-in-law's sent a car for me," he said.

"We're supposed to have someone meet us," Brian Hayes said. "I suppose I had better go look for him."

"You're going on to Berlin today?" Lowell asked.

"There's an eleven-o'clock plane," Hayes said. He put out his hand. "It was very good to meet you, Craig," he said. "And I hope you'll be able to come to Berlin. We'll be at the Hotel am Zoo."

"I don't really know—" Lowell said.

"It would please Georgia," Hayes said. "And when Georgia is pleased, I am."

"The Hotel am Zoo," Lowell repeated. "I'll see what I can do."

If you weren't such a nice guy, I would be happy to come to Berlin and jump your wife.

Georgia gave him her cheek to kiss and quickly groped him.

"Make an effort, Craig," she said.

There was another clean-cut, well-built young German standing by a Mercedes sedan.

"Ich bin Oberst Lowell," Lowell said.

"Welcome to Germany, Herr Oberst," the young man said, held the door open for him, and then climbed in the front seat. He picked the headset of a radio telephone up and spoke into it.

"What was all that about?" Lowell asked. "Why do I have the feeling that I'm under arrest?"

From the look on the German's face, it was perfectly clear that he didn't understand the attempt at a clever remark.

The chauffeur and the man who had met him inside appeared. The chauffeur put Lowell's luggage into the trunk and climbed behind the wheel. The man got in beside Lowell.

As the Mercedes drove away from the terminal, the policeman on duty to chase cars away saluted.

"We have a little brandy, if the colonel wishes," he said. "And we can get breakfast if the colonel has hunger?"

"Neither, thank you," Lowell said.

"In that case, how about the *Herald-Tribune?*" the man said and handed him a copy of the Paris edition of the New York *Herald-Tribune.*

Lowell took the thin newspaper, scanned the headlines, and flipped through it. When he looked up again, they were on the Autobahn, approaching the turn off to Frankfurt am Main. They were also, he realized, going like the hammers of hell. There was something in the German character that made them take personal affront at any car on the road ahead of them.

XI

(One)
Flughafen Köln
1550 Hours, 29 December 1961

The airplane, a Beechcraft King Aire, a small, eight-passenger turboprop, came in ninety seconds after a British Caledonian Airways Viscount; and while the larger aircraft was still taxiing to the end of the runway, it turned off onto a taxiway and stopped near a French Alouette helicopter.

Parked beside the Alouette were a Mercedes sedan and a yellow Volkswagen bus with the insignia of the customs service of the Federal Republic of Germany painted on its doors.

Without exception—for Germany is a democracy and everyone is equally subject to its laws—every aircraft arriving from a foreign country has to pass through customs. The King Aire had just come from Helsinki, Finland, and therefore it and its passengers had to comply with the procedure prescribed in regulations.

As Orwell pointed out, some animals are more equal than others.

The Volkswagen carried a customs officer, who was driv-

ing. It also carried the senior supervisor of customs on duty at
Flughafen Köln. When the rear door of the King Aire opened,
he was standing there. He saluted.

"How good to see you again, Herr Generalleutnant Graf
von Greiffenberg," he said to the plane's sole passenger.

"It's good to see you," Von Greiffenberg replied, offering
his hand. He was a tall erect man very close to sixty. He was
wearing a Homburg and a Chesterfield and was carrying a
heavy briefcase.

"If the Herr Graf will be good enough?" the senior supervisor
of customs said, extending a filled-out customs declaration on
a clipboard and a ball-point pen.

Von Greiffenberg handed the briefcase to one of the two
neat, stocky men who had been in the Volkswagen.

"Put the whole thing in the safe," he said. "I may call for
it."

"Jawohl, Herr Generalleutnant Graf," the man said. "Herr
Oberst Lowell is at the villa, Herr Generalleutnant Graf."

"Good," Peter-Paul von Greiffenberg said, and smiled as
he scrawled his name on the customs declaration. "Thank you,"
he said to the senior supervisor of customs.

"It is my pleasure, Herr Generalleutnant Graf," the senior
supervisor of customs said.

The pilot of the Alouette started the engine.

"Thank you all for your courtesy," Von Greiffenberg said.

The customs officer by then had taken the Graf's luggage
from the airplane and carried it to the Alouette. As he was
putting it in the backseat, the second man from the Mercedes
ran to the helicopter and held open the door for the Graf.

"Thank you," the Graf said as he got into the helicopter and
reached for the straps.

Flughafen Köln Departure Control cleared Helicopter FR-
203 for immediate takeoff to the East from the parking ramp
adjacent to taxiway thirteen.

The Graf took off his Homburg, put it on the seat beside
him, and then put a headset over his head. By then they had
enough altitude so that the Rhine was visible, as well as the
Cologne Cathedral and the new Rhine River Bridge.

"Nice flight, Herr Graf?" the pilot asked.

"A little bumpy," the Graf said.

"A front is moving in," the pilot said. "We were concerned that you would make it at all."

"God, it was cold in Helsinki," the Graf said.

As the crow flies, it is sixty-six miles from Flughafen Köln to Marburg an der Lahn. The route the pilot took covered about eighty miles, but from the time they left Flughafen Köln until they reached Marburg, they passed over nothing but the smallest of villages. It was a small point, but the Graf did not like to have his whereabouts known to anyone who didn't have to know where he was.

There was some gathering ground fog filling depressions in the terrain, and within an hour or so flight would be dangerous. Soon the medieval buildings of what had once been a cathedral and monastery—and, since the late 1600's, Philipps-Universität—appeared ahead, and a moment later, the pilot began to drop the helicopter toward the garden within the walls of Schloss Greiffenberg.

Schloss Greiffenberg was a villa, rather than what the word *Schloss* (castle) calls to mind. It was called *Schloss* because it had been built, in 1845, within the walls of, on the foundations of, and using material from the ruins of Schloss Greiffenberg (built circa 1380–85). In World War I the seventy-room (including outbuildings) estate had served as a rest home for officers, and in World War II it had been a neuropsychiatric hospital. After the war it had served as an office building for Kries Marburg until then Colonel Graf Peter-Paul von Greiffenberg had been released from imprisonment in Siberia.

Count von Greiffenberg had successfully sued the Kries Marburg and the state of Hesse for damages to the villa, for rent for the time the government had used the villa as offices, and for damages, alleging that the Kries and state had not met their obligation to search diligently for his surviving offspring after his death had been erroneously reported to them.

The state's defense did not impress the Supreme Court, even though Count von Greiffenberg's sole surviving blood kin, a daughter, could not be located after a reasonable search because she had married an American soldier and had been in the United States. Colonel (by then Generalmajor) Graf von Greiffenberg was awarded DM 870,000 for damages to the property and unpaid rent and DM 2,900,000 in punitive damages. He spent all of the money on refurbishing the villa, installing modern comforts, and in an attempt to furnish it as it had once been furnished.

It was not a case of him simply indulging an urge to attempt to restore things to a semblance of what they had been, but his duty, as he saw it, to provide a home for a number of his late wife's relatives (with the exception of his daughter, none of his own had survived both the Nazis and the Russians), whose property had suffered similar damage and confiscation in Pomerania, East Prussia, and Poland, and who were obviously unable to take the various People's Democratic functionaries to court and demand justice.

And then there was the question of Peter-Paul von Greiffenberg Lowell, who was the last male in whom there was the blood of the Von Greiffenbergs. Privately the Graf had often thought that it was rather a pity that the man who had married Ilse was so wealthy. If it had not been for that, it would have been easy to arrange for him to live in Germany and gradually instill in him the idea that the boy should take the German nationality that he could by right claim.

It was not that Graf von Greiffenberg did not like Craig Lowell. He liked him very much, and was pleased that since the Von Greiffenberg blood had been diluted by marriage to a commoner, that commoner was at least of English stock and a gentleman warrior, much as Von Greiffenbergs had been gentlemen warriors for centuries. The only real difference Generalleutnant Graf von Greiffenberg, Retired, had with Lieutenant Colonel Lowell was that Lowell simply would not consider the merits of having Peter-Paul take German citizenship.

While that question was still up in the air, Schloss Greiffenberg was the boy's home. Living there could not help but teach him something of his heritage.

The Alouette landed on a pad between the tennis courts and the apple orchard. The Graf took his luggage and started toward the villa. He had reached the tennis courts, and the Alouette had already taken off again when the butler came out to take the luggage.

The butler informed him that the Herr Oberst was in the crypt.

"We will not disturb him," the Graf said. "And my grandson?"

"He is in Kassel, Herr Graf, with his friends. Herr Ness drove them."

"I'd forgotten," the Graf confessed. "How long has Oberst Lowell been...down there?"

"About thirty minutes, Herr Graf," the butler said. "I gave him lunch when he arrived, and then he said he had work to do. Half an hour ago he went to the crypt."

The Graf went into the library and waited for his son-in-law to appear.

When Lowell came into the library a few minutes later, he went right to the whiskey cupboard and poured a stiff drink. He did not see the Graf as he entered, nor even when he went to the windows and looked through them, down to the ancient city of Marburg.

But he seemed to sense the Graf's eyes on his back and turned to look at him.

"I didn't know you were here," Lowell said.

"My dear Craig, I'm so glad to see you. Did you have a good flight?"

Lowell snorted. "Let's say 'interesting,'" he said.

"If I had known earlier when you were coming, I'd have had Peter-Paul meet you. I've been in Helsinki."

Anyone who really believed that the Graf had left the intelligence business when he had retired from the army probably believed in the Tooth Fairy and the Goodness of Man, Lowell thought.

"What's he doing in Kassel?"

"Something with friends, I don't really know."

"You don't seem very surprised to see me," Lowell said.

"Nothing you do surprises me, Craig," the Graf said.

"I have been run out of the country," Lowell said. "There are some people who are afraid I'll say something to the Secretary of Defense I shouldn't."

"And how did Mr. McNamara offend you?" the Graf asked with a laugh.

"They're afraid we're going to agree," Lowell said.

"No wonder they banished you," the Graf said. "For how long?"

"For thirty days," Lowell said.

"Well, it will give you a nice holiday, and you can spend some time with Peter-Paul."

"I'll be here about ten days if I'm welcome that long," Lowell said. "And then I'm going on to Indochina."

"That doesn't sound like a holiday," the Graf said.

"No."

"I think I'll have some of that whiskey," the Graf said. When he got close to Craig Lowell, he put his arm around his back and gave a little hug. It didn't take a second, but it was for Generalleutnant Graf von Greiffenberg a remarkable display of affection.

Lowell laughed. The Graf looked at him curiously.

"Courtesy would require," Lowell said, "that I ask you what you were doing in Helsinki. But I don't think you want me to ask, do you?"

"I was seeing friends," the Graf said smoothly. "May I ask why you're going to Indochina?"

"I presume that's a personal question?"

"Of course."

"I think we're going in there," Lowell said. "We just sent a bunch of airplanes over there."

"On an old aircraft carrier called the *Card*," the Graf said. "It stuck in my mind because it was a rather odd name."

"My, you do keep current, don't you?" Lowell asked, lightly sarcastic. "What else can you tell me that I didn't know?"

"How about a quote from MacArthur?" the Graf said. "'Don't get involved in a war on the Asian land mass.'"

"I like the other one better," Lowell said. "'There is no substitute for victory.' I'm afraid we're going to do the same thing we did in Korea. Spend a lot of money, kill a lot of people, and when the war is over, be just about where we were when we started."

"I was in China as a young officer," the Graf said. "A *very* young officer, come to think of it. I came away with the impression that there is no way western armies could win. It would be Russia times ten."

He waved Lowell into one of four identical high-backed red leather armchairs facing a low table and settled himself in an opposing chair. They both put their feet on the table.

"The only chance we have is mobility," Lowell said.

"I just came from Cologne by helicopter," the Graf said. "Thirty-odd minutes. By road it's two and a half hours. In this weather it would take four or five."

"I didn't hear a chopper," Lowell said, surprised.

"It was French, I'm afraid," the Graf said. "An Alouette."

"Wait till you see what we have on the drawing boards," Lowell said loyally. "And even starting to come off the line."

"I've heard," the Graf said. "Is that what they have you doing, Craig? War plans?"

"That's a tactful way of putting it," Lowell said. "I think of it more as paper-shuffling."

"And do you think it will work?" the Graf asked.

"Will what work?"

"The substitution of aircraft and helicopters for trucks?"

"I'm afraid not," Lowell said seriously. "The logistics to keep them in the air boggle the mind. But we have not heard, I don't think, the last bugler sounding the charge."

"Meaning what?"

"Despite reports to the contrary, cavalry is not dead."

"I still don't think I follow you," the Graf said.

"That frightens me a little, Herr Generalleutnant Graf," Lowell said, "if you, of all people, can't see where we're going."

"Tell me," the Graf said seriously.

"'Good afternoon, gentlemen,'" Lowell said, half mockingly. "'Our subject for the day is the role of cavalry in the modern army. There will be a verbal quiz following the lecture and a written examination on Friday.'"

Von Greiffenberg laughed.

"There have been from the earliest days three basic types of ground forces. These are the infantry, which takes and holds ground; the artillery, which bombards enemy positions prior to an infantry attack, or enemy forces when the enemy attacks; and the cavalry, whose primary characteristic is mobility. Mobility—originally with horses and later with tracked vehicles— gave the cavalry the ability to breach a weak point in the enemy lines and then to exploit that breakthrough by interrupting the enemy's lines of supply.

"From time to time, throughout history, well-meaning people have *upgefucht* cavalry's noble role."

The Graf chuckled. He knew what *upgefucht*, a word coined by American GIs in Germany, meant.

"The first such *upgefuching* occurred when the noble cavalry warrior was encased in several hundred pounds of armor, which required an enormous horse just to carry him and reduced his speed to about that of the foot soldier. He could no longer rush about, breaching the enemy's lines, and infantry soldiers found him an easy target. If all else failed, they could push him off his horse. Cavalry was dead.

"Nobody told the Americans this, however, and they used cavalry in their revolution—with great success. Cavalry was again alive and well, to the point where the Confederate cavalry of J. E. B. Stuart kept the Yankees from quickly winning the War Between the States for a longer period than the preponderance of forces indicated they should.

"In the American Civil War, too, the amateur soldiers came up with something that truly offended traditionalists. They bastardized artillery's noble role. Everybody but the Americans—on both sides—knew that one put artillery in place and kept it there until the battle was over. But not knowing this sacred rule, American cavalrymen hitched teams of horses to artillery pieces and galloped all over the battlefield with them, using them where they were needed at that moment, including, it must be noted, in the advance.

"Comes Brother Gatling, shortly followed by Brother Maxim and Brother Browning, with their machine guns. Horses made a splendid target, and cavalry again was dead.

"Comes a limey, name of Winston Churchill, who sees the requirement for a means of warfare to overcome his current problem, which is sort of a stalemate. Both he and the Germans are running out of infantrymen to send into the mouths of machine guns. Churchill's solution is a mechanical horse. It has tracks, which permit it to climb in and out of shell holes and across trenches. It has armor plate, which turns small-arms fire. It has the capability to move quickly about the battlefield and breach the enemy's lines at his weak points. He calls this strange device a 'tank.'

"After first making pro forma protestations that this device is the tool of the Devil and has no place in battle between Christian gentlemen, the Germans start building their own tanks. Too late. A name is needed for this new form of warfare, and since cavalry is obviously dead, someone decides that 'armor' has a nice ring to it. So the word is passed that cavalry is dead, and armor is born.

"Comes the second War to End All Wars. A German chap named Guderian, who understands the role of cavalry, attacks the French. Even though they have more and better tanks than he does, they do not understand the role of cavalry and think of their tanks as mobile pillboxes for support of the infantry. French tanks move at the speed of the French infantry. German tanks move like cavalry: They go as fast as they can move and to hell with their flanks. This, Herr Generalleutnant, is known as the *Blitzkrieg,* and shortly after Guderian puts it to work, the French are waving white flags."

"That's very good," Von Greiffenberg said, laughing. "You've given this speech before, I take it?"

"Have I ever? But indulge me, I'm not through."

"By all means."

"On the American side we have some interesting generals. One of them is sort of a cavalryman by the name of Patton."

"Sort of a cavalryman?"

"He was an infantry officer," Lowell said, "but understood this was a mistake of judgment on his part. In his heart he was cavalry. He was quite a polo player, you know. Polo is not an infantry sport. Infantry takes walks in the woods."

Von Greiffenberg chuckled.

"And who were the other 'interesting' American generals?"

"There were many, but for the purposes of this brief lecture, I will discuss only two. Both associated with the Second Armored Division. Ernest Harmon and his successor, I. D. White. Both cavalrymen. White, by the way, as a young aide-de-camp, laid out the golf course at Fort Knox from the back of a horse; and he, too, was one hell of a polo player. The important point here is that Harmon and White fought the Second Armored as *cavalry.* And Patton used his armored forces in the Third Army as cavalry."

"You really think that's the case?"

"White took a real screwing," Lowell said. "He should have gone in the history books as the first American general ever to take Paris and the first American general ever to take Berlin. He was outside Paris—Senlis, I think—when he was ordered to hold in place and let the Second French Armored pass through his lines for the honor of taking Paris. Later he had his first elements across the Elbe and was prepared to take Berlin when he was ordered to hold in place and let the Russians have it."

"That must have hurt," Von Greiffenberg said.

"Yeah, but I'm digressing. So far as I'm concerned, the greatest cavalry maneuver in history was Patton's. In the Battle of the Bulge he disengaged two divisions, moved them a hundred miles through a blizzard, and had them attacking in forty-eight hours. That's cavalry!"

"I agree, but I seem to be missing your point."

"Since our tanks, our armor, had done so well, everybody jumped on the bandwagon and decreed that armor was the force of the future. They had disbanded cavalry during the war, and now they came out with a new insignia for armor. A tank. I. D. White, who was arguably the best if not the senior armor officer on active duty, insisted—rather violently, I've been told—that cavalry was *not* dead and demanded that cavalry sabers be superimposed on the new tank of armor insignia."

"Was that White?" Von Greiffenberg asked, surprised.

"That was White," Lowell said.

"I never heard that before," the Graf said. "Odd. I should have thought Hasso von Manteuffel would have said something to me. He and White became close after the war, you know."

"That was White," Lowell repeated. "And now we're finally at my point. The lecture is about over. It has no more come down from Mount Sinai graven on stone tablets that cavalry has to be mounted on horses or tracked vehicles than it has come down that infantry has to be armed with pointed sticks or machine guns. Cavalry is a technique, a philosophy, not a particular tool."

"And you're saying the new cavalry horse is the helicopter?"

"Absolutely," Lowell said. "With what we have now, we can pick up a squad of troops and three days' rations and ammunition, and deliver them at one hundred miles an hour, rested and ready to fight, anywhere in a hundred-mile radius. We've got helicopters on the drawing boards that can pick up a 155-millimeter cannon, its crew, and its basic load of ammunition, and in an hour set it down on a hilltop someplace a hundred miles away."

"That sounds like artillery," the Graf said.

"Mobile artillery was stolen from cavalry in the Civil War,"

Lowell said. "It's time we took it back."

"You're talking about a division, aren't you? Maybe even *divisions?*"

"Absolutely," Lowell said. "Air cavalry divisions. The whole thing air-transportable."

"And you think they'll work against a guerrilla army in Vietnam?"

"I don't know," Lowell said. "We'll have to find out. I do know that conventional forces won't. If we use conventional forces, we'll have to carry the war to North Vietnam. Or even to China."

"'Don't get involved in a war on the Asian land mass,'" Von Greiffenberg quoted again.

"I don't think I'm personally going to get involved in a war anywhere," Lowell said. "I am the consummate paper-shuffler . . . and lecturer."

"You'll get a command," the Graf said.

"I am beginning to wonder if that isn't wishful thinking," Lowell said.

"Both Bob Bellmon and Paul Hanrahan have been named general officers," the Graf said.

"And Bill Roberts," Lowell said.

"And Paul Jiggs is a major general," the Graf said. "You are not without friends."

"There are a number of very powerful people in the army who think all of them are mad. Kennedy gave Hanrahan his star. He'd never have been recommended for it."

"The point is, they have their stars," the Graf said. "One day you will, I am sure."

"The eternal optimist. Or do I look that down in the mouth?"

"Neither," the Graf said. "A professional opinion."

"I don't believe that for a minute," Lowell said. "But I like to hear it. Where's the court?"

It was his son-in-law's very rude term for the dozen displaced East Germans and Poles who were related to the Graf and now made their home in the *schloss*. They demanded of the servants the respect due their titles, and Lowell found this amusing.

"Most of them went to Bavaria," he said. "Ludwig put it

rather cleverly. He said that the only reason Hessians pretend to enjoy Christmas and New Year's is because they know Lent will shortly follow."

"Ludwig is the fat Pomeranian?" Lowell asked, laughing.

The Graf nodded. "The Graf von Kolberg."

"Peter-Paul didn't go with them?"

"There's a good deal of you in Peter-Paul," the Graf said. "He tends to make sarcastic comments when my relatives are all gathered around remembering better days. Peter-Paul is much more interested in the films than in the Almanac de Gotha."

"The films?" Lowell asked. "Why did you say that?"

"It's true. Is that so unusual?"

"I have been invited to a film festival in Berlin," Lowell said. "I met an actress I know on the plane."

"How many actresses do you know?" the Graf teased.

"One," Lowell said. "That one."

"The one named after the state," the Graf said. "Tennessee, something? No, that's the writer."

"*Georgia* Paige," Lowell said.

"That's an extraordinary custom," the Graf said. "Is there an actor or actress named 'North Dakota' or 'Massachusetts'?"

"No, but there's an actor named Rip Torn," Lowell said. "And another one named Rock Hudson."

"'Rip Torn'?" the Graf parroted, laughing.

"You think Peter-Paul would like to go to this thing?" Lowell asked.

"I think he would prefer it to the alternatives," the Graf said. "Which are staying here with you or going to Bavaria with me for New Year's."

"I gather I'm not welcome at the palace?"

"Don't be silly. Of course you are. But it never entered my mind you'd want to go."

"I don't," Lowell said. "But I'm not exactly at home at a film festival, either."

"Peter-Paul would love it. If you could introduce him to a film star, he would be in ecstasy. And you—the both of you—should see the wall."

"You've seen it?"

"I watched them put it up," the Graf said. "In a morbid way, it's rather fascinating. It's an interesting insight into the working of their minds."

"Kennedy should have ordered it torn down," Lowell said.

"I don't think so," the Graf said. "There it stands, proof to the world that communism has provided such a better life for its people that they have to be kept in paradise by concrete walls topped with barbed wire."

"I hadn't thought of it that way," Lowell said. "I'm not sure if what you say isn't an accidental by-product of weak knees."

"There was nothing short of war that could be done to stop it," the Graf said, as if surprised he had to explain this to Lowell. "The Russians are scrupulously observing their obligations to the Western Allies. American soldiers can pass freely back and forth."

"Hello, Father," a voice in the process of changing said from the door. Lowell looked and saw Peter-Paul.

"I don't mean to say, of course, that you and Peter-Paul should cross into East Berlin," the Graf said seriously and very quickly.

Peter-Paul von Greiffenberg Lowell was a tall, slender fourteen-year-old, with a shock of light blond hair hanging over his forehead. His hair was too long on top, his father thought, and trimmed too short at the ears and neck.

There was a good deal of Ilse von Greiffenberg Lowell in him, in the cheekbones, in the eyebrows, and especially in the blue eyes.

Lowell swung his feet off the table and stood up. He held his arms out to his son, marveling at how much he had grown from the last time he had seen him. Peter-Paul von Greiffenberg Lowell walked across the room and extended his hand formally to his father. Lowell ignored it and wrapped his arms around the boy. The boy was stiff in his arms, and after a moment his father released him, feeling hurt and foolish.

"What were you doing in Kassel?" Lowell asked.

"I was there with friends," Peter-Paul said.

"Doing what?"

"There was a festival of Humphrey Bogart films," the boy said. "Are you familiar with the films of Humphrey Bogart?"

The little sonofabitch is being sarcastic.

"Yes, indeed," Lowell said. "I've been told there is a film festival in Berlin."

"December thirty-first to January five," the boy said, nodding.

"Would you like to go?"

"It is an industry affair," the boy said, "not open to the general public."

"I asked if you would like to go?" Lowell said, aware his smile was strained.

"Your father has been invited, Peter-Paul," the Graf said.

"By someone in the industry?" the boy asked. There was now a flicker of interest in his voice.

"Yes."

"May I ask who?"

"Does that matter?" Lowell asked, somewhat sharply.

"It would affect how much of the festival one could get into see," the boy said.

"Are you familiar with the films of Brian Hayes?" Lowell asked, mocking his son's question of a moment before.

"And he has invited you?"

"He has invited *us*," Lowell said.

"Phantastisch!" the boy said.

When he smiled, he looked very much like his mother.

(Two)
West Berlin
0630 Hours, 4 January 1962

When he paid off the taxi and was standing alone on a wide windswept road that a blue sign identified as Strasse des 17 Juni, Lowell decided that he had done a damned fool thing coming here. Here was somewhere near "the wall."

It was colder than the arctic, for one thing, and when he had seen what he wanted to see, he was going to have a hell of a time finding a cab to go back to the Hotel am Zoo. And if he had had the presence of mind, he could have had the Mercedes that had met them at the airport bring him here. It had been delicately put to him that the car would be available to him and Peter-Paul around the clock. Translation: The polite, taciturn young men driving the car were there to protect Peter-Paul. The Russians had no interest in an obscure American lieutenant colonel, but the grandson of Peter-Paul von Greiffenberg was another matter.

The Russians had had plenty of time and opportunity to reflect on their error in judgment in returning the Graf to the West.

Looking like hell, to tell the truth about it, Georgia had gotten out of their bed at half past five for a six-fifteen appointment with a faggot hairdresser with an apparently mystical skill. As a *personal* favor, the faggot had agreed to "do her" so that she would be at her best at a luncheon awards ceremony.

Lowell had pretended to be asleep—actually afraid that Georgia would like a quickie. The fear had been groundless. He suspected that Georgia had grown as bored with him in the sack as he was with her. All the ingredients were there: a healthy lustful male who had not been getting laid very much lately, and a healthy, lusty female who probably had but liked it anyway. Even the first time it had not been what he had fantasized. He told himself he should have known better.

If he had been alone, he would have found some excuse to leave. But Peter-Paul was having a ball. He had taken up with a photographer (a cinematographer, Peter-Paul had corrected him). Peter-Paul knew the name and his "credits," and the photographer had been flattered and impressed with Peter-Paul's European manners. The photographer, a burly, bald-headed man, had told Lowell he had two sons of his own who were neither impressed with their father nor well mannered. And they barely spoke English, much less German and French, as Peter-Paul did.

The two of them spent their days running all over Berlin, while the photographer took what he called "notebook shots." Peter-Paul was thrilled with the privilege of carrying battery packs and other photographer's impedimenta, and the photographer got, not only a coolie who spoke the native's language, but a chauffeur-driven Mercedes to haul them both around. When there was an official festival function, Peter-Paul went with the photographer. The photographer introduced him to the stars as "my assistant."

There was no way Lowell could have taken Peter-Paul away

from that sort of arrangement, and he had stayed.

Lowell looked across the street at the two Russian soldiers guarding the War Memorial. When he had been at Command and General Staff College at Leavenworth, most of the time bored out of his mind, he had made an unofficial study of the Battle of Berlin. He had drawn several conclusions, all firmly supported by little publicized facts: Eisenhower had been dead wrong when he ordered General I. D. White's Second "Hell on Wheels" Armored Division to halt in place on the Elbe. White could have taken Berlin. The German-Russian battle for the city had been largely a mop up operation of the Charlemagne Division of the Waffen-SS, Frenchmen who had enlisted in the Nazi cause. Although heralded as a great Soviet victory over fanatical Nazi forces, the truth of the matter was that the Germans involved in the battle were primarily concerned with trying to reach American lines so they could surrender.

The two Russian soldiers marching back and forth in front of the War Memorial did so with a straight-legged step, holding submachine guns diagonally across their chests. Lowell could see no difference between their posture and what he had seen in newsreels described as the Nazi goosestep.

He turned the fur collar of his overcoat up to keep the icy wind off his neck and walked down the Strasse des 17. Juni to the Brandenburg Gate.

That was the border, and there was a wall up. It was of crudely cast concrete blocks stacked on one another and topped with barbed wire. He walked to the wall, but had to retrace his steps when he saw that at this point there was no passage beside it. He turned left at the first intersection, walked through a recently planted grove of pines, four, five feet tall, and eventually came to the wall again.

The wall made a sharp zig here. On the far side of the turn he saw a rough-lumber arrangement that looked like an old-fashioned gallows. He walked around the corner. It was an observation platform, and the stairs to it were barred by a thin chain and a sign reading OFF LIMITS—EINTRITT VERBOTEN.

Nailed to one of the supporting timbers was a sign in English and German: OBSERVATION POST THREE. U.S. ARMY, BERLIN GARRISON. AUTHORIZED PERSONNEL ONLY.

Lowell ducked under the thin chain and climbed to the top. The first thing he saw was a Russian or East German observation platform, more elaborate than this one, with a roof and walls and a stove chimney. He saw two uniformed men examining him through binoculars. He was too far away to tell from their uniforms whether they were Russians or East Germans. He waved cheerfully at them, but there was no response.

And then he dropped his eyes to the ground and swore.

There was an area perhaps twenty-five yards wide on the East side of the wall. It had been bulldozed clear, and they were in the process of mining it. He found that difficult to believe, but when he looked around he could see, farther down the East side of the wall, the standard German triangular minefield sign, a skull and crossbones and the words *Achtung! Minenfeld!*

There was something really obscene about that.

He heard a familiar sound, the *fluckata-fluckata* of helicopter rotor blades. He looked over his shoulder for it, and after a moment found it. It was a Bell H-13E, with U.S. ARMY lettered on the bottom of the bubble.

It flew closer and then came to a hover perhaps fifty feet off the ground and about the same distance from the observation platform.

There were two people in it, one of them wearing the fur-brimmed winter service cap. The letters MP were on the front of it. The MP gestured to him, a clear signal that he was to leave the observation platform. Lowell waved as cheerfully at him as he had to the Russians, East Germans, or whoever they were in the East Zone tower.

The smart thing to do was simply get off the observation platform, but there was something about it that kept him there. He just did not want to leave yet, and there didn't seem to be anything the chopper-borne MP could do to make him. There was no place to set it down.

He leaned on the two-by-four railing and looked down at the minefield again, then farther into East Berlin, where for the first time he noticed that the windows of the buildings facing the wall were mostly bricked up.

Peter-Paul had refused several invitations to see the wall,

and Lowell had been unwilling to insist. He decided now that the boy was going to see this before he left Berlin, whether or not or he wanted to.

Peter-Paul had known nothing but comfortable circumstances. He hadn't been born when his grandfather had been in Siberia. He had been an infant when Lowell had been in Korea and when his mother had been killed. Perhaps that made him immune to rage at something like this. But he had to be exposed to it.

There was another familiar sound, the peculiar, unmistakable squeal of jeep brakes.

The MP in the chopper had apparently radioed the MPs on the ground. He didn't think there was much chance he would be hauled off in chains once he produced his AGO card, but he thought it was entirely possible that he would receive a letter through channels from the commanding general, Berlin Garrison, requesting that he reply by endorsement hereto why he had climbed a forbidden gallows and ignored the clear hand signals of a military policeman in the execution of his office.

The gallows shivered under the footsteps of two men running up the stairs. Lowell turned to face them.

Two MPs, in parkas and winter caps. One of them had warrant officer's bars pinned to the parka.

"My God!" the warrant said, in genuine shock. "It's the Duke!"

The other MP looked at him in surprise.

The warrant saluted.

"You are Major Lowell, aren't you, sir?" he asked.

"Guilty," Lowell said. "Nice to see you again."

He had no idea who the warrant was. Somebody from Korea, obviously. He couldn't remember a warrant who looked like this one.

"Stenday, sir," the warrant said. "I was with you on the Task Force."

"Yes, of course," Lowell said.

He didn't remember the name, either. There had been four hundred people in Task Force Lowell. He could not be expected to remember all of them. But he was shamed that he didn't remember this man at all.

He put his hand out. Warrant Officer Stenday jerked his

glove off and shook Lowell's hand enthusiastically. Then he remembered why he was here.

"Get on the horn and tell them it's an American officer," he said. Then he turned to Lowell. "Is there something you're after, Major?"

"No," Lowell said. "Nothing special. I just happened to be in Berlin, and I wanted to see this."

"Pretty fucking disgusting, isn't it?" Stenday said. "You see where the bastards are mining it?"

Lowell nodded.

"What we should do is get a dozen M-46s and knock the sonofabitch down," Stenday said.

Lowell quoted the philosophy of Generalleutnant Graf von Greiffenberg: "I don't know. It's sort of standing proof that communism has failed, wouldn't you say?"

"With all respect, Major . . . is that right, 'Major'?"

"I made light bird," Lowell said.

"With all respect, *Colonel*, you haven't seen those bastards shooting people—kids, some of them—trying to get over the wall. And we can't shoot back."

Lowell could think of nothing to say. He shrugged his shoulders helplessly.

They looked at each other for a minute.

"Can I offer you a ride to your car, Colonel?"

"I came by cab," Lowell said.

"Then I'll take you to Checkpoint Charlie," Stenday said. "That's on Potsdamer Platz. There's a phone there, and we got a hot plate. How about a cup of coffee?"

The other MP came back up the stairs.

"They want to know what he's doing," he said uneasily.

"Tell him he was pissing over the wall," Stenday said.

"I can't tell them that," the MP said.

"Just ignore them, then. Tell them we're going into Charlie, and then make believe the radio's broke." He turned back to Lowell. "No rush, Colonel. Take your time."

"I've seen all I need to see," Lowell said, and started toward the stairs.

There was a small, crude, tar-paper–covered shack near the MP checkpoint. Inside there was a two-burner gas stove with a coffeepot on the burner and a frying pan on the other. An

MP was frying bacon. There was a glass bowl full of eggs and a shelf with condiments. The bottles triggered memories of similar bottles on crude shelves in Greece and Korea . . . and a strange thought: The army might go into battle in worn boots and frayed uniforms and with worn-out equipment, but by God, they were Americans, and where they went, so did Heinz 57 steak sauce, Tabasco, catsup, and a hot plate.

The MP looked at Lowell curiously.

"This is the civilian infiltrator," Warrant Officer Stenday said. "Colonel Lowell. I was with the colonel in Korea."

"Can I fix you an egg sandwich, Colonel?" the MP said. "I got one just about done."

"Thank you," Lowell said. "My mouth is watering."

A captain wearing MP identification on the folded-up brim of his winter cap and the OD brassard of the Officer of the Day around his parka sleeve came into the hut as Lowell was being handed a steaming white china cup of coffee.

"Captain, this is Colonel Lowell," Stenday said. "He was the man on the observation platform."

"Good morning, sir," the captain said.

"Your people have taken pity on a freezing tourist, Captain," Lowell said, holding up the coffee cup.

"Is that what you're doing here, sir?" the captain asked.

"Actually, I came over here to find out how Mr. Stenday managed to stay out of the stockade long enough to become an MP," Lowell said.

"You know Mr. Stenday?" the captain asked.

"I knew him before he became respectable," Lowell said.

" 'You play ball with the Seventy-third Heavy Tank, or we'll stick the bat up your ass,' " Stenday quoted. It was the motto of the Seventy-third Tank Battalion.

Lowell chuckled. "It's been a long time since I heard that," Lowell said. "How did you wind up in the MPs, Stenday?"

"What they do with tanks in Berlin, Colonel," Stenday said, "is polish them. Once a month they take them out for a parade, and then they polish them again. I'm not much on that, so I wangled TDY with the MPs."

"I see."

"You want to know about Berlin tanks, Colonel?" Stenday went on. "They're kept ready to roll. And you know what we're going to do when the Russians come through the wall? We shag ass down to Berlin Military Post and assume a 'defensive position.' What that means is, we wait until they burn papers and blow up the RIAS* tower, and then we blow up the tanks and surrender."

The captain looked at Stenday and then at Lowell. American officer or not, Lowell had no Need to Know the details of what would happen if the Russians should decide to overwhelm the small American garrison. It was a clear violation of military security.

"I didn't hear him say anything, Captain," Lowell said.

"Neither did I, sir," the captain said after a moment. "What did you think of the wall?"

Lowell made a look of disgust. "What's the reason for the 'Off Limits' sign on that gallows?" he asked.

"They don't want any incidents, people giving the *Volks-polizei* the finger or throwing things at them," the captain said.

"I'm here in Berlin with a cameraman," Lowell said. "He's at the film festival. Could he get permission to shoot some pictures over the wall?"

"You'd have to get permission from PIO, sir, but that wouldn't be any problem."

"Where would I find the PIO?"

"I get off at 0800, Colonel," Stenday said. "I'll run you by there if you like."

The captain was wrong. Lowell encountered the bureaucratic mind when he went to the Public Information Division of Headquarters, Berlin Military Post. The PIO, a lieutenant colonel, said the decision whether or not a civilian photographer not accredited to Berlin Military Post would be allowed to climb the observation platform and take pictures would have to be made by higher authority. Higher authority turned out to be the Chief of Staff, a starchy full colone of infantry. After asking questions about what Lowell was doing in Berlin in the first place, he finally asked to see his orders.

Lowell gave him the single copy of his orders that he had folded into the shape of a dollar bill and put in his wallet.

The Chief of Staff's eyebrows went up when he read them.

---

*Rundfunk im Amerikanische Sektor, the American-backed German language radio station.

"Very impressive orders, Colonel," he said. "I can see no problem in letting your photographer take whatever pictures he wants to."

"Thank you very much, sir," Lowell said. He had no idea what had impressed the colonel. He hadn't even looked at his orders.

They left what had been the *Großes Hauptquartier* of the Luftwaffe and was now Headquarters, Berlin Military Post, trailed by an olive-drab Opel Captain bearing a Public Information Officer and his assistant. Once settled in the car, he took the orders out and read them. He smiled. No wonder the colonel had been impressed.

HEADQUARTERS
THE ARMY AVIATION CENTER AND FORT RUCKER, ALA.

Letter Orders: 26 December 1961

1. Ref TELECON Vice Chief of Staff, USA and CG Ft Rucker Ala 1545 hours 24 December.

2. Verbal orders V/C/S USA confirmed and made a matter of record:

LT COL C. W. LOWELL, 0439067 Armor, USAAB, Ft Rucker Ala is placed on TDY eff 27 Dec 1961 for pd not less than thirty (30) days in connection with activities of DCSOPS. Off will proceed at his discretion to Hq USAREUR, Hq USARPAC, Hq USA MAC(Vietnam). Off auth tvl by Govt and Civ air, motor, rail and water T. When utilizing Govt T Priority AAB. Off auth 200 lbs excess baggage. Off auth at his discretion up to fifteen (15) days lv at any point in his tvl. Off auth civ clothing. Off holds TOP SECRET sec clear. Questions concerning nature of asgmt will be referred to undersigned or V/C/S.

PAUL T. JIGGS
Major General, USA.

The nature of his assignment, of course, was quite simple: *Get the sonofabitch out of the country so that he won't be available to give the wrong answers to questions likely to be put to him by the Secretary of Defense*. But the words could be interpreted to mean that he was carrying out some high-priority and most secret mission for the Vice-Chief of Staff himself.

He found Peter-Paul and the photographer in the restaurant of the Hotel Am Zoo.

"Charley, I want you to meet an old friend of mine, Warrant Officer Stenday. He has some very interesting 'file shots' for you."

"Is that so?"

"He knows a place where you can take pictures over the wall," Lowell said.

The photographer's eyebrows went up.

"I think I'm going to like you, Stenday," he said. "Sit down and have some breakfast."

"This is my son, Stenday," Lowell said.

"How do you do?" Peter-Paul said formally, offering his hand. Then he turned to Lowell. "Father, one of Grandfather's men has a message for you."

"He does? Where is he?"

"I believe they went to get the car," Peter-Paul said in his British accented English.

Lowell saw the look of surprise on Stenday's face.

"Peter-Paul lives in Europe, Stenday," Lowell said, "to explain the accent."

"Oh," Stenday said.

One of the neat young German men came to the table.

"I have a message for you, Herr Oberst," he said. "I had no idea where you were." The last was a reprimand.

"I was safe in the hands of the MPs," Lowell said. He ripped open the envelope the man handed him. It was a photocopy of a cablegram:

> DOTHAN ALA 3 JAN 1962
> VIC RCA
> C W LOWELL
> SCHLOSS GREIFFENBERG
> MARBURG AN DER LAHN WEST GERMANY
> POPPA SAYS COME HOME ALL IS FORGIVEN
> MAGGIE

Poppa was obviously Major General Paul T. Jiggs. Maggie in the comic strip was married to Jiggs. Whatever it was, it was some sort of good news. He looked at his watch. It was nine-fifteen, or four-fifteen in the States. He was not going to risk Jiggs's ire by getting him out of bed. He would have to wait until Charley had taken his pictures over the wall to find out what was really going on.

The rest of the morning went very well. Charley was delighted to be able to photograph the minefields on the East side of the wall. He even took a few pictures of East Germans laying the mines. To Lowell's surprise and relief, his son was outraged at the notion that people should be kept behind a wall.

At half-past twelve he got through to Paul Jiggs at Fort Rucker. Jiggs had just walked into his office.

"That report you had something to do with was rejected as unacceptable," Jiggs said.

"Damn!" Lowell said, bitterly. "How badly was it cut?"

"It was returned for 'reexamination,'" Jiggs said.

"Oh. Christ. So that's why I'm forgiven. I'm the reexaminer."

"Yes, you are," Jiggs said. "Let me read you something, Craig. Quote: 'I shall be disappointed if the army's reexamination merely produces logistically oriented recommendations to procure more of the same, rather than a plan for employment of fresh and perhaps unorthodox concepts which will give us a significant increase in mobility.' End quote."

"Read that again," Lowell said. Jiggs did.

"Not to mention any names, was there once a band named after the man who signed that?" Lowell asked.

"I don't know about a band—Oh. Yes. There was a band by that name."

Lowell was exultant. Secretary of Defense McNamara had not only rejected the cutback request for 250 airplanes as being inadequate, he had as much as ordered plans for an air-mobile division.

"We won," Lowell said. "Presuming he means it."

"He means it. How soon can you come home?"

"Right away," Lowell said. "Just as soon as I can get on a plane."

Peter-Paul von Greiffenberg Lowell's only reaction to his father's announcement was anger: His father's departure would mean the end of his being Charley-the-photographer's coolie.

"Why don't you ask Grandfather if I mightn't stay?"

Peter-Paul sulked on the Pan American flight to Frankfurt am Main. He was still feeling sorry for himself and annoyed with this near stranger who appeared at odd intervals in his life when he got in the Mercedes that would carry him back to Marburg an der Lahn.

He did not look out the windows of the car, so he did not see his father waving good-bye to him.

(Three)
Pan American Flight 304
Clipper City of San Francisco
Above the Ruhr
2130 Hours, 4 January 1962

The Pan-American stewardess did the modesty squat in the aisle beside the next to the last double row of seats on the right. Lowell was slumped back in the chair, holding a legal pad against his knee. If McNamara wanted "unorthodox concepts," unorthodox concepts he would get; and there was no reason they should not be drafted on an airplane. He looked at the stewardess in annoyance.

"Excuse me, Mr. Lowell," she said, flashing him what he thought of somewhat unkindly as the Stewardess Smirk.

"Yes?"

"When all the seats in first class aren't taken, we usually move soldiers up from tourist."

He looked at her in some confusion. He had been deep in thought, trying to recall from memory the interlocking facts that affected the turning of a truck-transportable infantry division into a division capable of moving itself entirely by air. T-many troops could be moved by H-many Bell HU-1B helicopters. H-many Bell HU-1B helicopters required RWA-many rotary-wing aviators, plus M-many Maintenance Platoons, plus F-many fuel trucks plus SE-many spare engines. M-many Maintenance Platoons would require H-many more helicopters.

That was a nice thing for Pan American to do, he thought. *It would not occur to Lufthansa. But why tell me? Does she want me to give her a medal?*

She dropped her eyes to the empty seat beside her, on which he had placed his open attaché case.

"Oh, sure," he said. "Sorry."

"Thank you, sir," she said.

He closed the attaché case and put it under his seat. In every silvery cloud, he thought, there had to be a black lining. He was going to get as a seat partner some sergeant's wife with a babe-in-arms or, worse, some finance corps officer who would regale him with the intimate details of the burden he had shouldered paying the troops on alien shores. In either event, he would not be able to get much work done.

The soldier appeared three minutes later.

The soldier deposited an attaché case on the seat and then took off the uniform tunic. The soldier had captain's bars and a medical caduceus on her tunic, and a set of knockers that placed a severe strain on the buttons of her shirt.

"Hello," the captain said, displaying a mouthful of very uniform, very white teeth. The captain subjected her shirt buttons to another stress test when she reached up, unpinned, and then removed her uniform cap. The captain's hair was an admirable shade of red.

"Good evening," Lowell said.

The captain slipped into the aisle seat.

"I'm a little embarrassed at Pan Am's charity," she said. "But the alternative was remaining a sardine."

"I'm delighted to have you," Lowell said.

"I would be annoyed," she said, "if I had paid whatever it costs to ride up here, and someone appeared who was getting a free ride."

"We must all be prepared to make little sacrifices for the boys and girls in service," Lowell said.

The captain did not think that was especially funny. Her pale blue eyes, which were framed by dark red eyebrows, said so. But she said nothing aloud.

There are several reasons why I am suddenly overwhelmed with lust, Lowell thought. *For one thing, I haven't been laid in nearly twenty-four hours. For another, there is something erotic about a female in uniform, something like the eroticism of women running around an apartment in a man's shirt in lieu of pajamas. But what it really is is that I am excited about what McNamara wrote. That is probably the ultimate perversion.*

The captain decided to be gracious.

"Were you in Germany long?" she asked.

"A little over a week," Lowell said.

"Then you didn't get to see very much, did you?" the captain asked.

"I saw the wall," Lowell said.

The stewardess reappeared.

"We have cocktails," she said. "But you have to pay for them, I'm afraid."

"It will be my pleasure," Lowell said.

"You've made enough sacrifice for the boys and girls in service," the captain said. "I'll have a Scotch and water, please. And bring this gentleman whatever he'd like to have."

"His drinks come with his ticket," the stewardess said.

"Scotch," Lowell said.

"In that case," the captain said, "bring him a double."

Lowell chuckled, and the captain smiled at him.

When the drinks came, he raised his to hers.

"Can we start all over again?" he said.

"All right," she said.

"Tell me, Captain," Lowell said, "how do you like nursing?"

"I don't know," she said, smiling artificially, "I've never been a nurse."

"But I thought I saw a caduceus," he said, confused.

"You did," she said, smiling at his discomfiture. "But there was no *N* on it."

"You're a doctor?" he blurted.

"That really surprises you, doesn't it?" she asked.

"I didn't know the army had any female doctors," he said.

"They are trying very hard not to," she said, "Would you like me to tell you how that works?"

"Yes," he said. "If you're talking, I can't get my foot in my mouth."

"There are two kinds of officers in the army," she said. "Did you know that?"

"Only two?"

"There are regular officers and reserve officers," she said.

"Oh."

"But that's not as simple as it sounds," she said. "There aren't enough regular officers to go around."

"Why not?"

"They have sort of a club," she said. "They don't let a lot of people in the club. Like women."

"I thought there were women in the regular army."

"WACs," she said. "Not medical corps officers. Or for that matter armor officers or infantry officers. Just WACs."

"I see."

"So what happens, to cut a long story short . . . this must be boring you out of your mind."

"On the contrary, I'm fascinated," he said.

She smells of soap, he thought. It was a delightful smell.

"Because they don't have enough spaces for regular officers to go around, what they do is have reserve officers. When on active duty, reserve officers are equal to regular officers. Did you ever read any Orwell?"

"'Some animals are more equal than others,'?" he asked.

"Right," she said. "It's delightful to meet someone who reads books. I have been around people who don't read, period."

"Soldiers, you mean?" he asked.

"And officers," she said.

"Oh."

"As I was saying, about reserve officers and regular officers," she went on, "since the medical corps doesn't have women as regular army officers, and since the medical corps needs doctors, what they do is commission women as reserve officers and call them to active duty—temporarily—promising them the moon, plus two dollars."

"I see," he said. "I'm getting the feeling that you're not too wild about being in the army."

"Are you really?" she asked. "Well, what happens is that when a woman who is on active duty as a reserve officer completes her three years of service and wants to get out of the army, they suddenly realize they don't have enough people in her specialty, so they declare her to be essential."

"Is that what happened to you?"

"Uh-huh," she said. "I was supposed to get out of the army this month. Now I have to stay another year."

"I see."

"What really burns me up is that if I *wanted* to stay in the army," she said, "and applied for a regular commission, they would pat me on the head and say, 'Sorry, little lady, the army is a man's game, and you can't play.'"

"What is your specialty?"

"I'm a psychiatrist," she said. Then she saw the look on his face. "Why does that surprise you?"

"I don't know," he said. "You don't look like a psychiatrist."

"Very funny," she said. "But enough of this gay, idle chatter about girlish things. What were you doing in Germany? What do you do for a living?"

"I'm an armor officer," Lowell said. "Lieutenant colonel. Regular army."

She looked at him to make sure he wasn't kidding.

"Then what are you doing in first class, wearing a five-hundred-dollar suit and a thousand-dollar wristwatch?"

"I've also read a book or two," he said. "Observant little lady, aren't you?"

"Touché, *Colonel*," she said. "But that doesn't answer my question."

"I was sitting here minding my own business," Lowell said. "When Pan American dumped a charity case in my lap."

"Oh, you do play nasty, don't you?" she said. She seemed pleased.

"You said it, little lady," Lowell said. "The army's a man's game."

"If you call me 'little lady' one more time, I will pour my drink in your lap," she said.

"That would be assault upon a superior officer, and they would send you to Fort Leavenworth to make small rocks from big ones. That would be a good deal less pleasant than sitting in a comfortable chair, listening to people tell you all about their toilet training."

"You are such an all-around regular-army male supremacist sonofabitch," she said, "that I think I like you."

"You're just saying that to get me on your couch," he said.

"Your wife wouldn't like that," she said.

"How do you know there is a wife?" he asked.

"Are you saying there isn't?"

"How did a nice girl like you get to be a shrink?"

"If you ever say *shrink* to me again, you *will* get the drink in your lap," she said. "We were talking about your wife."

"No wife," he said.

"I get a lot of people your age who never married on my couch," she said.

"I didn't say I had never *been* married," he said. The stewardess walked past. Lowell snapped his fingers, caught her attention, and signaled for two drinks.

"If you had done that to me, you would have gotten the drinks in your lap," the captain said.

"Did you ever wonder if you might perhaps have a 'drinks-in-the-crotch' fixation?" Lowell asked.

"God!" she said, and then she laughed. "I suppose I asked for it."

She looked at him, and for a moment their eyes met. Then she flushed and looked away.

"What happened to the wife?" she asked. "She fled screaming home to mother?"

"She died," Lowell said.

She looked at him again, remorse on her face. She colored again, too, but this time she didn't look away.

"Let's try it one more time," she said. "Hello, there, my name is Joan Gillis. Is this seat occupied?"

"Please sit down, Doctor," Lowell said. "I'm grateful for the company. My name is Craig Lowell."

"I've very pleased to meet you, Colonel Lowell," she said, offering her hand.

"I'm very pleased to meet you, Dr. Gillis," he said. "Traveling far?"

Her hand was soft and warm, and he let go of it reluctantly.

"Fort Bragg, actually," she said. "Do you know it?"

"I get there from time to time," he said. "Perhaps we could have dinner or something."

"Or something," she said.

XII

(One)
U.S.N.S. CARD
10°30' North Latitude, 108°25' North Longitude
(The South China Sea)
1330 Hours, 10 January 1962

The choppers, the Piasecki H-21s, the Bell H-13s, and the Sikorsky H-34s had taken off first, without problem. There had been one almost-incident with an H-34. A helicopter has the ability of taking off vertically and of remaining motionless with reference to the ground, once it is airborne. When during takeoff a helicopter pilot detects or senses that something is not going exactly as it should be going, he can raise the forward end of the rotor cone, which reduces or eliminates forward speed, and he can thereafter make a powered or unpowered descent—an autorotation—to the ground immediately under him.

While taking off or landing, an experienced helicopter pilot is always aware of what is directly under him in case something goes wrong. If he has to land, in other words, he wants to land on the runway, or the taxiway, or the grass beside the runway, and not in treetops or on top of parked aircraft.

As one of the H-34s took off, a red Fuel Warning light on the instrument panel lit up. Very quickly and automatically, aware that he was then fifteen feet or so above the forward edge of the *Card*'s landing deck, the pilot raised the leading edge of his rotor cone and lost forward velocity. He then considered the problem. There are three reasons a Fuel Warning light will illuminate: (1) The fuel supply is near exhaustion; (2) there is some sort of problem in transferring the fuel from the fuel tanks to the engine; or (3) the goddamn light is broke.

The pilot has personally supervised the fueling of his aircraft, taking particular pains to ensure that there was no water in the avgas. If there was some sort of problem with fuel transfer, the engine would be running roughly or would have stopped. The engine was running like a Swiss watch. Ergo, the goddamned Fuel Warning light was fucked up.

It had taken the H-34's pilot no more than three seconds from the time the Fuel Warning light had started flashing to reach this conclusion, and he spent another second looking at his co-pilot to see if he had any idea. When the pilot shrugged and made an I-haven't-the-foggiest face, the pilot lowered the nose of the helicopter and resumed his takeoff procedure.

He had completely forgotten that the airfield from which he had taken off was unlike any other airfields with which he had experience. This one was moving in the same direction as he was, at approximately twenty-five miles an hour.

While he was holding the Sikorsky in a hover, in other words, the "airfield" with its armor-plated "island" was catching up with him at twenty-five miles per hour. Some of the seventy-five or so people on the *Card*'s deck held their breaths, some swore, and some averted their eyes in the time it took the pilot to make up his mind and resume horizontal motion.

Once it was clear that the H-34 was not going to be swatted out of the sky by the aircraft carrier's island, spewing flaming avgas over the deck and the people and aircraft on it, Major Philip S. Parker IV found himself chuckling. The two fat, dumb, and happy jackasses in the H-34 had no idea how close they had been to disaster. The proof of that came almost immediately, when the H-34 swung from side to side in a cheerful gesture of "so long."

The Cessna L-19s and De Havilland of Canada L-20s made their takeoffs without trouble. The two-place L-19 had been designed especially for Army Aviation, which meant it could take off and land from short dirt strips and roads at the front. The L-20 "Beaver" had been designed for civilian use in the wilds (the "bush") of Canada and Alaska. They became airborne somewhere between forty and fifty miles an hour. Since the *Card* was making twenty-five knots into a ten-mile-per-hour wind, in effect the L-19s and Beavers were almost at takeoff velocity when they were sitting on the deck with their brakes locked off and their engines not running.

The Beaver and L-19 pilots had been instructed to keep their wheels on the deck until their airspeed indicators indicated seventy miles an hour. They all took off without incident and disappeared to the West Southwest.

When the decks were cleared, the *Card* made a slow, ten-minute, 360-degree turn. While it was turning, the Mohawks were brought up from the hangar deck on the elevator and pushed and trundled to the aft end of the landing deck. There were seven of them.

The takeoff of the first Mohawk from the *Card* would be the first takeoff ever of a Mohawk from an aircraft carrier. There was absolutely no question in the minds of anyone connected with Grumman (there were two Grumman technical representatives—"tech reps"—aboard, one of whom was a retired naval aviator) that it should pose absolutely no problem. They had a good deal of experience in taking aircraft off from the decks of aircraft carriers, and the flight envelope of the Mohawk (how quickly it could become airborne) was better than the envelope of other Grumman aircraft, which routinely made hundreds of takeoffs every day from aircraft carriers around the world.

The theory that the Mohawks were capable of taking off from the *Card* had been tested at length at Fort Rucker and Bethpage, Long Island. It had been proved possible to get a Mohawk easily into the air from a runway exactly as long as the *Card*'s deck. Parker had made three such takeoffs himself.

It therefore logically followed that if the *Card* was headed at twenty-five knots into the wind, bringing the aircraft to a relative airspeed of thirty-odd knots before the brakes were released, it should be able to take off with no problem at all.

Theory was fine. But Phil Parker was worried—and about several things. He was the senior Mohawk pilot present, in effect the commanding officer. As such, he had wondered, what was his duty? To make the first takeoff himself, following the infantry school's "Follow me!" creed? Would that be inspiring his men to follow his example? Or would it inspire them to whisper that Phil (or "the coon") fixed it so that he would be the first man ever to take a Mohawk off an aircraft carrier?

Or should he send the best-qualified pilot up first? The best-qualified pilot was by definition the pilot with the most Mohawk time. The best-qualified pilot aboard had seven hours more Mohawk time than Parker himself did. That hardly made him that much better qualified.

If he himself went into the drink, the next best-qualified pilot was also the next senior in rank, and would therefore have the responsibility to decide whether to abort further takeoffs and take the Mohawks into Saigon on the *Card,* or to try it again.

Parker suspected that since taking the planes into Saigon would mean that they would have to take half their wings off (a hell of a job), so they could be trucked from the dock to Tan Son Nhut Airfield through Saigon, his successor would opt to try another takeoff. Which would likely put two Mohawks in the drink.

In the end, he had decided that he would make the first takeoff and then circle the *Card* until the other Mohawks had taken off. He was not at all surprised that the most experienced Mohawk pilot was miffed at the decision.

"Pilots, man your aircraft! Pilots, man your aircraft!" the loudspeaking system boomed.

With Parker's exception, all the pilots were sitting in their aircraft, not from any burning ambition to rush into the air, but because that was more comfortable than standing around on the deck.

"Launch helicopters!" the loudspeaker boomed. "Launch helicopters!"

Two H-34s had been kept behind, so they would be able to

do whatever they could if a Mohawk went into the drink. If all the Mohawks made it safely into the air, they would land and pick up the army personnel who had been needed to get the Mohawks running and into the air.

Parker climbed the little ladder and got in the pilot's seat, strapped himself in, and put on his helmet. He turned on the Master switch and watched as the instruments and the gyros came to life.

Then he looked down at the deck and made a circular motion with his index finger: "Wind it up!"

When he had closed the canopy, it was hot and muggy inside the Plexiglas, and he felt a drop of sweat roll down his back. He thought that it was probably going to be this way from now on in Vietnam—hot and steamy.

When all the instrument needles were in the green, he gave a thumbs-up signal to the Grumman tech rep. The retired naval aviator was functioning as launch officer. He had equipped himself with an old-fashioned cloth pilot's helmet, which Parker thought made him look like Amelia Earhart, and a pair of handheld flag signaling devices he called "paddles."

Faintly, over the whistle of the turboprops and the higher pitched whistle of the stubby propeller blade tips themselves, he heard the command "Launch aircraft!"

He checked the position of the flaps, reset the brakes, and then ran the engines up. He gave another thumbs-up signal to the Grumman tech rep, who then, enthusiastically, even violently, waved his paddles.

Parker flipped the brake switch off and felt himself being pushed back against the seat by the forces of acceleration. He was off the deck long before he ran out of it, and as the flaps and wheels came up the Mohawk quickly picked up speed and altitude. He began a slow, climbing turn around the *Card*.

He saw the second Mohawk take off. When he was sure that it was safe to distract the pilot, he pushed the Radio Trans button on the stick.

"Form up on me," he said.

"Gotcha," the pilot of the second Mohawk said, and then, as the third Mohawk was taking off, came back on the air.

"Hey, there it is," he said.

From this altitude they could make out the land mass of Asia. Specifically Vung Tau, Parker decided, also known as Cap St. Jacques.

One after the other the rest of the Mohawks took off without incident and climbed out and formed a *V* behind him.

He switched his radio frequency.

The sense of romance, of leading a flight of aircraft onto the Asian land mass, into the mysterious Orient, was shattered almost immediately.

"Tan Son Nhut Approach Control, Air France 404."

"Go ahead, Air France 404."

"Estimate Tan Son Nhut in thirty minutes. Have you got me on radar?"

"I have you, Air France 404, at two five thousand, heading 270, indicating 350 knots, distance 150 miles."

"Air France 404 requests landing instructions."

"Air France, maintain your present heading. Descend to five thousand. Radar indicates a Northwest Orient DC-8 inbound twenty miles to your right and several unidentified small aircraft flying in a circle at five thousand ten miles off Cap St. Jacques. Report passing through one zero thousand."

"Ah, Roger, Tan Son Nhut," Air France said.

We are not, Parker thought, *the forces of virtue and right flying in like Jimmy Cagney in* Devil Dogs of the Air *to the sounds of trumpets and drums to defeat the forces of evil and save the world for democracy, but "several unidentified small aircraft flying in a circle."*

(Two)
The Hotel Caravelle
(Military Assistance Command, Vietnam, BOQ #2)
Saigon, Republic of Vietnam
1705 Hours, 10 January 1962

Major Philip S. Parker IV felt tired, hot, and dirty when he finally got to his room. He quickly determined his priorities: (a) a bath; (b) a cold beer; and (c) several more of (b).

A little procession of vehicles had been on hand to meet the seven Mohawks from the *Card* when they landed at Tan Son Nhut Airfield. There was a colonel, the MAC-V aviation officer, who'd come more for personal curiosity and courtesy than anything else. The Mohawks of the Twenty-third Special Warfare Aviation Detachment didn't belong to him but to the Fifth Special Forces Group, whose colonel was also on hand. And there was a neat young man in a seersucker suit and with a Harvard nasal twang who said he was from "the Embassy."

He sounded, Phil Parker thought, the way Craig Lowell had sounded when he had first met Second Lieutenant Lowell at Student Officer Company, at the armored school, years before. Lowell sounded that way sometimes even today, especially after he and Toni Parker (who also sometimes sounded that way) had had enough very dry martinis to lessen their resolve not to talk like that in front of the peasants.

Parker did not like the young man from "the Embassy" but was able to resist the urge to clench his jaws and give his well-known and skilled imitation of his wife and his buddy in their cups. The young man from "the Embassy" was obviously from the CIA, and in his last briefing before going to California to board the *Card,* Parker had been told that the Twenty-third Special Warfare Aviation Detachment would be under the "operational guidance" of the CIA.

The primary reason Parker did not like the young man from the Embassy was that in a failed attempt to conceal his surprise and disappointment that the commanding officer of the Twenty-third Special Warfare Aviation Detachment was a big black buck nigger, he did everything short of saying some of his best friends were Negroes. It had been even more difficult to resist the temptation to do his famous impersonation of the southern darkie cotton-picker—foot-shuffling, moronic grin, the works— than to resist the temptation to clench his jaws while speaking.

But he had behaved himself. He had left the young man from the Embassy with the feeling that things were not quite as bad as he had thought they were when he had looked up at the Mohawk cockpit and saw that black face under the helmet.

The Special Forces colonel and the young man from the Embassy had somehow acquired the notion that the trip from the States on the *Card* and the twenty-minute flight had pushed the Mohawk pilots to the brink of exhaustion. Whatever else he might be, Phil Parker was a soldier, and smart soldiers never protest when their superiors have come to the conclusion that their duties have exhausted them and that they require several days of rest and recuperation.

When the Special Forces colonel told Parker to "get your people settled in the hotel, get your feet on the ground, maybe take a little look around Saigon, and then come to see me sometime Monday morning," Major Parker replied, "Yes, sir. Thank you, sir."

Parker sent the pilots into the hotel. He then took the bus with his enlisted men to the Special Forces compound to make sure they would have what they needed (and to make the point to the Special Forces first sergeant that he was concerned with their welfare, and that he had not just given a draft of coolies). And then he went on to the Hotel Caravelle.

The hotel was French Colonial. It reminded Parker of a hotel he and Toni had stayed in on leave in Morocco. That was a mixed blessing, he thought. The food would probably be very good, and the plumbing would probably not work very well.

He stripped to his shorts and then unpacked his luggage while he ran the water in the tub (the shower was a French "douche," a shower head on a flexible pipe), hoping that it would cool below tepid. It did not. When he came out of the shower, he felt cleaner but no cooler.

Civilian clothing was not only permitted but encouraged, the Special Forces colonel had told him; but he had not said, nor had Parker asked, what the civilian dress code in the hotel was. Could he get by in a polo shirt? Or, as a field-grade officer and gentleman, was he expected to wear at least a shirt and tie if not a jacket?

He had just about decided on the polo shirt when there came a knock on the door. The question was answered. His caller was a commissioned officer of the United States Army. He was attired in yellow Bermuda shorts, an open-collared sport shirt of many colors, and a straw beachcomber's hat.

"*Bienvenue à Saigon, mon major,*" Lieutenant Tom Ellis said, thrusting a bottle of beer at him. "*Voici une—*or is it *un?—bier.*"

"Where the hell did you learn to speak French?" Parker asked. "What the hell are you doing in Saigon?"

He took the beer and drank from the neck.

"I am in Saigon as a message center runner," Ellis said. "I even have one for you."

He handed Parker an eight-by-ten-inch envelope. It bore the printed return address "Station Hospital, Fort Bragg, N.C." and was addressed to him, somewhat vaguely: "Major P. S. Parker IV, Vietnam." It was obviously from Toni, and he tore it open eagerly.

It was a copy of the *New England Journal of Medicine*. The index was on the cover, and one of the articles had a stamped red arrow by it.

"Observed Resistance of Certain Strains of Oriental Gonococci and Spirochetes to Penicillium-Based Treatment" by Thomas P. Yancey, M.D., Chief of Venereal Disease Service, Massachusetts General Hospital, could be found starting on page thirty-two.

Parker chuckled and handed it to Ellis.

"Do you think the doc's trying to tell you something, Major?" Ellis asked.

"This isn't the only reason you came to Vietnam, to give me this?"

"Not the only one," Ellis said. "Put some clothes on, and we'll go to *'le cocktail'* and I'll tell you all about it."

"*'Le cocktail'*?"

"That's French for happy hour," Ellis said. "And they really do it right here."

"I'm not sure I want to be seen in public with you, Lieutenant, dressed that way."

"You don't like this? I bought it in Hawaii on the way over."

"In a place, no doubt, with a 'Tourists Welcome!' sign over the door?"

"At the airport," Ellis said. "I wasn't about to run around Hawaii with a briefcase chained to my wrist. Or take a chance on missing the plane."

"You're an officer courier? How did that happen?"

"I asked the general to send me to Vietnam," Ellis said. "This wasn't exactly what I had in mind, but as he pointed out, it's close."

Parker chuckled as he pulled the polo shirt over his head. He put his legs in a pair of chino trousers and then started to tuck the polo shirt in.

"If you do that, where are you going to carry your gun?" Ellis asked. The question surprised Parker and his surprise showed on his face. Ellis turned around and raised his shirt of many colors. He had a Colt .45 automatic pistol in the small of his back.

"We're supposed to go around armed?" Parker asked.

"We're supposed *not* to," Ellis said. "And I suppose if you looked long enough you could find one or two dummies who aren't."

"Are you playing cops and robbers, Ellis?" Parker asked.

"No," Ellis said simply, "I'm not."

"The only thing I've got with me is an old Colt revolver," he said.

"Well, take that, then, until you can get something better," Ellis said. "I was shopping before. There's a place selling aluminum-framed Smith & Wesson .38 Specials they stole from the air force. They want a hundred bucks for one."

"Where'd you get the .45?"

"At Bragg," Ellis said. "Issued."

"I'm not sure if you're pulling my leg or not," Parker said.

"I'm not," Ellis said.

"Shit!" Parker said and went to his attaché case, unlocked it, and took out a large revolver wrapped in an oiled rag.

"Where the hell did you get that thing?" Ellis asked.

"My grandfather carried it in the First World War," Parker said. "It's a 1917 Colt .45 ACP."

"And it still works?"

"It works fine, thank you, Lieutenant," Parker said. He sucked in his belly and slipped the old revolver under his waistband. This was not going to be a long-term solution to the problem. He was either going to have to get a shoulder holster or another pistol.

"Le Cocktail" was as nice as Ellis had suggested. There were white-jacketed waiters at your elbow offering hors d'oeuvres free and drinks at ridiculously low prices. There was a man playing a grand piano, and the room was full of attractive Vietnamese women. Some of them, Parker decided, were half white, which meant half French. Their skirts were slit on the side. He found them very attractive. He wondered how soon his resolve to be absolutely faithful to Toni would falter.

Over Japanese Asahi beer, Ellis told him that he had been bored with being the general's aide. . . .

"Bullshit," Parker said. "You weren't the aide long enough to get bored."

"Okay. For personal reasons . . ."

"Eaglebury's sister?"

"What makes you ask that?" Ellis asked.

"You didn't knock her up?" Parker asked.

"Jesus Christ!" Ellis flared.

"Sorry," Parker said, deducing correctly that Ellis's personal reasons were indeed Dianne Eaglebury and that he had in fact been in her pants. It was Parker's belief that never is a woman's virtue more strongly defended than by someone who has talked her out of it and is contemplating matrimony with the lady in question.

"She's not that kind of a girl," Ellis said, confirming Parker's analysis.

"Right," Parker said.

"Anyway, I asked to get transferred to Vietnam," Ellis said. "Most of my Cuba team is here."

"And the general said . . . ?" Parker asked.

"That luck was with me," Ellis chuckled. "He just happened to have a requirement for an officer courier."

"What did you bring with you?"

"Some stuff for First Group," Ellis said. "At least, that's where I delivered it."

"And when are you going back?" Parker asked.

"The general said I was to check with you before I went home, to see what you needed."

"Can't think of a thing," Parker said.

"Major, you just got here," Ellis said. "Why don't you think about it before you say that?"

"Think about it for how long?" Parker asked.

"Say, a week," Ellis said.

"What have you planned for the next seven days, Ellis?" Parker asked, smiling.

"I found out where three of my guys are," Ellis said. "Lopez, Dessler, and Talbott. They're with an 'A' Team in Kontum Province."

"Sure," Parker said. "Why not? I think we have to presume

that whatever's going on here is more important than passing canapes at Bragg."

"Thanks," Ellis said.

(Three)
Villa dans le Bois
Thu Sac, Kontum Province
Republic of South Vietnam
1630 Hours, 15 January 1962

The Villa in the Woods was no longer in the woods. Even before the building had been turned over to "A" Team Number 6, Company "A," First Special Forces Group, it had been in military hands. It had been put to use as Headquarters, Third Battalion, 119th Infantry Regiment (Separate), Army of the Republic of Vietnam; and ARVN riflemen had spent long and hot days chopping down the towering pines for a distance of one hundred yards from the big old house.

The better logs had been trucked into Kontum and sold, and the less valuable logs used to build frameworks for various sandbag structures on the perimeter of the compound, inside the compound, or attached to the villa itself. To the surprise of the men of the Third Battalion, 119th Infantry, ARVN, some of the money received from the sale of the logs had actually been spent for their welfare. Other commanders would have put all of the money in their own pockets, but their commander had actually bought rice with some of it, and used some of it to buy pigs and chickens.

When the Americans came, they made other necessary military improvements to the compound. They removed the forest to a distance of two hundred yards from the villa itself. The Vietnamese were impressed with how the Americans did this. For one thing, they did not ax or saw the trees to the ground. They wrapped the trunks, as close to the ground as possible, with primer cord, covered the primer cord with sandbags, and with cheerful shouts of "Fire in the Hole!" detonated the primer cord. There followed a sharp crack. The trees seemed to shudder, and then they started to fall. The explosive force of the primer cord cut the tree trunks almost surgically.

The timber thus obtained had been turned into lumber on a

barter basis. For every two tree trunks turned into construction lumber by an ARVN corps of engineers platoon equipped with a portable U.S. Army sawmill, the ARVN engineers got to keep one trunk for themselves. And since Master Sergeant Charles B. Dessler was supervising the lumbering operation, all the money from the sale of the tree trunks went to the engineers and not into the pocket of the ARVN engineer officer.

The primary purpose of the American timbering operation was the creation of a beaten fire zone, thus depriving the Vietcong of a place to hide closer than two hundred yards from the villa. But they also needed some of the lumber (the rest they sold) to reinforce the compound further. Six towers were erected, five on the perimeter of the compound, and the sixth in the center. All were protected by sandbags and equipped with machine guns and other weapons. The one inside the perimeter also served as a water tower, and the various antennae with which the "A" Team communicated with its headquarters and various ARVN units were mounted to it.

Water again flowed through the ornate faucets of Villa dans le Bois's faucets, and there was a sufficient quantity of it to permit a steady flow through otherwise unneeded bidets to cool wine.

There were three lines of coils of barbed wire surrounding the villa. This was called concertina, because it expanded from its shipping coil like the bellows of an accordion. Each coil was hung with beer cans and other light scrap metal so that noise would be created if the wire was disturbed.

Outside the exterior line of concertina, and between rows one and two and two and three, there had been emplaced both homemade (number ten cans filled with metal scrap and rocks and small charges of Composition C-3) mines and Claymore mines. These were a new and effective device that when detonated blew away everything in a cone-shaped pattern for about thirty yards.

The "A" Team was being "protected" by a company from the Third Battalion, 119th Infantry. They were housed in bunkers inside the inner ring of concertina, but, except for the company commander and half a dozen others, they were denied access to the villa itself. In the minds of the "A" Team, there existed some question of the resolve of the ARVN infantry company commander to give it the old school try in the event of an attack. He was therefore kept close at hand, where he could be watched and his resolve strengthened. The half-dozen other ARVN—five noncoms and an officer—both spoke English and had in various ways managed to convince the "A" Team whose side they were on. As a general rule of thumb, it had been concluded that the allegiance of at least half of the ARVN riflemen was dependent on who they thought was going to win the engagement then in progress.

Nine men, two officers, and seven noncommissioned officers made up the "A" Team. Three of the noncoms, Master Sergeant Charles B. Dessler, the operations sergeant; Master Sergeant Juan Vincenzo Lopez, the armorer; and SFC Richard L. Talbott, commo, had jumped into Cuba with First Lieutenant Tom Ellis. They were pleased and surprised when the twice-a-week supply convoy from Company rolled into the Villa dans le Bois compound and Ellis climbed down from the cab of the second truck.

The commanding officer (Captain Howard G. Fenn) and the executive officer (First Lieutenant Donald G. Crossman) had known Ellis while they were in training at Camp McCall. Their initial impression of him at McCall was that he was a nice kid, but they wondered what he was doing in Special Forces, which was supposed to recruit its officers from mature and experienced officers.

It had subsequently been brought unforgettably to their attention by Lieutenant Colonel Rudolph G. MacMillan, Deputy Commander for Special Projects of the Special Warfare Center (who had overheard them referring to him as the "Boy Wonder") that Lieutenant Ellis was in fact the guy who had fought his "A" Team through twenty miles of angry Cubans to a last-minute escape from the beach at the Bahia de Cochinos.

When they saw Tom Ellis climbing down from the supply convoy six-by-six, both Captain Fenn and Lieutenant Crossman, privately and independently, wondered if he had come to Villa dans le Bois to relieve and replace them. The team had been given a simple mission to perform: win the hearts and the minds of the people by providing, among other things, medical services. And they had been unable to do it.

On Christmas Eve the villagers of An Lac Shi had gone to

the Blessed Heart of Jesus Church for midnight mass and found Father Lo Patrick Sho, Mayor Song Lee Do, and four altar boys dead. The altar boys had been shot behind the ear, and the priest and the mayor had their throats cut open and their reproductive organs cut off. It was the Vietcong means of expressing their displeasure with lackeys of the traitorous anti–liberation forces who had encouraged the peasants to avail themselves of medical services offered by the Americans in the green berets.

The tactic had been very effective. When Staff Sergeant Robert Franz, the "A" Team's medic, had made his round that week, not only had no villagers of An Lac Shi appeared with sick children, or old people suffering from parasitic infestation, or any other illnesses, but no villagers in any of the other four villages in the team's area had shown up to take advantage of Staff Sergeant Franz's free and competent professional services.

Intestinal parasites causing rectal bleeding are bad, but not nearly as bad as a cut throat.

Captain Fenn truly believed he had done his best. He had even come up with the name of the Vietcong officer responsible, a Captain Van Lee Duc of the Ninth Company, Fifty-third Regiment. It was just that he couldn't find the sonofabitch, and God knows he had tried.

He had received simple orders from Captain Fenn: "You have to find that bastard, Don, that's all there is to it." Lieutenant Crossman also believed that he had done his best, and that his best simply hadn't been good enough. Yet, after spending ten days and nights in the jungle and forest, he had no better idea now where Captain Van Lee Duc was than he ever had.

He hadn't had so much as a sniff. All ten days and ten nights (in two five-day excursions) had done was to prove that somebody out there didn't like them. Two of his men had run feces-smeared punji sticks through their feet, and one of them had suffered a smashed upper right arm (he was lucky he wasn't squashed like a bug) when he tripped a wire and released an eight-foot section of tree trunk imbedded with more feces-smeared pointed sticks.

Lieutenant Don Crossman was very much aware that he had

sent three men to the hospital in Saigon, and all he'd gotten for it was a sense that Captain Van Lee Duc was sitting out there behind a tree, laughing his balls off at them.

There were, of course, extenuating circumstances. The natives were understandably more afraid of people who had proved their willingness to risk God's wrath by emasculating a priest in his own church than they were of Americans who were some strange combination of soldier and Good Samaritan. They were consequently not about to tell the Americans, much less the ARVN, anything at all about what they knew of the location of Captain Van Lee Duc and the Ninth Company of the Fifty-third Regiment of the People's Liberation Army.

On top of that, Captain Van Lee Duc and his small headquarters staff (estimates of his nucleus ranged from five to eleven; the truth was probably somewhere about eight) had an area of forest, jungle, and rice fields about ten miles by seventeen—170 square miles—to hide in.

But none of the extenuating circumstances mattered. They had been not able to find the sonofabitch, which meant that they could send Staff Sergeant Franz out every day for the next six months and he would have no patients.

Since Lieutenant Ellis had proven his own ability to command an "A" Team, it was entirely likely that he had been sent in to replace officers who were unable to comply with their orders.

But it was almost immediately apparent that Ellis was making a social call, nothing else. A not entirely happy social call to be sure: Over dinner Ellis told the story of getting Eaglebury's body back from the Cubans.

Obviously this was a gross breach of security on Ellis's part, for doubtless the file on the whole business was still stamped TOP SECRET. But as obviously that top-secret business was so much bullshit. The Cubans had had Eaglebury for sometime before they finally shot him. No man can resist torture beyond a given point. The Cubans almost certainly knew they had captured, interrogated, and finally shot a lieutenant commander of the U.S. Navy. And the Cubans damned well knew they had been paid fifty thousand dollars for his body, so who was that a secret from?

Toward the end of the first case of liter bottles of Asahi beer, the conversation turned to Captain Van Lee Duc and the altar boys with their brains blown all over the sanctuary. Captain Fenn and Lieutenant Crossman were a little uneasy having their failure dragged out in front of Ellis, but there was no way they could stop the conversation once it had started. Fenn thought that it was possible that Ellis would be able to think of something he hadn't.

He took considerable consolation from the fact that Ellis didn't have any more idea what to do than he did.

In the morning, however, Ellis did something Captain Fenn thought was a little strange. He asked SFC Talbott, the commo man, if he could get through to Saigon on his radio, and if he could, would the Saigon operator patch him through to the Hotel Caravelle.

Talbott told him he didn't know about the telephone patch and that Saigon was chickenshit, but he would find out.

"Tell him I want to talk to Major Parker."

The officers knew who Major Parker was. There weren't that many majors in Special Forces, and only one of these was an aviator, well over six feet tall, and as black as midnight.

Listening to the conversation, Captain Fenn thought that Lieutenant Ellis had a lot of nerve (Ellis told Parker that he was having trouble getting a ride back, and could Parker come pick him up?), and that Parker was what he had heard he was, a nice guy, maybe a little too nice for his own good. (Parker, his reluctance evident in his voice even over the frequency-clipped circuit, agreed to come get him at the airstrip in Kontum.)

"I don't know if this is going to work, Captain," Ellis said when he got off the radio. "The odds are that it won't. But have you got a spare map on which you could mark where you think this guy might be?"

"He could be in any one of a dozen places," Fenn said. "What are you up to?"

"Mark every place you think he might be."

"What the hell are you up to, Ellis?"

"If I'm not back tonight," Ellis said, "it will have been wishful thinking."

"What, goddamn it?"

"I think maybe Parker can find this bastard for us," Ellis said.

"How?"

"He has a very interesting airplane," Ellis said, "and that, no shit, is all I can tell you about it. It's classified 'TOP SECRET— Eyes of God Only.'"

"And you think he'll help?"

"I don't know," Ellis said. "If he does, he'll be sticking his neck out. But he might. I'm going to throw the altar boys with the bullets in their ears at him."

(Four)
U.S. Army OV-1A Aircraft Tail Number 92521
Heading: 030° True
Altitude: 3,500 Feet
Indicated Airspeed: 270 Knots
(Kontum Province, Republic of South Vietnam)
2035 Hours, 19 January 1962

"Spanish Harlem," the pilot said to his microphone, "Spanish Harlem, this is Father Divine. How do you read? Over?"

"Read you loud and clear, Father Divine, and God bless you," Spanish Harlem replied.

"Got a match, Spanish Harlem?" Father Divine asked.

"Roger, lighting match at this time," Spanish Harlem replied.

Spanish Harlem was sitting with his back against the enormous roots of a banyan tree. An AN/PRC-9 radio was on the foul-smelling rotted vegetation of the forest floor before him.

Lieutenant Tom Ellis was wearing a bulletproof vest, a pair of fatigue pants, and (because he had them, and nobody had his size to loan him), a pair of Corcoran jump boots, the gloss of which he'd now concealed beneath a layer of muck. Over the shoulder straps of the bulletproof vest was the canvas strapping of web gear. Suspended from the web gear were two canteens, two ammo pouches, and a .45 Colt pistol in a leather holster. Taped to the canvas straps of the harness were a canvas pouch holding two spare clips for the .45 and a first-aid kit. The pockets of the bulletproof vest each held a fragmentation grenade. Leaning against the tree was an M-14 rifle, an updated version of the M-1 Garand rifle of World War II and Korea. It fired the same bullet—a .308-inch-diameter 186-grain boat-tailed projectile—at just about the same ballistics as the venerable .30–06; but improvements in powder had permitted a smaller cartridge case. The Garand had fired its cartridges from an eight-shot clip. The M-14 had a twenty-shot magazine, which fed through the bottom. Ellis's M-14 had two clips taped to each other. There was another taped-together magazine in each of his ammo pouches. He had in all 120 rounds of 7.62-millimeter NATO (which is how the shortened .30–06 case was identified) for his M-14.

There was a dagger in a scabbard taped to his right boot. It was a British weapon, designed by a Shanghai policeman named Bruce Fairbairn for the commandos in World War II. It was made of high-quality steel, sharp-pointed and thin-bladed, long enough to penetrate vital organs and sharpened on both sides. It belonged to Captain Howard G. Fenn, and it had been something of an olive branch on Fenn's part to Ellis following a heated argument following Ellis's announcement that he, not Fenn, was going to take the hike in the woods.

"It's as simple as this," Ellis had said. "If you go and somebody hears about this, they'll know I told you about what the airplane can do. And my ass would really be in a jam. Either you and Crossman stay, or I call the whole thing off."

There had been heated words, but in the end Fenn had given in. The first priority was the elimination of Captain Van Lee Duc. He would just have to swallow the humiliation that somebody else was leading half his team and a half-dozen reliable ARVNs into the woods to do it.

When he saw that the knife Ellis intended to take on the walk in the woods was a nasty-looking switchblade, Fenn broke a long standing vow ("My toothbrush, sure; my wife, possibly; my limey sticker, never!") and pressed the Fairbairn on him.

Spanish Harlem took what looked like a stainless-steel mechanical pencil from one of the ammo pouches.

"Close your eyes," he ordered. "Here goes the match."

He closed his eyes, held what looked like a mechanical pencil over his head at arm's length, and lit it.

There was a hissing, and immediately a white light of terrible white brilliance at the tip of what looked like a mechanical pencil.

The light revealed the three other Americans of the patrol, Ellis's people from Cuba, and the half-dozen ARVNs. All were dressed like Ellis. All had their faces blackened with a non-reflecting paste. All sat with their eyes tightly closed, shielding them against the terrible brilliance of the burning thermite.

Ellis counted: "One thousand, two thousand, three thousand, four thousand, five thousand." Then he quickly jabbed the tip of the match into the muck between his legs. There was a hissing, and a smell of burning vegetation, and the white light disappeared. But not the red glow on his eyeballs, even though he had very carefully averted his eyes from the light.

"There it is," the co-pilot of the Mohawk said to Phil Parker. He was not looking out the window, but at a device mounted on the Mohawk's instrument panel. It was feeding a sheet of thin, slimy-feeling photosensitive paper to him. A small red light on a flexible steel mount gave him enough light to read it.

"Got you, Spanish Harlem," Phil Parker said and waited for the device to spew enough paper out so that he could tear it off. Then he studied it carefully. The Mohawk, on three-axis plus air-speed automatic flight stabilization, kept flying at precisely 3,500 feet at 270 knots on a course of thirty degrees true.

The Mohawk was equipped with several black boxes. One of them was a navigation device that determined the present location of the aircraft relative to the point of activation—in other words, relative to the airfield from which it had taken off. Another had in its electronic memory a map of the area over which the Mohawk was flying and the capability of locating the Mohawk's location on this map. Another black box, and its associated antennae and sensors, was capable of receiving thermal radiation and determining the location of the source of the radiation, its strength, and its frequency. Another black box electronically compared this data against known data, such as the known radiation patterns of various thermal radiation sources, and determined with remarkable accuracy whether the source of the thermal radiation was, for example, the exhaust of a truck, a campfire, or a thermite match.

Finally, another black box assembled all the data, the location of the airplane, the sources of thermal radiation, and its probable cause, and caused the on-board printing device to print a map on which was located the location of the aircraft and the sources of the radiation. There were little symbols identifying the thermal radiation sources. In this case, an asterisk identified Spanish Harlem's thermite match and the letters *WF* the source of other thermal radiation, most probably wood fires. The slimy printout in Parker's hands showed the letters *WF* twice in an area identified on the map as forest. There should have been no wood fire at all in that area, much less two of them close together.

"Let's make sure," Parker said to his co-pilot. "Set it up again at 2,500 feet."

The co-pilot disengaged the flight stabilization system, stood the Mohawk on its wing, and lowered the nose as he headed back toward where they had begun the run.

"Spanish Harlem, I'm going to need another light. I'll say when," Parker said to his microphone.

"Standing by," Spanish Harlem replied.

The only difference between the run at 3,500 and the run at 2,500 was that the slimy printout now identified four *WF*'s in the forest. At the greater distance the four fires had appeared as two.

"Spanish Harlem, I have you at Dog Four-Three-Six, Oscar Niner-One-Niner," Father Divine said. "Copy?"

"Dog Four-Three-Six, Oscar Niner-One-Niner," Ellis replied.

"Affirmative," Parker replied. "And I have four wood fires at position Dog Three-Niner-One, Mike Zero-Zero-Three, do you copy?"

"Dog Three-Niner-One, Mike Zero-Zero-Three," Ellis's voice came back.

"Affirmative," Parker said.

"God bless you and good night, Father Divine."

"Call collect if you find work," Parker said. "Father Divine clear."

"Now what?" the co-pilot said. "Home?"

Parker made a vague gesture toward the softly glowing instrument panel.

"I have just noticed an intermittent warning light, and I think we had better sit down at Kontum and check it out."

"Major, whatever those guys get themselves into, we won't be able to help."

"I like to be the first to know," Parker said. "Kontum, Lieutenant."

(Five)

With his flashlight held in his mouth like an oversize cigar, Tom Ellis, with Dessler, Lopez, Talbott, and Franz looking over his shoulder, very carefully marked their location, and then that of the four wood fires, on his map.

"That really works, Lieutenant?" Staff Sergeant Franz asked dubiously.

"I hope so," Ellis said.

According to his map, the fires were about a hundred yards off a path through the forest. There were four fires, which suggested at least eight or ten men, but possibly many more than that. He could think of no reason why eight or more men would be in the forest unless they were in fact Viet Cong.

He said aloud what he was thinking.

"Let's go get the bastards," Master Sergeant Dessler said.

"What do we do, Dessler?" Ellis asked. "Just walk down the path?"

"They don't know we can locate them," Dessler said. "They probably move every night. So I don't think they're going to spend a lot of time setting up traps."

"You want to take the point?" Ellis asked.

"Why not?" Dessler said, after a barely perceptible hesitation.

It was four and a half klicks from Position Dog Four-Three-Six, Oscar Niner-One-Niner to the four wood fires at Position Dog Three-Niner-One, Mike Zero-Zero-Three. The army was in the process of discarding miles, yards, and feet for the metric system of its NATO allies. *Kilometer* had stuck on the army tongue and become *klicks*.

A klick from their destination, Dessler held up his hand for the patrol to stop. When Ellis moved up to him, Dessler sniffed. Ellis sniffed, and he smelled it too. Wood smoke.

"I guess the canopy," Dessler said, pointing upward to where the interlocking branches of the trees blocked out the sky, "keeps it from getting away."

Dessler then took his M-14 from his shoulder and clicked the safety off. The others followed his example. Dessler started down the trail again.

Three hundred meters farther down the path, Ellis felt himself falling, and then a moment later a sharp tearing pain in his left leg and foot. He managed to bite off the scream that came to his lips by clenching his jaws, but he was not entirely successful in maintaining the absolute silence that he considered essential to their staying alive.

A strange sound, half moan, half pained yelp, escaped his lips.

"Whoa!" Dessler called.

Ellis tried to move his left leg. The leg was excruciatingly painful, and it would not move.

"Shit!" Dessler said over him, and then, "Christ, I'm sorry, Tom."

The apology was for his error in judgment. The Viet Cong had indeed set a trap, even though he was sure they wouldn't bother. Ellis had fallen into a punji-stick trap. Dessler had apparently just walked right over it.

"Franz!" Dessler called.

The medic appeared, and Dessler softly warned him to be careful: "Punji."

Franz carefully stepped around Ellis and dropped to his knees.

"Shit!" he said.

"Now what?" Ellis said. He felt faint and sick to his stomach.

Franz felt in the hole and then sat up.

"You've got one in your foot," he said matter-of-factly. "And another one in your calf."

"Goddamn it, I know that!" Ellis said.

"You're lucky you fell in it where you did," Franz said. "You only got two."

"Goddamn it, do something about it!"

"I can go two ways, Lieutenant," Franz said. "I can put you out, which is probably the best. Or I can give you a local, just put the leg and foot to sleep. That may not work."

"If you put me out, how long would I be out?"

"Couple of hours," Franz said.

"Then give me the local," Ellis ordered.

"That might not work," Franz said.

"Give me the goddamn local," Ellis said.

"Okay," Franz said, after a moment. Ellis realized with fury that Franz had made that decision. Franz was going to do what he thought could be done, and Ellis could not order him otherwise.

Franz took a hypodermic syringe from his kit, attached a very large stainless-steel needle to it, and then jabbed the needle through the rubber covering of a small glass vial.

"Hold a light, Dessler," he ordered.

Dessler held a flashlight with a red lense cover close enough so that Franz could see enough of the vial to make sure he was draining it.

"Before I give you this, Lieutenant," Franz said, holding the hypodermic up to get the air out of it, "I want you to understand that it's going to make you a little flaky. It'll numb the leg, but it will also affect your head. You understand that?"

"Give me the goddamned stuff!" Ellis ordered. He wanted to scream.

Franz leaned over the hole and shoved the needle into Ellis's calf, just where the calf muscle swelled below the knee. He was not at all gentle, and there was another blaze of pain.

"Somebody, I hope, brought cutters?" Franz asked. Ellis was aware of Dessler moving down the path.

The first sensation Ellis felt was a coolness in his leg, as if it had suddenly been immersed in cold water. It moved quickly down his leg. The pain was still there, but the coolness seemed to temper it somewhat. Then he felt suddenly very sleepy.

When he had fallen, he had thrown his arms out in front of him. Then he had collapsed. Next he had propped himself up on his elbows, because the pain seemed less excruciating in that position. Now he wanted to lie down again, and there seemed to be no good reason he should not. He rested his head on his arm.

Master Sergeant Dessler appeared with a large pair of commercial bolt cutters. They were the sort of tool you expected to see in a machine shop, not in the middle of the Vietnamese jungle. The more Ellis thought about that, the funnier it seemed.

He giggled.

The pain in his leg was down to toothache level.

"I'm going to have to cut all of those fuckers out of the way before I can get under his boot," Franz said. "And after I do that, you're going to have to hold him upright so I can get the one in his calf."

"I can pick him up," Dessler said.

"I'm perfectly capable of picking myself up, thank you just the same, Sergeant Dessler," Ellis said.

Dessler chuckled.

"Sure you are, Tom," he said.

"You really shouldn't call me Tom when the others can hear you," Ellis said.

"I beg your pardon, sir," Dessler said. "It won't happen again, sir."

"I don't mean to be chickenshit, you understand," Ellis said.

"I understand perfectly, sir," Dessler said. "Are you still in much pain, sir?"

"Nothing I can't handle; thank you for your concern, Sergeant Dessler."

"Christ, I'd like to know what kind of fucking wood they use," Franz said. "It's all I can do to cut the bastards."

"I'm perfectly all right now, Sergeant Franz," Ellis said. "Thank you very much."

"If he starts to move, hold him," Franz said. "I'm just about clear to get the cutter under his boot."

"I told you," Ellis said sternly, "that I am perfectly all right now."

"If he keeps that up, I'm going to have to put him out."

"If you put him out, we'll have to carry him."

"I know."

Sergeant Franz grunted. Ellis felt a tickle in his foot, and it made him giggle.

"Got it!" Franz said, and then called, "Lopez!"

"Yeah?"

"What I have to do is get the bolt cutter between the wall of the hole and the stake, you understand?"

"Yeah."

"But if the punji pulls back out, it'll really fuck up his muscle. It's got barbs."

"So what do you want me to do?"

"While Dessler picks him up, I want you to put your hand on the back of his calf, so it don't move. Can you reach him?"

"Yeah," Lopez said after a moment. "He's bleeding pretty bad."

"That's good," Franz said.

"That's a hell of a thing to say!" Ellis said indignantly.

"Pick him up, Dessler," Franz ordered.

"Why, Sergeant Dessler," Ellis said, when he found himself in Dessler's tight embrace, "I didn't know you cared!"

Lopez laughed.

Something bit Ellis's leg and he yelped in pain.

"Okay," Franz said. "Now pull him out of there and lay him on his back."

Ellis was aware that he was lying on his back and that Dessler, Lopez and Franz were on their knees by his leg.

"'Whenever two or three are gathered together in my name . . .'" Ellis quoted.

"Lieutenant, if you don't shut up," Franz said, "I'm going to have to put you out."

"Maybe you should anyway," Dessler said.

"*Mum*'s the word," Ellis said and put his finger before his lips. Franz seemed to be not only a nice fellow, but a competent noncom, and if he wanted him to be quiet, he would be quiet.

"What I'm going to do now is cut the punjis off as close to where they went in as I can," Franz said. "And then pull what's left the rest of the way through. You're going to have to hold him still."

I can't be very seriously hurt, Ellis decided. *I can't feel a thing.*

"Now what?" Lopez asked.

"Now I shoot his ass full of penicillin," Franz said. "And then we wait five, ten minutes. If he comes off cloud nine, I'll get a couple of ARVNs to help him walk. If he's still out of his gourd, I'll put him out and we'll have to rig a stretcher for him."

"What about coffee? Would that help?"

"I don't know," Franz said. "It's a stimulant. I don't know

what effect it would have on the narcotic."

"It wouldn't hurt to try," Dessler said. "I'd hate to have him unconscious."

Ellis became aware that Dessler was holding him in a sitting position and that Lopez was giving him something very bitter from his canteen cup.

What that is, Ellis realized after a moment, *is a packet of instant coffee mixed with very little water*.

Whatever effect the coffee was supposed to have, it didn't. Ellis felt himself falling asleep.

He opened his eyes. Dessler was methodically slapping his face.

Ellis put his hand up to stop him and then forced himself onto his elbows.

"How long was I out?" he asked.

"About twenty minutes," Dessler said.

"What shape am I in?"

"That's what I wanted to ask you," Dessler said. "We've got the punjis out and the wounds bandaged, and Franz gave you a bunch of penicillin. Do you remember what happened? Where we are?"

"I even remember you hugging me," Ellis said. "Help me up, please."

"You sure you're all right, Lieutenant?"

"We're among friends, Charley," Ellis said. "You can call me Tom."

Dessler chuckled. "I feel bad about this, *Tom*," he said. "Really bad."

"*I* fell in the goddamned hole," Ellis said. "Don't be silly."

Two of the reliable ARVNs were standing there, looking down at him.

"Let's see if you guys can help me walk," Ellis said.

They pulled him upright. He put his arms around their shoulders and supported himself on his good leg. The bad leg now felt as if it were on fire, and when he tried to straighten it, there was a sharp pain.

"This'll work," he said.

"I went and had a look," Dessler said. "I don't know if it's our guys or not, but it's the bad guys. They're armed. And they have sentinels out. There's about twenty-five, maybe thirty of them. How do you want to handle it?"

"Jesus, that many?"

Dessler nodded.

"Let's just take them out and see who they are later," Ellis said.

"They're keeping their fires going," Dessler said. "There's light."

"Grenades, and then shoot anybody who moves," Ellis said.

Dessler nodded, then asked, "What do we do with you?"

"Find me someplace where I can fire the M-14 prone," Ellis said.

"Why don't we just leave you here with a couple of ARVNs?"

"Because I am afraid of being alone in the dark," Ellis said.

"It would be smarter, Tom."

"As I have just proved by getting myself stuck with shitty sticks, I am not very smart," Ellis said.

"You're the boss," Dessler said.

"No, you're in charge," Ellis said. "If you really want to leave me here, go ahead."

"You mean that?"

"Yeah, I mean it," Ellis said.

"Then you stay, Tom," Dessler said. "We'll put you someplace where you can cover the trail, and then I'll put another M-14 on the other side. I think some of them will make it to the trail."

Ellis shrugged. There was no other real alternative. He could hardly rush the Viet Cong encampment on one leg.

Dessler found a place by the trail where he could rest the M-14 on a fallen log and left him there. He returned in several minutes and sketched the trail and the location of the encampment with a stick in the dirt.

"Franz is here," he said, pointing, "so make sure you keep your fire to the left of him. I sent a couple of ARVNs around on the other side, in case they head deeper into the forest. But I don't think they will. If they run, I think they'll run for the trail."

"Okay," Ellis said. "Go do it."

It seemed like a very long time before there was any sound but the creaking of limbs in the forest. Ellis's foot and leg felt more and more on fire, and when he felt (he didn't want to look) his trouser leg, it was moist with blood that had soaked the bandage.

Then there came the sound of grenades, muffled by the thick vegetation. There was first one grenade and then five or six more almost at once. Fifteen seconds after that, another continuous rumble of grenades lasted perhaps three seconds.

Then the faint sound of shouting, a pained scream, and the drumbeat of M-14 rounds, rapid-fire but not full automatic.

Then came, perhaps thirty seconds later, two separate bursts of three or four rounds each. Then the peculiar sound of an AK-47, firing full automatic, answered by a barrage of M-14 fire.

Then silence.

Then the sound of someone crashing through the forest, toward him.

He could see nothing. He couldn't even see the front sight of the M-14. He moved the lever to full automatic. There was a surprisingly loud click. If he was going to get a shot in, it would be for a fraction of a second, and he might as well throw as many rounds as he could as quickly as he could.

And then there were shadows moving out there.

He had the sudden chilling doubt that maybe they were his people.

But that was unlikely.

There was the glow of a muzzle burst as Franz opened up. Ellis squeezed the trigger and held it until the twenty-round magazine had emptied. When the recoil stopped, there was a sharp pain in his leg and foot. He felt a clammy sweat and was afraid he was going to pass out.

There was no more sound in the forest, no more gunfire.

Then Lopez's familiar voice.

"Coming through! Coming through!"

Lopez (Ellis knew it was Lopez, because his shadow was much larger than the shadows he had fired upon) appeared on the trail, followed by three others.

One of the three detached himself from the group and went to the two bodies on the trail and fired two rounds into each.

"You okay, Lieutenant?" Lopez called out.

"Yeah. Send somebody to help me up."

Two of the shadows detached themselves and came in his

direction. They were ARVNs, and they knew what was expected of them. They pulled Ellis to his feet and half carried him into the forest.

Dessler and an ARVN sergeant were squatting by one of the campfires, going through papers from a cheap cotton rucksack. The ARVN found something that interested him and chattered excitedly, first in Vietnamese and then in singsong English.

"Bull's-eye," Dessler called to Ellis. "We got the sonofabitch."

"He's sure?"

"What's he excited about is we got a visiting fireman too. A VC light bird."

"No kidding?" Ellis said, pleased. He urged the ARVNs forward to where Dessler was. Then he started to lower himself to the ground.

There was a bright orange light, and the jungle, the rude shelters the Viet Cong had built, the wood fire, and Dessler himself started to move in circles, and the ground came up and smacked him in the face.

Sixty feet above them, Captain Van Lee Duc, commanding officer of Ninth Company, Fifty-third Regiment, swung gently in a hammock suspended between branches of a large tree. He was bleeding slightly from several small wounds where small fragments of the hand grenades had struck him, but was neither seriously wounded nor in great pain.

From the first grenade, it had never entered his mind to fire his AK-47. If the attack failed, there would have been no need to, and he would have needlessly endangered his life by calling attention to himself in a position from which he had no means of withdrawal. And since the attack had succeeded, there were nineteen bodies on the ground, which meant that no more than eight or ten of his men had escaped. It would have been folly to expose himself.

His immediate problem, as he saw it, was to explain to the staff of the Fifty-third Regiment how the attack had happened in the first place, and why he had permitted the enemy to kill a senior staff officer.

There was no question in Captain Van Lee Duc's mind what had happened. It was just bad luck. The enemy had by chance passed close enough by to smell the smoke of the fires.

In the future, fires would be used only for cooking and then extinguished. In the future, he would also select campgrounds with more care.

For the time being, there was nothing that he could do but wait until the Americans and their puppet soldiers left.

Thirty minutes later they did.

XIII

(One)
Headquarters
U.S. Army Special Warfare School and Center
Fort Bragg, North Carolina
1645 Hours, 29 January 1962

PRIORITY
CONFIDENTIAL

HQ USARMY MIL ASSISTANCE COMMAND, VIETNAM
SAIGON RVN 1005 ZULU 27 JAN 1962
VIA CINC USARMYPAC

FOR DCSOPS DA WASH DC
INFO: SURGEON GENERAL
      CG XVIII AIRBORNE CORPS & FT BRAGG NC
      CG USASWS&C FT BRAGG NC
      CO USARMY STATION HOSP FT BRAGG NC
  1. 1st LT ELLIS, THOMAS J INFANTRY 0-326745 DET OF PATIENTS,
811TH FIELD HOSPITAL, SAIGON RVN HAS ABSENTED HIMSELF

WITHOUT PROPER AUTHORITY FROM 811TH FIELD HOSP AND IS CONSIDERED ABSENT WITHOUT LEAVE.

2. SUBJECT OFFICER, WHO PURSUANT TO PARA 31 GENERAL ORDERS 305 HG DA DATED 29 DEC 61, WAS PLACED ON TDY TO HQ USA MAC VIETNAM AS DCSOPS OFFICER COURIER WAS ADMITTED TO USA MEDICAL FACILITY KONTUM RVN 0545 HOURS 19 JAN 62 FOLLOWING MEDICAL EVACUATION BY HELICOPTER FROM POSITION NEAR AN LAC SHI. MEDICAL EVALUATION OF SUBJECT OFFICER AT THAT TIME INDICATED REQUIREMENT FOR TREATMENT BEYOND CAPABILITY OF USA MED FAC KONTUM AND SUBJECT OFFICER WAS TRANSPORTED BY USAF MED EVAC AIRCRAFT TO 811TH FIELD HOSP SAIGON WHERE OVER SUBJECT OFFICERS OBJECTIONS HE WAS ADMITTED FOR TREATMENT AND ASSIGNED DETACHMENT OF PATIENTS.

3. SUBJECT OFFICER SUFFERS FROM SEVERE PENETRATING LACERATIONS OF LEFT FOOT, WITH ATTENDANT DAMAGE TO MUSCLE, TENDON AND BONE AND SEVERE PENETRATING LACERATION OF LEFT CALF WITH ATTENDANT MUSCLE DAMAGE. PENETRATING WOUNDS WERE CAUSED BY SHARPENED WOOD, COMMONLY REFERRED TO AS "PUNJI STICKS," WHICH ARE CONTAMINATED WITH THE INTENTION OF CAUSING INFECTION BY HUMAN FECES AND OTHER UNKNOWN TOXIC SUBSTANCES. SUBJECT OFFICER HAD LOST SUBSTANTIAL QUANTITIES OF BLOOD, WHICH EXACERBATED HIS CONDITION. HIS CONDITION ON ADMISSION WAS "SERIOUS, GUARDED."

4. SUBJECT OFFICER WAS INFORMED THAT HE WAS UNFIT FOR DUTY, AND THAT HE WOULD BE CONFINED TO 811TH FIELD HOSP FOR A PERIOD OF AT LEAST TWENTY-ONE (21) DAYS, PRESUMING NORMAL RECOVERY, WHILE UNDERGOING MEDICAL TREATMENT TO REDUCE INFECTION AND WHATEVER SURGERY AND THERAPY WAS INDICATED. SUBJECT OFFICER WAS INFORMED THAT HIS OBLIGATION TO COMPLY WITH PROVISIONS OF PARA 31 DA GEN ORDERS 305 WAS OBVIATED ON HIS ADMISSION AND THAT FURTHER ORDERS WOULD BE ISSUED BY PROPER AUTHORITY WHEN HE WAS CERTIFIED AS FIT FOR DUTY BY MEDICAL OFFICERS OF 811TH STATION HOSPITAL.

5. FURTHER INVESTIGATION OF THIS INCIDENT BY 811TH STATION HOSPITAL AND HQ MACV HAS REVEALED THAT SUBJECT OFFICER WAS INJURED WHILE ENGAGED IN PATROL ACTION AGAINST VIET CONG FORCES IN VICINITY AN LAC SHI. COMMANDING OF-

FICER FIFTH SPECIAL FORCES GROUP STATES THAT SUBJECT OFFICER DID NOT REPEAT NOT HAVE AUTHORITY TO PARTICIPATE IN ANY ACTIVITIES OF UNITS SUBORDINATE TO FIFTH SPECIAL FORCES GROUP.

6. MEDICAL RECORDS OF SUBJECT OFFICER AT THE TIME OF HIS ABSENTING HIMSELF WITHOUT LEAVE INDICATE HIS CONDITION TO BE "RECUPERATING, STILL UNDER ANTIBIOTIC REGIMEN, WOUNDS HEALING NORMALLY, GOOD." IT HAD BEEN THE INTENTION OF MEDICAL OFFICERS TO CONTINUE ANTIBIOTIC REGIMEN FOR AT LEAST ANOTHER SEVEN (7) DAYS, TO ENSURE AGAINST A RECURRENCE OF INFECTION.

7. CRIMINAL INVESTIGATION DIVISION, PROVOST MARSHAL'S OFFICE, HQ MAC V HAVE DETERMINED THAT SUBJECT OFFICER LEFT TAN SON NHUT AIR TERMINAL SAIGON ABOARD NORTHWEST ORIENT AIRLINES FLIGHT 303 1305 ZULU 26 JAN 1962. SUBJECT OFFICER OBTAINED NECESSARY TICKETS BY PRESENTING HIS INVALIDATED DA ORDERS TO AIR TRANS OFFICER AT TAN SON NHUT AIR TERMINAL. ETA NORTHWEST ORIENT AIRLINES FLIGHT 303 AT SAN FRANCISCO CALIF IS 1715 ZULU 28 JAN 1962.

8. IT IS RECOMMENDED THAT IF POSSIBLE SUBJECT OFFICER BE MET AT SAN FRANCISCO CALIF BY COMPETENT AUTHORITY AND IMMEDIATELY RETURNED TO PATIENT STATUS. SUBJECT OFFICER HAS TICKETS FOR, BUT NO RESERVATION, FOR FURTHER TRAVEL TO FAYETTEVILLE, N.C.

9. IN THE EVENT IT IS IMPOSSIBLE TO RETURN SUBJECT OFFICER TO PATIENT STATUS AT SAN FRANCISCO CALIF IT IS MOST STRONGLY RECOMMENDED THAT IMMEDIATELY UPON HIS RETURN TO MILITARY CONTROL HE UNDERGO AN IMMEDIATE MEDICAL REEVALUATION AND BE SUBJECTED TO SUCH MEDICAL TREATMENT AS IS INDICATED, PRIOR TO WHATEVER DISCIPLINARY ACTIONS ARE DEEMED NECESSARY AND APPROPRIATE UNDER THE CIRCUMSTANCES.

10. PHOTOCOPIES OF ALL MEDICAL RECORDS ARE BEING FORWARDED TO THE OFFICE OF THE SURGEON GENERAL, DA, BY COURIER.

11. AFFIDAVITS FROM PERSONNEL FAMILIAR WITH VARIOUS ASPECTS OF SUBJECT OFFICER'S ACTIVITIES WHILE IN THE REPUBLIC OF VIETNAM ARE BEING PREPARED AND WILL BE FORWARDED BY COURIER AS THEY BECOME AVAILABLE.

12. IT IS REQUESTED THAT THIS HEADQUARTERS BE ADVISED

BY MOST EXPEDITIOUS MEANS OF SUBJECT OFFICER'S MEDICAL
CONDITION WHEN SUBJECT OFFICER IS RETURNED TO MILITARY
CONTROL, AND OF DISCIPLINARY ACTION TAKEN.

BY COMMAND OF GENERAL HARKINS:
ALEX W. DONALD, COLONEL, AGC

It thus came as no surprise to Paul Hanrahan when Lieutenant Ellis showed up, hobbling on crutches, in Hanrahan's
office. Lieutenant Ellis looked like death warmed over. When
he saluted, Hanrahan thought Ellis was going to fall over.

"Lieutenant Ellis," Hanrahan said, "pending a decision regarding charges which may be placed against you, you will
consider yourself under arrest."

As pale as Tom Ellis looked, Hanrahan was surprised that
his face could get any whiter, but it did.

"I thought it would be better if I came home, sir," Ellis
said.

"And you thought, 'What the hell, once I'm gone, what can
they do to me?' right?" Hanrahan said icily.

Ellis did not reply.

"Lieutenant Ellis, you will consider the following a direct
order," Hanrahan said. "You will report to the station hospital
immediately. You will inform hospital authorities that you are
in arrest status. You will remain in the station hospital, undergoing whatever medical treatment is prescribed, until released by
competent medical authority. Is that clear?"

"Yes, sir."

"Sergeant Major, would you please assist Lieutenant Ellis
to the hospital? You may use my car."

"Yes, sir."

"That is all, Lieutenant," Hanrahan said. "You are dismissed."

Ellis saluted. When he tried to turn around, he almost fell.
Taylor moved quickly and caught him.

Sergeant Major Taylor and General Hanrahan locked eyes.
Hanrahan shook his head.

When they were gone, Paul Hanrahan went to his window
and moved the curtain aside just enough so that he could see
out. Taylor had one hell of a time getting Ellis into the staff

car. Hanrahan wondered how the hell he had managed to get from the airport to Bragg.

Ellis's foot was wrapped in bandages. The bandages were dark with what looked like fresh blood.

Shit, I should have called for an ambulance, Hanrahan thought.

When the staff car finally drove off, Hanrahan dialed a number.

"Hello?" his wife's cheerful voice greeted him.

"Tom just walked in," he said. *"Hobbled* in."

"Thank God!" she breathed. "Is he all right?"

"No, he looks awful."

"You sent him to the hospital, I hope," Patricia asked.

"Yes," he said. "Under arrest."

"That was necessary?"

"Yes," he said.

"Can I go see him? Take him something?"

"I told you, he's under arrest," he said, more sharply than he intended.

Her reply was silence.

"Maybe tomorrow," he said. "He shouldn't have any visitors anyhow in his condition."

"All right," she said. Her tone made it evident that she thought he was a heartless sonofabitch.

"I've got to go," he said.

Patricia hung up without another word.

Hanrahan dialed another number.

"Liberty 7–2338," a female voice said.

"General Hanrahan for Colonel Felter," Hanrahan said.

"One moment, please," she said, and then: "I'm sorry, General. Colonel Felter is not in his office at the moment. Would you care to leave a message?"

"Please," Hanrahan said. "Tell him 'The Prodigal Son has returned.'"

"'The Prodigal Son has returned,'" she quoted. "I'll give him the message, General."

"Thank you," Hanrahan said, broke the connection, dialed a number from memory and got "Charley Company, 505th, First Sergeant, sir."

"Sorry," Hanrahan said, broke the connection, swore, and consulted the directory.

"Pathology, Sergeant Finster."

"Dr. Parker, please," Hanrahan said.

"The doctor is in the lab, sir."

"Get her on the phone," Hanrahan ordered. "This is important."

"Yes, sir."

"Dr. Parker?"

"Taylor is en route with Tom Ellis," Hanrahan said.

There was a pause before Toni Parker replied.

"Well, he won't suffer from lack of attention, Paul," she said.

"What does that mean?"

"I've been reading about those punji sticks and the infection they cause," she said. "I hate to use this word, but the infections are 'interesting.'"

"'Infections,' plural?"

"Several strains of unfamiliar bacillus and such that resist antibiotics," she said. "Some of them seem to cause morbidity in tissue that's hard to stop."

"Great!" he said.

"There's a couple of people here who are delighted he ran away from the hospital in Saigon. He'll be their first case."

"Which means they won't know what to do about it?"

"They don't know much more in Saigon, Paul," she said.

"Have a look when you have a chance, Toni, will you, and call me."

"I'll be there when they bring him in," she said. "I'll call you when I know something."

"Thank you, Toni," he said. "If you can't get me, call Pat."

"I was going to call her first anyway," Toni Parker chuckled and hung up.

General Hanrahan started to dial the operator, changed his mind, went into the outer office and poured himself a cup of coffee, and then set it down untouched and went back to his office and put in a call to Miss Dianne Eaglebury at the Delta Delta Delta House at Duke University in Durham.

When he got Dianne on the line, he told her that he had

nothing special in mind, except that he had sort of expected her to take the tour of the Special Warfare Center he had offered, and he just wanted to repeat the invitation.

She said that she really wanted to come down there, but one thing and another had come up, and she just hadn't been able to find the time.

"Well, whenever, we'll roll the carpet out," Hanrahan said.

"I appreciate the invitation," Dianne said. "One of these days, I'll take you up on it."

"Oh, incidentally, Tom Ellis's back. And doing well."

"Back? Back from where? 'Doing well?' Is something the matter with him?"

"I thought you knew," Hanrahan said. "He's been in Indochina."

"No, I didn't know," she said angrily. "What do you mean, 'He's doing well'?"

"He stepped on something over there," Hanrahan said. "They've put him in the hospital."

"There, at Fort Bragg?"

"Yes."

"Well, thank you for telling me, General," she said. "And thank you again for calling."

(Two)
The Oval Office
The White House
Washington, D.C.
1715 Hours, 29 January 1962

The President's secretary walked into the office with an envelope and extended it to him.

"Mr. Kennedy sent it over marked for immediate delivery," she said.

"Thank you," the President said, and tore the envelope open and read the typewritten sheet it held.

"I've got a message for you too," the President's secretary said to Lieutenant Colonel Sanford T. Felter, who was standing behind the President's desk. There was a stack of aerial photographs on the desk.

"Oh?" Felter asked.

"The switchboard asked me to tell you that General Hanrahan wants you to know the Prodigal Son has returned," she said.

"Why do I sometimes get the feeling that Senator Goldwater doesn't like me?" the President asked, and then he picked up on what his secretary said. "What Prodigal Son is that, Sandy? Your pal Lowell?"

"No, sir," Felter said, hesitated, and went on. "In this case the prodigal is Lieutenant Ellis."

"The boy-faced warrior? Where was he?"

"In Vietnam, sir."

"And General Hanrahan considered his return of such significance that he tells you via a cryptic message?" the President asked. "You can tell me, Felter. I'm the President. I can be trusted, despite the opinion of a certain silver-headed senator-general."

The secretary laughed out loud.

"He was over there as a courier," Felter said. "And while he was there, he went on a patrol he shouldn't have where he stepped on a punji stick. They put him in the hospital, and he left the hospital and came home."

"He just took off from the hospital?" the President asked.

"What's a punji stick?" the secretary asked.

The President told her, and then rephrased his question: "He went AWOL from the hospital? Why?"

"I would guess, Mr. President, that he hoped if he came home it would not come out that he had gone on the patrol."

"But he got caught?"

"The medics were concerned for his health, sir. He really should have been in the hospital. They sent a TWX."

"You think he's in the hospital at Fort Bragg now?"

"If he's at Bragg, Mr. President, he's in the hospital."

"Why do you suppose he wanted to go on a patrol?"

"Vietnam is nectar, Mr. President," Felter said, "and Lieutenant Ellis is a bee."

"Do I infer that he's in hot water with the army?"

"MAC V considers him AWOL, sir," Felter said.

"Well, far be it from me to interfere with good military order and discipline," the President said wryly. "But on the other hand, when you're going to be there anyway, I can't see any reason why you should not, Felter, express to Lieutenant Ellis my best wishes for his speedy recovery. Preferably in the hearing of whoever is concerned with the question of AWOL."

"I wasn't aware that I was going to Fort Bragg, Mr. President," Felter said.

"I've sometimes noticed that when I tell people to do something they don't really want to do, they tend to forget I told them. If you visited Bragg, I wouldn't be at all surprised that it would serve to keep memories sharp."

"I'm sure it would, Mr. President," Felter said. He wondered whether he was being sent to Bragg because something in Kennedy made him admire a young officer who went on a patrol he hadn't been ordered to go on and then went AWOL from a hospital, or whether it was because Kennedy meant what he said about jogging memories. He decided it was probably both, with emphasis on the latter.

Felter had come to believe that Kennedy hoped that he could solve the problem of Indochina with unconventional forces rather than getting involved in an all-out war. He suspected that this had a good deal to do with McNamara's ordering the army to come up with a proposal for an air-mobile division.

Felter did not believe that ten times as many Green Berets as were proposed, nor a dozen divisions, air-mobile or otherwise, would be of much use in Vietnam unless the decision were made to carry the war to Hanoi and, if necessary, to Peking.

But his opinions had not been sought, and he knew they would not be listened to if he offered them.

(Three)
Ward 3-B-14
Station Hospital
Fort Bragg, North Carolina
0930 Hours, 30 January 1962

The candy-striper was carrying a foil-wrapped flower pot. She went to the nurse's station.

"Lieutenant Ellis?" she asked when she finally had the nurse's attention.

The nurse looked at her in surprise.

"Flowers for Lieutenant Ellis," the candy-striper repeated.

"He can't have anything in there," the nurse said.

"Not even flowers?" a tall, sharp featured black woman asked. She was wearing a medical smock to which was pinned a name tag reading ANTOINETTE PARKER, M.D., CHIEF, PATHO-LOGICAL SERVICES.

"He's under arrest, Doctor," the nurse said.

"What's that got to do with flowers? You think she's got a file in among the roses?"

"I don't have the authority to pass anything in there," the nurse said.

"I think I do," Dr. Parker said. "Go ahead, honey, he's in 307, last door on the left."

"Doctor, I wish you'd put that you authorized that in writing," the nurse said.

"Sure," Dr. Parker said. "Why not?"

She took Tom Ellis's chart, which she had just put in the rack, opened the aluminum cover, and wrote "Delivery of flowers authorized. A. Parker, M.D., 0935 hours, 30 Jan." She showed it to the nurse and put the chart back in the case.

Tom Ellis was sick and uncomfortable. Flying halfway around the world with open wounds, a fever, and an infection that was not under control had been both insane and debilitating. His foot and calf were swollen, inflamed, and painful, and they weren't going to get much better anytime soon. He was subject to periodic sweats and chills, and they weren't exactly sure what were causing them, although infection and any number of odd Asiatic viruses were under consideration. He had intravenous systems in both arms, one feeding him antibiotics, the other feeding a saline solution in case something unexpected should happen to him. His electrocardiogram had shown certain irregularities. As a precaution, to rest his heart, they were feeding him oxygen through his nostrils. First thing that morning, they had given him a barium enema and subjected him to a painful and humiliating X-ray examination of his entrails.

Flowers, Dr. Parker decided professionally, and especially flowers delivered by a pretty young girl, were not contraindicated.

Dr. Parker was looking at her watch impatiently when an air force captain came to the nurse's station. She had hoped to see a bone-and-muscle guy and at least one of the four internal medicine guys who were working on Tom, to get their prognosis. But none of them were with him, and she had to get back to her lab.

"Flowers for Lieutenant Ellis," the air force captain said.

"Popular devil, isn't he?" Toni quipped, smiling sweetly at the nurse.

"Very popular, Doctor," the air force captain said. "With friends in high places."

"Oh?"

He pointed to the green stick in the pot of flowers. There were two pieces of paper wired to it. One read, "Capitol Florist, 13th and M N.W., Washington, D.C.," and the other was a small white envelope with gold embossing: THE WHITE HOUSE, Washington.

"Really?" the nurse squealed.

"Delivered to the plane by limo just before we took off to come down here," the captain said. "Where is he?"

"Right this way, Captain," Dr. Parker said. "I'll show you myself."

When she pushed the door to 307 open, a young woman who was not the candy-striper was in Lieutenant Ellis's room. He was still on his back, with the oxygen pipes in his nostrils, and the intravenous devices in each arm. The girl was sitting on the bed beside him, tenderly mopping his forehead with a washcloth. She had been crying, and her mascara had run, and her lipstick was mussed. There was lipstick on Tom Ellis's forehead and cheeks and mouth, and it looked as if he, too, had been crying.

"Miss Eaglebury, I presume?" Dr. Parker said. "General Hanrahan told me he thought you might drop by."

(Four)
Office of the Commanding General
U.S. Army Special Warfare School and Center
Fort Bragg, North Carolina
1245 Hours, 30 January 1962

Sergeant Major Taylor entered the office without knocking and closed the door after him.

"There's a gentleman from the CIA outside, General," he said. "I told him you were busy, but he insists."

General Hanrahan looked at Lieutenant Colonel Felter, who shrugged his shoulders.

"Ask him to come in, Taylor, please," Hanrahan said.

A man of about thirty walked briskly into the room. He wore a gray flannel suit, a white button-down–collar shirt, a red-striped necktie, and highly polished plain-toed cordovan shoes. He carried an expensive camel-hair overcoat over his arm and held a snap-brimmed hat in his hand. He looked, Sandy Felter thought, as if he were a bright and successful young stockbroker.

"General Hanrahan?" he said, extending a leather folder. "Thank you for letting me interrupt."

He didn't give Hanrahan what Hanrahan considered a long enough look at his credentials, and Hanrahan asked, "May I see that again, please?"

With visible impatience the credentials were returned to Hanrahan. The CIA man looked at Felter.

"Colonel, I don't mean to run you off, but I'll have to see General Hanrahan in private."

"I didn't catch your name," Felter said.

"I didn't give my name," the CIA man said.

"J. Croom Winston the Third," Hanrahan read from the credentials, earning him a look of displeasure from J. Croom Winston III.

"Colonel Felter," Hanrahan went on, "is authorized access to anything here, Mr. Winston."

"I'm afraid I must be the judge of that," Winston said. "Would you excuse us, Colonel?"

"Certainly," Felter said. He got up and walked out of the office and closed the door behind him.

"Was it all right, my coming in there?" Sergeant Major Taylor asked.

"How could you resist?" Felter asked. "Is there a scrambler phone around here?"

Taylor reached in the neck of his fatigue shirt and came out with his dog-tag chain. This held three keys in addition to his dog tags. He unlocked a steel credenza, took a telephone from it, and set it on top of the credenza.

"How does it work?" Felter asked, going to it.

"You tell the operator. You need a scrambler access authority code."

"Will mine work?"

"If it doesn't, I'll give you ours," Taylor said.

Felter nodded and dialed *O*.

"Able One-Nine Willy," he said. "Get me a military liaison at the CIA in McLean."

There was a pause as the operator checked the access code.

"One moment, sir."

There followed a series of buzzes and clicks.

"Military liaison, Martindale."

"You have an incoming, sir. Would you please engage your scrambler?"

"Engaged," the man said again in a moment.

"Go ahead, please; signal when finished. I am going off the line at this time."

"Sandy Felter, Marty," Felter said.

"What can we do for the White House?"

"Does the name J. Croom Winston the Third mean anything to you?"

"Never heard of him."

"He's got credentials, and he's waving them around to Paul Hanrahan. Find out who he is, will you?"

"Hang on. You seem annoyed."

"I am."

There was a ninety-second wait.

"He works out of Southeast Region, for the East German desk."

"Who's got the East German desk?"

"Hoare."

"Which would be quicker, you calling Hoare there, or me breaking this down and starting from scratch?"

"What do you want to know?"

"What he wants from Hanrahan, why, and who authorized it."

"Quickest is me walking down the hall and getting Hoare."

"Would you, please, Marty?"

There was another ninety-second wait.

"Joe Hoare, Sandy. What can I do for you?"

"You have an arrogant young man named J. Croom Winston the Third working for you, Joe?"

"I suppose, on balance, that *is* a reasonable description. I gather he's annoyed you somehow? How?"

"He just ran me out of Paul Hanrahan's office," Felter said. "Hanrahan told him I was cleared, but he announced he would be the judge of that. Is something going on that I don't know about?"

"I would be very surprised, Sandy, if anything went on anywhere that you didn't know about," Joe Hoare said. "Give me a minute to check to make sure, but I don't think Hoare has been assigned anything important."

"I'll wait," Felter said. "Thank you, Joe."

"Sandy, what he's doing down there is looking for a man named Karl-Heinz Wagner. Do you remember the East German Pioneer lieutenant who came through the wall in a truck?"

"No," Felter said.

"Well, this guy did and made it to the States, enlisted, and joined the Berets. We're still digging tunnels over there, and the action officer came up with this Wagner's name, and he wants to search his brain. He knows something about the other side, or the action officer hopes he does. Winston was sent down there to talk to him and, if he appears to have any information of importance, to ask the army if they can borrow him for a month or six weeks."

"That's all?" Felter asked incredulously.

"Yeah. You thought there was more?"

"The close working relationship everyone hopes can be maintained between the company and the army is not going to be helped at all, Joe, if you don't train your people to recognize the difference between a routine matter and something important."

"You are annoyed, aren't you, Sandy?"

"Or," Felter went on coldly, "if you permit them the misconception that because they have been hired and given a piece of plastic with their picture on it, that they have the authority to order sergeants major, much less general officers, around like clerks."

There was a pause before Hoare replied.

"I take your point, Sandy. Is he around there somewhere?"

"He's in with Hanrahan."

"Would you please call him to the phone?"

"I'm sure you understand that my concern is not solely with this young man," Felter said.

He covered the microphone with his hand. "Sergeant Major, would you please tell Mr. J. Croom Winston the Third that Mr. Joseph Hoare hopes he can be torn away from his duties to chat a moment on the telephone?"

"It would be my very great pleasure, Colonel Felter, sir," Taylor said.

He went to Hanrahan's door, knocked with his knuckles, and went immediately in.

"Mr. Winston has a telephone call, General," he said.

"That's a bit odd," J. Croom Winston said to General Hanrahan. "It must be important if they called me here."

He followed Sergeant Major Taylor out of Hanrahan's office.

"Is that line secure?" he asked the small, balding Jewish lieutenant colonel who held a telephone out to him.

"It's a scrambler line," Felter said.

"I'd like to take this in private, if you don't mind," Winston said. "I'm sure you understand."

"Perfectly," Felter said. "Would you come with me, please, Sergeant Major?"

They went into General Hanrahan's office and closed the door.

"Winston here," he said to the telephone.

"Joseph Hoare, Winston."

"Yes, sir?"

"Winston, there are half a dozen people who are put right through to the director when they call here."

"Yes, sir?"

"You have just made an ass of yourself, and thus of me, in front of one of them."

"Sir?"

"Your superiors will, I am sure, discuss this at greater length with you, but for the moment, all you have to know is that the lieutenant colonel you ordered from General Hanrahan's office is the President's personal representative to the intelligence community. He holds the opinion that you are an arrogant ass whose delusions of self-importance threaten the working relationship between the Company and the army. The only tiny sliver of silver in this black cloud is that he chose to telephone me and not the director."

While J. Croom Winston III was trying to frame a reply, the telephone clicked twice and Joseph Hoare said, "Break this down."

And then there was only the hiss of the carrier on the line.

(Five)
Known Distance Range Three
Camp McCall, North Carolina
1340 Hours, 30 January 1962

The range had changed a great deal from the time when thousands of basic trainees had fired Garand rifles at bull's-eye targets in World War II. The butts had been eroded by rain and time, and the target frames had long ago disintegrated. The area between the firing line and the butts at two hundred, three hundred, and five hundred yards was now crisscrossed with gulleys and grown heavily with weeds and trees, some dead, some cut off by bullets, and some miraculously intact. More than a dozen hulks of trucks, passenger cars, tanks, and armored personnel carriers, rusty and bullet-pocked, were scattered between what had been the firing line and the butts. There were bunkers, machine-gun emplacements, fox holes, and explosive-charge craters.

Despite the appearance of neglect and disarray, however, what had been Known Distance Range Three was in fact a carefully thought-out practical firing range. At some time during their Camp McCall training, Special Forces trainees, two at a time, in the buddy system, accompanied by an instructor, fired the course three times. They fired one course (M-14 rifle, grenade launcher, and M-60 machine gun) and then set up the range for the next firer.

Steel targets, outlines of torsos (in some cases, just of heads), were set up in the cabs of the trucks, where gunners would be in machine-gun emplacements, in bunkers, and in tank hatches. The targets would fall down when struck. The object of the exercise was to knock down all the targets with the ammunition provided, and to pass through the course in a specified period of time.

The instructor walked behind the trainees as they took one of five paths, chosen at random by him, making sure the steel targets of opportunity were struck. It was necessary to hit each target before moving on to the next. If the trainee ran out of ammunition before all the targets were struck, it was necessary for him to fire the course again, the next time during normal training hours, and the second and subsequent courses on Sunday, which was the only day the trainees were given off from training.

Private Geoffrey Craig had fired his first course and was reasonably sure that he could learn enough of it on his first (failing) run through so that he would possibly even be able to pass his second run, and more than likely pass it on his first Sunday excursion.

The first run was with the M-14 rifle. He had carried a double twenty-round magazine in the rifle and four more double magazines in pouches on his web harness. When that ammunition was exhausted, he would swap the empty magazines for full ones carried by his buddy, Private Karl-Heinz Wagner, for that purpose. He had been alarmed at how quickly he had exhausted his first two hundred rounds of ammunition, and he vowed to expend the second two-hundred-round supply with far greater care.

And then he had turned to the instructor for instruction, certain that with the hearing-protector ear sets in place that he had missed the instructor's right or left command.

The instructor signaled for him to remove the bright green ear protectors and then paid Private Geoffrey Craig the nicest compliment he could ever recall having been paid: "For a candy-ass, Craig, you're not a bad shot."

"That's it?" he had asked, in genuine surprise.

"That's it," the instructor said. "Clear the piece and hand me the magazine. I want to count the rounds."

Private Craig had then learned there was a more or less voluntary pool in effect. Everybody theoretically contributed to the pool a nickel for every round issued (four hundred rounds equaled twenty dollars) and was given a theoretical rebate of a nickel per round for every round left over when the course had been successfully completed. If you didn't have any rounds left over, no rebate. Craig had 106 rounds left over, and thus would be required to contribute "voluntarily" only $14.70 to the pool.

When all the trainees had successfully completed the rifle course (and the grenade launcher and machine-gun courses, which had different but similar rules, each requiring a maximum contribution of twenty dollars, less rebate) the money in the pool would be awarded to the three best (less expended ammo) shots on a ratio of 50:30:20.

It had been more or less tactfully mentioned that there was no reason the trainees could not afford the pool, since they were all, even Candy-Ass Craig, on parachutist's pay, and especially since the winners would almost certainly be happy to contribute half of their winnings to pay for a beer bust.

To Private Geoffrey Craig's genuine surprise and immense delight, he was the second best shot with the M-14, the best shot with the grenade launcher, and if luck was with him now and he didn't blow it, he was going to take the machine-gun course.

The only fly in the ointment was Karl-Heinz, who—in spite of the Expert Medal he'd been wearing when Geoff met him— had turned out to be a lousy shot, comparatively speaking. He had blown his first M-14 course and had only twelve rounds left when he successfully finished it on the second try. Thus he would be expected tomorrow on payday to contribute $39.60 to the pool for the M-14 part of it alone. He had made the grenade launcher the first time, but with only five rounds of fifty shells left (which meant that he would have to pay eighteen dollars into the pool). Geoff suspected that Karl-Heinz was not going to do much better with the M-60 machine gun than he had with the M-14, which meant that instead of having an extra fifty bucks jump pay on payday, his first jump pay would not even cover his contribution to the pool.

As he prepared to start the machine-gun course, Geoff psyched himself up for it. If he worried about Ursula and Karl-Heinz being so pathetically poor, he was not going to be able to take the machine-gun course. If he took the machine-gun course, he was going to walk away from the pool with close to five hundred bucks. Even after contributing half of it to the beer bust, he would then have $250 or so left over in "explainable" money. Which he could then tactfully press on Karl-Heinz to tide him over until they had graduated from John Wayne High School and they got their sergeant's stripes—and the pay that went with it.

He was very much afraid that if Karl-Heinz learned that money was something he didn't have to worry about, Karl-Heinz would break off their friendship. He was a proud sonofabitch, and Geoff had recently come to the unpleasant conclusion that he should have told them right off. Now, when it came out, Karl-Heinz was going to resent the deception.

But there was no solution to that that he could see. The only thing he could do was keep playing it by ear and hope for the best. The prospect of being denied Ursula was more than he could bear to think about. The only thing he'd actually gotten from her was a couple of sisterly kisses, no more than two or three on the mouth, but he could never get her out of his mind.

"If you think you can stagger through this thing, Candy-Ass," the instructor said, "without shooting yourself in the foot, I'm ready any time you are."

"Ready, Sergeant," Geoff said.

"Ready on the right, ready on the left, the flag is up, the flag is waving, the flag is down, commence firing."

The first target was a machine-gun nest, two torso silhouettes in a sandbag emplacement. It was one hundred yards from the starting point and was considered one of the easier targets. One simply assumed the prone position, supported the M-60 on its barrel bipod, and fired short, aimed, riflelike bursts at the torsos.

Geoff put the machine gun to his shoulder and fired two very short bursts. Both of the steel silhouettes fell down.

"Wise-ass!" the sergeant said, but he was smiling with approval.

Geoff ran onto the course, the M-60 at something like port arms, with Karl-Heinz carrying a can of ammo in each hand and the sergeant instructor trotting along behind him.

It was one of his good days. When he finished the course, Karl-Heinz hadn't even had to open the second can of ammo.

I think I have just won that fucking pool.

When they got back to the firing line, after setting up all the steel silhouettes Geoff had knocked down, there was a second jeep parked beside the jeep they had driven to the range. The driver was a young sergeant.

"Which one of you guys is Wagner?" he asked.

It was not required in the American army, and he tried not to do it, but habit was strong, and Karl-Heinz almost came to attention because he was being addressed by a superior.

"I am Private Wagner, Sergeant," he said.

"Get in: Colonel Mac wants to see you," the sergeant said.

"He's firing," the sergeant instructor said. "Won't it wait thirty minutes?"

"Colonel Mac said get him right away, I'm getting him right now."

"Shit," the instructor sergeant said. "Go ahead, Wagner."

When the jeep drove off, Geoff asked, "What was that all about? Who's Colonel Mac?"

"I don't know," the sergeant said. "Colonel Mac is the guy with the medal; he does all of the general's dirty jobs."

"What medal?"

"Jesus! The one with the little white stars—the Congressional."

"Oh."

Geoff decided to take a chance.

"Can I say something to you in confidence?" he asked.

"Go ahead."

"He can't afford this goddamned pool. He's supporting his sister on a private's pay."

"I heard," the sergeant said. "So what?"

"So look the other way and let me run this course for him."

The sergeant looked at him for a long moment.

"Fuck you, Candy-Ass," he said finally. And then he walked to the firing line, picked up the M-60, and felt the belt to it.

"You vill march behindt me vid your moudt shud," he said, in a credible German accent. "You vill speak only ven spoken to. You vill den call me Herr Feldwebel. If one liddle vord of dis gets oudt, I will feed you your balls. You understandt all dat, *Shiess*-for-Brains?"

"Jawohl, Herr Feldwebel," Geoff said.

"Vorwarts, marsch!" the sergeant said, and then, just to

keep Candy-Ass Craig in his place, he fired a six-round burst from the M-60, holding it against his hip, and knocked down the two torso silhouettes in the machine-gun nest.

(Six)
Office of the Deputy Commandant for Special Projects
U.S. Special Warfare Center and School
Fort Bragg, North Carolina
1425 Hours, 30 January 1962

"But my uniform, Sergeant Major," Private Karl-Heinz Wagner said to Taylor. "And my appearance."

He was in mussed and soiled fatigues and field jacket, and badly shaven.

"They know where you've been," Taylor said. "Don't worry about it. Just knock at the door and go in when you're told to."

Karl-Heinz marched to within three feet of Lieutenant Colonel Rudolph G. MacMillan's desk and saluted, staring six inches over MacMillan's head.

"PFC Wagner, Karl-Heinz, reporting as ordered, sir."

Mac returned the salute.

"At ease, Wagner," he said with a smile. "Were you doing something interesting, or were you glad to be hauled off from McCall?"

"I was about to fire the M-60 machine-gun course, sir," Wagner said.

"Well, I expect you've fired machine guns before," Mac said. "This is Colonel Felter and Mr. Winston. They want to talk to you."

Felter went to Wagner with his hands extended and spoke in German.

"You're a very interesting man, Wagner," he said. "I'm happy to meet you."

He has a Berlin accent, Karl-Heinz thought. And he thought that the little colonel was an interesting man too. He was unquestionably an infantry officer of considerable experience and personal courage. He wore, among other decorations, the second highest American award for valor.

"It is my honor, Herr Oberst," Wagner said.

"And this is Mr. Winston," Felter said.

Winston smiled but did not offer his hand.

"Do it in English, Sandy, please," Mac said.

"As often as the colonel has been in Germany," Felter said, "his German is limited to 'Another beer, Herr Ober,' and 'Where is the men's room?'"

"That, Herr Oberst," MacMillan said, in not at all bad German, "I understood."

"We are about to have coffee," Felter said in English. "Will you have some, Wagner? It must have been cold in the jeep."

Why not? Wagner thought. *They are buttering me up for something, but there is no reason I shouldn't take the butter.*

"Thank you, sir," Wagner said.

"There is a CIA officer in Berlin," Felter said abruptly, "who believes that you may possess certain information concerning the wall, areas near the wall, and presumably East German Pioneer equipment, which would be useful to him. Mr. Winston is here to ask you if you are willing to go to Berlin and provide such information. Are you?"

Wagner was spared the necessity of an immediate reply by the appearance of Sergeant Major Taylor and a clerk carrying a stainless-steel pitcher of coffee, cups, and doughnuts.

"Sit down, Taylor," Felter said. "I want you in on this."

"Yes, sir."

"I just asked Wagner if he will go to Berlin and make himself useful," Felter said. "I'm waiting for his reply."

"Do I have a choice in the matter, Colonel?" Wagner asked.

"Yes, of course," Felter said.

"Then, with respect, no, sir."

"Okay," Felter said. "That's it."

"Colonel!" the civilian protested.

Felter looked at him.

"You have something to say, Mr. Winston?" he asked coldly.

"May I ask Wagner why not, sir?"

"You may ask him," Felter said, "but he is under no obligation to answer. Do you understand what I said, Wagner?"

"It is a matter of honor, sir," Wagner said.

"Didn't you make that decision when you came over the wall?" Winston said.

"That was a decision to leave," Felter said. "Which is a

different matter. Wagner is, I believe, thinking about the oath he swore to the DDR when he was commissioned. Is that correct, Wagner?"

"Yes, sir."

"May I speak, Colonel?" Taylor asked.

"I hoped you would," Felter said.

"There's a conflict of oaths," Taylor said. "The one he swore when he was commissioned, and the one he swore when he enlisted."

"When I enlisted, Sergeant Major," Wagner said, "it was with the understanding that I would not be sent to Germany."

"And you won't be," Felter said, "not involuntarily."

"We are not asking him to take up arms," Winston said. "All we want him to do is help us with the wall. And he knows from personal experience what a moral abomination that is!"

"I will ask you for your next contribution to this discussion, Mr. Winston," Felter said. "Is that clear?"

"Taylor's right," MacMillan said. "If he doesn't think he broke once and for all his East German oath, then the one he swore when he enlisted can't count."

"He swore to defend the Constitution and to obey the orders of officers and noncommissioned officers appointed over him, that's all," Felter said. "And it was with the understanding that he would not be sent to Germany."

"Bullshit, Sandy," MacMillan said. "He also swore that he had 'no mental reservations whatsoever.' Now, he either did or he didn't."

"I grudgingly grant the point," Felter said. "But someone made him the deal—no Germany—and I won't see him ordered there."

"Colonel MacMillan, with your permission, may I ask what you would do in my circumstances?" Wagner asked.

"I'm not a West Pointer. You want to ask about the fine points of officers' honor, ask Colonel Felter. He's a West Pointer."

"What's that got to do with it?" Felter said impatiently.

"What would you do as a man?" Wagner blurted.

"What would *I* do? I'd ask what was in it for me," MacMillan said.

"With respect, I don't understand," Wagner said.

"You're a lousy PFC," MacMillan said, "without a pot to piss in. You used to be an officer, so you're obviously smart enough to figure that out for yourself. You should also be smart enough to know when a couple of light colonels and somebody from the CIA call you in and ask you to do something that they think what you have to offer is valuable. If I were you, I'd ask what the deal was."

Wagner saw that Felter and the sergeant major were embarrassed by MacMillan's speech and that it angered the civilian.

"I am not interested in a deal, Colonel," Wagner said.

"You're not an officer now," MacMillan said. "Don't get on an officer's high horse with me. You're in no position to reject a deal until you hear what it is."

"I repeat, sir, it is a matter of honor."

"Bullshit!" MacMillan said angrily. "You brought your sister with you. You're responsible for her. You're living on baked beans and bologna. You make me more than a little sick."

"You're offering me money?"

"I'm offering you early graduation from the course. That would make you a sergeant. I'll sweeten that by making it staff sergeant. I'll have Taylor exercise his considerable influence with post housing to get your sister into an on-post apartment. And all I'm asking of you is that you go over there and help the spooks figure out a way to get other people through the wall. If that offends your sense of 'officer's honor,' so far as I'm concerned, you can go fuck yourself, Herr ex-Oberleutnant Wagner."

"Take it easy, Mac," Felter said.

"Bullshit. He pisses me off!"

MacMillan's anger, Wagner saw, was genuine. The man held him in contempt, and that wasn't fair. By what right?

He looked at him, and then his eyes dropped to the rows of ribbons on MacMillan's tunic. Even as a young enlisted man, when first called to service, he had had an interest in the enemy's decorations and insignia. He had later prided himself on being able to identify them and to know what their equivalents were.

The ruddy-faced lieutenant colonel glowering at him was an American *Fallschirmjäger* of some distinction. His parachutist's wings were studded with five stars, each signifying a jump into combat. There was a wreathed star on his Combat Infantry Badge, which meant he had been awarded the American equivalent of the Close Combat Badge twice. He had the ribbon of the French Croix de Geurre (Iron Cross). He had a leaf-studden Purple Ribbon, the equivalent of the War Wound. And up on top, the first Karl-Heinz Wagner had seen one anywhere except on a decorations-and-awards poster, was a blue ribbon with a number of small white stars on it. That was the American Medal of Honor, the equivalent of the Knight's Cross, with swords and diamonds, of the Iron Cross.

The conclusion Karl-Heinz Wagner reached was that he could not afford to offend such an officer. He was, as Colonel MacMillan had pointed out, a PFC literally living on beans and bologna, whose only chance to improve his position was by graduation from the Special Forces school and getting the promotion that would bring him to sergeant. It was possible that if he continued to defy this officer, he would be dropped from the Special Forces school and from Special Forces. They would then probably assign him to the Eighty-second Airborne Division, with some comment on his service record that he had been found "unsuitable" for Special Forces. It would, under those circumstances, be a long time—if ever—before he could win a promotion to corporal, much less sergeant.

He really had no choice. He thought that it really had been naive of him to think that he would not be asked to do whatever the army wanted of him, and that what they would want of him would involve his former comrades in arms in the army of the German Democratic Republic.

"When will I go to Germany?" he asked.

"I repeat, Wagner," the small Jewish lieutenant colonel said, "that if you don't want to go, you will not be ordered to go."

"Yes, sir," Wagner said. "I understand that, sir. I am willing to go, sir."

"Don't do us any goddamned favors, Herr Oberleutnant," Colonel MacMillan said.

"That's enough, Mac," Felter said. Wagner was surprised at both the icy tone—"I *will* be obeyed"—in his voice, and at the reaction to it by Colonel MacMillan. It required great effort on his part to keep his mouth shut, but he managed it.

"When would you like to have Wagner, Mr. Winston?" Colonel Felter asked.

"As soon as possible, Colonel. Today preferably."

"That's out of the question," Felter replied immediately. "He has his personal affairs to put in order. We'll leave when he leaves up to Sergeant Major Taylor."

Winston nodded. There was no longer any question in Wagner's mind that the little man was in charge.

"If we put him on TDY 'to Washington, D.C., and such other destinations as directed,'" Felter asked, "can we pay him per diem?"

"Instead of to the Seventh Group?" Sergeant Major Taylor asked as his brain searched his encyclopedic knowledge of regulations. "Yes, sir. 'Exigencies of the service.' The General will have to okay it."

"What about civilian clothing, Mr. Winston?" Felter asked.

"I hadn't really considered that, Colonel," Winston said after a pause.

"Perhaps you should have," Felter said dryly. "Taylor, get him the civilian clothes allowance."

"Yes, sir."

"Winston, I think that's all we need you for," Felter said. "Wagner will be sent to Washington as soon as his affairs are in order. Unless you have something else?"

(Seven)

PFC Karl-Heinz Wagner stood beside Sergeant Major Taylor in front of the personnel sergeant's desk as Taylor ticked off from memory, and the personnel sergeant wrote down, what was required bureaucratically.

By the authority of the commanding general, having considered previous experience, PFC Wagner was determined to have completed the requirements for graduation from the basic course of the Special Warfare School. In consideration of his performance while a student, and of his demonstrated qualities of leadership, he was to be immediately promoted to staff sergeant. He was awarded a primary Military Occupational Specialty of Special Forces operations sergeant, and a secondary MOS of engineer demolitions specialist (Special Forces).

Staff Sergeant Wagner was to be placed on Temporary Duty with the Defense Intelligence Agency, Washington, D.C., for a ninety-day period. Travel by personal automobile and/or by military and civilian motor, rail, ship, and air transportation was authorized.

Inasmuch as the exigencies of the service made it impossible to determine the exact nature of his duties or their location, he was authorized the appropriate Zone of the Interior or Foreign Service per Diem allowance in lieu of rations and quarters, thirty days per diem to be paid in advance. Inasmuch as the nature of his duties would require the wearing of civilian clothing, payment of a three hundred dollars' civilian clothing allowance was authorized. Finally it had been determined by the commanding general that the peculiar nature of Staff Sergeant Wagner's duties were such that quartering of his dependent in on-post government housing was necessary for both security and compassionate reasons, and the post housing officer, Fort Bragg, North Carolina, was to be requested to inform the commanding general if there was any reason why Staff Sergeant Wagner's dependent could not be assigned the next noncommissioned-officer's-dependent housing to become vacant.

"Can you think of anything else?" Taylor asked the personnel sergeant.

"Advance pay?"

"Thirty days advance pay," Taylor said. "Do all that right now, Phil."

"Can't you hear the rattle of my typewriter?"

"Now we'll run you out to McCall and you can pick up your gear," Taylor said to Wagner as he led him out of the headquarters toward a jeep. "In the morning the paperwork will be done. I know the sergeant in post housing, so you can move your sister in tomorrow, get her settled, and then go to D.C. the day after tomorrow. Sound all right?"

"Fine," Wagner said. "Thank you very much, Sergeant Major Taylor."

"Listen, don't let what Colonel Mac said bug you too much."

"I understand him," Wagner said.

"I don't think you do," Taylor said. "I soldiered with him in War Two. When he was an enlisted man. I was with him at Anzio. We were Pathfinders. What it was, Wagner, believe me, was that he knows what it's like to be busted. He thought you were just being a little stupid about not taking a good deal when one was offered."

"With respect, Sergeant Major," Wagner said, "I think you are wrong."

"I am?"

"Lieutenant Colonel MacMillan is a soldier. A very good soldier. In almost direct proportion to how good a soldier a man is, he has contempt for a turncoat. I am in the unfortunate position of having to agree with him."

"I think you're full of shit, *Sergeant,*" Sergeant Major Taylor replied. "And also dumb, if you haven't figured out yet that we're the good guys and they're the bad guys. Or did you come through the wall because they caught you with your hand in the officers' club cash box?"

"Of course not," Wagner said.

"So far as I'm concerned," Taylor said, "a turncoat is somebody who changes sides when it looks like his side is about to lose."

"Perhaps you are right," Wagner said.

Taylor did not feel that Wagner had been altogether convinced of the logic of his argument.

XIV

(One)
Camp McCall, North Carolina
2005 Hours, 4 February 1962

Private Geoffrey Craig had been retired for the evening for almost an hour when he was summoned to duty. It was the first time in forty-eight hours that he had either undressed before retiring or slept within the relative comfort of a sleeping bag, mountain; on a cloth, ground; beneath a shelter half. It was in fact the first time he had had his clothes off in forty-eight hours, the previous two days having been spent acquiring the skills necessary to move cross-country under adverse conditions (in this case, snow mixed with freezing sleet), using a compass.

Before retiring, it had been necessary for him to infiltrate into the cadre area to steal a second shelter half from the supply room. Following the sudden and unexplained departure of PFC Karl-Heinz Wagner, he had no buddy, and thus only half of the two shelter halves necessary to form a pup tent. The cadre having proven themselves totally unconcerned with his problems, he had the option of finding what shelter he could from his shelter half or of acquiring a second half.

It had been constantly reiterated that the first qualities a Green Beret must have were self-reliance and resourcefulness. He had taken that to heart, his conviction buttressed by his awareness that unless he got the second half to make a pup tent, he was going to sleep under a blanket of snow and freezing rain. The obvious thing to do was steal a shelter half, and he had, and he was not going to concern himself for the moment with the shit that was going to hit the fan when the cadre supply sergeant found that the padlock had been torn off the supply quonset, a shelter half had been stolen, and a case of ten-in-one rations broken into and pilfered.

Also, Private Craig had had damned little to eat in the past forty-eight hours, and he had concluded that it was just as well to be hung for a wolf as a lamb. After all, what could they do to him? Send him to the John Wayne Course at the Camp McCall School for Boys?

"Drop your cock and pick up your socks, Candy-Ass," the cadre sergeant said to him. "Your beloved country has need of your services."

"Oh, for Christ's sake!"

"Yours not to reason why, Candy-Ass," the cadreman said. "Yours but to get your ass out of that bag before I shovel snow in it."

He wondered if the theft had already been discovered and if he had been discovered to be the culprit. If that was the case, they were liable to roast his ass over a slow fire.

Under the circumstances, he decided, that might not be as bad as it sounded.

He dressed in winter underwear over his T-shirt and shorts, and with difficulty managed to get his feet in his mostly dry and thus quite stiff jump boots. He had a great deal of difficulty in lacing the boots. It was as dark as the womb in his pup tent, and his fingers were wooden from the cold.

Finally he zipped the sleeping bag shut, crawled out of the pup tent, and put on his field jacket. It was hard as concrete, and he wondered if the goddamned snow-soaked sonofabitch was actually frozen. He had a hell of a time getting the zipper ends together with his wooden fingers.

"One must always try to remember, mustn't one," the cadreman said, "that it is extremely difficult to shoot the bad guys if one has forgotten one's rifle?"

"Shit!" Private Craig said. He bent over and pulled his M-14 from beneath the pup tent and slung it over his shoulder, then followed the cadreman off into the dark. He had been issued a flashlight, but he had forgotten it, and he couldn't go back for it now.

"Where are we going?"

"*I* am going to bed," the cadreman said. "*You're* going to Fort Bragg."

"What the hell for?"

"The way this system works is that the privates have to do what the sergeants want them to do," the cadreman said. "You may have noticed that you are a private."

A supply detail, Private Craig decided, a one-man goddamned supply detail. He was going to be put in the back of a three-quarter-ton truck and have his ass frozen off between here and Bragg, where he would load something heavy, like cases of groceries, onto the three-quarter-ton and then have his ass frozen all the way back to McCall, where he would then be permitted to unload the heavy cases of groceries.

When they got to the motor pool the first sergeant was there. For a moment, until he realized that the cadre had all sorts of things, like electric lights, that made it possible for them to stay up after the sun went down, he was surprised to see him up so late.

"Two envelopes, Craig," the first sergeant said to him, holding one up in each hand. "One goes to Headquarters, and the address is on the other side. You will deliver them and then return. Can you remember all that, or would you like to take notes?"

"I think I can remember it," Geoff said.

"You'd better," the first sergeant said. And then he said something that for him was extraordinarily compassionate and tender. "You don't have to rush back here. Why don't you take a shower and a shave while you're on post? You smell like a leprous goat."

"Who's going to drive me?" Craig asked.

"I couldn't steel myself to ask one of my delicate cadreman

to drive all that way through the ice and snow," the first sergeant said. "Take my jeep."

It was as cold as a witch's teat on the twenty-mile trip back to Fort Bragg, even though Geoff put up the hood on his field jacket and pulled the cord so tight that only his nose stuck out of the opening. He had to hold his head very carefully so that he wouldn't be blinded if he moved it within the hood.

He delivered the envelope to the Charge of Quarters in the headquarters building, and then asked if there was someplace he could take a shower.

"You better deliver the other envelope before you worry about taking a shower."

Geoff looked at the other envelope. It was addressed to Apt 2C, Building Q-404, 14 Carentan Terrace.

"Where is this?" he asked, showing the envelope to the charge of quarters.

"NCO housing area," he was told. "Go onto the main post, drive past the main post theater on your left, and then turn left toward the division area."

"What the hell is this, anyway?"

"How the hell would I know?"

Building Q-404 turned out to be a two-story frame building—a duplex, if that was the word—with two apartments on each floor of each half of the building. Deciding he didn't dare leave the rifle in the jeep, he slung it over his shoulder and climbed the stairs to the second floor.

The door of 2-C had a sign on it: S/SGT. WAGNER.

He wondered who the hell Staff Sergeant Wagner was, and what was his importance to the system that he got personal messenger service from Camp McCall. He knocked at the door and waited. He could hear the sounds of television in other apartments and the sound of a kid giggling in delight, and then he heard footsteps inside the apartment, and the rattle as a door chain was unlocked.

"Ach du Lieber Gott!" Ursula said when she saw him. She covered her mouth with her hands.

"Jesus Christ!" Geoff said.

Ursula surprised him by throwing her arms around him, right around the dirty, cold field jacket.

In a moment, as if suddenly aware of what she had done,

she said, "I'm so glad to see you." There had been time, before she broke away, for him to feel the warmth of her back through her bathrobe.

"Where's Karl-Heinz?" he asked.

"I don't know," she said. "They sent him someplace he couldn't tell me."

"Whose apartment is this?"

"His—ours. They made him a staff sergeant, and I am entitled to live here." She looked at him, met his eyes, and asked, "What are you doing here?"

He took the envelope from his field-jacket pocket and handed it to her.

"What's this?"

"I have no idea."

"Come in, God, what's the matter with me? You look frozen. Let me get you a cup of coffee. You want something to eat?"

She led him into the kitchen, put water in a kettle, and turned the stove on.

She turned to look at him, and there was movement beneath her nightgown and bathrobe, and he knew that she was naked beneath it.

"Take off your jacket," she said. "You're not going anywhere until you're warmed up."

"I think I'm in love with you," he said.

"You're a fool," she said. "A young boy and a fool. I don't want you ever to say something like that again." She paused, as if considering what she had said. "Love? How can you even think of love? You're a fool!"

She turned angrily from him and found a small jar of instant coffee.

"Do you want me to go?"

"I want you to take off your jacket and warm yourself," she said.

He took the field jacket off and hung it on the back of a chair. The apartment was completely furnished, simply but completely. He decided that since they didn't have any money, the furniture belonged to the army.

"Tell me about Karl-Heinz," he said.

"What do you know?" she asked.

"All he said to me was that he was going on TDY and could he borrow the Volkswagen."

"It's in back," she said. "I run the engine every morning to keep the battery charged. It was dead when he went to get it."

"You're not driving it? Why not?"

"Because I am not the good driver, and I could not pay if I hurt it."

"It's insured, you drive it," he said. "It's better for it if you drive it, and I'll be out in the woods for another goddamned month."

"If that would be best," she said.

"Tell me about Karl-Heinz," he said again.

"He wouldn't tell me where he was going, but I think Germany."

"Why do you think Germany?"

"Because he did not want to go."

"Then why did he?"

"Stupid question," she said. "Because he was told to go. Sometimes you're a fool."

"He told me he had made a deal that he wouldn't go to Germany," Geoff said. "A deal's a deal."

"And a fool is a fool. He is a soldier, and he goes where he is told to go."

The kettle whistled, and she poured boiling water and made instant coffee for him.

"I'll make you a sandwich. Or soup? You want soup? I have made a soup."

"See what's in the envelope," he said. "Then give me some soup, please."

She tore the envelope open. It contained two letter-size envelopes. She opened the thicker one. It held a stack of twenty-dollar bills. She looked at him to see his reaction, and he looked in her eyes and thought, *Shit, I do love her. That's all there is to it.*

"What's this?" she asked.

"I told you, I don't know."

She tore open the other envelope, took out a sheet of paper, read it, and handed it to him.

"What does this mean?" she asked.

It was a short, typewritten note:

Dear Miss Wagner:

    S/Sgt. Wagner won third place in the pool. I thought I had better give you this, since he is on TDY.

                         Yours sincerely,
                         Scott Tourtillott, 1/Sgt.

She counted the money. There was just over three hundred dollars.

"We don't need this, we won't take this, you take it back and say thank you very much."

"He won it, Ursula," Geoff said. *In a pig's ass, he did. He can't hit the broad side of a barn at ten yards with an M-60.*

"Won it? What is a 'pool'?"

He explained it to her, and in the explanation got his own explanation. First Sergeant "Indian Joe" Tourtillott had had him deliver the money because he knew that he would be able to think of some way to get her to take it.

"He was an officer," Ursula said. "He is a very good shot."

"I know," Geoff said.

"He should have won this money when we needed it so badly," she said. "Now there is money enough, and more."

"Is there?"

"Mrs. Sergeant Major Taylor came to see me, and she told me exactly how much money Karl-Heinz will now make, and that the army will send me a check next month, on payday, that he has made the allotment."

"We don't give the woman the husband's title in this country, Ursula," Geoff said.

"You don't?"

"No. When you marry me, for example, you will simply be Mrs. Geoffrey Craig."

"I told you once I don't want to hear any more of that foolishness," she snapped. "You must be crazy."

"What's that got to do with anything?"

"You don't stop it, once and for all, you go," she said. "If Karl-Heinz hear you even talking like that, he be very mad."

"You said something about soup?"

The soup was delicious.

"Can I tell you something?" she asked.

"Anything."

"You stink, you need a bath."

"I know."

"And your clothes are filthy rotten stinking," she said. "You have to go right away?"

"No."

"You take a bath. I wash the clothes," she said.

"How are you going to dry them?"

"There is the machine," she said.

"I said 'dry,'" he said.

"There is the machine," she said. "You put the clothes in, and it spins around with heat, and the clothes are dried. Mrs. Sergea—Mrs. Taylor showed me how to work it."

"And in the meantime, while the clothes are drying, I get to chase you naked around the apartment?"

"Don't be silly!" she snapped. "I give you something of Karl-Heinz to wear."

There were a pair of panties, labeled THURSDAY and embellished with hearts; a brassiere; and a slip hanging from the shower curtain. He had never seen anything so erotic in his life.

She gave him a shirt and a pair of pants to wear while the washer and dryer were operating. They didn't fit, and they were of a strange, cheap material. He asked if Karl-Heinz had brought them from East Germany.

"Not good, are they?" she asked, nodding.

"Never look a gift horse in the mouth," he said. "I wasn't criticizing. I was curious."

She had, he thought with regret, taken his joking remark about chasing her naked around the apartment at least half seriously. She had dressed while he was bathing in a sweater and skirt, and she'd done her hair up in the back.

"They're no good," she said. "Everything back there is cheap. I mean cheap-made, not cheap to buy."

"I understand," he said.

"Do you think Karl-Heinz will be back when they say?"

"Sure," he said. "How long did they say?"

"Ninety days," she said, and then added happily, "Mrs. Taylor says that if I want, I can get a job in the PX."

"Doing what?"

"Working as waitress in snack bar, to start."

Fuck that! he thought angrily.

"Do you need the money that bad?"

"I want to help," she said. "You know, we're poor."

"Well, you'll get a chance to meet a lot of men in the snack bar," Geoff said. "Try to meet a rich one."

She thought it over and decided to consider it a joke.

"What would a rich man want with me?"

To love you, to worship you, to hold you in his arms, to buy you expensive underwear and quart bottles of musky French perfume.

"You make pretty good soup," he said.

She smiled at him.

"Don't look at me that way," she said.

"What way?"

"Like a puppy dog," she said.

"I can't help it," he said.

"You're a fool, Geoffrey," she said. "A fool."

He loved the way his name sounded when she said it. And he was aware that she didn't seem quite so absolutely certain that he was a fool as she had earlier.

"Actually," he said, "I'm not such a bad fellow. Most dogs, except Dobermans, like me...."

At that moment the dryer, with a squeal and an off-key bell, announced that it had completed its assigned task.

They both looked at it as if annoyed by the distraction, but there was nothing for Geoff to do but go to the damned dryer, confirm that his goddamned uniform was clean, dry, and as warm as toast, and carry the goddamned thing into the bathroom and get dressed.

She went with him to the door.

"Can I come back?" he asked.

"Sure, why did you have to ask?"

"Because now that I've told you I love you, I thought maybe you wouldn't want to have me around."

She looked up at him and met his eyes, and as he fell into them, she said, "I don't even want you to go now."

"I don't really have to go now," he said.

"You don't?"

"No, I don't," he said.

"There's something I think you should know," she said. "I never do this before."

"Are you sure you want to now?" he asked, very softly.

"What do you think?" she asked, and then she walked away from him, across the little living room and into the bedroom. His heart beating heavily, in sort of jumps, he went after her.

"Don't look," she ordered.

He cheated, he turned his back, but he saw everything she didn't want him to see in the mirror. And she caught him.

"Well, you satisfied?" she asked, her face coloring.

"Is it all right, now, if I tell you I love you?"

"Oh, my Geoffrey!" she said, and went to him.

A minute or so later, he was able to remove his jump boots with considerably more speed than he had earlier been able to put them on. And it hurt her, as it was supposed to hurt virgins, but she told him that if he stopped, she'd kill him.

(Two)
U.S. Army Station Hospital
Fort Bragg, North Carolina
0830 Hours, 6 February 1962

When Dianne Eaglebury parked Tom Ellis's Jaguar in the visitors' parking lot and reached in the backseat for the doll, her breasts fell out of her brassiere, and after she had the doll sitting on the roof, she had to put her hands under her sweater again and, desperately hoping that no one was watching, put things back where they belonged.

The reason her breasts had come out of the brassiere, she was well aware, was that the brassiere was not designed to hold things in place, but rather to sort of put things on display. It was of thin, lacy material, and the cups were one quarter of an orb rather than a hemisphere. When properly in place, it lifted the lower portion of her breasts while leaving the upper portion, down to the nipple, exposed.

She had seen it in the window of a store on Book Row in Durham and bought it for $29.95, even though that seemed like a hell of a lot of money for a bra and panty set that contained in all about as much material as a man's handkerchief. She thought that it was entirely likely that she would be able to display the bra—and what it offered—to Tom. It made her feel delightfully wicked. Finding the opportunity to give him a look at the black, transparent panties seemed less likely. There was no lock on his door, and while she was prepared to be shamelessly lewd for him, she was not willing to do it for an audience of nurses, ward boys, or anyone else who might come sailing into the room without knocking.

The doll had begun life as a cutsey-pie little girl in darling little pigtails, a skirt beneath which white-ribboned pantaloons could be seen, and with an adorable little pink beret perched cutely atop its head. The beret had inspired her. The beret was now green, the result of thirty minutes' careful labor with a green Magic Marker. Hours of additional careful labor had created a miniature Special Forces flash on the beret. The blond nylon pigtails had been carefully untwisted, combed, and re-fashioned into a rather good representation of Dianne's own coiffure. The skirt had been cut off above the knees, and the white-ribboned pantaloons were now black-lace panties about as brief as the ones she was wearing.

Tom would be amused, Dianne believed.

God, she hoped so. Tom wasn't doing well.

Dr. Parker had called her the night before and warned her that Tom might be a little "strange" when she saw him. He had some kind of a fever, and a perfectly ordinary to-be-expected symptom of this was a degree of irrationality.

It was nothing to be concerned about, Dr. Parker had told her, but she wanted Dianne to be prepared for it. It would pass when the fever was reduced, and it might very well be reduced by the time Dianne came down from Durham.

Dianne could not bring herself to call the lanky physician "Toni," or even think of her as "Toni," although the physician kept telling her to, and they had become friends. Antoinette Parker had insisted that Dianne stay with her in her quarters. With a good deal of wine in her to give her liquid courage, Dianne had asked for, and Dr. Parker had delivered, a lecture on the fine points of birth control, accompanied by both the appropriate prescription and the confession that she, too, had been greatly surprised with the ease and abandon with which, prior to marriage, she had presented Phil Parker with her pearl of great price.

"One week, I was a high—and virginal—priestess of medicine at Mass General, devoutly convinced that carnal desires were an affliction of the less intellectually endowed, and the next week I was a card-carrying camp follower, slinking around a motel room in Manhattan, Kansas, in black underwear, praying the sight would convince a soldier that life without me was unthinkable."

Dr. Antoinette Parker seemed to understand how Dianne felt about Tom. Dianne did not think that understanding was going to come that easily, if at all, from her mother and father.

She didn't have to sneak in the hospital today the way she had on her first visit to see Tom, when they wouldn't let her in to see him and desperate measures had been required. Dr. Parker had arranged for family status for her with the hospital administration. Dianne sensed that that wasn't a routine thing, for she got a strange look from the soldier at the visitors' desk before he gave her a visitor's badge to pin on her sweater and asked her if she knew where the ward was.

"I know where it is," she said.

Dr. Parker was in the corridor by the nurses' station when she got to the ward, talking to a tall, good-looking Irishwoman just starting to turn gray and, Dianne thought, so confident of her good looks that she wasn't going to try to dye the gray away.

"Good morning," Dianne said cheerfully.

"We've been waiting for you," Dr. Parker said. "This is Patricia Hanrahan, another friend of Tom's."

"Hello, Dianne," Patricia Hanrahan said softly.

Dianne made the connection.

"You're the general's wife," Dianne said. "Tom's told me about you."

"He talked to me about you too," Patricia Hanrahan said.

Dr. Parker had taken her arm and was leading her off the corridor.

"Where are we going?" Dianne asked.

"We have to talk, and I don't want to do it in the corridor," Dr. Parker said.

"Talk about what?" Dianne said as uneasiness swept through her.

They were now in a small room furnished with chrome pipe

vinyl-upholstered furniture, two small tables, and a Coke machine.

"Tom's gone, Dianne," Dr. Parker said.

"Tom's gone? What do you mean, 'Tom's gone'? Where did he go?"

"Tom died at seven-fifteen this morning," Dr. Parker said.

"I'm so sorry, honey," Patricia Hanrahan said.

Part of Dianne's brain told her this couldn't be true. Another part told her it was.

"What the hell happened?" she asked, barely audibly.

"Nobody really knows," Toni Parker said.

"What the hell happened?" Dianne repeated angrily.

"It was probably the infection . . ." Toni Parker said.

"Probably? He's dead, and you don't *know* what killed him?"

"Oh, God!" Patricia Hanrahan said, and sobbed.

"Yesterday morning, early yesterday morning, his temperature began to rise to a dangerous level," Toni Parker said. "We managed to reduce it during the day. When I called you, we thought we had it under control. And then it went up again, and we were unable to reduce it."

Dianne looked at her.

"Do I have to say they did every thing humanly possible?" Toni Parker asked, having considerable difficulty keeping her voice under control.

"You weren't there?" Dianne accused.

"I was with him most of the afternoon," Toni Parker said. "And last night. I was there when he died."

"What *happened?*" Dianne asked.

"There was interference with the nerve system," Toni Parker said in a flat voice. "And with the chemical balance of the body. I don't know what the autopsy will reveal, if anything."

"Autopsy? Oh, *God!* They're going to cut him open?"

"Maybe we'll find something that will help the next time," Toni Parker said.

"I can't tell you how sorry I am," Patricia Hanrahan said.

"Why didn't somebody call me?" Dianne asked very softly. "I could have come yesterday, last night."

"I made that decision," Toni Parker said.

"Thanks a lot," Dianne said bitterly.

"He was comatose," Toni said. "He was in intensive care. You wouldn't have been allowed in there. I thought—we all thought—that we would be able to reduce the fever. I prayed we could."

"I should have been here," Dianne said, and then more angrily: "I should have been here!"

"I'm sorry," Toni Parker said. "Good God, I'm sorry!"

"Where is he? Can I see him?"

"No," Toni Parker said quickly, positively, as if she had anticipated and dreaded the question.

"Why not? Why can't I see him?" Dianne said. "Jesus Christ, why can't I even *see* him?"

For the first time she wept. Toni Parker put her arms around her and held her. Patricia Hanrahan, biting her lips, dabbed at the tears in her eyes.

A minute later, still holding her, Toni Parker said slowly, levelly, as if carefully choosing each word, "Tom's father is here, Dianne. When Tom's condition was considered to be life-threatening, he was notified, and he flew down here."

"You told him? He was ashamed of Tom, and Tom couldn't stand him, but you told *him?* And not me?"

"That was done by administration," Toni said.

Dianne pushed herself away from Toni Parker and went into her purse for a handkerchief.

"What happens now?" she asked, after she had blown her nose.

"When the body is released—"

"Released?"

"After the autopsy," Toni said. "There is some concern about contamination."

"What about *'when the body is released' ?*" Dianne asked.

"Oh, Mary, Mother of God!" Patricia Hanrahan said.

"We think it's best if the remains are cremated," Toni Parker said. "Mr. Ellis has agreed."

"So?" Dianne asked. "What difference does that make?"

"Mr. Ellis has decided to place Tom's ashes in the VA cemetery in Fayetteville," Patricia Hanrahan said. "There will be a military funeral, of course. Tom is considered to have died as the result of wounds suffered in combat."

"I don't know what the hell you're leading up to," Dianne said, "but something."

"Mr. Ellis has been asking about Tom's things," Patricia Hanrahan said. "He's asked about Tom's car."

"The sonofabitch walked out on him, had nothing to do with him when he was growing up, but he shows up to get Tom's car, right?"

"Tom made a will before he went to Vietnam," Patricia Hanrahan said. "We don't know yet what's in it. It's with the Judge Advocate General. I don't know...Is it possible he made provision for you?"

"I don't think so," Dianne said bitterly. "He went over thinking I was too good for him."

"Oh, my dear!" Patricia Hanrahan said.

"Will he sell the Jag to me?" Dianne asked.

Toni Parker and Patricia Hanrahan exchanged glances.

"I'm afraid not," Patricia Hanrahan said after a moment.

"How will we know until we ask him?"

"My husband asked him," Patricia Hanrahan said. "My husband told him about you and said that he thought you might want to buy the car."

"And...?"

"Tom's father said that this was probably the only chance he would ever have to own a car like that, and if he sold it, his wife would just spend the money."

"It's outside," Dianne said.

"The funeral will be at ten tomorrow morning," Patricia Hanrahan said.

"The funeral or the cremation?" Dianne asked.

"The cremation will be today," Toni Parker said.

"I know," Dianne said, bitterly bright, "as soon as *'the body is released.'*"

"You can stay with me," Toni said.

"Is his mother coming?" Dianne asked.

"She said she can't afford to come," Patricia Hanrahan said.

"Would she come if I sent her a ticket and paid for a motel?"

"I don't know," Patricia Hanrahan said. "I could call and ask if you want me to."

"She was hardly what you could call an ideal mother," Dianne said. "But she was his mother. Would you, please?"

"I'll do it right now if you'd like," Patricia Hanrahan said.

"Can I get you anything?" Toni asked. "You want a pill, or a chaplain? Anything?"

"No," Dianne said, and a moment later: "Thank you."

Patricia Hanrahan called Sergeant Major Taylor and got the number, then she told the operator to charge the call to his quarters phone and called Tom Ellis's mother and told her that if she could come, there was a fund that provided transportation for next of kin, and motel expenses.

"You're very good at that, aren't you?" Dianne said admiringly when she had told Tom's mother she would get back to her within the hour with the details.

"I try to be," Patricia Hanrahan said. "Honey, if Tom's car is important to you, perhaps you could talk to Mr. Ellis or Tom's mother after the will is probated. Or my husband could. Maybe you could say something at the funeral, to both of them."

"I'm not going to the funeral," Dianne said. "I'd spit in his eye if I went to the funeral."

"Are you sure?" Toni Parker asked. "About not going to the funeral, I mean?"

"I said my good-byes to Tom, my hello and my good-bye, down the hall," Dianne said.

"You're going back to Duke?" Patricia Hanrahan asked. "Or home?"

"Back to school," Dianne said. "I don't want my father feeling sorry for me."

"I'll take you," Patricia Hanrahan said.

"You don't have to do that," Dianne said. "I'll rent a car."

"I'll take you," Patricia Hanrahan said. "Tom would want me to."

She picked up the doll with the black lace panties and the green beret and handed it to Dianne Eaglebury.

* * *

(Three)
Office of the Commanding General
U.S. Army Special Warfare School and Center
Fort Bragg, North Carolina
1130 Hours, 2 March 1962

First Lieutenant Charles J. Wood, Jr., Infantry, aide-de-camp to Brigadier General Paul T. Hanrahan, jumped to his feet when the tall mustachioed officer entered the outer office.

"Good morning, Colonel," he said. "May I help you?"

Tom Ellis, Craig Lowell saw, had been replaced by a proper aide-de-camp. This one was everything a good aide-de-camp was supposed to be and probably everything that Tom Ellis was not. This one was a ring-knocker—on whose hand was proudly displayed the ring signifying graduation from the United States Military Academy at West Point. He was erect, looked as if he had shaved ten minutes ago after a daily haircut, and was bright-eyed and bushy-tailed.

He had probably been selected, Lowell thought, because he would not remind Hanrahan of Tom Ellis.

"Good morning, Lieutenant," Lowell said. "My name is Lowell, and if the general is not tied up, I'd be grateful if he could give me a moment of his time."

"I will see if the general is occupied, sir. Would you care to tell me the nature of your business?"

"I'm paying my respects, Lieutenant, while here on temporary duty."

Lieutenant Wood went to the general's door, knocked, was told to enter, entered, and closed the door behind him.

"I'll bet he makes life interesting," Lowell said to Sergeant Major Taylor.

"The lieutenant does make us all toe the line," Taylor said.

"Isn't that Tom Ellis's car outside?" Lowell asked.

"Yeah."

"Mrs. Hanrahan told me his mother came down for the funeral."

"Very nasty, Colonel," Taylor said. "Both of them thought the car, and the rest of his stuff, was theirs."

"Isn't it?"

"Not until the will's probated. They were both highly pissed when they couldn't take his stuff home with them."

"Christ!" Lowell said.

"I hope his mother finally gets it," Taylor said.

"She was, I gather, the nicer of the two?"

"No. On a 'nice scale' of one to ten, they'd both run about one and a half. But the mother would sell the car to Ellis's girl. His father wants to play sport with it."

"How did Dianne take it?"

"She paid for the mother to fly down for the funeral, but she didn't go herself."

"A brother and a boyfriend buying the farm in a year is tough," Lowell said. "How long is the legal business going to take?"

"I don't think the JAG* is busting their ass to hurry anything. Ellis's father as much as accused them of trying to steal his stuff."

"The general will see you now, Colonel Lowell," Lieutenant Wood said from the general's open door, and then, when Lowell got to the door, he formally announced him: "General, Lieutenant Colonel Lowell."

Lowell marched in, stopped three feet from General Hanrahan's desk, saluted stiffly, and announced, "Lieutenant Colonel Lowell, C. W., sir, requesting an audience with the commanding general, sir."

General Hanrahan returned the salute.

"I would hate to think you're making fun of my aide, Craig," he said.

"No, sir," Lowell said.

"You are being then a paragon of military courtesy, which makes me think you want something I'm not going to want to give you."

"You have always had a suspicious nature, General."

"Where you're concerned, I have every justification. Charley, this is Colonel Lowell . . ."

"The colonel and I have met, sir," Wood said.

". . . whom I have known since he was younger than you. If he ever asks for anything, you check with Sergeant Major

---

*Judge Advocate General, the army's legal staff.

Taylor, Colonel Mac, or myself before you give it to him. He is not a nice man."

"Yes, sir."

"Tell Colonel Mac, please, what the cat has dragged in, and ask him if he is free," Hanrahan said.

"Yes, sir."

"Nice boy," Lowell said.

"What do you want, Craig?"

"Nice to see you, too, sir."

"What do you want, Craig?"

"Can you tell me all about HALO in thirty minutes?"

"Why should I want to?"

"Because then we can go to lunch and talk about something pleasant," Lowell said.

"I don't know if I can tell you about HALO in one afternoon, much less thirty minutes, and I won't tell you a thing about it until you tell me why you want to know."

Without knocking, Lieutenant Colonel Rudolph G. MacMillan walked into the office.

"Uh-oh," he said, "what's he after?"

"Aside from offering to buy us lunch, he wants to know all about HALO."

"I didn't say anything about 'us' for lunch," Lowell said. "Mac can buy his own lunch."

"Will you require anything else, General?" Lieutenant Wood asked.

"Stick around, Charley," General Hanrahan said. "Colonel Lowell is taking us all to lunch."

"Yes, sir," Lieutenant Wood said.

"Why do want to want to know about HALO, Craig?" MacMillan asked.

"Odd that you should ask," Lowell said. "It happens that General Roberts has decided that it is a blank in my military education that has to be immediately filled in."

"And how did that come to pass?" Hanrahan asked.

"We were having a conference," Lowell said. "I've been doing that a *lot* lately in case no one has heard, and Brigadier General Jack Holson made the astonishing announcement, apropos of nothing special that I can recall, that the army, specifically Special Forces, possessed the capability of exiting a jet at thirty thousand feet and landing in the pickle barrel of their choice."

"What's so funny about that?" Mac bristled. "We can."

"So General Holson, who thought he saw disbelief on my face, somewhat pointedly informed me," Lowell said. "He then observed that I really didn't know much about airborne capabilities, did I? To which I responded I knew as little about airborne operations as I could manage. My aversion to exiting airplanes in flight is well known, I went on to say. For some reason, General Holson took umbrage at what I hoped would be considered an amusing reply."

Hanrahan chuckled. Brigadier General Jack Holson was an old paratrooper and later a convert to Army Aviation and air mobility. But he was first of all a paratrooper who had jumped a company of the Eleventh Airborne Division onto Corregidor to take it back from the Japanese. It was not hard for him to imagine just how "pointed" Jack Holson's remarks to Lowell had been.

"At which point," Lowell went on, "in what I thought at the time was spreading oil on troubled waters, Brigadier General Bill Roberts announced that just as soon as there was time, I would bring myself up-to-date on airborne operations."

"And he wasn't kidding. . . . There is now time?" Hanrahan asked.

"He was not kidding," Lowell said. "Yet another draft of the air-mobility business has been sent around for criticism, and Roberts sent me up here to learn all there is to know about HALO."

"Not about regular operations?" Mac asked.

"I was able to make the point, Colonel, that anyone who had served with you for any length of time had all the details of World War Two or conventional parachute operations burned indelibly in their memory."

"Screw you, Lowell," MacMillan said, laughing.

"But you're serious about HALO?" Mac asked.

"I believe there will be both a multiple choice and an oral quiz on my return," Lowell said.

MacMillan went to the phone and dialed a number.

He was calling an expert, Lowell thought. The expert would give him a quick briefing, taking no more than an hour, probably. He would be finished then at, say, half past two or three, and then he could call the hospital and see if Captain Joan Gillis, Medical Corps, was free for cocktails with him and his very good friend, Antoinette Parker, M.D. If Antoinette was part of it, he believed, Joan Gillis would agree to come. And since Toni Parker was indeed a very good friend, she could be expected to find excuse to leave them immediately after dinner.

He had telephoned Joan Gillis five times since he'd met her coming home from Frankfurt. They had always been pleasant, amusing conversations, and he thought that tonight might be the night. This insane idea of Bill Roberts that he find out all there was to know about HALO might have a happy ending after all.

"Roxy," Mac said to the telephone, "put a dress on, pick up Patricia Hanrahan, and meet us at the main club. Lowell's here and he's buying lunch. Half an hour."

"I thought you were calling a HALO expert for me," Lowell said.

"There he is," Mac said, pointing at Lieutenant Wood. "Before he went to work for the general, he was assistant HALO project officer. He's made sixty? Wood?"

"Sixty-four, sir," Wood said.

"Sixty-four HALO's," Mac said.

"Strange, Lieutenant," Lowell said. "You don't look insane."

"It's a very interesting capability, Colonel," Lieutenant Wood said.

About which, beyond any question, I am about to learn more than I really care to know, Lowell thought.

Hanrahan put that into words: "After lunch, Craig, I'll have Charley brief you and run you through the training program."

"Show me the program, you mean," Lowell said. "'Running me through it' has an entirely different connotation."

Lunch was mostly pleasant. Lowell really liked Roxy MacMillan and was fond of Patricia Hanrahan. But neither was pleased with his solution—his having landed at Fayetteville and rented a car and a motel room—to the problem of whose feelings would be hurt if he spent the night with somebody else. And Roxy MacMillan, who was still angry about the way

Tom Ellis's father had gone through his BOQ "like a vacuum cleaner," talked about that.

"I'm not sure if I should call up Dianne Eaglebury and ask her down for a weekend or whether that would be opening the wound again," Roxy said.

"Leave her alone," Mac said. "She's lost a brother and a boyfriend. If you were her, would you want to come down here?"

"I didn't ask you," Roxy said.

"Mac is right, Roxy," Lowell said.

Roxy thereupon announced that she would get some steaks and call Toni Parker, and they would have a barbeque.

"Can I ask somebody?" Lowell asked. There was no way out. Refusing Roxy would hurt her feelings, and he was unwilling to do that, no matter what the damage to his seduction of the lady shrink.

"I'm afraid to ask who," Roxy said. "But I will."

"A doctor I know at the hospital," Lowell said.

"Who is he?"

"He's a her," Lowell said.

"Sure," Roxy said.

"She's a shrink," Lowell said. "She can ask Charley Wood what has driven him to jump out of an airplane at twenty-thousand feet sixty-four times."

"*Thirty*-thousand feet, Colonel," Wood corrected him. "They call it 'jump pay.'"

Lowell chuckled. Now that he'd been around him a little, he liked the starchy little West Pointer.

"Are you making your paratrooper cracks again?" Roxy said. "Don't you ever knock it off?"

"Only when I am offering observations about people who wear girl scout hats," Lowell said.

"Well, we're all sick of that too, Lover-Boy," Roxy said. "Knock it off."

"When Tom's girl came to the hospital," Patricia Hanrahan said, "she had made him a doll with a green beret."

"Oh, hell," Roxy said.

"Let's change the subject," General Hanrahan said.

"Think of something funny," Roxy said.

"Like throwing Lowell out of an airplane?" Mac said.

"That's funny," General Hanrahan said. "The idea has a certain appeal."

"Is there any way I could see my cousin without causing any trouble?" Lowell asked.

"He finishes McCall today," Mac said. "They get their berets tomorrow. Being the louse that you are, you could and probably will see him when they come in from McCall. If you were a nice guy, you'd go to the graduation parade and leave him alone tonight."

"What's wrong with tonight?" Roxy asked. "What the hell, bring him to the steak broil."

"No, Roxy," Mac said.

"Why not? I mean after all he's family. I remember when *you* brought PFC Lowell to a steak broil in Bad Nauheim."

"I was ordered to," Mac said. "General Porky Waterford ordered me to."

"So order him, General," Roxy said.

"No, Roxy," Mac repeated.

"Why not?" Roxy demanded.

"Because tonight they let them go," Mac said. "Tonight they have a few beers and chase girls. He don't want to be with a bunch of officers and their wives."

"I hate to say this, but he's right again, Roxy," Lowell said. "Maybe I can buy him lunch tomorrow."

"Well, okay," she said, genuinely disappointed.

From 1415 until 1730, with time out only for a telephone call to Toni Parker to make sure that she would bring Dr. Gillis with her to the MacMillans, Lieutenant Colonel Lowell was briefed by First Lieutenant Charley Wood on HALO operations, techniques, and capabilities. Lieutenant Wood was indeed an expert on High-Altitude, Low-Opening parachute techniques and seemed possessed by a burning desire to impart all that he knew to Lieutenant Colonel Lowell. He did indeed learn a good deal more than he wanted to know.

Some of it he found interesting. He had had no idea how great a distance HALO parachutists could move over the ground. The special parachutes were in fact more like an inefficient wing than a parachute. They could achieve speeds approaching

twenty miles per hour in a chosen direction across the ground
as the parachutist descended.

They could, in other words, be dropped well within friendly
lines and land well inside enemy territory. That was an interesting capability. And according to Wood, they really could,
with a little practice, land in an area the size of a pickle barrel.
There were many interesting military applications of that capability, and by the time the briefing session was over, Lowell
found himself paying rapt attention to what Wood told him.

He had believed his enforced familiarity with HALO was
nothing more than a pointed lesson from Bill Roberts that one
should be very careful what one said about parachutists in the
presence of a general officer who happened to be a distinguished parachutist. That belief changed.

When Lieutenant Wood told him that a HALO was scheduled the next morning and that he could actually watch them
jump, he quickly accepted the offer.

The steak broil was very pleasant. Toni had a couple of
drinks and related the romantic nature of her proposal of marriage while Phil Parker and Lowell were sharing a picture-
window house in a housing development outside Fort Riley.
Everyone from Joan Gillis to Hanrahan (who had heard the
story a half-dozen times before) laughed out loud at her recitation of their bachelor quarters, and how they had left the
MODEL HOME sign on the lawn because they got to meet interesting engaged young women that way.

As she prepared to return to the hospital with Toni, Joan
seemed to squeeze his hand when she quickly agreed to have
dinner with him the next night.

At 0510, Lowell met Lieutenant Wood at the mess hall, had
a forty-five-cent breakfast of bacon and eggs and hash-browns,
and then was driven to Pope Air Force Base, where a group
of twenty-one Green Berets were about to make their first
HALO jump from a C-130 at thirty-thousand feet.

They all had their equipment laid out on the concrete beside
the aircraft, and Lowell suspected that if they had not known
he was coming, they would have been suited up long before
now.

He was introduced to the jump master, a competent-appearing master sergeant as old as he was, and to his staff of instructors. There was one instructor per trainee. The jump master told him they went together to the open rear door of the aircraft. The trainee, on command, went off backward, and the instructor then jumped after him, "flew" beside him, and made sure that everything was all right and that the trainee pulled the D-ring, which would deploy his parachute, when he was ordered to do so. There was as a safety measure an atmospheric pressure-controlled device that would open the parachute at five thousand feet. If something went wrong with that, there was an emergency reserve parachute.

"I understand you're going up with us, Colonel, to observe?"

"If I won't be in the way."

"Not at all, sir," the master sergeant said. "Glad to have you."

"Thank you," Lowell said.

"I understand you and Mr. Wojinski and the general all served together in Greece, Colonel?"

"Yes, we did."

"Ski's an old friend of mine," the master sergeant said. "Glad to have you, Colonel. And now, if you'll excuse me, I'll check things here. Lieutenant Wood will see that you're properly suited up."

"I'm to be suited up?"

"Colonel, without leathers and oxygen, it gets pretty uncomfortable at thirty thousand feet."

"I suppose it does," Lowell said, more than a little uncomfortable that he had exposed his ignorance and stupidity before the jump master.

The "leathers" to which the jump master referred were a sheepskin-lined jacket and trousers. To this was added a sheepskin-lined helmet, much like those worn by aviators in the days of open-cockpit airplanes, and an ordinary pair of jump boots. Lieutenant Wood told Lieutenant Colonel Lowell that it was necessary for him to wear the jump boots because at the temperature they were going to encounter, he would frostbite or freeze his ankles unless they were covered and the cuffs of the sheepskin trousers were closed tightly over the boots.

The helmet was equipped with goggles and a face mask, through which oxygen was fed, either from one of the two portable bottles fastened to the parachute harness or from the aircraft's oxygen system. There were two parachutes: the controllable chute and the hemispherical canopied reserve chute. Just walking around "suited up" was difficult. Lowell did not envy the jump master and the instructors who had not only to worry about themselves, but to keep an eye on their students.

Thirty-five minutes into the flight, the order was given to change from the aircraft oxygen supply to the portable oxygen bottles. As soon as the jump master was making sure that everybody's portable oxygen equipment was functioning properly, there came a hydraulic whine and the sound of rushing air. The rear door of the aircraft opened, forming a shelf.

Lieutenant Wood removed his oxygen mouthpiece from the leather face mask of the helmet long enough to tell Lowell to come with him. He led him three feet out on the now horizontal door and guided Lowell's hand to a fuselage frame. He was really going to get a good look at these courageous—or crazy—young men as they took a thirty-thousand-foot step, Lowell decided.

He could see the instructors checking the equipment of each trainee, then the trainees and instructors forming a two-man column in the fuselage, getting ready to make the jump.

It was *both*, Lowell decided. These people were demonstrably *both* courageous and crazy.

The jump master came out onto the horizontal door, put his hand on a frame, and nodded at Lowell. Then Lieutenant Wood came out on his side. They looked like 1930's high-altitude balloonists, Lowell thought. He remembered pictures from *National Geographic* magazine.

The jump master beckoned to him to come over to him.

He's out of his mind if he thinks I'm just going to walk over there. I have no intention of falling out of this airplane. I would get exactly in the middle of the door when the pilot of this thing would decide to raise the nose a little, and I would go sliding out like gravel from a dumptruck.

He shook his head violently, "No."

Lieutenant Wood tapped his shoulder and pointed to the jump master and signaled urgently for him to cross over to him.

Lowell shook his head violently again.

Lieutenant Wood pointed to a flashing red light, then made gestures indicating that he would literally hold his hand if Colonel Lowell was so chicken as to be unwilling to walk across eight or ten feet of perfectly level floor so as to get out of the way in order to let the *men* get on with their business.

Lowell saw that the jump master had similarly seen that he was afraid. He was now at arm's length from his side of the door, stretching out his hand toward Lowell.

What the hell, if I screw things up and they have to abort the jump or something, I'll never hear the end of it from Hanrahan and MacMillan.

With considerable willpower, he loosened the viselike grip he had on the frame and put his hand in Lieutenant Wood's. He moved very carefully toward the center of the door, his other arm outstretched toward that of the jump master.

He finally reached it and grasped it as firmly as he could.

Whereupon the jump master and Lieutenant Wood let go of the aircraft frame, moved quickly to Lieutenant Colonel Lowell, lifted him off his feet with all the skill of longtime bouncers evicting an undesirable customer, and, carrying him backward between them, trotted the eight feet to the edge of the horizontal door and jumped off.

XV

As he walked through the main door of the open mess, a graceful old building that always reminded him of the Winged Foot Country Club, Lowell was stopped by an officious club officer, a captain, who asked if he could help him.

"Thanks, I know where the bar is."

"You are a member?"

"I'm on TDY here."

"The dress code requires a necktie, sir."

Lowell was wearing a dark green blazer, flannel slacks, a soft plaid shirt, and had a British civilian trenchcoat over his shoulders. There was an ascot around his neck.

He found nothing at all wrong with the way he was dressed.

"It's all I have," Lowell said simply.

"Then I'll have to ask you to leave, sir."

"You're neither senior enough nor large enough, Captain, to throw me out," Lowell said.

"Then I should have to inform your commanding officer, sir," the captain said. "May I please see your identification?"

Lowell handed him a calling card.

"I'm on TDY to the Special Warfare Center," he said. "My commanding officer is Brigadier General Hanrahan."

The captain wrote Lowell's name in a notebook. Lowell had the feeling the club officer disapproved of Brigadier General Hanrahan and correctly suspected that Hanrahan would ignore this notice of his flagrant disregard of prescribed sartorial standards.

Barbara Gillis, in uniform, was sitting at the bar.

"We're going to have to stop meeting this way," Lowell said when he walked up to her. "A man can ruin his reputation going out with soldiers."

The bartender raised his eyebrows. He had taken Lowell at his word. In his expensive civilian clothing, with ascot, Lieutenant Colonel Lowell looked more like a civilian than he did a soldier in civvies.

"God!" Barbara Gillis said.

"If you promise to be good and not to try to take advantage of me, I *will* have one teensy-weensy little drink," Lowell said. He looked at the bartender. "Wave the neck of a vermouth bottle over a large glass of gin," he said. "And then serve it over ice."

The bartender nodded and walked away.

"Why do I feel he disapproves of me?" Lowell said. "You're a shrink—tell me."

"Do you drink martinis all the time?" she asked.

"Only after I have been mugged," he said.

"I have the strangest feeling that's close to the truth," she said. "You look strange. Were you really mugged?"

"Twice," he said. "Once just now, and once earlier by friends."

Her eyebrows went up in question. Beautiful eyes, he thought.

"There I was," he said as the drink was delivered, "minding my own business, trying to mind my own business, when I was brutally assaulted and thrown out the door."

"What door?"

"The back door of a C-130," he said. "It was a long fall."

"I haven't the foggiest idea what you're talking about. Are you drunk?"

"Not yet," he said cheerfully. He raised the martini to his lips and took a healthy swallow. "Not *quite* enough gin," he said, "but it will do."

"Start all over again," Barbara Gillis said.

"It's too painful to think about," he said. "You should understand that."

She shook her head.

"I don't suppose you have anything lethal in your purse, do you, Doc?" he asked quickly.

"Now what?" Barbara asked.

"Failing strychnine or something really good, how about a good laxative? Something that works infallibly and instantly?"

"Maybe you do need my professional services," Barbara said.

"Among the other things that have gone wrong today, my plans to get you alone and ply you with spirits to overcome your maidenly inhibitions have gone awry," Lowell said. "The gorilla making his way toward us is an old friend of mine who said that he had to 'talk to me in private.' I didn't know how to tell him no."

"Good evening, sir," Warrant Officer Stephan Wojinski said. He was wearing a shirt and tie and a multi-hued plaid sport coat. He was accompanied by a tall, sharp-faced woman with a beehive hairdo, in a slinky black dress cut low enough to reveal a spectacular freckled bosom and the black undergarments that kept it more or less restrained. She looked more than a little ill at ease.

"Hello, Ski," Lowell said warmly, shaking his hand. "Captain Gillis, may I present Warrant Officer and Mrs. Wojinski? Ski is one of my oldest and best friends."

Mrs. Wojinski, Barbara thought, seemed almost pathetically pleased at the way Lowell had described her husband.

"Mrs. Wojinski, on the other hand," Lowell went on, "thinks I am a bad influence on her husband. Before he met me, she says, he was a tea-totaler."

"Like hell he was," Mrs. Wojinski said. "I never said nothing like that."

"Speaking of drinks," Ski said, and turned to the bartender, "Nelson, bring the colonel and his lady another round of whatever it is they're having, and me and the missus a couple of CC's and Cokes."

"Whoa!" Lowell said. "One double martini is enough. When I finish this, I'll have a Scotch. And put whatever poison you happen to have handy in Mr. Wojinski's drink. Anything, so long as it's either lethal or will make him very sick."

"I didn't have nothing to do with that, Duke," Wojinski said, very seriously. "So help me Christ! I guess they figured I'd tell you."

"Is somebody going to tell me what all this is about?" Barbara Gillis asked.

"They threw the colonel out of a C-130," Mrs. Wojinski said, matter-of-factly.

"Actually, they carried me out," Lowell said.

"They did what?" Barbara asked.

"They tricked him into getting suited up," Ski said. "And then they took him to thirty-thousand feet and jumped out with him."

Barbara saw that Wojinski thought this was funny and was making a valiant effort not to show it.

"Whatever for?" Barbara asked. And then she thought of another question, and asked it before there could be a reply. *"Thirty-thousand* feet? You can't live without oxygen at that altitude."

"They gave me oxygen," Lowell said. "They thought of everything."

"Yeah," Ski said, laughing, "they did that."

Lowell gave him a dirty look.

"No wonder you wanted a double martini," Barbara said.

"Enough of this idle conversation," Lowell said. "What's on your mind, Ski?"

Warrant Officer and Mrs. Wojinski both looked uncomfortable.

"The bar isn't really the place for it," Ski said finally.

"Well, I would suggest the dining room," Lowell said. "But that pompous little sonofabitch at the door is the assistant club officer, and I'll give you three to five that he's waiting to tell me he's checked with higher authority and I can't come in with my ascot."

"What's an ascot?" Mrs. Wojinski asked.

"That thing around his neck," Ski explained.

"Oh," she said. "I always wondered what they called those."

"Is that lobster place in Fayetteville still open?" Lowell asked.

"Yeah, but it's expensive as hell," Ski said.

"Lobster all right with you, Barbara?" Lowell asked.

"I didn't even know there was a place to get lobster," she said. "I'll pay. Just take me there."

"No," Ski said immediately, flatly. "My treat. Ain't every day somebody gets to be an instant paratrooper.'

"If that's the case," Lowell said, "you can split it between you, and we'll all have two lobsters."

Halfway to Fayetteville in the Wojinskis' Oldsmobile station wagon, Mrs. Wojinski, who to Lowell's annoyance had insisted "the ladies" ride in back together, pushed herself forward on the seat.

"This is as good a place as any," she said. "And I suppose that the captain, being a doctor, isn't going to be all that shocked."

"Go right ahead," Dr. Barbara Gillis said. "I'm unshockable. And please call me Barbara."

"Colonel, your cousin is fooling around," Mrs. Wojinski said.

"Is he?" Lowell asked. "With women—*a* woman, you mean?"

"Before Ski got the warrant, we used to live on Carentan Terrace," Mrs. Wojinski said, "and we still got friends there, of course. And, well, they thought I should know so I could tell Ski. They told me and I told him, and he said we had better tell you."

"Tell me what, exactly?"

"That he's fooling around," she said.

"With somebody's wife?"

"With a German girl, sister of a guy named Wagner."

"Isn't that their business and nobody else's?" Lowell asked.

"Ordinarily it would be, Duke," Ski said. "But there's two

things. First, there was a bunch of wife-swappers over there, and they got caught at it. Hell of a mess. They gave half a dozen couples six hours to get off the post."

"Geoff is involved with wife-swapping?" Lowell asked. "How did he manage to do that without a wife to swap?"

"Craig," Barbara said sharply. "God!"

"And there's also a bunch of Christers over there," Ski went on. "They got a new Come-to-Jesus chaplain, and he got them all fired up. Real bunch of dingbats. They sent a letter to the post commander complaining that the high school cheerleaders' dresses were too short, that kind of crap. And after the wife-swapping, they appointed themselves in charge of morals in the NCO housing area. They're going to turn the kid in."

"Turn him in for what?"

"For spending his nights in Sergeant Wagner's quarters," Mrs. Wojinski said. "He's not here."

"Where is he?"

"In Berlin, on TDY," Ski said.

"Oh," Lowell said, understanding.

"Once it gets official, the army's going to have to get moral," Ski said.

"Okay. I'll handle it," Lowell said. "Thanks for letting me know. Do I have to do anything tonight, do you think?"

"Tomorrow, for sure," Ski said.

"He graduates tomorrow," Lowell said. "Can you arrange to have him sent to see me, Ski?"

"I already done that," Ski said.

"In that case, I'll pay for the lobsters," Lowell said.

"Can I ask who you're all talking about?" Barbara Gillis asked.

"The Duke's cousin," Ski explained. "He's in training. We been sort of keeping an eye on him."

Barbara said what she was thinking: "You people really take care of each other, don't you?"

"Sure, why not?" Ski said. "I've known the Duke a long time. He takes care of me, and I look out for him."

"How does he take care of you?" she asked.

"I take him on airplane trips to the Caribbean," Lowell said. "That sort of thing."

Mrs. Wojinski laughed and snorted. "You damned near got him blown away doing that," she said.

"Got him promoted, too, don't forget that," Lowell said.

"I think I would have rather took the warrant exam," Ski said.

"You couldn't pass the warrant exam," Lowell said. "You have to read and write to *take* the exam. Face it, Ski, without me, Ski, you'd still be on Carentan Terrace, throwing your house keys on the floor."

"Well, Jesus, one of them wives was a real looker . . ." Ski said.

"The both of youse," Mrs. Wojinski said, "can go to hell."

In the Lobster House, while they were powdering their noses, Mrs. Wojinski told Captain Gillis that she was the first of "the Duke's girls" she had ever met.

"He likes you," she said. "I can tell by the way he looks at you."

"I'm not one of his 'girls,'" Barbara said.

"You could do a hell of a lot worse," Mrs. Wojinski said. "Don't knock it until you've tried it."

"Because he's rich?"

"They don't come no nicer," Mrs. Wojinski said. "Rich goes on top of that."

Dr. Antoinette Parker had also discussed Lieutenant Colonel Lowell with Dr. Barbara Gillis.

"As a shark swims through the sea, automatically eating everything that comes his way, Craig paddles around, genetically compelled to copulate with everything female he can get in a horizontal position. Once you understand that, everything else about him falls into place."

"Then why should I go out with him?"

"Well, for one thing, he's a very nice guy," Toni Parker had told her, "and from what I hear, he has received very few bad comments on the postcoital critique."

"Will he take no for an answer? Or am I going to have to wrestle with him?"

"I don't know. I don't think he's ever been turned down," Toni said.

"I think I have just been told I have the duty tonight."

"Oh, I think you should go," Toni said. "As Oscar Wilde pointed out, Doctor, celibacy is the most unusual of all the perversions."

"Very funny."

"And maybe you're the one," Toni said. "He was looking at you very strangely last night."

"What makes you think I would *want* to be the one?"

"Psychiatrist," Dr. Parker had laughed, "heal thyself."

Dr. Gillis was surprised and disappointed when they drove back to the officers' open mess from Fayetteville. Lowell did not suggest a nightcap, and when he walked her to her car, he didn't so much as touch her arm.

"I'm glad you were free," he said. "We'll do it again sometime."

The more she thought about it, the more the truth became evident.

She had been examined and found wanting by Duke Lowell.

God damn him, the arrogant bastard!

And then she had another thought.

Maybe the reason he hadn't tried to get into her pants, or even acted as if that idea had any appeal to him, was that he thought she was different from other women. She *had* caught him looking at her strangely several times, and she didn't think that was because she had seaweed from the steamed clams stuck between her teeth.

But if that was the case, why the "We'll do it again sometime" remark? *Sometime* was pretty damned vague.

The bottom line in the second line of reasoning was the same as the first: *God* damn *him, the arrogant bastard!*

There was only way, Dr. Barbara Gillis decided, to handle Lieutenant Colonel Craig W. Lowell. When he called—*if* he called—she would have other plans.

(Two)
Office of the Commanding General
U.S. Army Special Warfare School and Center
1040 Hours, 3 March 1962

"Come in, Craig," General Hanrahan said. "Sit down on the couch beside Mac."

Lowell went to the couch and sat down beside MacMillan on the couch. There were two green berets on the couch, both with the silver leaf of a lieutenant colonel pinned to the flash. A set of silver paratrooper wings, pinned to a piece of cardboard, sat on top of one of the berets.

"You seem extraordinarily quiet, Craig," Hanrahan said.

"I've been had," Lowell said. "With great skill and obviously after a good deal of careful planning. What is there to say?"

"While there are humorous elements, you'll notice we are not smiling, nor do either of us intend to crack wise about what you did," Hanrahan said.

"What was done to me," Lowell corrected him, and then the anger took over. "I hope you don't really think I'm going to pin those wings on me, much less wear that absurd hat."

"I'm sorry you feel that way, Craig," Hanrahan said seriously.

"Getting thrown out of an airplane does not a paratrooper make," Lowell said.

"Sometimes it does," Hanrahan said.

Lowell looked at him with his eyebrows raised but said nothing.

"Tell him, Mac," Hanrahan said.

"I don't understand the point of all this," Lowell said.

"Tell him, Mac," Hanrahan repeated.

"I had to throw Paul out his first time," MacMillan said reluctantly.

"What?" Lowell asked. Brigadier General Paul T. Hanrahan's parachutist's wings carried two stars for two combat jumps into German-occupied Greece during World War II. He and MacMillan had become paratroopers when the Eighty-second Airborne Division was still the Eighty-second Infantry Division, and the entire airborne forces of the United States Army had been two test companies.

"I said he froze in the door the first time, and I had to pry him loose and throw him out," MacMillan said. "For Christ's sake, don't make any smart-ass remarks about it."

"And with all the imaginative devices that come to someone who is afraid, I have been putting off making my own first HALO," Hanrahan said. "So you're one up on me, Craig. You've made yours."

Hanrahan was obviously telling the truth.

"I was thrown out," Lowell repeated.

"You made the jump," Hanrahan said. "After a special course of instruction conducted by the former assistant HALO project officer, you made a HALO descent by parachute. You are on TDY orders here. We will cut special orders stating that you are now HALO-qualified and that, in consideration of your previous experience commanding indigenous troops in combat, you have been certified as Special Forces–qualified."

"I wish you wouldn't do that, Paul," Lowell said.

"I'm sorry you feel that way, but it's too late," Hanrahan said. "The orders have been cut."

"I keep asking why," Lowell said.

"There are a number of reasons, some of them selfish, and some of them accruing to your advantage."

"My advantage? A lot of people are going to get a big laugh out of this."

"I just got off the horn from Jack Holson," Hanrahan said. "I led him to believe that once it had been explained to you, you were so enthusiastic about HALO that you insisted on getting qualified. He seemed quite pleased. In fact, General Holson offered the opinion that under your layer of smart-ass, you've always been a pretty good officer."

"There's a layer of dishonesty in all this," Lowell said.

"Let's say 'irregularity,'" Hanrahan said. "To reiterate, you did make the jump. And the element of irregularity is nothing compared to the way I understand you got your first commission, or the irregularity with which Paul Jiggs elected to give you command of Task Force Lowell. Irregularities are sometimes necessary for the good of the service."

"And how is this going to be for 'the good of the service'?"

"Craig, you if anyone should understand what we're trying to do here. You should not be standing on the sidelines, making cracks about the berets. You should know better, damn it."

Lowell did not respond.

"The first obligation of an officer is to defend his country,"

Hanrahan said. "His second obligation is to keep his men alive while doing so. You tell me anyone in the army who is more dedicated to that than we are. My selfish reason for all this is that you are presently in a position with your mouth close to the ear of the Secretary of Defense. I had hoped that doing this would make you remember that you had once been one of us, that we still think of you as one of us, and that you would represent our interests accordingly. Apparently, I was wrong."

Lowell stood up. He looked at General Hanrahan. Then he bent over the table and picked up the green beret and walked to the mirror on the back of General Hanrahan's door and put it on.

"Now that I'm a Green Beret, I presume I am permitted to kick in the balls anybody who laughs at me wearing this?"

"We expect it of you, Colonel," MacMillan said, then stood up and went to him and pinned the parachutist's wings to his tunic pocket.

(Three)
Apartment 2-C, Building Q-404
14 Carentan Terrace
NCO Housing Area
Fort Bragg, North Carolina
1045 Hours, 3 March 1962

Ursula Wagner came out of the bathroom wearing a pair of pants labeled SATURDAY and nothing else. Geoffrey Craig, who was lying in the bed naked under the sheet, had several thoughts. He first wondered idly if it was coincidence or Teutonic orderliness that had her wearing Saturday's pants on Saturday. Then he wondered if her odd modesty was Germanic or a personal quirk. She seldom took her pants off where he could see her without them. On the other hand, possibly because she had the most marvelous set of boobs he had ever seen in his life, she had from the first been wholly unconcerned with her nakedness above the waist.

"I have something to tell you," Geoffrey Craig said.

"Tell me after you get dressed," she said. She went to the closet door. On a hanger on the doorknob was his freshly pressed class "A" uniform. It had on it the Special Forces insignia and the three stripes of a sergeant. She lay it on the bed.

Last night he had lay in the bed and watched her sew the patch and the insignia on. His emotions had been ambivalent. It was a touching, tender scene of the woman doing for her man. He had also been able to see her breasts under her bathrobe, which had given him an enormous erection.

"You have marvelous teats," he said to her.

She shook her head in exasperation.

"Get dressed," she ordered. "You can't be late."

"I'm rich," he said.

"Get dressed," she repeated.

"Did you hear what I said?"

"I'm rich too," she said. "I am very happy, and I am rich too."

"I mean *rich* rich," he said. "Money-type rich."

She looked at him strangely.

"Which means, among other things, that you can go with me to Belvoir," he said. "I think it would be better if we got married before we went, or as soon as we get there, but your argument that we can't afford it is now invalid."

"What are you saying?" she asked, concern in her voice.

"Let me put it this way," he said. "My income from the trust funds I have now, which does not include, of course, the trust funds I will come into possession of at age twenty-five, gives me an income that is at least as large as what the post commander is paid."

"You do not fool me?" Ursula asked.

"I do not fool you," he said.

"Oh, mein Gott!" she said tragically.

"It's not a social disease," he said. "Why does it make you unhappy?"

"That is why you never talk about your family," she accused.

"No, it isn't," he said.

"Yes, it is," she accused. "And you have been talking of marriage!"

"That's exactly what I am talking about," he said.

"And what will your family say when they hear you want to marry somebody like me? Oh, damn you, Geoffrey!"

"Actually," he said, "I was thinking the best way to handle

that is with a fait accompli. 'Hi, there, Dad. Say hello to my wife.'"

"And he would think, and your mother would think, that I am some cheap foreigner who has married you for their money."

"No they wouldn't," he said, although he considered that a very likely possibility. "And it's my money, not theirs. And besides, you wouldn't be the first kraut in the family."

"'Kraut,'" she quoted bitterly. "You see!"

"The second German lady," he said.

"What are you talking about?"

"My cousin Craig, the one who's a colonel, was married to a German woman," Geoffrey said. "She was killed in an automobile accident a long time ago."

"He's an officer, he married a German lady," Ursula said. "He would think what your mother and father would think."

"Well, we'll find out soon enough," Geoffrey said.

"What do you mean?"

"I am not to 'run away' after the parade. Tourtillot said that a 'Colonel Lowell' wants to see me."

"I am not going," she said.

"You'll go if I have to carry you over my shoulder," he said.

"I don't want to go," Ursula said, tears in her eyes.

"There's only one thing you have to make up your mind about," he said. "Do you love me or don't you?"

She looked at him and sobbed.

"Do you or not?"

"What's that got to do with anything?"

"Yes or no, goddamn it, Ursula!"

"Yes. You know that, yes."

"Well, in that case, it's you and me, sweetheart. Fuck everybody else, including my parents, Staff Sergeant Karl-Heinz Wagner and Colonel Craig W. Lowell."

(Four)

It wasn't much of a reviewing stand, but then, it didn't get much use, and there weren't all that many Green Beret graduation ceremonies.

The usual procedure was for the graduating class to march

onto the parade ground (normally the athletic field) and then, on command, to file onto the reviewing stand, where they shook hands with the commanding general. He congratulated them by name. They took two more steps, and in a complicated (and thus previously rehearsed) maneuver, they shook the right hand of the Deputy Commandant for Special Projects while simultaneously reaching out with the left for the diploma. They then reformed where they had been.

When they had all reformed, Sergeant Major Taylor would give the command to "Discard hats," the hats would be thrown into the air, green berets would be put on, and the formation would be over.

This was the end of the first phase of training. Unless they were already qualified, the graduates would next be trained in a specific MOS and then cross-trained in a second MOS. Every member of an "A" Team had to have two MOSs. During the period between this graduation and the final graduation (which was most often unmarked by ceremony), when they had become fully qualified, the trainees could wear the green beret, but not the flash sewn to it by fully qualified Green Berets.

This graduation, however, marked the end of the chickenshit. Once they had graduated from John Wayne High, as Camp McCall was somewhat irreverently called, they were considered to have proven themselves extraordinarily well qualified in basic soldierly skills. In further training, from now on, they would be treated as responsible noncommissioned officers.

The ceremony went less smoothly today than it usually did. The strange light bird who was passing out the diplomas instead of Colonel Mac (the light bird had been identified by somebody as "one of the real old-timer Green Berets," some guy who had been in Greece with Warrant Officer Wojinski and the general even before there was such a thing as the Berets) did not have the simultaneous right-hand–shake, left-hand–here's-your-diploma routine down pat. He kept dropping the rolled-up diplomas, or in one case jabbing a master Sergeant accidently in the crotch with one.

Finally, Geoffrey Craig faced the clumsy colonel.

"Congratulations, Sergeant," the clumsy colonel said.

"Thank you, sir," Sergeant Craig said.

"Stick around afterward, I want a word with you."

"Yes, sir."

Sergeant Craig wondered again why he had never seen Cousin Craig wear a beret before, or for that matter jump wings; but he had more important things on his mind. When he came off the little platform, Ursula was not standing where she had been.

They caught up with her in Geoff's Volkswagen on the road from Smoke Bomb Hill to the main post and Pope Air Force Base.

"Honey, get in the car," Geoff said.

Ursula shook her head and refused even to look at the car.

"Fräulein," Lieutenant Colonel Lowell said in impeccable German, "if you don't come get in the car, I am going to get out, boot you in the ass, and throw you in the car."

She looked at him in shock and anger and a little fear. But he was smiling at her, and she threw her hands up in resignation and got in the car.

(Five)
The Tri-Delta House
Duke University
Durham, North Carolina
1320 Hours, 3 March 1962

Dianne Eaglebury had not felt very hungry, so instead of eating lunch, she had made a quick swoop through the kitchen and returned with two pears and an apple.

When the army staff car had pulled to the curb outside, she had been sitting on her windowsill, watching the wind move the limbs of the trees in front of the house. She hadn't paid much attention to the staff car after the driver got out. He was a captain who wore regular shoes (what Tom would have called a "straight-leg") and a hat with a leather brim and carried a heavy briefcase. There were no parachute wings on his tunic. He was, she concluded, one of the ROTC officers who wanted something from the Tri-Delts. As long as they didn't try to get her involved, she didn't give a damn who he was or what he wanted.

The housemother knocked on her door a minute later.

"There's an officer to see you, Dianne."

"Who is he?"

"He said he's from Fort Bragg," the housemother said.

Dianne went down the stairs. The captain was a bookish type, she thought.

"You wanted to see me?"

"Miss Dianne Eaglebury?" he asked. She nodded. "I'm Captain LeMoyne from the Office of the Judge Advocate General at Fort Bragg. Is there somewhere we can talk?"

She didn't want to take him into the sitting room because she thought she might start crying. She didn't even trust herself to speak now. She made a waving motion with her hand, signaling him to follow her, and went back up the stairs and to her room.

She sat on her bed and waved him into the chair by her desk. Then she stood up and went to her dresser and picked up the doll in the short skirt, black panties, and green beret and carried it back to the bed.

"Miss Eaglebury, I am an army lawyer," Captain LeMoyne said, "and I have been assigned the job of settling the affairs of the late First Lieutenant Thomas G. Ellis, with whom I believe you were acquainted?"

"Yes," Dianne said, surprised at how natural her voice sounded, "we were acquainted."

"Shortly before entering upon a Temporary Duty assignment, Miss Eaglebury, the late Lieutenant Ellis prepared a last will and testament, and left it in the custody of the adjutant of the Special Warfare Center at Fort Bragg. It was ultimately placed in my hands for action. Here is a copy of Lieutenant Ellis's last will and testament."

"Put it on the desk," Dianne said. "I'll look at it later."

"In his last will and testament, Miss Eaglebury, Lieutenant Ellis identified you as 'his very good friend'—"

"'Very good friend?'"

"—and left you his entire estate," Captain LeMoyne concluded. "The estate has now been probated. There is not much, it consists in the main of his personal effects, a stereo and a television, his uniforms, that sort of thing . . . his pay to the day of his death. But there is a Jaguar automobile. In addition, Lieutenant Ellis named you as beneficiary of his National Service Life Insurance, and I have that check with me, and a check representing his final pay and allowances."

Captain LeMoyne did not like Miss Dianne Eaglebury. She obviously did not give much of a damn for the late Lieutenant Ellis. She'd probably given him a little pussy, and now she was going to get about fourteen grand and a Jaguar.

If she had cared about the late Lieutenant Ellis, Captain LeMoyne decided, she would have shown some emotion, not just sat there on the bed, playing with a vulgar doll and not even looking at him.

(Six)
The Oak Room
The Plaza Hotel
New York City, New York
1330 Hours, 3 March 1962

Porter Craig went from his apartment to the Plaza by taxi. He disliked taxis and for that reason if they stayed in the city over the weekend, he seldom left the apartment to go any farther than the Gristede's on the corner. There was no help in the apartment over weekends, neither maid, cook, nor chauffeur. It would have taken a half hour or more to get the car from the garage, and then he would have the problem of parking it himself. So he had taken a cab, and it had been just as dirty and battered inside as it had looked when it pulled up in front of the apartment.

He entered the Oak Room.

Craig Lowell was staying at the Plaza, possessed of a "lady" he wished Porter to meet and a report on Geoff. If it wasn't for the report on Geoff, Porter told himself, he would have told Craig Lowell to piss off. If he had something to say to him, he could come to the apartment and say it. But Craig had said that what he had to tell him about Geoff he would rather tell Porter privately and have Porter decide when, how, or if Geoff's mother should be told.

So he had come to the Oak Room and was standing by the end of the bar, and Craig Lowell was nowhere in sight.

Porter decided that patience was the best course. He walked almost all the way across the room to a table by the window in the corner. One of the waiters (he looked German but was doubtless Puerto Rican) came for his order, and Porter decided on a Scotch and water rather than a Bloody Mary. He suspected that what he was going to hear from Craig, coupled with the acid in a Bloody Mary, would give him heartburn.

Craig Lowell arrived as the Scotch was delivered. He was in civilian clothes, a tweed jacket, and a turtleneck sweater, and if you weren't supposed to come into the Oak Room tieless, that rule had been waived by anyone in a position to throw him out.

He was holding the hand of a blonde. The blonde was hatless but wearing a mink jacket. As they got closer Porter saw that the blonde was a young blonde, much too young for Craig Lowell. The blonde was spectacular, however, giving credit where credit was due. Craig knew how to pick them. He wondered, unkindly, if the blonde had gotten the mink the way the minks got theirs. Then he realized that was unkind and unfair. Craig Lowell had never had to purchase a woman's favors with mink coats or jewels.

Porter Craig stood up as they got to the table.

"Ursula, this is my Cousin Porter," Lowell said. "How are you, Chubby?"

"Hello," said Ursula, smiling shyly at Porter Craig. She gave him her hand. There was a diamond ring on it, emerald cut, maybe three carats, and on the third finger, left hand. An engagement ring.

"I'm happy to meet you," Porter said, "lovely ring."

"Isn't it?" Craig Lowell said. "It's new. Bought this morning."

"This morning? How did you do that? It's Sunday."

"There was a little card in the window of Van Cleef's," Lowell said, matter-of-factly, "giving a number to call in case of emergency. This was an emergency, so I called and gave them your name."

"And they opened the store for you?"

"No, but they did send a charming little pansy to the hotel with a briefcase full of rings. This one doesn't quite fit, but they said they'd shrink it for Ursula on Monday."

"Congratulations are in order, I gather?" Porter Craig said.

"I would say so, yes," Craig said. "I didn't know how you were going to feel about this."

The waiter appeared.

"Scotch for me," Lowell said to the waiter. "Ursula?"

"Nothing for me, thank you," she said in a German accent, confirming Porter's suspicion that she was a foreigner. That wasn't surprising, he realized. Craig's wife had been German. While it lasted, Craig had been happy, and now he'd found himself another German girl. It was really about time, and if there was a considerable difference in their ages, that was their business.

"Nonsense," Lowell said. "We have a family rule that no one ever has to face Porter completely sober. You're soon going to be a member of the family, so you might as well take advantage of it. At least have a glass of wine? Or a beer?"

"If you insist," Ursula said.

He browbeat her into that, Porter thought angrily. *He should not treat a nice young woman like this one that way.*

"What about Geoff?" Porter asked.

"What about him?" Lowell asked.

"You said you had something to tell me about him," Porter said.

"Oh, yes, I did say that, didn't I?" Lowell said. "I saw him yesterday, as a matter of fact."

"And you are going to tell me how he is?"

"Fit," Lowell said. "Very fit. They've had him running around in the woods and sleeping on the ground. I understand that's supposed to be good for you."

"What do they have him doing?"

"He's on his way to Fort Belvoir."

"What's at Fort Belvoir?"

"The Engineers."

"He's in the Engineers?"

"Actually, he's a Green Beret," Lowell said.

"Is that some sort of a joke?" Porter asked.

"Not at all," Lowell said. "He has a green beret and shiny jump boots and everything. He looks quite good in a uniform, actually. He's a sergeant now, you know."

"What the hell is this?" Porter said. "Forgive me, Miss . . ."

"Ursula," Lowell corrected him. "Now that she's going to be in the family, you're just going to have to learn her name."

"Craig!" the girl said, embarrassed.

"What the hell is what, Porter?" Craig asked.

"How can Geoff possibly be a Green Beret and a sergeant? Three months ago . . . You know where he was three months ago."

"I don't think it was easy," Lowell said. "But blood tells, I suppose. There is a strain of warrior in the clan, you know."

"Why is he going to . . . where did you say?"

"Fort Belvoir."

"Why is he going to Fort Belvoir?"

"They are, I suppose, going to teach him to blow things up," Lowell said. "We Green Berets do a lot of that sort of thing, you know."

"Where is this place?" Porter Craig demanded.

"In Virginia," Lowell said, "not far from Washington. You could go see him, I suppose, if you wanted, instead of spending your weekends in a smelly apartment."

"Why couldn't he come home?" Porter demanded. "Is he on some kind of restriction or something?"

"The thing is, he's got himself a girl," Craig said. "Actually, she's a bit more than just a pretty face. He says he's going to marry her."

"Jesus Christ! Is he out of his mind?"

"I don't think so. I've met her, and I rather like her."

"If she wears a skirt, you'd like her."

"You will be delighted to learn, I'm sure, that she didn't know Geoff is—'comfortable'—until the romance was in high gear. He could, in my judgment, have done a hell of a lot worse."

Porter Craig was not entirely a fool. His head snapped toward Ursula.

"It's you, isn't it?" he challenged.

Ursula flushed but did not avert her eyes. She nodded.

"And you love my son?" Porter Craig asked gently.

She nodded again.

"You're German?" he asked. "The accent?"

"I'm German," Ursula said.

"We had another German girl in the family," Porter said. "Unfortunately we lost her."

She nodded.

"Geoff told me," she said.

"Geoff's mother is not entirely the fire-breathing dragon

Craig has obviously painted her to be," Porter Craig said. "I'm sure she will be as happy to know you as I am. I suggest we get in a cab, go to the apartment, introduce you two, and then see if we can't get Geoff on the telephone. Can we do that, Craig? Can we at least get him on the telephone?"

Lieutenant Colonel Craig W. Lowell raised his right hand in the air above his shoulder, made a fist, and then a pumping motion.

"What the hell are you doing?" Porter Craig asked. -

"That is a military signal," Lowell said, "given by a commander to order his subordinates to form on him."

"Geoff's here?"

"Uh-huh," Lowell said.

But it was a female, a good-looking one, who came to the table.

"Porter, this is Captain Dr. Gillis," Lowell said. "She has a dual role in this. She is the chaperone, for appearances' sake, and she is a shrink, which I thought was a good safety precaution to take."

"I never know when to believe him," Porter Craig said.

"I'm here as a friend," Barbara Gillis said, "but I am an army doctor."

"This is her coat," Ursula said.

"You didn't have to tell him that," Lowell said.

And then, across the room, Porter Craig saw a soldier walking toward them. There were sergeant's chevrons on his sleeves, silver parachutist's wings on his breast, and a green beret on his head.

Porter Craig's eyes blurred with tears.

Sergeant Geoffrey Craig reached the table and put out his hand to his father.

"Father," he said.

"You're actually a sergeant," his father said.

"He missed being best in his class by only two," Ursula said, with quiet pride.

Porter Craig saw that his son's hand had dropped protectively to the girl's shoulder. He reflected that he was glad that he had followed his urge to approve of the girl. To do otherwise, to judge by the look in Geoff's eyes, would have been futile.

"Don't order anything," he said. "We're going home."

"Don't look so distressed," Lowell said. "Oddly enough, your father can handle your mother. And never forget the Green Beret psalm."

Geoff chuckled. Ursula looked uncomfortable.

"I'm afraid to ask what that is," Porter Craig said, "but curiosity overwhelms me."

"'For yea,'" Colonel Lowell quoted, "'tho I walk in the valley of the shadow of death, I will fear no evil...'"

"'...for I,'" Sergeant Craig joined in, "'am the meanest sonofabitch in the valley.'"

"That's terrible," Barbara Gillis and Ursula Wagner said, almost in chorus.

Sergeant Craig and Colonel Lowell, very pleased with themselves, laughed happily.

"What we're going to do now," Porter Craig said, "is go over to the apartment."

"You all go ahead," Barbara Gillis said. "I don't want to intrude."

"Don't be silly," Geoff said.

"Craig and I will be over in a while," Barbara said. "For one thing, we have to check out of here, and really, I don't think—"

"We have fourteen rooms," Porter Craig said. "There is absolutely no reason for you to be in a hotel in the first place."

"I'm not even sure Craig and I will be staying over," Barbara Gillis said firmly. "The only thing I am sure about is that I don't belong there when you spring this on Geoff's mother."

"Neither do I," Craig said. "You go ahead. We'll have a drink, check out, and take a cab over there in an hour or so."

"If you insist," Porter Craig said.

"I leave the coat," Ursula said.

"Take the coat," Craig said.

"I don't want to lose it," she said.

"Sit on it," Lowell said. "Go!"

When they were gone, he looked across the table at Barbara Gillis.

"I owe you one," he said.

"Don't be silly," she said.

"I don't think we could have carried this off without you."

"He is not half as bad as you said he was," Barbara said.

"I mean loaning her the clothes and holding her hand. She was scared out of her skin."

"If I was able to help, I'm glad. They're sweet, and I have the feeling they'll make it."

"Yeah, I think they will," he said.

The waiter appeared.

"Decision time," Lowell said.

"Order one of the same for me," Barbara said.

"If I have another, I won't be able to fly," Lowell said. "Which means we'll have to spend the night."

"Have another, you're entitled, Cupid. I thought you handled the whole thing very well."

Lowell gestured for another drink.

"Porter has a very nice apartment," Lowell said, "with a lovely view of the reservoir. If the moon is full, we can watch muggings in the park."

"I don't think we should stay in their apartment," Barbara said.

"Why not?" he asked. "It's really quite nice. And Geoff's mother, while a little flaky, isn't really all that bad."

"A girl has to draw the line somewhere," Barbara said.

"Between what and what?"

"A suite in the Plaza is one thing," Barbara Gillis said. "Somebody's apartment is something else."

"Aware that I have a lewd and lascivious mind," Lowell said, "I'm very much afraid I have put a meaning to you that you don't have in mind."

"I have in mind room service and champagne and cavorting around in my birthday suit," Barbara Gillis said. "Since you didn't ask, I thought I had better."

She stood up.

"Are you coming, Craig? Or do I still frighten you?"

She walked away from the table.

He took money from his pocket, dropped it on the table, and ran after her. He caught up with her at the door, and they walked hand in hand to the elevators.

• • •

(Seven)
21–29 Sven-Hedin Strasse
Lichtefelde-West
West Berlin
0740 Hours, 9 March 1962

The message came in with the first batch of the day's routines, and it was the first of these, and thus the first through the decryption process, and thus the first routine that came to the station commander's attention. He habitually read the routines while he was having breakfast, before going to his office for the rest. The station commander read it, raised his eyebrows, and ordered its immediate delivery.

"I mean *now;* don't just put it in his box."

The communications officer walked across the dining room and handed Staff Sergeant Wagner the teleprinter printout.

CIA LANGLEY 1915ZULU 8MAR62
ROUTINE ENCRYPTED

STATION COMMANDER FOXTROT
DIRECTION DEPUTY DIRECTOR DELIVER FOLLOWING SOONEST S/
SGT
KARL-HEINZ WAGNER, USA

SERGEANT GEOFFREY CRAIG AND URSULA MARRIED THIRTY MIN-
UTES AGO NEW YORK CITY PROTESTANT EPISCOPAL SERVICE VES-
TRY SAINT BARTHOLOMEW'S CHURCH. DEPARTED IMMEDIATELY
FOR STUDENT DETACHMENT USA ENGINEER SCHOOL FT BELVOIR
VIRGINIA. THEY WILL ATTEMPT TELEPHONE TOMORROW. NICE
WEDDING.
REGARDS. S. T. FELTER
LTCOL INF

His first reaction was rage, then despair.

They were both children, too young to get married.

How the hell were they going to feed themselves?

He decided he would have to think this thing through, but that he could not think it through here in the compound, which was both American and intelligence. He did not feel at all at home here.

He went to his action officer and asked permission to take the morning off, telling him that his work was all done.

"Go ahead, sure. Where are you going?"

"I don't know, for a walk."

"It's cold. Too cold to walk. Take a car. If you don't have anything better to do, go have a look at the wall."

"Thank you, sir."

"Wear your uniform, Karl," his action officer said.

That was an order. The suggestion to take a car (which meant one of the chauffeured Opel Kapitans with which the station was generously equipped) to go have a look at the wall was a suggestion.

"Yes, sir," he said.

He was in civilian clothing, a shirt and trousers and a sweater. He could wear whatever he wanted within the compound, but if he stepped out of the compound, he was to be in uniform. There was some sort of unwritten protocol between the West and the East that personnel in uniform were not to be molested in any way so long as they were on their side of the border. They were fair game in civilian clothing.

He had worn his uniform very rarely since he had been in Berlin, because he had rarely left the compound. He had gone to the PX at Truman Hall and to the American movies, but mostly he had stayed in the compound or gone no farther than the *gast haus* on the corner, which was unofficially thought of as part of the Sven-Hedin Strasse compound and where he could go in his civilian clothing.

What they had wanted of him was what they had said they wanted of him: technical information about the wall. He had no idea why they wanted what they did, but he gave them as much information as he could from his own memory and from examination of an incredible number of photographs.

He had not gone to see the wall, although they wanted him to go see it. They told him he was absolutely safe as long as he wore his uniform.

"We're better snatchers than they are, Karl," his action officer told him. "They like the agreement. And you're really not that important to them."

They thought he was afraid, and in a way he was, but that wasn't the reason he hadn't gone to see the wall. They wanted him to go to jog his memory, but they were wrong about that. He had seen more of the wall on Sven-Hedin Strasse by photograph than he had seen when he had helped build it.

The reason he hadn't gone to see the wall was that he didn't want to see the wall. He thought it would trigger some kind of reaction—he didn't know exactly what—that he didn't want to have. He might, he thought, see someone he knew on the other side of the wall, one of his men (although his men, contaminated, had probably been sent far from Berlin the day after he'd crossed into West Berlin) or an officer that he had known, who would see that he had violated his oath and was working for the Amis.

He had been given a small but comfortable room on the top floor of the main building. He climbed the stairs and stripped off his civilian clothing and put on his uniform.

When he started out of the compound on foot, one of the Opel Kapitans started its engine and came after him.

"You're authorized a car," the driver said to him in German, "I was told."

He got in. It was easier to give in than to argue with the driver.

"Where do we go?"

"Go to the wall," Karl-Heinz Wagner heard himself say, "by the Brandenburg Gate."

As the Kapitan went down Onkle Tom Allee (named for the American Civil War *Schwartze*) and onto Clay Allee (named for the American general, Lucius D. Clay, whom the Berliners believed had kept them from being swept behind the Iron Curtain), he told himself that if he got the wall business out of the way once and for all, then his mind would be clear to deal with the immediate problem of Ursula and Geoff getting married and thus proving their mutual insanity.

Clay Allee turned into Hohenzollern Damm, named after the ex–royal and imperial family, and then they rolled past the Kaiser Wilhelm Gedacht, the ruins of the church left in ruins as a memorial, and wound up on the Strasse des 17. Juni.

He knew this area quite well on a map but much less so on paper. He became more and more interested in what was going on than he thought he would be. With the Brandenburg Gate directly ahead, the Red Army War Memorial should be right about here. . . .

"Stop!" he told the driver.

"You're going to look at the Russians?" the driver asked, and spat.

Karl-Heinz walked across the street and looked at the Russian soldiers marching stiffly and with great precision back and forth in front of the monument.

One part of his mind (he had marched with that stiff-legged step) approved. They could march very well. And then he had an odd thought: What else could they do?

He watched them for ten minutes, until he became aware that he was very cold, and then he got back in the car and had himself driven to the wall in front of the Brandenburg Gate.

"Is there some way we can follow the wall?"

"You tell me where you want to go, we'll go there."

"Find someplace you can drive along the wall," Karl-Heinz ordered.

Five minutes later he ordered the driver to stop again. They had come to an observation platform where the wall formed a *V* near Leipziger Strasse in East Berlin.

There was a sign on the rough wooden stairs saying it was off limits except to authorized military personnel.

He climbed over the light chain, telling himself he was both American military personnel and authorized. His action officer had told him to have a look at the wall. And that's what he was doing.

He had climbed to the top of the platform before he realized that was the kind of thinking he would expect from Geoff, not from himself. *Geoff—my brother-in-law, Ursula's husband, but at least he married her in a church.* American GI–type thinking. Unless it is specifically forbidden, it's authorized.

He had been trained in the other way. Unless it was specifically authorized, it was forbidden.

He looked down at Leipziger Strasse, and saw with his eyes the minefield he had seen in photographs late last night and would see again late tonight.

What a stinking thing to do!

No wonder the Americans weren't enraged. They couldn't

believe it. He had trouble believing it, and he had helped draw the minefield plans.

He looked across the wall at an East German observation tower.

They were looking at him through binoculars.

There was nothing really wrong with Geoff. He was really a nice fellow, and he would be kind to Ursula, and he had seen it coming, he might as well admit that. He should not have been surprised.

They would need a little of his help to get themselves started, and he would help them. He could afford to now, on jump pay, as a staff sergeant.

There were officers watching him now.

He saw a camera on a tripod, with a telephoto lens.

Were they taking his picture because they didn't see that many Green Berets? Or had they learned he was back?

He looked at the East German tower for a long moment, his arms folded across his chest. Then he took his green beret off.

"Get a good look!" he shouted in German, although he supposed they were too far away to hear him.

He had an unpleasant thought. Colonel Felter's radio had said Geoff and Ursula would try to call him tomorrow. That was today, that was now, and if he wasn't there when they called, they would worry and call back, and they didn't have the money to do that.

Staff Sergeant Karl-Heinz Wagner of Special Forces put his green beret on his head. Then he put his thumb to his nose and wiggled the fingers so that the East German photographer would get an interesting picture.

Then he went down the steps and got in the Opel Kapitan and told the driver to take him home.

(Eight)
An Lac Shi
Kontum Province
Republic of South Vietnam
1615 Hours, 10 March 1962

Captain Van Lee Duc, commanding officer of No. 9 Company, Fifty-third Regiment, had had the Blessed Heart of Jesus Roman Catholic Church under surveillance by his men for four days. Neither they nor he had entered the village, but had instead studied it from an observation post on the edge of the rice paddies, where the forest began.

He had not yet had time to establish a relationship with the new mayor, and under the circumstances, not making his presence known until the time was right was clearly the way to handle the situation. Until the time was right, he could not rely on the villagers of An Lac Shi to keep their mouths shut.

After the Americans had had the extraordinary good luck to come across his headquarters in the jungles, his headquarters had been reduced to seven men, and he had been unable to entice one villager to leave his farm and join the forces of national liberation.

Both the forces of the puppet government in Saigon and the Americans in the green berets obviously believed that because they had eliminated the company they had done more damage than was the case. The Americans had started sending the Green Beret sergeant who was some kind of doctor back to An Lac Shi immediately after the firefight in the jungle. At first he had come with a protecting force—several other Americans in two jeeps, followed by three-quarter-ton trucks carrying puppet soldiers.

Because Captain Van Lee Duck had neither the forces to attack a force that strong, and because it really would have accomplished little if he had the forces, this little convoy had not been attacked. The Americans and the Saigon puppets had obviously seen this as proof that the forces of national liberation no longer posed a threat.

One day, just after the American had left, Captain Van Lee Duc had sent a sergeant to throw a torch onto the thatch roof of the Blessed Heart of Jesus Roman Catholic Church.

The villagers would think one of two things: that the People's Liberation Army had set the roof on fire, because the villagers had permitted the American soldier to use the church for his medical office; or that the American or the puppet soldiers had set it on fire carelessly. It didn't matter what they thought. There was no longer a roof on the church building, and the pews had been burned, and it did not make for a very good medical office.

After that, he had done nothing as he waited for replacements to come to him except watch.

The first time he saw the Senegalese, he thought that the Catholic church had sent a replacement for Father Lo Patrick Sho. But the Senegalese turned out not to be a priest but a brother. He could not celebrate mass or hear confessions, which would have been a bad thing. All he was was a brother, and all he was doing in An Lac Shi was arranging to repair the roof of the Blessed Heart of Jesus Church and fix whatever other damage he could.

Captain Van Lee Duc told himself he should have known the Senegalese was not a priest. For one thing, he had ridden into An Lac Shi on a bicycle. A priest would have at the very least a Vespa motor scooter. For another, he should have known that a Senegalese would not be a priest. The Senegalese were animals, recruited in Africa as cannon fodder for the French army. They did not have the brains to be priests.

The Senegalese didn't even speak Vietnamese, just French and whatever language those African savages spoke. He had with him an interpreter, a young Vietnamese, who, Captain Van Lee Duc learned, was from one of the Catholic orphanages and soon was to enter the seminary himself.

But the Senegalese was determined, Captain Van Lee Duc had to admit that. He immediately went to work by himself. Stripping down to a pair of pants, he took down the burned rafters that had held up the roof and then sawed new ones from pieces of lumber the Americans sent him.

He worked all day in the hot sun. Sometimes the young Vietnamese interpreter helped, but most of the time the Vietnamese went and begged money for materials from the villagers. He did not have much success, for the villagers could see no point in contributing to a new roof, since it would soon be burned down again.

But the Senegalese didn't quite fail. Slowly he managed to saw rafters from the huge timber the Americans gave him. One by one, the rafters went in place. He had trouble at first getting money for the thatching material, but then the American medical sergeant gave him money to buy the material and to pay the women of the village to prepare it.

Captain Van Lee Duc knew that he could not permit the roof to be completed, and he thought the best way to handle this psychologically was to wait until it was almost completed, by which time the villagers would have their hopes high, and then burn it again.

It would also be educational to kill the Senegalese and his interpreter, and Captain Van Lee Duc planned to do that. But then something fortuitous happened: The guard that accompanied the American medical sergeant diminished in size until, like water in the hot sun, it simply disappeared. The medical sergeant arrived once a week alone, unarmed, in his jeep, and set up his place of business in the walls of the church.

Sometimes, when there was a long line of people waiting to take his medicine or have their teeth pulled, he even stayed overnight. Sometimes he did not.

In the end Captain Van Lee Duc decided that it would be better if he could kill the American at the same time he burned the church and killed the Senegalese brother and his interpreter. He would not let the fact that the American was not present keep him from burning the church just when the roof was about complete.

He had been disappointed today when the line of people waiting to see the American medical sergeant had been much shorter than usual; by half past four, there was only a tubercular old woman and two mothers with diarrhea babies in line. The sergeant would be through with them by five o'clock, and then he would get back in his jeep and leave.

At five o'clock Captain Van Lee Duc decided that luck was going his way today. When the American got in his jeep to leave, he couldn't make the engine start, not even after the Senegalese and his interpreter pushed it all over, trying to start it.

The American was stupid, Captain Van Lee Duc thought. He did not realize how much face he was losing by losing his temper in public and swearing and then actually kicking the jeep when he couldn't get it to start.

Now he could kill all three of them.

Captain Van Lee Duc sent his runner into the forest and

told him to find the lieutenant and tell him that he would need five men. They were to come armed with AK-47 automatic rifles and bring with them one thermite hand grenade apiece. It was almost certain that he could fire the church with a cigarette lighter, but it was always good military practice to prepare for any eventuality.

He toyed with the idea of putting the bodies of the Senegalese, the interpreter, and the American medical sergeant in the middle of the church, one on top of the other, and then setting off a thermite grenade on top of them. The grenade would burn right through their bodies, and the smell would go all over the village.

When the men came, the lieutenant was with them, and Captain Van Lee Duc was furious. He had not ordered him to come and he should not have come. He slapped his face three times to humiliate him in front of the others. Then he told him he was to stay where he could watch, but he was not allowed to participate in the operation.

Captain Van Lee Duc waited until almost eleven P.M. by his wristwatch. He wanted to be sure the villagers as well as the Senegalese brother, the interpreter, and the American were asleep. There were two reasons for this: He wanted them to be terrified when the noise awakened them, and he did not want them—out of some idiotic obligation to their faith—to have time to run to the aid of the Senegalese brother.

There were two doors to the Blessed Heart of Jesus Church, the main door in front and a side door. The side door was blocked with piles of thatching, which meant that there was only one door, which made the operation that much simpler.

He made each man recite out loud what his role in the operation was to be. They would rush the door in pairs, opening fire as soon as they were inside, spraying the interior from side to side.

If the Senegalese and the interpreter and the American had not been killed by the spraying fire from the AK-47s of the first pair, they would be killed by aimed fire from the second pair. There was still enough of a hole in the roof to provide sufficient light.

Once the people inside were dead, Captain Van Lee Duc

would enter the church and make sure that they were in fact dead. He would put their bodies together in the center of the aisle, light the thatch from inside, and then pull the pin on the thermite grenade sitting on the bodies.

Within three minutes they would be back in the jungle at the edge of the rice paddy.

Not even a dog barked as they made their way to the front door of the Blessed Heart of Jesus Church. They tried the door, and it was fastened from inside. Captain Van Lee Duc thought that was stupid. A sick old woman could force the lock by leaning on the door.

He gave the hand signal, and the first two soldiers broke through the door, stepped through the vestibule, and sprayed the interior with short bursts from their AK-47s.

Then the second pair of soldiers rushed inside. But they did not fire, and when Captain Van Lee Duc rushed in after them, angrily shouting at them to fire, they were looking at him in confusion. There was no one in the church.

Captain Van Lee Duc looked up the roof just in time to see the first hand grenade drop into the church. He was so surprised that he just looked at it as it fell and then as it lay on the floor. He was looking at it when it went off.

He felt himself being thrown up against the wall of the church; and then there was a brilliant fire at his shoulder and incredible pain. The thermite grenade he had in his shirt pocket had ignited.

He screamed and rolled around on the ground.

Something stopped him.

He looked up and saw the Senegalese. The Senegalese, naked to the waist, was holding him still with a foot on his shoulder. He had a very large pistol in his hand, aimed at Captain Van Lee Duc's face.

The medical sergeant came over.

"Let the motherfucker burn, Phil."

"I wish I could," the Senegalese said. "I hope you understand me, Captain," he said. "This is for Tom Ellis."

That was the last thing Captain Van Lee Duc heard. The last thing he saw was a yellow-orange flash at the muzzle of a Colt Model 1917 .45-caliber ACP revolver that had previously seen service in the Marne, in War I; in North Africa, France, and Germany in War II; and most recently in Korea. The bullet struck him just above his nose and, because of hydrostatic action of the projectile upon brain tissue, created an exit hole about three inches in diameter at the rear of the skull.

ABOUT THE AUTHOR

W.E.B. Griffin, who was once a soldier, belongs to the Armor Association; Paris Post #1, The American Legion; and is a life member of the National Rifle Association and Gaston-Lee Post #5660, Veterans of Foreign Wars.